SONG

of the

SUN
GOD

Published by the Perera-Hussein Publishing House, 2017
www.pererahussein.com

ISBN: 978-955-8897-28-7

First edition

Song of the Sun God by Shankari Chandran is a work of fiction.
Names, characters, places and incidents,
especially those of historical persons and/or events,
either are the product of the author's imagination
or are used fictitiously, and any resemblance to actual persons
living or dead, events, or locales is entirely coincidental.

The right of Shankari Chandran to be identified as the Author
of this work, has been asserted by her in accordance with
the Copyright, Designs and Patents Act.

Printed and bound by Thomson Press.

To offset the environmental pollution caused by printing books,
the Perera-Hussein Publishing House grows trees in Puttalam –
Sri Lanka's semi-arid zone.

SONG
of the
SUN
GOD

SHANKARI CHANDRAN

PERERA-HUSSEIN PUBLISHING HOUSE
COLOMBO

'Why at the beginning of things, is there always light?'
The Narrow Road to the Deep North – Richard Flanagan

To Haran,
for reading this faster than TKAM,
and loving it more.

FAMILY TREE

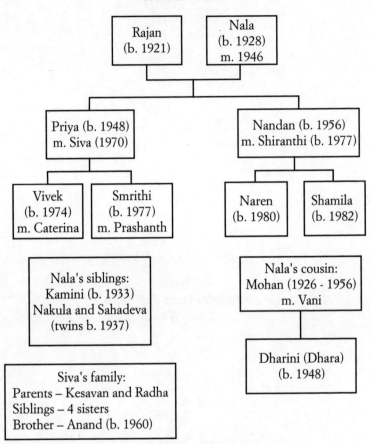

Rajan
(b. 1921)

Nala
(b. 1928)
m. 1946

Priya (b. 1948)
m. Siva (1970)

Nandan (b. 1956)
m. Shiranthi (b. 1977)

Vivek
(b. 1974)
m. Caterina

Smrithi
(b. 1977)
m. Prashanth

Naren
(b. 1980)

Shamila
(b. 1982)

Nala's siblings:
Kamini (b. 1933)
Nakula and Sahadeva
(twins b. 1937)

Nala's cousin:
Mohan (1926 - 1956)
m. Vani

Dharini (Dhara)
(b. 1948)

Siva's family:
Parents – Kesavan and Radha
Siblings – 4 sisters
Brother – Anand (b. 1960)

OTHER FAMILY MEMBERS
Archi – Nala's grandmother
Lali – Rajan's elder sister (1916 – 1931)
Devaki – Rajan's mother (d. 1965)
Ayah – Nala's nursemaid

FRIENDS
Rita Matthews – Nala's best friend
Dr Fonseka and Dolly Fonseka – Rajan and Nala's neighbours in
Cinnamon Gardens, Colombo

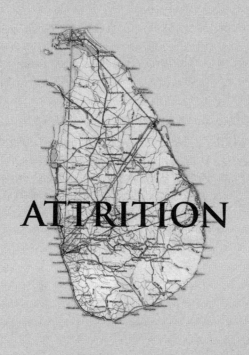

ATTRITION

The Bhagavad Gita, *or sacred 'Song of God' contains a discussion between* Lord Krishna and the warrior prince Arjuna, on human nature and the *purpose of life. It forms an important chapter in the* Mahabharata – *a Sanskrit epic about a great war between two sides of the same family.*

1

COLOMBO, 1932

'If you're going to do something, son, you should do it properly,' he said to Rajan. The boy had never seen a monk like that before – completely naked, his light brown skin unimpaired by clothing. At his feet lay the orange robe of his order. He had taken it off and making sure the edges were aligned into a perfect square, had placed it neatly on the pavement. His movements were slow and deliberate.

In books, Rajan had seen human anatomy in all its simple and complex artistry – but only in books. He had seen monks in Jaffna, but this one was different. This one was young and surprisingly muscular. The sunlight wrapped itself around him like his orange robe. He looked beautiful. The boy watched fascinated, as the monk wiped his shorn head with the palm of his hand. It came away damp. It was a dry day: not too hot, not too humid.

Rajan's mother thought it was a perfect day. She took him to the stalls outside the hospital and gave him two cents for a treat. He wanted to buy a glass of faloodah with it, to share with his sister, Lali. She had been unwell for several weeks and Rajan knew it would help her.

There was nothing like faloodah: flavoured, coloured gelatine suspended in milk on a bed of rose syrup, topped with swollen basil seeds. It was the perfect combination of colour, flavour and texture. Years later, when Rajan became a doctor, he would reassess the nutritional impact of the drink with educated eyes. Protein, calcium, sugar and starch were bound together in a cocktail of artificial colour and sweetness. Milky pink remained his favourite colour in adulthood long after he stopped drinking faloodah. He would start drinking it again, much later in old age, when he dared death to take him.

Lali loved faloodah and little Rajan loved her. He was only eleven, and had never been given pocket money before. The two coins felt heavy in his hands. He placed them in his shallow pocket and then took them out again. He was afraid they would fall out. Lali laughed at him weakly from her hospital bed.

'You always expect the worst,' she whispered, her lips cracking as she spoke. He loved her so much because she only expected the best.

Up north, she had been treated by the local apothecary whose miracle tincture was supposed to 'purge' her fever. Rajan who read a lot had never read of purging as a cure for fever. His sister hadn't eaten in weeks and finally the little boy convinced his mother that Lali needed help. Fearfully, they brought her to Colombo.

He was sure now, that faloodah would save her. It would provide hydration, energy and happiness in equal measure. Its milky pinkness made her smile. He was on his way to buy it from the teahouse when he saw the monk undressing quietly on a side of the street.

The monk wiped his shorn head again with his palm. Once more it came away damp. He sat down on the pavement in the lotus position. To the little boy, the monk looked like Lord Buddha himself, who had found an answer to the suffering of mankind and shared it with the world. Their country was the keeper of that answer; an island citadel that protected the Buddha's ways and His wisdom.

The monk began chanting slowly and clearly. Rajan couldn't understand the words but he understood their tone. It was peaceful. The boy felt calm watching the monk close his eyes, oblivious to the gathering crowd. People were watching and whispering. People were always watching and whispering in the capital.

Rajan had seen angry monks walking the streets shouting about something, anything. Usually it was about the British but lately it was about the Tamils. The monks hated Tamils even more than they hated the British or the Muslims.

The monk in front of him didn't seem angry though. He was happy, sitting quietly on the pavement. Rajan wanted to talk to him, ask him what he was doing. He had opened a bottle of water and was pouring it on himself, as though he were bathing. Rajan's eyes started to sting. 'You should stand back, son,' the monk said to him as he smiled and rubbed his body with the water. The water; something was wrong with the water.

Rajan was about to speak when his father touched his shoulder. What was his father doing here? He was supposed to be with Lali at the hospital. They were all taking turns to sit with her: she never liked being alone, even though she was the eldest child.

For the first and last time in his life, Rajan saw his father cry. He didn't say anything: there was no need. He looked for his mother and saw her crumpled on the ground, her mouth open but the cries trapped in her chest. She was beating herself, trying to free her voice. His father raised her up and they began the slow journey back into the hospital. Behind them, Rajan heard screams. He turned around to see the young monk who had been meditating – naked and peaceful – still seated, still silent, but now glowing. People screamed as tall flames wrapped themselves around him like an orange robe.

✧

ALLEVADDY VILLAGE, JAFFNA PROVINCE IN THE NORTH OF CEYLON, 1932

Before he went to sleep, Rajan prepared wood for the kitchen fire and thosai batter for breakfast. Appa liked to start the day with fermented pancakes.

Lying in bed, he stared out of his window, unable to sleep. His mother used to sing him a lullaby. She called out to the moon, '*nila nila*, run quickly. Don't stop until you reach the mountain peak. There are jasmines, they are fallen from heaven. Bring them back, *nila nila*. They will help us sleep.' He tried humming the lullaby quietly to himself.

In the morning, he woke up at the same time as his father. Appa drew water from the well in the courtyard they shared with their cousins. He stood in his sarong and poured cold water over the little boy's head; two buckets every day. Then Appa bathed himself leaving Rajan to make breakfast.

Rajan's thosais were not as crispy as Amma's but Appa said they were very tasty. Sometimes their neighbour, Aunty Savitri, brought over a bowl of potato curry to eat with the pancakes. She showed Rajan how to swirl the batter on the flat iron pan without burning himself. He tried to create the concentric layers of thosai, the way Appa liked it – a thick central moon orbited by thin, brittle rings.

'Don't worry, mahan, your Amma will be back soon,' she said, kissing his head. After Lali's funeral, Amma had stayed in Colombo with relatives.

Rajan served the steaming pancakes onto Appa's plate and sat next to him. They ate in silence, the only noise coming from the street as the village cocks crowed, waking the rest of the neighbourhood.

He stood up, reaching over to take his father's empty plate back to the kitchen. Appa stopped him, touching his arm tentatively. Rajan wanted his father to hold him.

'Amma is coming back tonight, mahan. We must help her. We must help each other.'

'Yes Appa,' he tried not to cry. He wanted to vomit out his pancake and the sick feeling he carried with him every day.

'Go and get ready mahan, you'll be late for school. By the time you return home, Amma will be here. Everything will be better.'

When Amma arrived that night, she kissed him quietly, whispering his name and nothing more as her tears fell. She held his face, stroked his cheeks and smoothed his hair, as if remembering him with her hands. He pulled her towards the settee but she shook her head and prised her hand from his. She drifted away towards her bedroom, faltering briefly outside Lali's doorway.

Rajan stared out of his window that night. His mother cried herself to sleep, calling, *ende kollonthai, ende kollonthai,* my child, my child, while he watched the moon. It floated above them like a glowing pancake.

Every day, Rajan read until it was dark and then he read by candlelight. He meticulously scraped wax from the bottom of the dish with his foot-ruler. He would reuse it with a new wick tomorrow. Years ago, Lali had shown him how; she was very careful. For his birthdays he never asked for books because they were so expensive – he could borrow books – instead he asked for candles.

His grandmother laughed when he told her he had finished all of the school textbooks by the age of fourteen. She looked at him with pride, spat three times to ward off the evil eye, and asked him, 'Rajan, what are you studying? If you've finished all the books from school, what else is there to learn?' His mother never asked him this. She said every generation should have the chance to be better and freer than the one before it. So she kept buying him candles and, when she could, she bought him books.

His cousins laughed and rolled their eyes whenever Amma quoted Auvayar saying: '*Katrathu Kai Mun Alavu; Kallathathu Ulahalvu* – what we have learned is the size of a fistful of earth; what we haven't learned is the size of this world.' Rajan loved the legendary poetess, whom the gods allowed to live on the moon so she would always be with the Tamils.

Rajan's classes were taught in English at the local American missionary school. He learnt Sinhalese as well, but Tamil was the language he loved most. When he called out to his mother in the middle of the night, it was in Tamil. When he remembered his sister, it was in Tamil.

After Lali's death, Amma rarely left their house, but once a month she travelled to Jaffna town to visit relatives and buy medicines. Appa didn't allow the village apothecary into their house anymore so Amma's medicine box had to be stocked by the town doctor. Rajan was quick to help his mother with her errands and during school holidays, he was allowed to stay in town with his cousins for a few weeks longer. Amma smiled, knowing why he wanted to join her. He loved the library and its endless shelves of Tamil literature – manuscripts that chronicled the history of the Tamil people.

The library was open only until three o'clock, but Rajan, in his neatly pressed shirt, would disappear quietly behind the piles of books. They formed tall, haphazard towers, like anthills all over the rooms. He would emerge hours later and disappear outside just as quietly. The curator, Mr Kanagasabai, noticed and followed him one day. The old man found him organising the books.

'You're not supposed to be here son – there are rules about opening hours and there is a committee…the committee won't like it,' he said without much conviction. Rajan looked up at him, surprised to be interrupted. He was reading Gray's Anatomy again. He had memorised all of the body's systems; he was mapping the trajectory of different diseases so that he would be prepared the next time sickness came to his home. It took several moments for him to find his voice.

'Iyah,' he addressed the curator respectfully. 'I was just reading,' he offered as a full response.

'I know, son. I can see that,' the old man replied. 'I love to read too; although my eyes are not as good as they used to be. My Amma told me I went through her candles too quickly.'

'Me too,' Rajan relaxed a little. 'Will I get in trouble if I stay here?'

'No,' Mr Kanagasabai replied. 'But I will.'

The old man looked at the order Rajan had created and sighed, finally saying, 'Come back tomorrow. Bring a notepad and pen, and some cloths. We need to clean the manuscripts before we file them.'

Rajan closed his book and blew out the candle. Tomorrow he would go with Amma to Jaffna town again.

TELLIPPALAI VILLAGE, JAFFNA PROVINCE, 1936

Nala balanced precariously on her cousin-brother's back, peering into her mother's window. Mohan had positioned himself on all fours, amongst the tickling fingers of their grandmother's fern shrubs. He was only two years older than Nala but at ten he was already much bigger and stronger than her. Mohan liked to lift sacks of coconuts to grow his muscles. He told her that was what MG Ramachandran did before he became an actor. Nala's parents had gone to see MGR's first film with Mohan's parents. Nala asked if they could go too, but her mother had said, 'Chee chee, it's not for children.'

Nala wasn't sure why or what *was* for children. As usual she wouldn't listen to Mohan when he told her that spying on her sick mother probably wasn't for children either. She climbed down from his back and sat next to him under the window.

'It's her presha,' she composed her face into her best medical expression.

'Her presha?' Mohan questioned.

'Yes, her presha.' She rolled her eyes as though everyone was supposed to know what 'presha' was.

'It's like demensha,' she continued.

Whenever their grandmother Archi cursed Nala's father, he said 'demensha' and rolled his eyes the way Nala did. Her mother would shush him but the children could see she was trying not to laugh. According to her mother, Archi was too young to have dementia; she was forty-eight-years-old. But Nala's father liked to remind her that it ran in the family and cursing could be the first sign. Amma would shush Appa again.

'Her presha was too high and the baby came too early,' Nala continued her medical report. She heard the doctor say that high presha ran in their family: like demensha.

She opened her notebook and started writing. Her father had given it to her for her birthday, because she was good at drawing. She liked to carry it around with her everywhere. Pressing hard with her pencil, she wrote '18th April 1936, Amma has hi presha.' It was a few days after Tamil New Year but no one had celebrated this year. Amma couldn't go to the temple or anywhere for thirty-one days after the baby.

'Where's the baby?' Mohan asked quietly.

'Dead,' she replied. She wanted to cry. Amma had been in her room all week and Nala knew she wasn't eating or sleeping; only crying. Amma had been certain the baby inside her this time was a boy.

Nala's younger sister Kamini was born three years ago. Amma had cried then too. The little girl was beautiful and healthy but Amma didn't care. She remembered hearing Archi try to comfort Amma. 'It will happen mahal, soon, it will happen.'

But it didn't happen soon. It took a long time for Amma to have babies. Some of Nala's aunties had babies every year. That was why she had so many cousins. Mohan was her favourite. She was convinced that Amma's babies took longer because they came out fairer, like her.

Amma's next visitor was the family astrologer. Amma wouldn't listen to Appa or Archi or the doctor. In desperation, Archi had called Mr Viswanathan. He used to be the family tailor but his hobby had turned out to be surprisingly accurate. He had given up tailoring and taken up full-time astrology. It was Mr Viswanathan who had read and matched Amma and Appa's charts, when Appa's family first proposed to Amma's family. Both families trusted Mr Viswanathan; they knew it would be a good match.

Standing on her cousin-brother's back again, Nala watched the astrologer. He sat on a chair next to Amma's bed and opened up his books. Amma stirred but still didn't move.

'*Thangachi*, little sister,' said the old man, 'your Sanni period has ended now.' He leaned forward to show her a chart with twelve boxes on it. He pointed to the different boxes.

'Saturn is moving out of the fifth house, the house for family and children.' He tapped the fifth box. 'Jupiter is moving into this house next month. You will be blessed with sons soon. These things, they are written in the planets thangachi, and when the planets move, our destiny moves too. Your sons will come.' The old man patted Amma's hand and left the room.

Nala grabbed Mohan and raced around the house to watch the astrologer leave. They ducked beneath the large verandah and crawled, until they were almost under the old man and her father.

'Stay back Nala, they'll see you,' Mohan whispered. She laughed; he was constantly afraid of getting in trouble. 'Your father will get angry!' She wasn't afraid of her father; she was his favourite.

'All the very best for your move, thambi,' said the astrologer, 'God bless you, and be safe in Colombo; things are changing in the south.'

Colombo? What was the old man talking about? She had never been to the capital city. Appa tried to pay him but the old man shook his head and put his hands together to say goodbye. Appa did the same. She laughed again, the men looked like they were praying to each other.

'Shh, Nala!' Mohan whispered. 'What's wrong with you? I'm going to get a caning, and you will too if you're not careful. This is no laughing matter.' Mohan sounded just like his father, making her laugh once more, this time louder.

As the astrologer walked down the verandah steps, Archi came running out and gave him a tiffin carrier. Nala could smell the fried okra through the steel. She wondered what other curries the compartments contained.

'Careful, it's hot. Thank you again, Iyah,' Archi said as she handed the old man the food.

Appa stood on the steps and watched the astrologer walk slowly away. Without looking down at the children, he said, 'Nalayini, why don't you go and sit with Amma? She's feeling a little better; she could do with your company. You too Mohan, your back must be hurting.' He smiled as he walked back into the house.

COLOMBO, 1937

Nala inspected her brothers. The babies stared back, blankly. They looked like two dumplings with their puckered, shiny faces and the lazy folds of paper-white skin. She wanted to touch the hair that feathered their bodies. It looked soft.

Amma said 'No touching, not yet, they're too small.' She meant *special*. Whenever Amma wasn't looking, she inched her face closer to theirs. She wanted to smell them. She had seen her mother pick them up and place her nose in the space between the babies' jaw and neck. Amma would close her eyes, breathe deeply and sigh. Nala wanted to try.

Amma saw her. 'Move back, Nala,' she placed a hand on her shoulder and gently but firmly pushed her away. 'They need air.'

She wasn't stealing the babies' air. Perhaps she was breathing too much around them. She tried to take short, shallow breaths.

'Nala, what are you doing? If you're going to behave like a monkey then could you please go outside.' Usually Amma didn't let her play outside in the afternoon sun. It made her skin darker and Nala had beautiful fair skin. Not as fair as the babies, but still fairer than her younger sister's.

She left the room and found the new servant girl. Nala had already forgotten her name but the young woman was happy being called Ayah. She sat on the kitchen floor, deftly peeling the violet skin from small bulbs of onion. She couldn't cross her legs properly underneath her, they were bowed like the arches of the Pillayar temple.

'My bones are bent but my teeth are straight,' she had explained when she first moved in.

From time to time she adjusted her body and sat on her haunches, throwing the cleaned onions into the small hammock her lungi skirt made between her knees. She changed her position back and forth, but she never dropped an onion or lost the rhythm of her work.

'Sit, Nala bubba,' she said in Sinhalese, motioning to the low stool next to her.

'I'm not a baby. I'm nine-years-old,' Nala replied, perching herself on the wooden seat. It was smooth and heavy. On one end was a small, serrated blade, shaped like a peacock's tail. Every morning Ayah straddled the seat and held the half-moon of a young coconut on the blade. She would briskly scrape out the milky flesh for the chilli sambal they ate with breakfast. Ayah had wrapped an old sarong around the blade.

'Don't touch,' she warned Nala.

'I know, I'm not allowed to touch anything,' the little girl complained.

'Have they named the babies yet?' Ayah asked, switching to English as she shelled the last onion.

'Nakula and Sahadeva,' Nala replied. 'They're named after the twin brothers in the *Mahabharata* – the youngest Pandavas. Do you know the story?'

Ayah shook her head and Nala summarised for her: 'Five Pandava brothers fought against their one hundred Kaurava cousins, and won. It was an ancient battle but I'm not sure it really happened. I think Archi might be exaggerating.'

Ayah laughed, revealing her full set of straight but discoloured teeth. She pulled a piece of betel leaf from her sari blouse. 'We have stories like that too, in the *Mahavamsa*. Men fight and people die.' She chewed hard on the leaf, the red pulp muffling her voice. 'We're supposed to learn something from the stories but I can never remember what.' She stood up, carrying the onions to the table protectively in her lungi.

'Me neither,' Nala said. The twin brothers in the *Mahabharata* were boring. That was all she could remember about Nakula and Sahadeva.

TELLIPPALAI VILLAGE, 1939

Nala was thrilled to return to the family home and to Mohan. She wasted no time, immediately exploring the old house and garden with him. The place looked different, her eleven-year-old eyes noticing for the first time the red dust that settled on everything from the furniture to the plants. Appa said he missed the redness of Jaffna. She had only missed Mohan.

The monsoon was coming and everyone watched the skies, like guests at a wedding, waiting for the groom to make his triumphant entry. The garden was parched but still overgrown. Archi's magical fingers could coax okra, onions and gourds from the small vegetable patch. Mohan had cut channels into the soil. 'It will capture the rain water without letting it wash away Archi's seedlings,' he told her proudly, stroking the funny faint hair on his upper lip, and taking her on a tour of her former home as if he were now its maharajah.

Amma said she was too old to play hide-and-seek but she rarely listened to her mother. Mohan teased her. 'Three years in Colombo have turned you into a little princess,' he said, flicking her collared frock and the bows in her hair that matched the bows on her socks. She replied, 'I was born a princess.' He ran off to hide before she could finish her mocking but pretty curtsy.

Nala opened every cupboard and checked under every bed in the house. Despite having grown taller, Mohan was still an excellent hider. She was still a terrible loser.

'Mohan, Mohan come out now, I'm tired of looking!' she shouted at him. She sat on the steps of the front verandah and examined her legs. They were pocked with mosquito bites; red, angry welts rising up from her fair skin like small volcanoes.

'Don't scratch!' Archi said. Her grandmother sat in the usual place on her rocking chair, her legs covered with a light blanket. In the late morning, after she had finished all of her cooking for the day, she would sit and watch over her garden, her street and her grandchildren.

'Don't scratch!' Archi repeated, more imperiously, 'You'll scar yourself. It will be malaria season soon, you should be more careful.'

Nala was afraid of malaria. One of her younger cousins had died of it in the last monsoon. The rains left fetid pools of water in the streets and gardens, creating the perfect breeding ground for mosquitoes. Amma was so worried she left the twins and Kamini back in Colombo. The boys were only two-years-old and had never been to Jaffna. Appa said Amma fussed over them too much but Nala was quite happy to be free of her siblings and have Mohan to herself.

She was inspecting her skin when Archi let out a long kusu. The old lady gave a wicked giggle as her chair and blanket began to move with a life of its own.

'Aaaarchiii! What did you do that for?' Mohan shouted as he stumbled out from under the rocking chair, coughing and laughing.

'Found you!' Nala cried with malicious delight. Archi's kusus were legendary.

'That's not fair,' he replied, breathing the humid, clean air deeply. 'It doesn't count.'

He sat himself next to her and she began to show off her battle scars.

'Mine are definitely better than yours,' she pointed to her left calf. 'See how these bites merge into each other, making one big bumpy line. It looks like the Himalayas.'

Mohan usually laughed at her jokes, even when they weren't funny. But he wasn't listening to her; he was concentrating on the raised voices coming from inside the house. Appa and Mohan's father, Nirmalan mama, were arguing again, although they weren't angry at each other yet.

'What was he thinking, thambi?' Nirmalan mama asked Nala's father, '*Was* GG Ponnambalam even thinking when he made that speech?'

She moved closer to the door and crouched next to Mohan. Everyone was talking about GG Ponnambalam, the leader of the Tamil Congress Party. He had made a speech and afterwards, Sinhalese people had rioted, attacking Tamils.

Her uncle didn't give Appa time to answer. He continued, 'the Buddhists say the *Mahavamsa* gives them a historical claim to the country – it is their history of the Sinhalese kings of Ceylon. GG Ponnambalam went to Navalapitiya, into the *heartland* of the old Sinhalese kingdom, and told them that most of the Sinhalese kings mentioned in *their* sacred chronicle were actually *Tamil*. What did he think was going to happen when he said that?' Nirmalan mama was angry now. 'He was stirring up trouble and other people paid the price for it.'

'He wasn't stirring up trouble,' Appa replied. 'Trouble is already upon us. If the Buddhist monks and politicians want to use the *Mahavamsa* to take sole ownership of this country then we have a right to challenge the chronicle and them. We should talk about our ancient Tamil kingdom and the richness of Hinduism. We should tell them that the Sinhalese and Tamils lived together peacefully for centuries. We should put forward our side of history.'

'History, exactly!' Nirmalan mama laughed even though her father hadn't told a joke. 'It's just history, thambi. It doesn't matter who arrived first or which kings fought with each other. That is the past and what matters now is the future.'

'You should tell that to the bhikkus and the politicians,' Appa said quietly. The children had to move right up to the door to listen. Archi wouldn't normally allow them to eavesdrop, but she too was listening. She looked sad.

'In Colombo,' Appa continued, 'it's everywhere. It's in the newspapers, there are posters, and bhikkus hand out leaflets. The monks are telling people about the greatness of Buddhism – telling Sinhalese Buddhists who ten years ago barely cared about their own religion.'

'I know, but Ponnambalam's speech did more damage than good. He was trying to make the monks angry.'

'But the rioters weren't just monks,' Appa replied. 'Normal Sinhalese people are starting to believe that Ceylon is only for the Sinhalese, not the Tamils.'

'Don't worry thambi. We will find a way to live together, we always have,' her uncle replied. 'We will pacify the monks and this will pass. You worry too much, like Ponnambalam. For now, Ceylon is for the Ceylonese – the Tamils and the Sinhalese. But mostly, it is for the British Empire.' Nala could tell he was trying to make Appa laugh, but it didn't work.

2

Steep steps led down from the temple courtyard to the water's edge. The women, wrapped in layers of luminous silk, had developed the art of lifting their saris high enough to let them navigate the steps safely, but not so high as to reveal the soft skin above the ankle or the hint of a petticoat – things only a husband should see. They learned to walk these steps elegantly, no longer running and jumping down them as they did when they were girls.

Nala had come to the Pillayar temple with her mother to pray for a good husband. She was seventeen and it was time to beseech the elephant god. She was relieved when her parents started to talk about marriage. Her cousin-sisters were teasing her about Mohan; he was her mother's brother's son – a 'marriageable cousin' – but he was a brother to her. Archi had overheard the talk and slapped her cousin-sister, hard. '*We* are not villagers,' she declared.

At the temple, Nala offered a plate of sweet rice and garlands to the deity and a portion of her father's wages to the priest in order to secure her marriage.

She then crossed the courtyard to the temple pond, with an offering of jasmines from her mother's garden. She sat on the final step, carefully gathering her new sari closer to her feet. She arranged the pleats of peacock blue silk neatly, as her mother had taught her, pressing them with her palm and turning them in the sunlight to watch the hibiscus pink shimmer through the blue weave. Her mother called it 'silk shot'. The new sari had been a gift from her father.

Playing with her outfit, she was distracted and never said her final prayers to Lord Ganesha. Instead, she admired her pale skin in the unpolished mirror of the water's surface. A jealous cousin once told her this colour could only come from an illicit colonial gene. Her father said she was as beautiful as an Apsara, a celestial dancer. Her mother had disapproved, spitting three times and making him do the same. The evil eye hovered closely around the beautiful.

She had a long symmetrical face with a smattering of freckles that danced when she laughed. She surveyed her full lips and uncommonly white teeth. Appa made them all brush their teeth and tongues daily. Her eyes wandered down to her chest and the beginnings of the curves she would inherit from her mother, not like her poor flat-chested friend Rita.

She fiddled with the medallion on her necklace as she sat. It was St Christopher, the Catholic patron of travellers, given to her by Archi. Her grandmother was a devout Hindu who unashamedly prayed to all gods and saints, just in case. Her grandfather overlooked this religious indiscretion on the grounds that Jesus lived with his mother, so he seemed like a good Hindu boy anyway.

A sudden wind blew the jasmines out of her lap and into the water, breaking her reflection and reverie. She held a few flowers back and placed them in her thick plaited hair, pushing stray black curls into submission. She turned to go and looked up into the eyes of a dark young man across the pond.

Rajan sat on the steps, waiting nervously. His mother had sent him to the temple with Uncle Ramanathan, who had suggested the girl as a possible match. She came from a good family and her astrological chart was compatible with his. He asked to see her before he would agree to a first meeting, but no-one had a photograph. A visit to the temple was easily contrived and after making his own contribution of flowers to Lord Ganesha, he sat with his uncle on the other side of the temple pond.

'There she is Rajan, there she is,' his uncle whispered. Rajan laughed – there was no need to whisper. The girl couldn't hear them and as he watched her study her own reflection, he realised she couldn't see them either.

'What do you think?' Uncle Ramanathan asked excitedly. Rajan hadn't thought much about marriage, he'd been studying too hard. But his mother told him it was time, and looking at the beautiful girl by the water, he blushed and agreed.

✿

'Amma, it hurts,' Nala complained. Her mother was too rough with her. 'It's your own fault. I don't know why you can't keep it properly. What's the point of having all this hair if you can't look after it?' Amma snapped, pulling hard with a steel comb. She was massaging sesame oil into the thick mass, untangling and deciphering the curls into a braided message of wifely order and propriety. Sitting on the verandah of their home, Amma adjusted her cane chair to get a better grip, punctuating her lecture with sharp tugs.

'Tomorrow we will wash it and by Saturday it will be clean and tidy, all ready for the viewing.'

'You make me sound like a bullock being traded – a fine white bullock with good hair.'

'Don't be ridiculous,' her mother retorted with more retaliatory combing. 'You say such silly things. You are not a bullock and you are not that fine.'

Amma paused for a moment to survey her work before continuing. 'Ayah and I are going to teach you how to cook next week. Just the basics, we can't teach you everything in a week. But you can't show up at your in-laws' house not knowing how to make a simple sarakku spice mix. What will they think of me if you can't roast coriander and cumin seeds without burning them?'

Amma shook her head as she contemplated her daughter's ignorance. 'Imagine if they asked you to prepare a chicken curry and paruppu – you would have to ask them how to boil dhal. I would be shamed – shamed I tell you. God help you if they like crab curry. I told you to spend more time in the kitchen and less time playing badminton. Of what use is badminton to your husband?'

Mohan said badminton was an important skill. He had moved in with her family while studying at university in Colombo. Sometimes he let her win their weekly competitions. Her twin brothers were only eight and sometimes she let them win.

'Amma, I don't even have a husband yet, or in-laws.'

'That's right, and you never will if you keep talking back. Saturn is in your eighth house at the moment; that's why everything you say comes out badly.'

She opened her mouth but closed it again, it was pointless. Emboldened by her silence, Amma continued. 'I wish you would learn from me. Your words don't become a girl like you.'

'You mean a girl like *you* were. I am not you, Amma. I'm not you!' Nala's nose reddened as she felt her tears betray her. She hated crying in front of her mother.

'Yes mahal,' Amma replied, using the perfunctory endearment. 'I can see that very clearly. This man is special. He's the first doctor from his village – he was only sixteen-years-old when he entered medical school. He has already been accepted into a training programme in England - he will be the youngest qualified surgeon in Ceylon when he comes back. Old Uncle Ramanathan says he has a brilliant future ahead of him *and* he's a good person, from a good family. The doctor has seen you already but I don't think it's necessary for him to hear you before you marry. When he arrives on Saturday, please just smile sweetly and keep your mouth shut.'

Rajan was accompanied by his parents and Uncle Ramanathan for the first meeting. The parents talked, not involving the prospective bride and groom, until his mother, a square stout woman, asked Nala what her favourite colour was.

'Blue,' she replied.

'You can't have a blue wedding sari,' the old lady laughed.

'Then crimson, I like crimson,' she said firmly.

Her mother intervened, not wanting her to appear fussy, 'She likes red. A red wedding sari would be wonderful, thank you.'

'She can have crimson,' Rajan spoke for the first time that afternoon. His voice was not what Nala had imagined. His accent was clear and clipped, his voice quiet. Not soft – it was a strong voice – but quiet.

'She should have crimson if she likes,' he said, settling the matter.

Four months later, Nala thought about this, their only conversation, as she walked down the aisle towards him in a crimson sari. He was seated under a canopy of garlands. The priest sat on the dais offering flowers and ghee into the small sacrificial fire. He muttered prayers to himself, while the crowd of well-wishers chatted amongst themselves, paying little attention to the ancient ceremony that was taking place. The nathaswaram player sat with his drummer on the side. He played his trumpet enthusiastically, nodding his head and swaying in time with the drummer as he belted out the strident wedding tune.

'Keep your eyes down,' Amma whispered as Nala left the changing room.

Her father guided her footsteps and, despite the heavy sari and borrowed jewellery she wore, she didn't falter. Appa helped her onto the small seat beside Rajan. He arranged her elaborate floral head-dress, kissed her tearfully and stepped back, leaving her with her husband-to-be.

She found that if she kept her head straight but dropped it a little and moved her eyes as far left as they would go, she could make out the lines of Rajan's hands without being detected. Or so she thought. Her mother nudged her from behind. 'Plenty of time for peeking later,' she had said earlier, laughing and scolding simultaneously in the changing room. Nala hadn't seen his face again, except in his graduation photograph. He looked serious in sepia.

She pulled at the gold threads on her wedding sari. Amma had told her not to but she couldn't help it. The embroidery spread like a forest of flowers over a deep crimson earth, telling a story no-one but the weaver understood. She picked a golden flower, then traced the thread of the petals to the leaves down to the stem. Amma nudged her sharply again.

The ceremony was long and Nala struggled to stay focused. Leaning back a little, she tried to catch her cousin-brother's eye. Mohan was standing behind Rajan on the other side of the canopy and he was probably laughing at her. He was Rajan's groomsman. The position should have been given to one of the twins but she had argued convincingly that they were only eight-years-old and too young for the job. It would be unfair to choose between them. When Amma finally conceded, Nala winked at Mohan behind Amma's back. She knew she would feel better if Mohan was there on the dais with her.

Not that she felt bad. Amma had tried to reassure her as she was getting dressed, 'Don't be nervous mahal, everything will be fine today and tonight. He's a good man, your Appa has chosen well. He'll be kind. And you must be kind...and quiet too Nala, not all men will listen to your talk like Appa and Mohan. You listen to him, you be what *he* needs.'

After a while, she had stopped listening to her mother who continued to dress her and scold her. Instead, Nala had sat at the changing room mirror and admired the bride that was emerging. Her wedding sari was tightly pleated at her waist and across her chest, making her look more womanly than she was. The vibrant colour suited her. She hoped Rajan would like it.

The ceremony had almost ended and although Nala and Rajan had sat next to each other for four hours, they were yet to look at each other directly. Finally, the priest nodded at her. The musicians took their cue, and accelerated the wedding song towards its frenetic peak. Amma nudged her and she straightened her back, leant towards the man next to her and bowed her head. He reached around her neck with the thick gold wedding chain. Once tied it could never be untied. His fingers fumbled against the back of her neck and she felt her mother bend down to help him. As Amma closed the chain's clasp, the crowd showered them in flowers, and she could hear Amma stifle a sob.

Rajan dipped his finger into the pot of kunkumam powder the priest held out to him. Slowly and carefully, he placed a small red moon on her pale forehead.

She was married.

After the hundreds of close friends and distant cousins departed, Nala and Rajan retired to their bedroom. A thoughtful aunty had thrown frangipani flowers over the bed and her mother had left a tumbler of warm milk on the nightstand.

She reached prettily for the silver cup: her dowry bangles falling over themselves to her slim wrists, disrupting the graceful movement she was attempting. She passed the tumbler to Rajan as her mother had instructed her.

He cleared his throat nervously, drank the cup of milk and handed it back to her. There was a piece of sugar candy at the bottom to sweeten it. It shone dully, like an unpolished diamond. She wanted to pull it out and eat it but he was looking at her.

Until now, she had understood, even enjoyed her part in the wedding ceremony, but in the quiet of their bedroom, she wondered what would happen next. How should they begin a life together? Amma had reassured her that Rajan's years of medical training would have prepared him properly for his duties. Apparently he had done a rotation in obstetrics and even won a prize in midwifery.

She looked hopefully at her husband. Her black curls were fighting to release themselves from the elaborate but dying flower arrangement. She would need his help to remove the jewels that were woven into her braid. She blushed at the thought of his fingers in her hair.

'Thank you for the milk, Nala,' he said finally. 'You must be very tired.' He moved to the far side of the room and quickly changed into the plain sarong and night shirt he had brought with him. He got into their bed and turned his back to her, leaving her, still wrapped and trapped in her heavy wedding clothes.

After two weeks, Nala began to worry. The couple had moved into Rajan's parents' home in Wellawatte, only six blocks from her parents. Every evening he would return from work and the family ate dinner together. Her mother-in-law Devaki served the food, heaping steaming hot curries onto her father-in-law and Rajan's plates. As both men began to eat, Devaki would motion to Nala to join them. She served her own plate and only started to eat when her mother-in-law did. After the meal, she and Rajan would retire to their room, where he read and then formally wished her good night.

By the third week, she decided it was time to seek advice. She visited her own family daily, often meeting them at the nearby Pillayar temple for a chat and a quick prayer. On one such visit, she quietly pulled her grandmother aside and confessed her concern.

'Archi, it's been weeks since the wedding and...nothing has happened,' she began tentatively.

'Nala, it's far too early for you to be pregnant,' her grandmother replied.

'No Archi, I mean *nothing* has happened that could make me pregnant...' she blushed. 'I don't think he...likes me.'

'Nonsense, all men like women, especially a woman as beautiful as you. What happens when you go to your room?' Archi asked.

'He just reads for a little while. Sometimes his mother brings him a cup of warm milk before she sleeps. After that he goes to sleep.' She described their nightly routine tearfully.

'That's unusual, perhaps he is-' Archi stopped in mid-sentence. 'Nala, where *exactly* is your bedroom?' she questioned.

'It's at the back of the house, next to his parents' room. Why?'

'Well then, that explains it,' Archi declared. She paused before lowering her voice, 'In three days time it is the Shivarathri poosai. I will ask Devaki to join me for a midnight vigil at the temple. I'll tell her we must pray all night together and seek Lord Shiva's blessings for our future grandchildren. You must take your husband to your bedroom and well, you know...' Archi's voice trailed off. The old woman looked around to make sure no-one was listening.

Nala's face was ablaze at the thought of seducing her husband and making the god of destruction an accomplice in her grandmother's plan. Archi took her face in her hands.

'You have a lifetime of difficult moments ahead of you Nala; that is marriage. As the *Thirukkural* says, you must begin each journey as you intend to continue it. Take control now, with love in your heart and a smile on your pretty face.'

Nala rolled her eyes and laughed. Archi often quoted from the ancient poem, confidently misquoting it to suit her own purposes.

'Archi, I doubt the *Thirukkural* has anything to say about overbearing mothers-in-law and shy husbands!'

'Nala, the *Thirukkural* has something to say about everything,' Archi replied, winking at her as she popped a shaving of areca nut into her mouth.

Later that week, her in-laws and parents attended the temple, at Archi's request. It was the full moon of Shivarathri, when offerings were made all night long to Lord Shiva. Rajan and Nala ate dinner at home, alone and in silence. After dinner, Rajan undressed and slipped into their bed with a PG Wodehouse novel. She took a deep breath and sat next to him, on his side.

'What are you doing?' he asked.

'I don't know.' Her heart raced uncomfortably. 'You don't seem to know either so I thought perhaps we could work it out together.' She reached over and took the book away from him. He smiled nervously and blushed even more deeply than her.

Nala excitedly prepared for their honeymoon. Five weeks had passed since the wedding and they were no longer complete strangers to each other.

Rajan had been selected by his consultants at Colombo General Hospital to present a paper on the effectiveness of Ceylon's smallpox vaccination programme. The conference was in Delhi and he had agreed to take her with him although he refused to use the word 'honeymoon' outside the refuge of their bedroom.

Nala was one month short of her eighteenth birthday. Eighteen: one plus eight added up to nine. Everyone told her this was a good age to begin a journey. She checked her handbag again, laying out her precious cargo on the bed. First, she took out the important documents: the brand new passports, tickets, itinerary and traveller's cheques – all carefully preserved in a special plastic wallet and filed neatly by Rajan's meticulous, excited hands. He had proudly explained to her that he would be able to find any document and any traveller's cheque of the desired denomination in the dark, under pressure, perhaps even under water. She watched with hidden amusement as he rehearsed different scenarios in which he would need to produce a document quickly, applauding his successful drills.

Next, she took out a small, embroidered purse given to her by her mother. It contained a standard issue packet of holy ash, folded tightly to keep its contents from spilling, and a creased picture of Lord Murugan, her mother's personal deity. She pulled at the medallion that was trapped in the lining of the purse: it was St Christopher, from her grandmother – just in case.

She flicked through the empty notebook her father had given her. 'Write down everything you see and feel Nala, I want to know all about it when you get back.' She had tried to touch his feet but he held her and kissed her forehead.

On top of the notebook she placed the package from Ayah: cumin, chilli powder, mustard seeds, root ginger, five betel nuts, two small tins of mackerel, and a tin-opener that doubled as a betel nut cracker. There was also a packet of coriander seeds in case she got sick. The nursemaid was determined to ensure that her charge didn't suffer from malnutrition while she was away. Outside Ceylon, food was very bland.

Finally, she admired the gifts from her husband for this trip: a pair of large tortoise-shell sunglasses and, most surprisingly, pink frosted lipstick. Rajan had shyly offered it to her saying, 'I thought you might like this.'

She had laughed with delight and kissed him forcefully on the cheek. He laughed back and looked around to make sure no-one was watching.

She hadn't used the lipstick yet but she had admired its creamy, shiny pinkness many times. It smelled faintly of lychees and her mouth watered at the thought of wearing it. She was saving it for the Taj Mahal and for just the right moment.

3

KANDY, 1947

Sitting high, watching over the island imperially, Kandy and the surrounding hill-country had reason for its pride. It was beautiful. Mist lingered lightly over the hills, kissing their contours. Their many nuances of green, giving way to emerald terraces, some sharp and some shallow, changed colour in the light. They were flecked with people in the distance, picking the tender leaves of the tea plantations.

Kandy offered Nala a surprising adventure. She found herself living alone with her husband for the first time since marriage. The hospital had given them a house with a housekeeper. It was smaller than her mother-in-law's house where she'd lived for the last year, but she didn't care. It was hers; hers and Rajan's. She could be as untidy and as unruly as she wished; she could tease and flirt openly with him; she could regale him with stories and scandals she learned from her weekly art class.

'Don't be seduced by those ladies,' Rajan warned her about her new friends: the well-dressed wives of Sinhalese landowners, English diplomats and exiled aristocrats. He was particularly scathing about Philomena de Silva and her husband Melvin, who owned the largest tea estate in the area. Philomena was a tea party politician.

'Melvin humours his wife's interest in politics because he married her for her connections. He's a clever man. He knows that if he wants to do as well under the new party as he's done under the British, he'll need the right blood. Blood is as much currency as currency itself. The new democracy won't be too different from the old autocracy, Nala,' Rajan lectured her. He admired Melvin's shrewdness as much as he was repulsed by it. 'There'll be a transfer of power from one self-interested master to another. The country will be defined by men like him.'

'I think he's very smart in his tailored English suits,' Nala replied. She refused to be swayed, she looked forward to her art classes with the ladies. Sitting, chatting and sipping tea, they laughed their carefree, tinkly little laughs. They peppered their sentences with 'You must' – 'You must try this blend of tea my husband is developing'; 'You must see these shoes I bought in London'; 'You must go to this new dress shop in Madras.'

Many of the ladies were well-travelled. They had been to Europe and seen the paintings she loved. They moved in interesting circles even if they weren't actually interested in them. Their boredom was a pre-requisite for their sophistication. Nala was far too excited to feign boredom.

Rajan had asked her to do him a favour. He never asked for favours.

'I have to go back to Colombo for a fortnight. The Royal College of Surgeons wants me to invigilate the written examinations. I wouldn't ask you to do this Nala, but this patient needs my help.'

He said he had taken care of everything. Their driver Vijay had been instructed to take Nala every day at eleven o'clock from Kandy to the village.

'It's only a thirty minute drive but you would never know the village is there – it's on the other side of the main plantations.'

The servant girl had been instructed to cook and fill two tiffin carriers as well as four canisters of water from their kitchen pump.

'Do not carry the canisters – let the driver do that Nala. You must be careful not to strain yourself in your condition. Wait in the car. Don't accept any food or water from the family – even cooked food – just say that you've already eaten at home. Or eat the food you've brought, if you have to. But don't wash your hands there.

'I've already given the family a box of sterile dressings and napkins. All you need to do is accompany the driver and make sure the family gets the food and water. I've told Mr Thambiah what to do if his daughter develops a fever but he may need help. That is the *only* time you should get out of the car. He'll be afraid to use the syringe so I'll need to teach you.'

Rajan spread a cloth on the dining table and carefully placed a glass syringe, a needle, a glass of water and a plump aubergine in front of him.

'This needle needs to be boiled every time you use it, even if you're using it on the same person. Please wash your hands and use my rubber gloves before you do anything. Now, attach the needle to the syringe. Listen for the click.'

She leaned in closer and pushed the needle gently onto the nub of the syringe. Her heart was beating so loudly she wasn't sure she'd be able to hear anything.

'There. Good, Nala,' he smiled proudly. 'That's the hardest part – people are usually afraid of sharp objects.'

'You're a sharp object,' she replied.

'True,' he laughed. 'Now, insert the needle into the glass of water and imagine you're loading it with penicillin – draw the syringe slowly and fully. If you see air bubbles, raise the syringe vertically, needle facing upwards. That's it. Then slowly press the syringe and let the air out. Stop when you see the liquid at the tip of the syringe.'

She did as he instructed.

'Good. Now for the easy part – imagine that aubergine is the buttocks of your patient, and push it in. One quick stab and push and you're done.'

Gluteus maximus, he called it. For a man of few words, he used complicated ones. She had done many things to an aubergine but never that – injecting it with pretend penicillin was much easier than cooking.

Nala had seen poorer villages. As a child she'd visited relatives, usually at funerals, and she'd been aware that some people had harder lives than her. She knew her parents weren't wealthy like Rita Matthews', but they were the growing middle class. Ceylon was proud of its middle classes. Politicians boasted about them. The country's streets were not littered with its poor, the way they were in India.

No, the streets of Colombo and Kandy were clean.

'Just make the delivery and leave, Nala.' That was the last thing Rajan said to her when he boarded the train for the capital. The car climbed higher into the hill country. With each turn, the roads became narrower, as though seeking level ground between the angles of the implacable mountain.

The homes she passed were fragile huts, some steadied across wooden frames, others just propped against the sharp gradient of the mountain.

When she looked out of the car window, she could glimpse Philomena de Silva's plantation between huts. The blanket of camellia plants looked different from this side of the valley, the thick green rows sitting like fat toupees in a shop window.

'Wait in the car Madam,' Vijay said, turning off the engine. 'I'll give them everything and come back.'

'No. I'll come,' she replied.

She wasn't prepared for the smell. She could taste the foulness when she swallowed.

'Madam, please – Doctor will not like this. He was very clear.'

'Doctor is not here,' she replied lifting her sari to mid-calf as she stepped over potholes of feculent water.

Mohan had married an Indian Tamil – Vani – a low caste, quiet girl. She wondered if Vani's family lived like this.

The driver strode ahead of her confidently with a canister of water in each hand. The door to the hut was a striped sarong. He set the water down and lifted up the sarong to allow Nala in.

'Shouldn't we knock first?' she asked.

'No, only the girl will be here. The others will be on the plantation. It's picking season.'

She followed Vijay into a small, dark room. A pulp of shredded coconut husk and cow dung had been applied to the walls to strengthen them. Woven bed mats lined the edges of the swept dirt floor. Against the far corner lay a girl, no more than fifteen, asleep on a mattress made of kapok fibre rolled up in an old sari.

Nala bent down and sat next to the girl. Her skin was hot and wet.

'Madam, please,' Vijay said nervously.

'Bring the things Vijay, do as Doctor asked. And candles – I think my husband keeps candles in the glove box. In fact, check the whole car and bring anything useful he keeps in there. Leave it by the door and wait outside.'

Nala pulled the stained bed sheet back and inspected the girl. She stirred and opened her eyes.

'Amma?' she asked softly.

'No rasathi, my name is Nala. I am the doctor's wife. Dr Rajan – you know him don't you?'

'Yes. He comes here. He helps us.'

'Yes. What's your name rasathi?' Nala began to wipe the girl, gently starting with her face.

'Meenakshi, after the goddess.'

'I know the goddess. I went to the Meenakshi Amman temple once,' Nala slowly took the girl's dress off. It was dark and crusted in places. She wiped her carefully between the thighs. Large clots came away in her hands. She remembered the gloves too late.

'You've been to India?' the girl asked, trying to raise her head.

'I have – I went after Doctor and I were married. Have you been?'

'No. But my thatha was born there.'

'Is your grandfather still there?' Fresh, thick blood had started to trickle.

'No, the British brought him to Kandy when he was a little boy. He died here.' The girl closed her eyes. 'Appa says we'll all die here.'

Nala returned the next day with food and as many canisters of water as the driver could fit into the car. She went the day after that with their spare mattress and a pillow. And the day after that with old clothes.

Nala held the glass thermometer up to the lantern. It read just over forty degrees.

The man sat on his haunches next to his daughter. He wiped his face with his faded sarong. The skin on his forehead had thickened, from the cloth rope that tied the basket to his back. Tea was heavy when it wasn't steeping in a bone china pot.

'Do you know what to do madam?' he asked. His Tamil was faster and shorter than hers. Born here, he still spoke like an Indian.

'I think so. Doctor taught me,' she replied, clenching and stretching her fingers in the rubber gloves. She surveyed her instruments, all lined up on the cloth next to her. The syringe was loaded and ready. Rajan said he had 'procured' the penicillin from the British Army's supply. Very few Ceylonese had access to it and, as she had proudly told her art class, Rajan was the first doctor to administer it to civilians. She hadn't told her art class that she would also be administering it.

She inhaled deeply and exhaled slowly. The girl's temperature had been high for too long. The man reached out and steadied Nala's arm. His skin was black and cracked like desiccated tamarind paste, scorched by the sun.

'Meenakshi is my only child. Her mother died long ago. I should have let her keep it but I didn't know – I didn't know she would do this to herself – or the baby.' The man held his daughter's hand.

'What about the father of the baby?' Nala asked, exhausted. She had been sitting there for hours, taking the girl's temperature, and praying for the fever to ease.

'The father of the baby has many children in this village – far away from the manor where his wife cannot see.'

She looked at the girl and cleaned the curve of her bottom. She imagined the aubergine and she did as Rajan had instructed her.

The ladies stood facing their easels as Master William Baptist inspected their work. They had been attending classes together for several months at Philomena de Silva's house and their uniquely similar masterpieces were shaping up. Standing on the verandah of the stately house, the group looked over the tea estates that formed the subject of their artistic efforts. They mixed their palette as he instructed them, some more confidently than others.

Nala was 'a natural talent' according to the master. The others hid their smiles behind their easels while she blushed prettily, her fair skin revealing the rush of blood underneath. She knew what they were doing – and thinking. She didn't mind their jealous whispers, she was used to it. It was hard being the envy of others but she would rather be beautiful and envied than ugly and overlooked like Felicia Gunawardene, Judge Gunawardene's wife. *And* she couldn't paint.

The weekly classes gave her a chance to chatter endlessly to an eager and more responsive audience than her husband. She had recently announced her first pregnancy and much of each week's conversation was devoted to whether she was carrying the son she desperately wanted. The ladies were full of questions and comments.

'How did Rajan become a consultant at such a young age, Nala? He must be terribly clever. He's very handsome for such a dark man.' Before she could boast about his honours from the Royal College of Surgeons in London, they had moved onto the next question.

'And darling, how did you become so fair-skinned? Are all your relatives like you?' they asked as they kissed her, leaving their waxy lipstick and Chanel perfume on her coveted skin.

On that day, Philomena was entertaining them with tales of the parliamentary debates that were taking place in Colombo.

'The new constitution still hasn't been finalised. That's what happens when you let men negotiate.' Everyone laughed and Philomena continued, 'I think the British should just give the United National Party what it wants. It did win the general election after all.

'As you know, my father is a member of the UNP. We are *close* personal friends with the Senanayake clan,' she reminded them. She stepped back to admire her painting. 'DS Senanayake will become Prime Minister when the British finally go.'

'Do you think the British will really leave?' Felicia Gunawardene asked. 'What would they do with all their properties? Their businesses and their big houses?'

'They'll sell them back to us, of course. Britain is tired of war and tired of freedom movements,' Philomena declared, flourishing her paintbrush like a sword. 'It's an ageing master, feeling the weight of its years.'

Nala hid behind her easel as Philomena's voice rose, 'Nehru and India have had their 'tryst with destiny' and now the time for ours has come too.' That tryst ended in a great deal of bloodshed for the Hindus and Muslims but she didn't dare remind Philomena.

Inevitably, Viktoria Khilkov started baiting their hostess. The older woman's aristocratic upbringing should have given her a better sense of politeness.

'Philomena, you are sweet, but I've seen all of this before in Russia,' Viktoria said, interrupting her flow. 'I've heard the talk about giving power back to the people. People are stupid and those who know better should rule them. In this case, those who know better also know how to harness people with rhetoric that has far too much resonance. It's no wonder that Tamil politicians are worried.'

Nala avoided looking at either of the ladies; embarrassed for Philomena and afraid of Viktoria, she kept her attention firmly on her palette and the hill country green she was trying to re-create.

'Exile has made you hard Viktoria,' Philomena responded. 'This is a chance for our nation to-'

'Philomena, this island has never been a nation,' Viktoria interrupted her again. 'It was just three separate tribal kingdoms. You should know that – you've heard the hill country Sinhalese talk about wanting a state for themselves; they want their old Kandyan kingdom back. Ceylon was forced together as one colony, not a nation – a zone really, for administrative convenience, run by one of the finest civil services in the world. Ceylon is the spice shelf in the Empire's pantry cupboard, nothing more.'

'We will be more, the Sinhala nation will…' Philomena stopped and looked around, suddenly self-conscious.

'Oh yes, the *Sinhala nation*. You really have been reading too much propaganda – UNP or bhikku, it's all the same. Let me guess, the *Mahavamsa*?' Viktoria asked.

The bhikkus had been using the ancient text to prove that Ceylon was a Buddhist and therefore Sinhalese nation. Rajan said the bhikkus, despite being monks, excelled even more than Viktoria at stirring trouble.

'Don't speak about our history like that,' Philomena replied. Her pink blush deepened to a defensive red, tears catching on her long, carefully coiffed eyelashes.

'It isn't history or even literature,' Viktoria argued. 'It's a call to arms, a questionable account of racial superiority, couched in the rhetoric of religion. Every race has its own version, mind you – the problem here is that yours is being used as a political manifesto in Colombo.'

Nala was now completely confused by both Philomena and Viktoria. She knew that the Tamil politicians wanted the new constitution of Ceylon to guarantee them an equal status in the new country. GG Ponnambalam, the leader of the Tamil Congress, had proposed 50-50 representation in parliament but no-one had taken him seriously. Even Rajan thought giving all of the minorities in Ceylon equal representation with the Sinhalese was preposterous in a democracy. She laughed whenever Rajan used the word 'preposterous'.

Viktoria's haughty matter-of-factness was too frightening so she turned to Philomena.

'What do you mean, Philomena? It won't be the Sinhala nation: it will be Ceylon – for all of us.' Nala intended the last part of her sentence to come out as a statement but it sounded more like a question. Maybe she wasn't sure after all. Looking around, none of the ladies looked sure, except for Viktoria who looked at her pityingly.

'Of course it will be a country for all of us,' Philomena replied too hastily, too soothingly. 'The Sinhalese, Tamils, Muslims, and Burghers – we've lived together for such a long time. We are Ceylonese and we need a democracy that will govern us. That's what the UNP is negotiating for at the moment with the British.'

'And what is the Tamil Congress negotiating for?' asked Viktoria.

'I beg your pardon?' Philomena's face reddened further.

'You know what I'm talking about. The UNP won't agree to the constitution because the Tamil Congress is negotiating with the British for minority protections. Why do the Tamils think they need protection?' Viktoria goaded.

Nala spoke up again, this time more confidently. She felt so much smarter when Rajan wasn't around to correct her. 'I just can't imagine that there will be any problems. I'm sure the British will create a system that protects everyone. The Tamil people wouldn't need *special* protection.'

The silence was becoming uncomfortable and made her want to chatter nervously on into the abyss. 'There is no majority or minority surely, just Ceylonese – we're all Ceylonese, aren't we.'

This time, she was able to control her voice and lower the pitch at the end of her sentence – it was a statement, not a question. Surveying her friends for agreement not reassurance, she gave them what she considered to be a politically wise smile. They looked away, unable to make eye contact with her.

'Enough talk of politics!' Philomena clapped her hands and her maids brought out a fresh pitcher of chilled lime cordial.

'I want to tell you about my new project. It's called the Mahatma Gandhi Foundation,' she said, the shards of chipped ice knocking each other as she raised her glass to her shiny lips.

'We owe so much to the Mahatma, it's the least I could do. I'm going to throw a spring ball with an auction. Melvin will invite his set from Colombo and of course the Senanayakes will come. *Everyone* will come.

'The money will go to projects for the poor in India. There has been so much trouble since Independence. Such a tragedy,' Philomena shook her head and wiped her mouth delicately.

'There are projects here in Kandy you could also support,' Nala spoke softly.

'What?'

'There are projects – here in Kandy,' she repeated. She thought of Meenakshi, who now worked for her and Rajan as their new servant girl. 'You could put some of the money into helping the Indian Tamils here.' When no-one responded, she continued, 'You know how they live Philomena. Their children are always sick. Perhaps we could do something for their children?' Her hand went protectively to her belly.

Viktoria laughed loudly. 'Why Nala, I think that is a brilliant idea! Philomena, what do you think?' she asked, arching one eyebrow at their hostess.

'I – I don't know what to say, Nala darling. Thank you for that idea – I will certainly give it some thought. Now, who would like more tea?' Philomena clapped for her maid again.

☼

Nala lay on the hospital bed, propped upright by pillows. Her parents had come from Colombo for her confinement. Amma sat on the bed with her, fanning her slowly. The windows in the room were open but the air was still, humidity sitting heavily on her belly.

Her contractions had started but it was too early, the baby wasn't due for another four weeks. Rajan said her blood pressure was high – *eclampsia* he called it, not staying to explain what that meant.

A week ago, he had been conducting his daily medical examination of her at home. He kept looking at her swollen feet, which she tried to hide from him.

'Stop fidgeting!' he almost shouted as he steadied the stethoscope. His fist clenched the rubber pump, inflating the cuff around her arm. It strangled her painfully. She was too afraid to ask him to stop. He had taken her pressure three times, watching the mercury rise to the top of the meter, then fall slowly down.

'We're going to the hospital, now,' he said. Several weeks before, he had packed her hospital bag, which he gave to the servant boy. Amma started to cry but Appa ushered her out of the room.

'We'll meet you at the hospital, mahan,' Appa said to Rajan. Nala had seen that look on her father's face before and she put her arms on her belly, around her child, as she too began to cry.

At the hospital, Rajan had politely but firmly requested a private room. It had two windows and a small bathroom. It was the room reserved for the MPs and estate owners of Kandy. Amma slept on a small cot bed by her side. Appa visited during the day, staying with her for hours and, on Rajan's instructions, bringing all her meals from her home. Rajan visited regularly, asking her terse questions. Did she have a headache, did she feel dizzy or nauseous, and how was her vision? He wouldn't stay to talk or eat with her. He lingered just long enough to examine her, read her chart, inspect the cleanliness of the room and bathroom and get an update from the staff. Although she had an obstetrician at Kandy Hospital, Rajan had instructed him that he would deliver his own child. The doctor had acquiesced immediately, neither of them referring to the hospital policy against this.

As Amma fanned her, Appa scoffed into his newspaper.

'What is it Appa – more bad news?' Nala asked, breathing deeply between contractions; they were slow but consistent. Appa had been scoffing all week while he kept her company.

'No, just more of the same,' Appa replied. 'People are saying GG Ponnambalam will align the Tamil Congress with the UNP. It seems he will support the Citizenship Act.' Appa shook his head. 'That man is a fool, a damn fool.'

She rarely heard Appa swear, but she understood her father's anger. Prime Minister Senanayake and his ruling United National Party were about to enact legislation. The act would strip the Indian Tamils of their citizenship and right to vote in Ceylon.

'My friends at my painting class are talking of little else,' she said.

'I'm sure they are, Nala. There are almost one million Indian Tamils in Ceylon and most of them work on your friends' plantations. If the Indian Tamils can't vote, then the Ceylon Tamils will never hold enough seats in parliament. There aren't enough of us without the Indian Tamils. We will always be at the mercy of the UNP or whatever Sinhala party comes to power. The Ceylon Tamils – the Tamil Congress – must block this, not support it!'

Appa threw the newspaper on the floor. Amma clicked her tongue at him and he bent down to retrieve it.

'Appa, please don't get upset, you'll make yourself sick,' Nala said to her father. He had his own health problems. His stomach was paining him and he had blood in his toilet. Rajan had taken him to see a British specialist in Colombo. Appa wouldn't talk about what the old gentleman had said, dismissing it as a waste of time.

'I'm alright mahal. You concentrate on yourself and the baby,' he smiled at her as he refolded the paper.

'What does Rajan say about all of this madness in Colombo?' he asked.

'Rajan? Rajan doesn't say anything about anything, at least not to me,' she replied, trying to control the resentment in her voice.

'Maybe you talk too much, Nala. Maybe he doesn't have a chance to talk,' Amma suggested. She adored Rajan. Nala was about to respond angrily when Appa spoke.

'Mahal, don't judge him by his words. Judge him by his actions. He is good to you and to us. He is good to his mother-'

She interrupted her father. 'He is *very* good to his mother. She can do no wrong in his eyes.'

'That is as it should be, Nala,' her father continued. 'His mother has no other children but there is a big family. Rajan has obligations – duties – to them and you shouldn't stand in the way of those.'

Rajan had cousins, many of whom had grown up in his home. He never mentioned the money he gave to his mother but she knew about it.

'He is good to you. You'll learn in time to understand what he's saying to you, even when he doesn't speak.'

Appa turned the paper to the social pages. 'Shall we see what parties we are not invited to?' he asked, trying to make her laugh. She didn't respond; she felt a sharp pain, a cold knife, slicing through her lower back. It was not like the other contractions.

'Call Rajan, call Rajan,' she whispered, saying his name over and over again, like a prayer.

Sweat trickled down, pooling in shallow wells at the base of her throat and the pit of her belly button. Her body finally relaxed, the tension shuddered from her arched back one last time. Her clenched fists released the thick, hospital sheets, and she held out her arms to Rajan.

'Let me see, let me see – is it a boy?' she asked breathlessly. He didn't hear her, his eyes and fingers quickly scanning the baby, assessing it for any abnormalities.

'Rajan, show me – is it a boy?' she repeated, more desperately this time.

'No Nala, it's a girl. She's fine,' he said, not taking his eyes off his new daughter. Her arms dropped a little. She cleared her throat before asking for the child again. He placed the baby gently in her arms and wrapped a blanket around them both. He sat on the bed next to her, tired but smiling. He had delivered many babies before but she could tell he had been anxious about this one.

She traced the baby's face. It was creased and crumpled like an aged passion fruit. Her skin was milky white except for the soft hair on her cheeks. She ran her hands over the baby's head. It was sticky.

'The nurses will clean her,' he explained.

'Are you disappointed?' she asked.

'Disappointed?' Rajan was confused.

'Yes, because she's a…girl.'

'No, Nala, don't be silly,' he laughed but stopped when he saw tears in her eyes.

'I've thought of a name for her,' he said.

'Already?' she was surprised. She held her breath as she waited for him to say *Lali*, the name of his sister who inhabited the locked core of his life.

'Yes, already. We've had nine months to think about it. I'd like to call her Priya. It means –'

'*Beloved* – I know. It's beautiful.' Embarrassed by the tears that were flowing freely now she touched the baby's downy face and whispered, 'Archi says that even the blackest mother crow thinks its chicks are golden.'

'Yes, but you are no crow and she is beautiful, just like you,' he replied.

'Thank you, Rajan.'

'I'll get the nurse,' he turned to go before either of them could say more.

✿

The months swam by in a haze of relentless feeding. Her daughter's insatiability was beyond her understanding. The baby wrapped soft, pink pincers around Nala's nipples and reached deeply into her, sucking out her marrow. She felt herself fading into a flaccid attachment to a new organism that was thriving, but demanding more and more of her.

Every morning she vowed to try harder with the baby: to love her more freely, to be more patient with her cries, to offer her breast and her body more readily. But by midday, she found herself watching the filigreed hand of the clock in her drawing room, willing Meenakshi to return from the market, so that she could pull herself out of her child's orbit and hand her over. She fought against the glorious gravity of blood that kept her tied to Priya and to her house.

Philomena de Silva visited her occasionally, bringing love cake and news from their circle of friends.

'I'm fundraising for my new Mahatma Gandhi Foundation, may God rest his soul,' she said, offering Nala a large slice. 'Eat. I hear you're feeding the baby yourself. You'll need your energy.'

'We've decided that the money will go to projects in Gujarat. That was Bapuji's home state, you know,' Philomena smiled, referring to Gandhi by his pet name.

'I want you to join the committee, of course Nala darling, whenever you feel ready,' she added, eyeing the state of her hair. She kissed her goodbye, leaving behind a cloud of Chanel that lingered for days.

Nala found herself resenting Rajan. Surely it was so much easier to love someone if you didn't have to be with them all of the time. Every evening he came home, eyes barely glancing at her, searching instead for the baby. Before he touched her, he washed his hands, as if preparing for surgery, meticulously sanitising himself in a familiar routine. And then he held her, smelled her, tested her strength and motor function, tickled her and kissed her. The affection that Nala had to wrest from her husband was showered like rice on a bride, to their child.

For Priya's first birthday, they returned to Colombo and celebrated with the usual visit to the temple, followed by a gathering of family and friends. Nala had wanted to hire Saraswathi Hall for the event but Rajan refused, declaring it an unnecessary expense. 'It's a birthday, not a wedding,' he said. He was right, but she hadn't been to Colombo for over a year, and there were so many people to see.

Priya was dressed in a French lace frock with matching bloomers; a gift from Rita Matthews who had recently returned from a tour of the Continent. The baby spent most of the afternoon scratching and pulling on the frilled collar, until Rajan could bear her pain no longer, and ordered Ayah to change her into a simple cotton dress. Archi made an enormous butter cake for the guests. She had been baking batches for weeks and freezing them at the houses of friends. The night before the party she connected them together, gluing the pieces of cake with a rich mortar of butter icing.

Ayah and Amma were charged with the task of chaperoning the baby as she was passed from aunty to aunty. Nala put her foot down when Rajan tried to insist on a pre-holding hand washing rule. 'It's ridiculous and offensive. I don't know about your relatives but there is nothing infectious about my family.'

With the baby safely entouraged and occupied, she was free to roam, a happy whirlwind of turquoise silk. People pressed gold sovereigns into her hands, gifts for Priya that Nala would save for her wedding dowry. They kissed her cheeks, told her she looked beautiful and asked her when she was planning another baby. She laughed off the question. They would start trying again soon but Rajan wanted to wait. He said 'higher rates of pregnancy increase the chances of maternal mortality and morbidity,' quoting from some research paper. She was, for once, very happy to defer to his superior knowledge on the matter. That night she enjoyed just being herself, without a baby at her breast or in her belly.

Before they left Colombo, Nala asked her mother for a favour. Rajan's contract with Kandy Hospital ran for two more years and she needed help. Ayah packed a small suitcase and returned to the hill-country with her.

4

COLOMBO, 1951

The cancer had moved with stealth. It feasted and grew without remorse. Nala held her father's frail hand. She could see the pain etched into his handsome face. It had replaced his smile lines with harsher, deeper ones. He was not an old man yet, but he had the frailty of a newborn.

'Don't cry, mahal, it's alright,' Appa whispered. 'Promise me you will look after your brothers and sister. If you swim, swim together. If you sink, sink together.'

'Don't worry Appa,' Rajan reassured her father. 'Nala and I will stay here. We'll take care of them. You have nothing to worry about.'

Appa's eyes filled with tears. 'You're a good boy, mahan. I knew from the beginning.'

He was breathless. He nodded at Rajan who rolled Appa's sleeve up to the wasted muscle of his shoulder. Collapsed blue veins sat with resignation.

Appa craved death, even more than the morphine Rajan had been giving him quietly over the last few months. Nala begged, with words, then tears and then screams.

'Let him go,' she cried. 'Help him, if you care for me at all, you will help him.'

Finally, Rajan relented. He put the cap back on the syringe. She rolled Appa's sleeve down again and placed his hands gently onto his sunken chest. Its rise and fall slowed to a steady rhythm, and then slowed and slowed.

✧

After Appa's death, Nala and Rajan offered to remain in her parents' home. Rajan had taken over the household expenses for her father during his illness and he continued to look after these. She didn't feel like the mistress of the house though. She still found herself deferring to her mother on domestic matters. She desperately wanted her own home but didn't know how to approach Rajan about it. Certainly she couldn't leave Amma and her siblings just yet; they needed her. Her father still needed her.

Nala stopped outside the Kathirgamam temple and breathed in the chaos. She was surrounded by thousands of pilgrims. Many of them had come on foot from all over to this remote southern corner of the island. Pilgrims even came from South India to see where Lord Murugan had met his divine consort Valli. The land was sacred and loved by worshippers from all religions. She had promised her father before he died that she would honour his last wishes and donate a bell to the temple.

It was the largest bell the priest had ever received. Nala had commissioned it a few weeks earlier, through her friend Rita Matthews. Rita was one of the Cinnamon Gardens Matthews, but they knew each other from Holy Family Convent, the Colombo school for girls they had both attended. Rita knew how to get things done; even as a child she had connections.

Although Nala had grown up in the middle-class Tamil suburb of Wellawatte, she knew Rita's elegant Colombo 7 neighbourhood well. Over generous morning teas, Rita introduced Nala to her world of parties and pretty things. Appa was fond of Rita but cautioned his daughter: the Matthews were once named 'Muthiahs' and their privileged life at Cinnamon Gardens had come at the price of their faith.

The thought of Appa made her sad again. He would have liked that the Matthews had made his bell for him. He would have seen that as a sign. Old habits and old cultures died hard despite religious conversion. Rajan said Appa would have found it ironic; Rajan thought everything was ironic.

She stood at the altar watching the priest. He was hunched over, holding her father's bell awkwardly. Its weight and curved shape defied him. He stumbled and both the bell and the priest's sarong started to slip down his body. She wasn't sure if she was going to laugh or cry out. A young Buddhist monk who had been watching the proceedings rushed forward and caught the bell while the priest caught his sarong. Together, they steadied the bell on the priest's sturdy paunch and he carried it alone behind the curtain that was drawn across the deity's enclave.

She sat down on the side of the temple, leaning against its cool stone wall. She tried to pray for Appa's soul but her eyes wandered over the other worshippers. She saw the young monk who had saved her gift. He was a handsome man, almost pretty. His head was shorn and he wore the saffron robes of the Buddha, denoting his path of austerity and detachment. He was with a group of other bhikkus, monks who worshipped here regularly.

She wondered if the bhikkus were the same ones who had tried to give them flyers at the temple gate. Rajan had politely declined, not just because he didn't support the newly formed Sri Lanka Freedom Party, but because, as he often liked to tell her, he didn't approve of political activism at temples. The temple was not the place to talk about the superiority of the Sinhala language or Bandaranaike's plans for a new order to the country.

Of course Rajan didn't approve of socialising at temples either, which showed a clear misunderstanding of one of the main purposes for which God had created places of worship.

Breathing back tears she remembered one of the last times she had spoken to Appa. He had patted her cheek when he saw the familiar discolouration of her nose.

'Don't cry, mahal, it's alright. Promise me you will look after your brothers and sister. If you swim, swim together. If you sink, sink together.' The thought of her three siblings sinking together made her laugh. None of them could swim except for Nakula, the older twin, who was an excellent athlete. She had only ever waded in the ocean and as a young woman she always wore her sari. She could drown in her modesty, she thought.

Speaking of modesty, she must remember to tell Rita that her bell had almost disrobed a priest at one of Ceylon's greatest temples. Rita and her family would make a pilgrimage here next month for Easter and she knew Rita wouldn't be able to keep a straight face at the altar. Nala was smiling to herself as the group of bhikkus moved past her. The handsome monk caught her eye and smiled back, motioning to the priest who was fortuitously still fully clothed. They both laughed, trying hard not to think about a fallen bell, or worse, a fallen sarong.

She tried once more to pray for her father and her nose reddened. She silently asked Lord Murugan to grant her a son. She was ready to have another child. She imagined herself holding a boy who would be like Appa in appearance and character: someone handsome, strong and kind, who made her laugh and understood her nature.

Blades of afternoon light cleaved through the closed timber shutters of Nala's room. She sat upright in her bed, forlornly pressing the chikan embroidered shawl on her lap, pushing the furrows away until a smooth skin of cream cashmere surrounded her. It had been a gift from Rajan on their honeymoon. They had bought it together from a man at the bazaar who pulled down shawl after shawl from high shelves, unfurling them with a flick and flourish of his wrists. She laughed as colour burst around her, each shawl brighter and more elaborate than the last.

Finally, Rajan said to the man, 'No, not these.' He shook his head. 'Something beautiful: something simple; like her,' he pointed to Nala and smiled. She smiled back. The man nodded, not understanding English but not needing to. He went to the workshop behind him and returned with material, buttery soft. Silver-white thread weaved an intricate shadow across its body, a flowering vine that moved gracefully from one end of the tapestry to the other. Rajan wrapped his cashmere arms around her tightly and she felt safe, full of hope for the future that sprawled out in front of her like a thousand vibrant shawls.

After Priya's birth, there had been two others who had not stayed inside her long enough to live. She named the first baby Murugan after her favourite deity. She named the next baby Keshava, after Lord Krishna. Rajan had been upset when she told him. He said she shouldn't do that. She shouldn't name a child before it was born but she couldn't help it.

She thought of all the times she had complained about Priya and suffered her clinging kisses with irritation; all the times her period had come and she'd been relieved. She was being punished. She never discussed it with Rajan, too afraid to know what he thought. For once, she didn't resent his silence, keeping it safely between them.

He spoke to colleagues at Colombo General and called colleagues in Madras and London about the 'problem'. He sought reasons, explanations for the loss, while she sought comfort and the courage to try again.

Her friends offered advice and prayers. Everyone had a story to tell, about women who had tried to have children for years, who had performed the right poosai at the right temple on the right day, imploring the planets to align and a baby to be born. She barely listened as they spoke, her eyes wandering over the wealth of children that filled the houses of these women; women who did not know the depth of her yearning; women who had never felt the bitter thrill of regularly conceiving but not consummating life.

Nala pulled the shawl around her but she couldn't feel its warmth; she had been spotting flecks of dark, clotted blood all morning and a familiar cramp in her belly had started to pulse slowly, quietly. She tried hard not to name the baby within.

'Don't move.' Nala's eyes darted between her palette and her subject. They were sitting on the shaded verandah at the back of the house. Since her last miscarriage, she hadn't left the house, often not leaving her bedroom for hours. Finally, Rajan had pulled out her easel and paints from an unpacked box. He requested a portrait of himself. It was so unlike him that she conceded and began to look forward to their daily sitting.

She added more red and white into the brown paint; she was struggling to create his skin colour. He was dark but the base tone was softer and lighter. When he smiled, his lips parted, revealing clean, straight teeth. He said dental and oral hygiene could never be prioritised too highly, the mouth was the gateway to the body. She wished it was the gateway to his soul.

She had sketched his outline already, faintly tracing the lines of his face onto the canvas: the stern clench of his jaw, the heavy eyebrows and the straight nose. But the eyes and the lips, she was having trouble with those. They were capricious conspirators, the features working in tandem, sometimes serious, sometimes fierce, occasionally warm but always resolute.

'Rajan,' she repeated, 'please – I'm concentrating.'

'Yes, I can see you're concentrating,' he responded.

She looked up to see him trying not to smile.

'This is actually quite hard. I know it's not surgery but it's difficult to capture someone – their *essence* as Master Baptist would say. You have to really know someone to paint them properly; otherwise you might as well just take their photograph. Paint has texture and tones. Master said with great paintings you feel like you're looking at a living moment in that person's life that will breathe forever because of the way the artist has painted it, even more than because of how the person has lived it. Master Baptist could have been a poet as well as an artist.'

Rajan relaxed his pose and looked directly at her. 'Master Baptist is a drunkard. Now you're quoting him about living moments and lecturing me on art? I knew we spent too long in the hill country.'

'Never mind,' she said, hiding her face and her tears behind her canvas. 'I'm almost finished for today. I just want to get your skin colour right so I can paint when you're not here. And I need to sketch your mouth.'

'My mouth?' he repeated, self-consciously licking his lips.

'Yes, your mouth, so if you could stop moving it that would be helpful,' she retorted not daring to peek out from behind the canvas.

'We do need to talk about something,' he replied, ignoring her instructions. 'I spoke with your Amma yesterday, about Kamini. She's twenty years old now.'

Nala's younger sister finished school the year Appa died and for the last two years she had been studying home economics at a local college. Appa would have organised a marriage for her by now. He had some savings and a pension that Amma could live on, but she knew there was not enough to provide for the dowry and the wedding.

She put her palette down; she had ruined the skin-brown and would need to start again. She braced herself for the conversation with Rajan. Talking about money made her nervous; sometimes talking to him about anything made her nervous. Before she could speak, Rajan began – 'I've asked your Amma to look for a husband. We mustn't wait too long, Kamini is getting older. She will finish studying soon and I'm sure she's keen to start her own family. I told Amma that the dowry can come from your Appa. Your father wanted to do his duty. This house – *his* house – will be more than enough. I will pay for the wedding and other things. Kamini will have a good start in life, Nala.'

She tried to speak but he raised a hand, a gesture she usually found upsetting.

'Your brothers,' he continued, 'they're doing quite well in their exams – Sahadeva is better than Nakula as usual. Nakula spends too long on the track, running races and showing off to his friends. He doesn't do all the extra homework I set him. He'll need to buckle down for his A-Levels. I told Amma that I will help with their university expenses.'

'Rajan, I...don't know what to say. Thank you-' she stood up, unsure of how to express her gratitude, her relief. She wanted to put her arms around him but he looked away.

'There's nothing to say,' he said quickly, closing the sliver of a moment that had opened up between them. He cleared his throat as if the conversation had irritated it; the words a mucus that needed to be expelled. She resumed her seat behind the canvas.

'One last thing, Nala – if we give this house to Kamini, then Amma and the twins can move in with us, when we set up our own home.'

'Our own home?' she repeated.

'Yes, our own home. We need a little more space, and there will be...more children, God willing. We should move, don't you agree?' Before she could respond, he said, 'I'll stop talking now, so you can paint me; you can *capture my essence* if you wish.'

God willing.

More children.

Our own home.

She looked around the canvas to see if he was making fun of her. Rajan's eyes were serious but his mouth soft. His dark skin was tinged by an unusual pink; he was the colour of palm sugar.

ANNAMALAIYAR TEMPLE, TAMIL NADU PROVINCE IN SOUTH INDIA, 1954

Nala breathed deeply, willing herself not to cry.

'Rajan, I'd like to go to Annamalaiyar Temple.' She didn't wait for him to refuse; to make excuses about work. 'Amma has agreed to look after Priya and walk her to kindergarten. Rita will visit the family every day to check on the house. Even the twins have promised they will come home on time so that Amma won't be alone for long. And of course Ayah is here to supervise them all.'

He looked at her hard and she raised her face to his, ready for his response, his scorn.

'Yes, we can go to Annamalaiyar, if you like. It's supposed to be a beautiful temple. I'll talk to the hospital about taking a little time off.' He walked away, but she didn't need more. She called Rita and made the travel arrangements for South India.

She looked sadly at the tree in the temple courtyard. Its magnificent branches were covered in tiny cradles, tied by other childless couples. Like her, they had made the pilgrimage to Annamalaiyar, a few hours from Madras. Like her, they had tied their cradles to the temple tree and prayed – begged – for a child. From a distance, the cradles looked like a flock of parrots, nestling in the boughs of the ancient branches. Each contained the last hope of thousands of women. Behind the temple, the dusty hills of Annamalai stood, watching the worshippers. Lord Shiva descended to the earth, on those hills. He took the form of a pillar of fire, bringing light to the world.

She said her final prayers as a hot wind lifted her cradle and the others, making them swing wildly. She stepped back from the temple tree. *Maghizha* – the tree had a name. She had given her children names too. As she tied the cradle to the temple tree, she told it what she had chosen for her next baby, if only Lord Shiva would hear her prayer. 'Sivanandan' she whispered, not daring to say it too loudly in case the evil eye heard her; in case the planets knew how she hungered. Amma said the planets could be fickle.

Rajan was waiting for her in the temple hall. It was called the hall of light but as she stepped inside, it felt dark and cold. She narrowed her eyes trying to see him but there were too many people. They drifted in and out between the carved pillars that held the temple dome above them. Suddenly, someone took her hand and she pulled away, instinctively afraid.

'It's only me,' Rajan said, dropping her hand. People didn't touch at the temple. 'Shall we go?' he asked.

'Yes. Thank you for bringing me here,' she said quietly.

'There's no need to thank me, Nala. We both want the same thing,' he replied.

'Sivanandan' she whispered again – the son of Lord Shiva. 'It will work this time Rajan, I know it will. I'm going to name him Sivanandan. Nandan for short.'

He nodded, his eyes shining in the shadows. He took her hand and led her from the hall of light.

COLOMBO, 1956

Violence happened quickly. The Tamil Federal Party had staged a sit-in, in front of the parliament house, protesting against the new Prime Minister's language policy. Peaceful sit-ins had worked for Gandhi, they agreed, as they set up a large camp of Tamil leaders, politicians and others. A minister from the Sri Lanka Freedom Party formed his own mob. They turned on the Tamil sit-in first and then later rioted, destroying local Tamil businesses.

Nala had asked Rajan why they targeted the Tamil businesses. He mumbled something about common criminals and petty jealousy. 'It was like this for the Jews in the beginning,' he said. She didn't know what their riots had to do with the terrible things that had happened in Germany, but she didn't want to probe him. Surprisingly, the violence ended in Colombo almost as quickly as it had started.

Rajan returned home late again, tired and breathless. 'Turn on the radio,' he said, more curt than usual as he unbuttoned his shirt. He was the only surgeon at Colombo General to wear a full-sleeved shirt, despite the heat. Tonight as he peeled off his shirt, she could see the shine on his short, compact body. The hairs on his chest were starting to grey and they were wet now, with a mixture of sweat and monsoon rain.

'The radio, turn on the radio,' he barked again.

She hated it when he talked to her like that. Why couldn't he talk in full, loving sentences? How hard was it to start with *cunju* and end with *please*? Her friends' husbands all had pet names for their wives. Rajan just started his sentences with, 'I say,' if he was in a good mood. 'I say, could you bring me my coat?' 'I say, could I have some more kadalai curry?'

'My name is not 'I say," she would retort in the early years, but she had given up now. It was the closest she was going to get to *darling* and she had come to expect it, perhaps even like it a little.

She certainly preferred it to the tone he was using now, the brusque, almost rude tone of a man whose mind was elsewhere, who was constantly busy or distracted and had no time for small talk.

'What is the matter with you?' she demanded.

'Shush!' he replied, his fingers adjusting the knobs of their radio. He was looking for a different channel.

'Don't shush me, Rajan. Why can't you talk normally? I've been waiting all day for you and now you can't even greet me properly.' She hated that she sounded like a hysterical pregnant woman, but she was hurt.

'Not now, Nala!' He pushed her voice away with one irritated hand as his other fiddled with the knobs again. He finally found the channel he was searching for.

'Riots,' he said.

She stopped talking and sat down next to him. The news came crackling through, but with a clear message. There was rioting now in the east of the country, in a Tamil province. The violence which ended in Colombo had moved on to Gal Oya.

The radio presenter was saying something about a Sinhalese girl being raped by Tamils and made to walk naked in the town of Batticaloa. The local Sinhalese were retaliating with government vehicles and dynamite from the dam. The police were refusing to intervene, claiming to be outnumbered by the mob. Tamil politicians in Colombo were calling for the army to be sent in to help, but for now, Prime Minister Bandaranaike and the government wanted to 'wait and see'.

The Gal Oya dam.

Finally she understood what Rajan was upset about. Her cousin-brother Mohan had moved to Gal Oya with his young family, shortly after her father's death. He was a civil engineer working on the reservoir project.

Even as a child Mohan had been good at building things. He was the one who built their first fort in Archi's back garden. He was an inspired designer for whom an empty old suitcase and travel chest held endless potential.

His parents had not been happy with his choice of wife. He had married a lower caste girl, Vani, because he loved her – and he thought the new start in Gal Oya would be good for all of them. A chance to live where no-one knew them and no-one asked questions. The couple had a young daughter, a few months younger than Nala's, and she knew Mohan was thinking about the future.

Gal Oya was the future, he had said. There would be more settlements like it in the previously barren provinces of their small country. With new engineering and irrigation, anything was possible. In this case, even damming a river and clearing a jungle was possible.

Mohan had worked on the dam because irrigation was his expertise and he was seduced by the ambition of mastering a river. Later, he was asked to turn his hand to more civil engineering projects and it was then that he understood why his parents and so many others had resented the initiative.

The trickle of people into the area quickly became a river with a powerful current of its own. More than fifty new villages were built from the ground up and given to local Tamils, Muslims, and even the indigenous tribes' people from the area. An equal number of Sinhalese people were also brought in from poorer provinces. These people had no ties to the land in the east. But they were given villages too, in the more fertile parts of the development near the headwaters.

Mohan had been awed by the audacity of the government to attempt such regeneration. Later, he just stopped talking to Nala about his work or his life in Gal Oya. There was nothing to say. He had believed that engineering could change people's lives, but now he could see that the government was using engineering – using him – to change his country's demography.

Mohan had once told her that he thought irrigation was beautiful. Beautiful. She laughed at him. He tried to explain it to her. 'Bringing water to people is a gift, Nala. God has given us the knowledge and skill to manipulate water and make it grow things in places that couldn't grow things for hundreds, maybe thousands, of years. If we can irrigate, we can grow, then we can feed and we can live,' he said.

Remembering his words, she swallowed hard against the tightness in her throat. She listened to the radio. Rajan looked at her but he didn't need to speak. She said a prayer for her cousin-brother in Gal Oya, for the child inside her and for the husband who never called her cunju. Her husband, who had known from the first news report that Mohan was in danger.

Rajan reached out to touch her, to hold on to her reassuring warmth, but she was already up, heading for the phone.

✣

After the riots ended in Gal Oya only government vehicles were allowed into the area. At Nala's tearful insistence, Rajan called a colonel whom he had treated in Colombo for many years and reluctantly asked for a favour. The colonel got him a seat in an army van.

'Do whatever you have to do Rajan, please just help them,' Nala begged. He held his wife and stroked her hair slowly as she cried goodbye. Ayah handed him a tiffin carrier of food for the long journey and two more for him to share with the soldiers he was travelling with. He nodded his thanks to Ayah. He pressed his lips to the top of his wife's head briefly and placed his hand over her belly for a moment longer, but he couldn't say a word.

On the trip to Gal Oya, the soldiers gratefully received their food and chatted amongst themselves. Occasionally they looked over at him but they left him alone. They knew why he was coming and who had approved his seat.

At Gal Oya, he was taken to a school hall that had been converted into a hospital ward. He explained whom he was looking for to the old man in charge. The man was wearing a doctor's white coat and carried a clipboard which he would refer to from time-to-time as he weaved Rajan through the rows of makeshift beds.

'The little girl is alright, frightened but alright. I put her with the other children to give the mother a chance to rest,' the old man said, stopping at the first patient Rajan had come for. Dhara, Mohan's eight-year-old daughter, was lying on a woven palm-leaf mat, with a group of girls. Her body was curled tightly into itself. He knelt down beside her and she shuddered as he touched her. She turned to look at him and recognised him immediately, crawling quickly into his arms. She didn't cry but her small body shook uncontrollably.

'Put your head against my chest Dhara and concentrate on my breathing,' he said as he began to tap a rhythm on her back. 'Listen to that rhythm and only that rhythm,' he whispered. When she finally began to relax into his arms a little, he picked her up and placed her gently back on the mat.

'I will get Amma, mahal. Then I will come back for you,' he said to her. She wouldn't let go of him and he gently prised her arms away, placing one of her hands on her own chest. 'Tap the beat on your chest. Focus only on that – I'll be back for you as soon as I find Amma. I promise.'

He stood up and asked, 'Where is the mother?' The old man was still standing awkwardly next to him.

'The mother, well the mother, the mother has been…' the old man stumbled, not comfortable saying the word aloud to Rajan. 'She will heal,' he pushed on, 'but it will take more time. I can give you dressings and napkins for the…the wound. But her mind, Dr Rajan, I'm not sure about her mind. It would be good if you could take the family back, they can't stay here indefinitely,' the old man finished, relieved to be at the end of his report. He hated these conversations and there were too many of them lately.

They finally stopped at Vani's bed where she was sitting quietly. Rajan thanked the old man who excused himself and left. He touched her lightly on the shoulder and she stared at him, not recognising him. He wasn't sure if she recognised herself, she seemed confused and uncertain of her surroundings. Her clothes were torn and bloodstained, shreds hanging as limply as her bruised arms and matted hair. She had been hurt in the oldest way by the oldest weapon.

'Vani, it's me, Rajan,' he said softly, 'Nala's husband.'

She looked at him closely and said, 'Thank you for coming.'

He still wasn't sure if she recognised him. 'Vani, I've come to take you back to Colombo.'

'Colombo?' she repeated. 'No, no, I'm waiting for Mohan.'

Rajan blinked back his tears. 'Come Vani, I'll take you to him.' He reached out his arms to her.

The mourners gathered at the small field next to the hospital. The dead had been brought there, their mangled bodies piled together, like siblings sharing a bed. Vani was a small woman, about the same age as

Nala. Rajan didn't hold anyone in public, with the occasional exception of his wife, but he held Vani awkwardly as she cried.

There were too many bodies and not enough facilities, so the best that could be done was mass cremation. Many of the bodies had already been burned, some recognisable, others not: cremation of the living followed by cremation of the dead. Mohan was recognisable to Rajan but he thought it best if Vani didn't see his face. She should remember him differently, as he was.

The priest had been forced to change the funeral ritual and he called on someone from the gathering to act as the son for all of the dead. He needed one man to perform the rites on behalf of them all.

Rajan gently helped Vani to the ground where she sat, like an injured bird, her arms occasionally flapping at her sides. He controlled the rising emotion and stepped forward.

The rites began. The priest poured rice into a large mortar made of stone. The rice had been husked and was ready to cook, not paddy rice that was still wrapped in its husk. Paddy rice was used at weddings.

'If you sow paddy rice it will grow fields and fields of more rice: paddy rice is living. Husked rice, like this, is dead,' the priest said as he asked Rajan to pound the husked rice with the heavy pestle.

'The body is dead and the soul needs to be released.'

Rajan wondered if Mohan had been pounded by stone.

The priest then lifted a clay pot onto Rajan's shoulder and told him to walk slowly, anti-clockwise around the enormous pyre. Somewhere in the crowd, a man began to sing, his voice cascading over the tones and semi-tones of prayers, descending in mourning and ascending in worship. Rajan walked and the priest followed him, hitting the pot two times from behind, with a small scythe.

'The body is only a vessel, a pot that holds our souls until we are liberated by death,' the priest intoned. The holes in the pot symbolised the release of man's three desires for wealth, property, and carnal love.

'These desires should not tie the soul to its body,' the priest said as he hit the pot with his scythe one last time.

Rajan wondered if Mohan had been touched by a scythe.

At the end of the ceremony, the priest began the final funeral prayer, the *Ashtothram*. He chanted the one-hundred-and-eight names of Lord Shiva, the god of destruction, whose cosmic dance sustained the universe and whose one word could end it. Rajan repeated after the priest, *Hara, hara Mahadeva...* I bow to the Destroyer, as he set fire to the pyre. An orange robe wrapped itself around the bodies.

☼

Nala ignored Rajan and boarded the *Yal Devi* to Jaffna. He accompanied her, silent and angry. With every jolt of the train, his hands tensed and reached forward, ready to catch the baby as though it would slip out of her, in contravention of every obstetric case study known to the medical profession. She didn't look out the window. For the first time in her life the beauty of the hill country passed her by, like pages of a magazine, flicked by an indifferent reader.

In her handbag she held a small brown paper bag; the kind used by street vendors to package honeyed cashews. It was the only thing Rajan could find after the funeral to contain the ashes, picked up from the litter on the ground. From the cindered debris, he had taken a warm, powdery handful and put it in the sticky paper bag to bring back. It still smelled sweet, like burnt, salted sugar. Nala's hand rested on her bag. She didn't know which part of Mohan she was taking home.

When Rajan returned from Gal Oya with Mohan's family, she forced him to tell her what had happened. She wanted to know and remember every detail: the mass of broken people stacked in an unruly heap; the flames that spread their fingers, embracing the dead before consuming them; the skin blistering and melting, revealing muscle, followed by bone; the many fused into one. She had thrown Rajan's clothes out but she could still smell the smoke; it was all around her whenever she closed her eyes.

She leaned back into the frayed leather seat. Rajan had insisted on a first class sleeper cabin. It contained just the two of them, the only sound the clatter of the train against the northbound tracks and the low, rhythmic growl of the engine as it ached towards Jaffna. From there, a cousin would drive them to Tellippalai, her village; Mohan's village. She wanted to place his ashes in their grandmother's garden.

The terrain changed gradually. The central highlands and their emerald fields flattened into jungles of the Northern Province. Moisture in the air was replaced by dust. The train slowed as it approached Kilinochchi, the last major town before entering the Tamil peninsula. She watched as groups of children ran along the track with the crawling train. They were waving to the passengers and laughing. Some were running with boxes of food – mangoes, rhambutan and fried lentil cakes – shouting outrageous prices and negotiating down when no-one shouted back. Some were running with home-made kites, flying like a skein of ragged birds, swirling hungrily above them. She closed her eyes and remembered. She was playing with Mohan's kite. He had made it himself from ekels, the thin sticks that were used to scrape the morning moss from their tongues. He formed a crucifix first, binding it with jute. Then, adding more ekels, he transformed the cross into a diamond.

'It's a *rhombus*, Nala,' he explained importantly as he pulled out a piece of silk from his pocket and stretched it across the frame. It was a delicate yellow, the colour of the heart of a frangipani.

She gasped, horrified. 'That's from Archi's sari! Your Appa is going to cane you,' she declared smugly.

'Archi gave it to me, Nala, don't be such a mami.'

'I am not a mami,' she bristled. Her mamis were all fat and bossy.

On its maiden voyage, the kite darted and dragged erratically, more like a flower tossed along the roadside, than the eagle Mohan assured her he was constructing. Undaunted, he ran as fast as he could, up and down their street with Nala behind him, struggling to keep up. The kite had to be dismantled, redesigned and reassembled several times, its shiny silk body coated in ochre dust from the street. Eventually Archi agreed to take the exhausted children to the beach. Nala begged Mohan for a turn.

'Hold on to it tightly,' he warned, worried as her feet became entangled in the kite's leash. They stood as close to the water's edge as Archi would allow them, waiting to catch the wind as it galloped in from the ocean. It didn't take long, the wind lifted the kite off the ground and she released more and more string from the spool in her hands. The children watched, laughing with Archi as the kite finally soared over the water, an amber flower against the taut pink skin of the twilight sky.

Suddenly, the air was still again, as though the ocean had held its breath, and the kite plummeted into the waves. Nala shouted and ran towards it, desperate to retrieve it. Mohan had worked so hard to build it. She would get it for him. She couldn't swim. She remembered this as she inhaled the caustic salt of the water all around her, inside her. She tried to cough but swallowed more water. She tried to cough again but she was crying too hard. She tried to call for Mohan but realised he was right there already, his arms wrapped around her waist, pulling her up and against his small strong body.

'Hold on to me, Mohan, hold on to me,' she whispered, crying.

She opened her eyes and saw Rajan watching her, sadly.

5

COLOMBO, 1956

Priya sat cross-legged on her mother's bed, quietly watching her sleep. Her beautiful face was whiter than usual, as though someone had drained the pinkness and laughter from it. At home, Nala laughed in her sleep but here in the enormous white bed, strapped in by stiff sheets, she only whimpered, her hands resting protectively over her belly.

On the bedside table Rajan had left Nala's powder, toothbrush, comb and kunkumam bottle. Priya carefully opened the bottle and took out the nail that was resting inside. She licked the head of the nail the way she'd seen her mother do it, and dipped it into the vermillion powder. She carefully pressed the nail to Nala's forehead, placing a red sun to watch over her pale moon face.

Nala stirred.

'I'm sorry Amma, I didn't mean to wake you.'

'No, it's fine. Where's Appa?' Nala asked.

'He's seeing patients. He said he'll be back soon.' She held onto the cold railing and adjusted herself on the bed, careful not to lean on Nala or the baby inside.

'Come, slide next to me,' Nala said, pulling back the sheets and making space for her. Priya fit her small body to the warm curves of her mother and closed her eyes for a moment.

'When are you coming home, Amma?' she whispered.

'Soon, I promise. Appa wants me to stay here until the baby comes, just to make sure there are no problems this time. What have you been doing at home? Not fighting with your cousin or making trouble for Ayah I hope?' Nala's voice smiled.

'Never,' Priya smiled back. 'I've been helping Ayah in the kitchen, she's teaching me. We do our homework every day. Appa makes sure.

Dhara's very clever. She and I are going to be twin sisters. She's going to tell everyone her birthday is in June even though it's in December. She's very sad about Mohan mama so Appa and I try to take extra care of her, Ayah too. And I'm reading the comic books Sahadeva mama bought me, you know, the ones about the *Mahabharata*.'

'That's wonderful mahal. Which part are you up to?' Nala sank deeper into the bed. Priya put the palms of her hands to her mother's stomach. It felt like a hot stone. She felt a sudden kick and jerked her hands back. Nala laughed.

'Don't be scared, that's the baby moving. Tell me, what's happening in your *Mahabharata*?'

Priya settled back in the bed. 'The princess Draupadi has just married the warrior Arjuna. She's beautiful and dark-skinned, just like Dhara. Arjuna had to fight for her in an archery competition. He beat all the other princes because he's the best. Then he took her home to his mother.'

'And what did his mother say, mahal?' Nala asked.

'It was very funny Amma – she said, 'share it equally with your brothers.' So Arjuna had to share his wife with his brothers and poor Draupadi married all five Pandava princes! Imagine that,' she said, laughing.

'Imagine that,' Nala echoed. 'I don't think I could cope with more than one husband, especially if they were all like your father.'

'Amma, you're so funny,' Priya wriggled down in the bed and gently kissed her mother's belly. It moved again underneath her touch.

'Do you know what that story is trying to teach you Priya?' Nala asked.

Priya's ear was resting on her mother, listening hard for a message from her new sibling. She didn't hear Rajan walk in until he answered for her:

'That you should always do what your mother tells you, even if it's ridiculous and morally suspect.'

Priya didn't understand her father but she could tell when he was making a joke and she laughed anyway. Nala laughed too, a faint blush of colour returning to her face.

'Don't listen to him, mahal. The moral of Draupadi's marriage, is that you should share everything you have with your siblings – your burdens as well as your blessings. And let me tell you, marriage is both.'

Priya looked at her parents who were laughing at each other. She was confused but happy. She laughed with them.

☼

Rajan arranged the muslin canopy around Nala and the baby. She stirred and laughed. He froze, not wanting to wake them. He still liked to watch her. He liked the way she reached for her wedding pendant when she was nervous, the way her wide lips parted when she smiled, and the way she would immediately close her lips again, remembering what her mother had said about not showing all of one's teeth. She had freckles on her nose that dived into the creases of her face when she laughed. He observed her more than he talked to her. He straightened the canopy once more, checking for holes, before retreating to his study.

Rajan rarely missed eating lunch at home. It offered him a hot meal and, during school holidays, a chance to see the children before Ayah put them all to bed for their naps. They would be waiting at the front window as his car pulled in: two little girls with palm trees of hair shooting from the sides of their heads, their skin shining from their daily massage of sesame oil, their eyes shining with joy. As he entered the house they would come running out, the strong one dragging the shy one. Priya raised her arms first so he could lift her and throw her into the air. Dhara held back, raising her arms tentatively, after he had put Priya down. She had been living with them since Mohan's death. Vani had moved into her mother's home in Kotahena. They visited her often but she still wasn't ready to take Dhara back.

He could see Nala tense as he swung the girls up and they left his hands for a brief moment. She would relax and smile as he caught them again. Back on the ground, the girls searched his pockets for the two Bultos he had hidden there. The dark caramel squares were impossible to break with your teeth, they had to be sucked. The girls could keep a piece of it in their mouths, tucked away in a cheek compartment, sucking hard for an hour. His sister used to make hers last for two hours; she said the key was to take the caramel out every twenty minutes and let it dry and re-harden, before returning it to her mouth. Lali had lots of tricks.

He made sure the girls ate the Bultos after their lunchtime nap. He didn't want them falling asleep with caramel in their mouths and choking.

It was one o'clock now and everyone was sleeping after lunch. He brushed his teeth quickly, tipping the Gopal's Pal Podi onto his new toothbrush, careful not to spill the blue powder. He liked the brushes: they were expensive but more effective than the margosa twigs he had used as a child, or the burnt paddy husk he had used as a student. He checked his clock to make sure the alarm was set for two o'clock, took off his shirt and trousers, and pulled on his sarong. He lay down on the divan, closed his eyes but couldn't sleep, troubled by the usual thoughts.

Prime Minister Bandaranaike's Sinhala Only language policy had made Sinhalese the sole, official language of the entire country. The policy would change everything for the Tamils; the riots that killed Mohan were only the beginning.

Lying on the divan, Rajan willed his mind to pause on its fearful path; to let him rest for just an hour. He heard the study door open quietly and locked his fingers across his stomach, trying not to smile. Small feet padded slowly around the edge of the room. Lifting his eyelids slightly, he watched as they crept towards him. He clenched his jaw to stop himself from laughing. He should have stretched and warmed up his feet.

As Priya and Dhara stepped forward, he smiled. The little girls were focusing on his toes so intently they didn't see his face as they reached out with tiny fingers. Priya suddenly remembered to look, but it was too late – his toes had spread open and then snapped shut, trapping them. His toes were almost as dextrous as his surgeon's fingers, he thought proudly. The girls shrieked with laughter, waking up their Ayah, Nala and their new baby brother.

Nala and Ayah sat on the top step of the back verandah, each with a fine-toothed comb in their hands. Dhara and Priya perched on the lower step, squatting between the legs of the older women. Ayah muttered in Sinhalese as she pulled the comb quickly through Priya's hair. She isolated and captured the lice, squeezing them between yellow thumbnails. As she crushed yet another insect to its death, the satisfying popping sound it released made her snort victoriously. She flicked the body away. Her feet were littered with the corpses of her handiwork.

Nala was not as well-practised as Ayah. She combed Dhara's thick, black hair slowly, taking care not to hurt the nine-year-old. Segment by segment, she untangled her niece's curls and scraped the small colonies of eggs away, wiping the comb on a white rag that was now speckled with the brown roe. As she pulled the comb down from the hair root, she could see the tiny insects disturbed from their homes, fleeing. Some landed on Dhara's slender neck. She bent down and blew, tickling the child and making her laugh. Dhara leant back into Nala's chest, and she embraced her, closing her arms and legs around the child for a moment.

'Nala mami, tell us a story, please – from the *Mahabharata*,' Dhara asked, straightening up and returning to the proper de-lousing position.

Nala smiled. Dhara and Priya loved stories from the *Mahabharata*. Children were fascinated by the epic war between cousins who fought each other for a kingdom they refused to share.

'Of course, which one, mahal?' she asked. There were thousands of stories to choose from. Hindus talked a lot.

'The one about Arjuna and how he won his wife! It's so romantic,' Priya chimed in, freeing herself from Ayah and her powerful thumbnails.

'No, no, Arjuna is such a goody-goody. He's boring,' Dhara shook her head, 'Tell us the one about Karna, mami. He's my favourite character.'

'I know he is Dhara. He's mine too. Where shall I begin?' Nala gave up the combing. Ayah handed her the bottle of margosa oil, which she trickled carefully into Dhara's curls. The pungent green liquid ran down the canals of hair she had created, and she massaged the child's head gently.

Dhara sighed and relaxed into Nala again. 'Start at the beginning, when he was born, mami. Start with his mother and the Sun God.'

Nala began the story. 'Karna's mother, Kunti, was a Pandava princess. Many years before he was born, Kunti had been given an ancient prayer by a sage. It gave her the power to call any god she chose and conceive a child.'

'Conceive?' Priya asked. Ayah had trapped her once again between her legs and was smothering her hair in oil.

'Conceive means to have a baby. We talked about that last time Priya, pay attention please,' Nala gently reprimanded her scowling daughter. She leant over and wiped the oil from Priya's eyebrow before it could drip into her eyes.

'Before Kunti married her husband, she called on Surya, the Sun God. Poor Kunti hadn't realised the power of the prayer; she didn't know it would give her a baby with Surya.'

'Maybe Kunti should have paid attention too,' Priya whispered to Dhara. The girls giggled as Nala continued.

'Kunti had the baby Karna. The Sun God gave his young son earrings and impenetrable armour. Impenetrable means that nothing could break it. Wrapped in his father's protective cloak that shone like the sun itself, Karna could not be killed.

'Kunti was young and unmarried. She was frightened when she had the baby so she gave him up. She placed him in a basket with the gifts from his father and surrendered him to the will of a river. Karna was found by a charioteer who raised him.

'Eventually Kunti married a prince and had more sons, the famous Pandava warriors. Once again, these children were conceived through other gods, using the ancient prayer.

'When Karna met his five brothers, they didn't know his true identity – they laughed at him and looked down upon him because he was 'merely' a charioteer's son. Only Duryodhana, the Kaurava king, who was hated by so many, accepted Karna as his friend and equal.

'Later, when war broke out between the Pandavas and the Kauravas, Kunti revealed herself to Karna and begged him to join his Pandava brothers against their Kaurava cousins. But Karna had promised his loyalty to Duryodhana; and he would not betray him. However, Karna promised Kunti that of her sons, he would only fight Arjuna. One of them would die - she would always have five sons as she did now.

Dhara turned around and looked at Nala thoughtfully. 'It must have been very sad for Karna, to find out that his mother had given him away.'

'Yes, Dhara, I think Karna must have been sad. The charioteer and his wife who raised him, loved him though. They loved him like he was their own. Karna had many moments of happiness in his life.'

'He still died though, didn't he?'

'Yes, but we all die,' Nala stopped, as a dam somewhere in the east opened and swept away a different cousin-brother. The dam closed just as quickly and she could breathe; she could speak again.

'Karna chose a warrior's life and a warrior's death,' she didn't finish the story. They all knew how it ended. Karna was cheated by Arjuna's father into giving away his celestial armour. He fought Arjuna on the battlefield, and without the breastplate forged by the Sun God to protect him, Karna was doomed to die. Perhaps he had been doomed from the very beginning.

'I love Karna,' Dhara said, rubbing the tears of margosa oil from her forehead, streaking it across her face.

'Me too, mahal,' she said, taking the girl's small face in her hands. She gently pressed her forehead to Dhara's, leaving an imprint of her red potu on the child's forehead.

'There,' she said. Priya moved over to receive her shadow of a potu. Nala rubbed noses with her daughter. 'I love Karna and I love you,' she said, looking at both the lustrous little girls. The children ran off to admire her handiwork in the mirror.

✡

Ayah ran from the main house into the surgery and burst into Rajan's office. Her words tumbled out as disjointed as her body, in a mix of Sinhalese and English, falling all over the room. She kept repeating, 'Nandan Baby, Nandan Baby'.

Rajan was too stunned to reprimand her for disrupting his consultation. It took him a few moments to realise that there was danger in the house and her Nandan Baby was its target.

He nodded and stood up silently, his mouth suddenly dry. Ayah ran the length of the path faster than he thought her bowed legs could carry her. Following her, he entered their shrine room to see his wife frozen by the doorway, the words caught in her throat and her arm outstretched towards their little son, Nandan.

'Nobody move,' he whispered.

Breathe, breathe, he told himself.

Breathe. Now slowly, quietly breathe. In and out.

'Nobody move,' he said again.

What was that noise? Why was there so much noise in the room?
Breathe.

He realised the noise was his heavy, frightened breathing. The room was silent, both women paralysed with terror.

Little Nandan sat at the altar of their shrine room. He was sitting on his bottom with his chubby legs bent in front of him, his belly hanging over his nappy and rolling into the space between his thighs. There was a king cobra standing over him. Rajan couldn't think. The cobra's hood was splayed out, casting a shadow on the baby's smooth belly. He could see the markings on its majestic head shimmering in the afternoon light. He couldn't tell if the snake's mouth was open. It was standing between him and his son.

Nandan's body *was* covered in holy ash. He looked like a contented little Buddha in a loin-cloth nappy. He had loaded the offering of jasmines into the container that previously contained the holy ash and, judging by the mango debris strewn around his body, had eaten the fruit that was intended for Lord Shiva.

Nobody move, Rajan prayed.

Nobody.

The cobra moved.

He started calculating – he had polyvalent anti-venom in his fridge, he had a tourniquet and a scalpel, he would need 20ml for the first dose, administered at a rate of one ml per minute.

Where were his needles? Where were his needles?

Breathe.

His needles were where they always were: the cupboard on the left, second shelf. He could run, load, and inject within minutes. He could do this. He could do this.

The cobra retracted his hood and moved again, watching the baby as it slid towards the image of Lord Shiva: the Lord who had answered his wife's prayers and given them this son, a son to bear his name and bring joy to them all.

Please Lord, Rajan prayed.

Please, not this child too.

The cobra, king amongst predators, reared his head and opened his hood again. There was deference in the snake this time. Ayah would swear in years to come, when this story was retold and relived, that the cobra had prayed to Lord Shiva and left. People would look at Rajan in disbelief as Ayah talked and wiped her eyes with the corner of her sari. He would smile indulgently and look away. But at night when he prayed, when he remembered his dead and his living, he thanked the Lord Shiva for sparing his son and he too was sure that the cobra was there not to attack, but to pray.

Dhara lined the bottles up in a row against the back fence. From the bottom of the garden they could still hear Ayah shouting at Vasanthi, her young niece who had started working as the new servant girl.

'Where did you get so many bottles from?' Priya asked, counting eleven.

'From the bins on the street and at Galle Face Green,' Dhara replied proudly. 'Whenever mami and mama aren't looking, I put them in my school bag. Lanka Lime, Orange Barley, and Vimto – every flavour.'

'Appa's going to be so angry. You know he doesn't like dirt. He says it makes you sick.'

'Other things make you sick too acca, and I'm going to protect us from them,' Dhara replied.

'What are you talking about?'

'Never mind, help me fill them.' She gave Priya a large spoon, and together the little girls scooped earth from the bed of anthuriums.

'Will it hurt the plants if we take their dirt?' Priya asked, eyeing the shiny pink leaves nervously. 'Archi loves these ones. She said you can only grow them in the south. There's not enough rain in Jaffna.'

'They'll be fine acca, just fill the bottles. You worry about the strangest things.'

'So do you Dhara – what are we doing?'

'We're making weapons.'

'What?'

'*Weapons.* Honestly, you are going to be impossible to protect.' Dhara filled her bottles with a mix of pebbles and soil, testing each bottle for its weight. She then pulled her arm back and pretended to throw the bottle, repeating the motion several times.

'I asked Rajan mama to buy a gun but he said no. He said we would never keep a gun in our home and if the mob comes he will tell them to take whatever they want but to leave the family alone.'

Dhara put the bottle down and wiped her eyes, her tears streaking brown stolen soil down her face.

'It won't be enough.'

'What's happening Dhara, you're scaring me.'

'Nothing is happening – yet. But something always happens,' she replied.

☼

Priya moved the arm and leg off her body. They were small and skinny like her own, but heavy. Appa said people were heavier in their sleep, especially Amma, which was why he didn't like to hug or be hugged by her at night. Amma said Appa didn't like to hug because he lacked warmth. Priya thought that if Appa was cold, he would want to be hugged even more.

The little girl slipped out of bed quietly, careful not to wake her sleeping cousin-sister. Dhara often woke up at night, screaming and crying out for her parents. Nala reached her first, holding her, soothing and rocking her for hours until she slept again. Priya surveyed Dhara's face once more – she didn't want her to wake up alone.

She tip-toed quickly over the cool cement floor. It shone like the surface of a temple pond in the moonlight. The large, bronze statue of the goddess Lakshmi sat impassively by the front door, her silhouette framed against the wide window. Priya squeezed herself behind the goddess' pedestal and took her place on the window sill, her legs bunched up to her chest, her chin resting on her knees as she watched and waited. She bit the nail of her index finger. It was the longest one she had left but still it hurt a little. Appa would be annoyed. She tried to sit on her hands but nearly toppled over onto the statue. She steadied herself against the window, pressing a small nose to it, breathing out hot steam circles in a different pattern from the night before. She waited again.

Finally, she saw the white lights of the car flash outside their gate. She was blinded for a moment but felt herself relax against the glass, eyes closed. She knew he was getting out of the car, thanking the driver politely, unlocking the padlocked gate, relocking it carefully, checking it twice, before walking slowly to the front door.

She heard the key turn and the heavy door open. Moonlight entered the foyer and wrapped itself around the goddess, spilling over onto her upturned face.

'Have you been waiting long?' Rajan asked, bending down and helping her out.

'No, Appa,' she replied, reaching forward. He held her fingertips in his palm and looked at the torn stubs of her nails. She waited for the admonishment.

'Come, it's time for you to sleep. You mustn't worry. I'm fine, mahal. I'm fine,' he said, taking her hand gently in his.

This time, the riots spread across the whole country. Dr Karunatilake, the director of Colombo General, called all the Tamil doctors when the troubles started, warning them not to leave their homes. Some, like Rajan, travelled to work in marked, government vehicles and ambulances. Nala begged him to stay but he wouldn't leave his patients. Nor would he tell her what he saw on the streets or in the wards.

The violence was short-lived, lasting only a week in May, but people were still afraid. Prime Minister Bandaranaike was noticeably incapable or uninterested in using the police to stop the mobs as hundreds of Tamils were killed and their homes destroyed.

Many of Nala's cousins stayed with them during the riots. Mohan's widow, Vani, joined them too and Dhara was thrilled to be living in the same home as her mother again. Nala gave Vani her guest bedroom so that Dhara could sleep with her.

Cinnamon Gardens was a pleasant neighbourhood of diplomats and doctors, and its pedigree seemed to protect it from trouble each time. They had other family and friends in Colombo who had fled north, to the safety of Jaffna. They would return when the capital quietened down. Rajan had laughed bitterly to her when he heard that expression. He said 'quietened down' described the nature of violence in Colombo perfectly. It would just *quieten down* for a little while until it rose up again – fuelled by bhikkus and politicians who goaded people into becoming rampaging mobs. Once more Colombo would be filled with the cries of dying Tamils. The cycle of violence in Ceylon was turning ever faster now: the years were different but the problems were the same.

Nala didn't share his bitterness. She had even managed to enjoy herself a little this time, almost forgetting why her cousins and their children had come to stay with her. Almost.

They had played cards and told old family stories. Some were about Mohan, and Nala was finally able to say his name out loud. For the last two years she had let any mention of him drift away like smoke; a smoke that curled around her and tasted like burnt, salted sugar.

A few times, she even felt he was still there, teasing her for her dismal poker face when she was both winning and losing at cards. She would laugh and look up from her hand, expecting him to laugh back, finding nothing but a deceitful, painful emptiness.

Rajan's surgery had been closed for several weeks during the riots and he would now have a backlog of patients to deal with. The doors to his clinic would open in two hours and there was still some preparation to do.

She arranged her husband's instruments the way he had taught her. Carefully, with steel tongs, she pulled them steaming out of the steriliser and placed them on his surgical tray in the right order. The metal caught the early morning light, reflecting it around the neatly ordered clinic, creating its only chaos. She checked that the water dispenser was full and equipped with enough cups for today's patients. She put out a tray of biscuits, love cake and milk toffee, and straightened his copies of Reader's Digest magazines, the only reading material for the waiting patients.

She checked his patient list to see if there was anyone special she should greet herself. His practice was thriving and it was not uncommon for clergymen, politicians and ambassadors to want to see him. Although he made no distinction between his patients, Nala enjoyed the celebrity of their life. He had earned it, and she had earned it too. Without her, how would he know how to receive these people, how to engage and entertain them? They lived in Colombo 7 and they had to act accordingly.

She frowned as she read the morning's patient list. Rajan continued to see his old patients, their children, and their children's children.

Payment would be offered in blessings, contributions of small livestock, or food and invitations to weddings in distant villages. Many of them had travelled for days to see him, exhausted and hungry when they arrived. He insisted that these patients were treated and fed with the same generosity and grace as Cardinal Bartholomew, whose tonsils he would be taking out later that afternoon. *When would Rajan learn?* She sighed. She would have to instruct Ayah to make extra food for the day.

Suddenly, she heard banging at the front gate of the house.

'Iyah, Iyah, open the gate please sir, open the gate!'

She ran to the front verandah, closely followed by Rajan and Ayah. They were cautious, even though the voice was calling Rajan by his respectful title. The man banged on the gate again, desperately this time.

'Nala, get back inside. Take Ayah,' Rajan said fearfully. She sent Ayah into the house but she stood her ground next to her husband.

'Iyah, Iyah, please, I beg you, open the gate, I have the Prime Minister. He's hurt!'

The car in the driveway turned off its blinding headlights and in the early morning light, Nala could see the man help another older man out. It was indeed the former Prime Minister of Ceylon, John Kotelawala, Ceylon's third Prime Minister: the nephew of the country's first prime minister, DS Senanayake, and cousin to the country's second, Dudley Senanayake. None of them had any blood relationship with the current Prime Minister, SWRD Bandaranaike that they would acknowledge.

Rajan opened the gate quickly and helped the Prime Minister and his driver into the house. As Nala liked to tell it, Rajan had already saved the Prime Minister's life once, years before, when he was suffering from an unstoppable and potentially fatal nosebleed. Despite the ministrations of a team of doctors, ayurvedic physicians, astrologers, and a host of bhikkus, Kotelawala had bled for days. He was eventually brought to Colombo's youngest and finest general surgeon, Rajan, who dismissed his entourage. Using only his attractive and excited young wife as his nurse, he cauterised the Prime Minister's nose, stopped the bleeding, saved him from certain death and raised Nala's social standing in Colombo considerably.

Of course, Rajan's cousins up north felt he should have plunged the cauterising iron into the Prime Minister's eye or a vital organ – that might have stopped Kotelawala from betraying the Tamil people. At the last election he had caved into pressure from Bandaranaike's then opposition party and adopted his own Sinhala Only policy. He had lost the election anyway.

Nala laughed at Rajan's typical rejoinder to his cousins – firstly he said, assassinating anyone could only lead to bloody retribution; secondly, assassinating the only politician who could marginally pass for a moderate instead of a raving, frothing-at-the-mouth Sinhala nationalist, was simply stupid; and thirdly, assassination as a surgical technique was a violation of his Hippocratic Oath and bad for future business.

And so when Sir John Lionel Kotelawala was ushered once more into Rajan's surgery, he greeted him as kindly and politely as he would any other patient. Only this patient had recently represented Ceylon at the United Nations and now had a small cockroach stuck in his ear.

On the road back from Kandy to Colombo, Kotelawala had stopped at a rest house for tea and a short nap. While sleeping, a cockroach had flown into his ear and become trapped in the esteemed canal, somewhere between the outer ear and the tympanic membrane. Unnerved and off-balance, Kotelawala had insisted that his driver take him to Dr Rajan immediately.

Months later, Rajan received his second letter of thanks from Kotelawala, hand-written on official paper, emblazoned with the family-crest. Rajan threw the letter away, saying the family-crest may as well be adopted as the official state-crest; leadership in Ceylon was more a dynastic struggle than a democratic process.

Nala saved the letter and showed it to her siblings and friends who all agreed that her husband was a very important man. She quietly reassured her cousins in the north that Rajan would never save the life of the new Prime Minister, Bandaranaike, should he ever find a cockroach stuck in his ear.

Despite Rajan's mortification, she framed the letter and hung it proudly in her husband's surgery, just below his certificates from the Royal College of Surgeons and above the merit certificates that he received in primary school. Her mother-in-law had kept those and insisted that they too be framed. But it was Kotelawala's letter that she directed patients to: the letter and the legend that propelled her husband's reputation and career into loftier circles.

All because Rajan, with the aid of his nurse Nala, had deftly removed an offending insect and cleaned out the former Prime Minister's ears so that he could enjoy Colombo's quiet while it lasted; and hear the noise of violence properly for himself, when it inevitably started again.

Why was Nala taking so long? Why did it take women so long to go to the toilet? That was the third time this evening. Rajan was sure their host would notice soon and become worried. Perhaps they would think she had a stomach problem. His nose wrinkled. He preferred to use his own toilet at home. It was something his mother had impressed upon him as a boy, the importance of using one's own toilet. She was such a clever woman, he thought, momentarily distracted from his wife's mysterious and alarmingly frequent disappearances to the toilet.

On her return Nala smiled sweetly at him, making him even more suspicious. She whispered something to Myrtle, Dr Jansz Vanderstraaten's wife whose finely manicured eyebrows rose in amazement. A moment later she too excused herself to go to the bathroom. What in God's name was going on with these women and why was his wife always the instigator?

They were dining at John Kotelawala's house while holidaying in the ancient royal capital of Kurunegala. Kotelawala no longer lived in the area permanently but he was still a high-profile member of the local intelligentsia who fawned around him now. Decked in his military finest, he imposed his personal space on others as confidently as he imposed his opinions. His British medals glittered like the lights of his enormous ballroom chandelier as he talked to his adoring guests.

'The Chinese are hypocrites! Look at them with their Marxist morality and the atrocities they've committed in Tibet. Those people deserve to be free,' he raged passionately. 'They were meant to be an independent country, they are their own people.' The audience murmured its agreement. 'The Chinese talk about equality – empty rhetoric, empty rhetoric. The people of Tibet have not been equal; they are second-class citizens in a country they didn't want to belong to. It's an outrage' – people tried to applaud but he continued, cutting them off as he approached the climax – 'and it is a shame on all of us that the world has watched for so long, without intervening to protect those poor people.'

Rajan wanted to turn away but Kotelawala was hypnotic. He didn't care about the machinations of Colombo politicians or Sinhala nobility. Ceylon's politics was dominated by the same class that had probably ruled it in ancient times. Power didn't change hands in their little democracy, it just got passed down the generations. Rajan was more interested in how it affected the price of rice and sugar and whether their island would get drawn into foreign wars again. It wasn't just spices that made them a valuable piece of the former empire; it was their position at the tip of India.

Kotelawala took a breath and motioned to the audience who were poised to applaud. He was nodding his thanks to the appreciative crowd, deflecting their compliments and shushing their praise with a pained but proud smile, when Myrtle Jansz Vanderstraaten returned from the toilet, giddy with excitement. She sat down and huddled with Nala and the ladies, who all stared at the sweeping staircase leading up to the bathroom, in wonder. One by one they all casually went to the toilet – as casually as ten ladies dressed in their finest saris and dresses could.

The former Prime Minister moved on from Tibet's right to self-determination. Inevitably, he was talking about Bandaranaike's failed language negotiations with the Tamils. Prime Minister Bandaranaike hadn't been as committed to the hard line of his Sinhala Only language policy after he defeated Kotelawala with it.

'I can't believe I'm saying this – and no-one tell my Senanayake cousins I said it – but Bandaranaike was right. He should have compromised and allowed the Tamils their regional councils. They could have used their language in their provinces. I have many fine Tamil friends whom I'm sure would agree with me,' Kotelawala said, searching the crowd for Rajan's face and smiling at him. Rajan nodded and smiled tightly back.

He found himself agreeing with Kotelawala for the first time that night – the bhikkus held too much power in Ceylon. They had sabotaged Bandaranaike's attempted compromise.

'Sinhala Only' the monks said, was not just about language, it was about Buddhism's return to greatness. Rajan could see it was about racial supremacy, hidden in the rhetoric of religion and the fine detail of domestic policy.

When Nala returned from the toilet, he took her aside before she could disappear into the whispering circle of silk and taffeta.

'What is going on?' he hissed. 'Why are you all going to the bathroom?'

'It's the toilet,' she exploded.

'Shh, shh, what are you talking about?' His wife was *non compos mentis* – the short period of decadent exposure to these ninnies had rendered her either simple or insane.

'It's the toilet,' she repeated, as if that explained everything. And then looking around to make sure they weren't being overheard, she conspiratorially dropped her voice and whispered, 'It's gold-plated. The toilet is gold-plated. It's –'

'Yes, yes, I heard you.' At least he thought he had heard her. Did she just say the toilet was gold-plated? He had to see this for himself.

6

COLOMBO, 1959

Nala loved everything about their new home in Cinnamon Gardens. She loved its internal courtyard and the verandah that started at the front door and hugged the body of the house all the way around. She loved the upright toilets and running water in the bathrooms – and what that said about them. She feigned enthusiasm for the small open-air kitchen at the back where Ayah could deep fry, and the larger, covered kitchen next to it. She wouldn't know what to do in either but Ayah and her new protégé Priya would. She was bemused by her eleven-year-old daughter's interest in all things domestic – Priya must have inherited it from the other side of the family.

She was proud of Rajan's new surgery and waiting room that had been built on a side of the house. It was clean and organised. She had never been entirely happy with him working from home but he had insisted on having his private surgery at the house. He was hardly the type to suggest mid-afternoon hanky panky – he was far more likely to offer instructions on how she could improve the running of the household, and she certainly didn't want that.

But Rajan's practice was growing. She wandered around the empty waiting room imagining herself greeting his patients, shaking hands like the sophisticated lady she was, laughing at their compliments, blushing modestly. 'No, no, Mr Seneviratne, you are too kind. This old thing? We've had that Victorian table for years,' and, 'Yes, Reverend Niles, I painted that myself. Oh, you are lovely to say that. I just dabble a little in painting; I'm not *really* an artist.'

She made a list in her notebook about furniture. Dr Fonseka's wife down the road had some beautiful English pieces: dark wood tables, cane chairs, almirahs, ornate mirrors, and a grandfather clock. Nala would need all of that now that they had the house. She would have to speak to Dolly Fonseka about where to shop.

Rajan would disagree of course; he could be such a villager at times. He hated to spend money but she would convince him. It was for his own good.

She walked down the corridor, past the bedrooms for her children – each had their own room but she knew Priya and Dhara would insist on sleeping together. She had ordered an extra large bed for Priya's room and another for Dhara's room. Rajan and Nala had asked Vani to move in with them, instead of simply sleeping over sometimes. Vani had cried and apologised for not taking Dhara back. Nala cried too, and reassured her that they loved the child and wanted to do what was best for her. Vani's physical injuries had healed a long time ago but Gal Oya had changed her. Living with Nala was what was best for Dhara.

Nandan had his own room too, but at only three-years-old, he made his way into her bed every night. She looked forward to his sweet moon face peering into hers, just before he jumped in and put his little arms possessively across her belly. Rajan didn't mind Nandan coming into their bed as long as the boy didn't wet himself. *That's very practical of you*, she thought, irritated.

At the end of the corridor were two rooms for their relatives: her mother, her grandmother – Archi, and her mother-in-law. She sighed at the thought of her mother-in-law. She would have to do her duty. Her father had raised her properly. He would have been proud of her, especially if he knew what a difficult woman Devaki turned out to be.

She sighed again as she walked into the final room. It was also empty but soon she would fill it. Against the back wall, were four large shelves for her deities and a small shelf underneath for photos of her Appa, Mohan, Rajan's Appa and Lali. She was excited about the new shrine room and the statues it would house. There was lord Ganesha – all prayers started with an invocation to the serious elephant headed god – Rajan's favourite deity of course. She preferred Ganesha's younger brother, the handsome lord Murugan. Her mother had given her a new statue of lord Krishna. The young lord was standing, playing his flute, his traditional white clothing contrasting against the beautiful blue of his skin. She thought about putting the statue in the hallway so that all of her visitors could see it, but Amma had asked her to keep it in the shrine room where it would be safer, away from Nandan. Her shrine room would also have the Virgin Mary and a beautiful picture of our Lord Jesus Christ, along with St Christopher. Her new neighbours had thoughtfully given her a statue of Lord Buddha meditating peacefully, which she would include too. All gods were welcome in her home; she wanted everyone's blessings.

She was counting the weeks for the house to be ready. Amma would do the milk boiling ceremony and stock her kitchen with rice, salt, sugar, turmeric, coriander, and cumin seeds – all the essentials. The temple priest had offered to do a more detailed 'moving-in' poosai with offerings to Lord Ganesha, to remove the obstacles from their life here – in their new home. She couldn't wait.

☼

Nala glided along the polished cement floor. She lifted her sari ever so slightly when she stepped from the main hall to the corridor that led to the bedrooms. The corridor and bedrooms had wooden floors and she didn't want the hem of her sari to get caught – it was deep blue in colour, fashionably called Royal Blue, and matched the Ceylon sapphire necklace she was wearing. Apparently the queen of England was partial to Ceylon sapphires too. She liked the young queen; she was so pretty and poised. They had a lot in common.

She shut the door to the corridor behind her, muffling the noise from the party a little. Everyone was there: Rajan's colleagues, their neighbours, and a few of their cousins. He hadn't wanted to host the celebration.

'It's showing off, Nala,' he said, embarrassed at her suggestion.

'No it's not. You're the youngest doctor to be promoted to Chief Consultant at Colombo General – and the first Tamil. I'm proud of you and we should celebrate,' she insisted.

The house was perfect. Even her children were perfect: the girls in their new matching navy and white dresses that made them look like they were heading off on a sea voyage; Nandan, so handsome in his printed shirt and polished shoes. The children had been allowed to join the party for an hour, on the condition that they behaved and retreated to their bedrooms as soon as Ayah came for them. There was to be no resistance or there would be no further parties.

The guest list was more Sinhalese than it was Tamil, which was why not all of her cousins had been invited. They didn't understand. Rajan and Nala had Sinhalese friends – many of them had helped Rajan throughout his career. She wasn't going to ignore or offend them because of what was happening in the country.

Amma had been annoyed with her, saying that she should invite all or none of her cousins. Kamini agreed, saying that the ones who hadn't been invited would call her a snob, too big for her chappals.

She wasn't a snob. She got along with everyone, but she knew her cousins didn't. They were right to be angry with the government and perhaps they were right to be angry with some of the Sinhalese. She had her own anger, which she carried more quietly. She had tried to bury it; kneading it with bare hands into the lifeless soil of her grandmother's neglected garden. But it followed her silently, like smoke.

She shook her head. Hesitantly, she opened the door to her mother-in-law's room. Devaki had been given the largest spare bedroom with an attached bathroom. It was sparsely furnished, at Devaki's request, with a low double bed, a writing desk and a rocking chair. Rajan had asked the carpenter to build wooden railings near each piece of furniture so that when she needed to get up, she could hold onto it and pull herself up. She was a stout, short woman whose body was failing her. Childbearing, illness and age had added layers of flesh to her small frame and it could no longer bear her weight comfortably.

On entering the room, Nala paused: it took a moment for her eyes to adjust to the muted lighting. Ayah was waiting for her and her mother-in-law was sitting on the edge of the bed, her nightdress stained and smelling. She tried not to wrinkle her nose.

'Amma, what happened?' she asked. It was a stupid question but Nala didn't know what else to say.

'Nothing, nothing,' Devaki replied, looking down, 'Just a little accident. I will clean myself.'

'Let Ayah help you Amma. She can wash you and change the sheets.'

'No, no. I'll do it mahal,' Devaki replied, looking suspiciously at Ayah.

'Please Amma, you can't do it. Ayah knows what to do.'

'Where is Vasanthi?' the old lady asked. Vasanthi, their servant girl, usually tended to her mother-in-law's needs but she had returned to her village for the Buddhist festival of Vesak. Every second day, Vasanthi and Ayah would bathe the old woman. Both of them were needed to lift and move her.

'Amma, it's late, Vasanthi has gone home. She'll be back in two days. There are other helpers out in the hall. They're here for the party; I'll get one of them.' She was irritated now; she couldn't leave the party for long.

'No, no. I'll wait for Vasanthi,' Devaki insisted.

'Amma, you can't wait for Vasanthi. You can't sleep in this,' Nala said, pointing to the brown stain that was spreading down her nightdress.

'No, no-one else. No-one else can see me. I'll wait,' Devaki turned her head away but not before Nala saw the tears.

She shook her head. Her mother-in-law was more stubborn than her husband. For a moment she contemplated calling Rajan. Devaki would listen to him but she wouldn't want her son to see her like this.

'Ayah, help me quickly,' she started unpinning her sari. She slipped off her new sandals, wincing as she pulled the strap over her blistered heel. Semi-naked, they dragged the old lady to the bathroom and seated her on a chair in the middle of the tiled floor. Ayah had already prepared large buckets of water and together they stripped Devaki. Nala took a wash cloth and rubbed her mother-in-law's body quickly but gently, wiping off the faeces from her privates and the folds of her thick legs. She stepped back, keeping a hand on Devaki to steady her, while Ayah poured water over her. Together, they rubbed her with soap and one more bucket of water.

She dried her mother-in-law's thin hair and was tenderly plaiting its greyed remains when Rajan entered the bedroom. He was confused by what he saw – his mother on her rocking chair, Ayah changing the bed sheets and his wife standing over them both, regally, in her brassiere, underskirt and Ceylon sapphires.

☼

Fear sapped his hopes for his children, and was replaced with a growing, and exhausting anxiety. At Priya and Dhara's primary school, children no longer studied in English. They had been segregated by ethnicity and taught in their *swabasha*: their own native tongue – either Sinhalese or Tamil. Sinhalese was now the language of the civil service, the courts and the country. If the Tamils didn't learn Sinhalese in school, then eventually they wouldn't be able to speak it, and wouldn't be able to work – or live – as equals in Ceylon.

He woke up in the middle of the night again, adrenalin rushing through him like a cold fever in his blood. He slipped out of bed and went to check on the girls. Nandan was already in their bed on Nala's side, wedged tightly into the curve of her body.

The girls slept huddled together under a large mosquito net. He touched the muslin lightly without lifting it. He didn't want to wake them, especially Dhara. At twelve-years-of-age, Priya was already beautiful. She looked just like her mother, only far more serious than most girls her age – more serious than Nala ever looked at any age. Priya even slept gracefully, just as she walked and talked. He was not a superstitious man but looking at his children he was tempted to spit three times to ward off the evil eye, the way his mother did whenever people complimented them.

He straightened the canopy so it completely covered the girls. From time to time he would check it and sew up any holes or tears. Nala laughed at him and told him to leave that to the servants. But he liked to sew; his mother had taught him and he knew he was more thorough than the servants. His sewing was versatile and not limited to sutures and mosquito nets; he could even make his own undershorts. Whenever Nala saw him doing this, she laughed so hard that her eyes filled with tears. What other surgeon in Colombo 7 stitched his own undershorts, she would ask? He loved to watch her laugh and so he continued to sew his own, long after he could afford to buy them from Marks & Spencer in London.

Priya, Dhara and Nandan. His heart picked up speed, carrying adrenalin through his body and mind into frightened places – places where his children could be hunted down and hurt; where a monk's burning robe curled around them all. Cinnamon Gardens was safe for now, but for how long? He couldn't tie the children to this house and its high gates. There would be school, university, jobs, marriage and eventually, children of their own.

Unable to go back to sleep, Rajan sat in his surgery looking at a map of the world. It had been a gift from the old curator of the Jaffna Library, when he left the north to study in Colombo. The map stretched, inviting and blue across the wall. It was such a vast place, surely there was somewhere they could go: somewhere they would be safe from riots and growing rage.

✪

Nala watched him push the remains of his rice, snake beans and aubergine curry to the side of his plate. He hadn't even touched the fried bitter gourd curry. She made a mental note to talk to Ayah about her cooking. The old maid was getting a little lazy and today's aubergine curry could have been better. The bitter gourd was too bitter and the beans were too salty. She had told Ayah over and over again, Rajan's mother had high blood pressure and salt made her dizzy. She would have to start supervising Ayah again.

'We need to leave,' Rajan said quietly in Tamil instead of English. Vasanthi, the young servant girl, was still clearing the plates and he waited for her to finish.

'Leave? We don't have plans tonight do we?' Nala replied, confused. Why was Rajan always so thrifty with words? He could never explain anything properly.

'I mean that we need to leave Colombo,' he said.

His attempt at elaboration was frustrating her further.

'What are you talking about, Rajan? We don't *need* to leave anywhere.'

'We do. We need to get out of Colombo; there is nothing here for us.'

Now *that* was dramatic. Finally, he was showing a little flair, after only fourteen years of re-training.

'Everything is here for us. Where would we go? Kandy?' she asked hopefully. She loved her years in the hill country and still missed her old friends, the sophisticated ladies and lifestyle, even her old painting master. Perhaps she could start painting again. In recent years, between Rajan's busy practice and the children, she hadn't had as much time to paint as she would have liked. She suddenly caught herself. Why was she planning a new life in Kandy; what was wrong with their current one?

'What are you talking about?' she asked again. He wasn't making any sense, which was unusual for him. She watched him as he rubbed the sides of his head and exhaled slowly.

Before he could answer, Vasanthi returned with a plate of mangoes and a small knife. Nala took the plate and motioned to Vasanthi to leave. She peeled back thin strips of skin. Usually more adept, she was holding the soft fruit too tightly, its juice trickling between the taut tendons of her forearm.

'Have your dessert,' she said, brusquely placing the mangled fruit on his side plate.

'We need to leave Ceylon, Nala. You know exactly what I mean and you know why.'

She sighed deeply. 'You always fear the worst, Rajan, always. Bandaranaike is dead and a new parliament will give us a new chance.'

'Yes, Bandaranaike is dead,' he replied. 'And his widow is already making public appearances and rallying his party. Sirimavo Bandaranaike won't be joining a Buddhist monastery for a life of spiritual contemplation. She's even better at Sinhala chauvinism than he was. It's only a matter of time before she 'reluctantly' accepts her husband's mantle,' he added bitterly. 'The leader of the Sri Lanka

Freedom Party might have been assassinated, but the party is very much alive.'

'Where would we go? Have you thought of that?' she could see that anxiety was distracting him away from her, pulling him inward. 'Where would we go?' she repeated, desperately hoping he didn't have an answer.

'London or Toronto perhaps. Your brothers want to go there. Kamini too – she said Gajan's engineering qualifications would be recognised in Canada. But you know how Gajan hates the cold.'

'You've spoken to all of them?' she asked, incredulously. 'Without speaking to me first?'

'Yes – I just asked them Nala. You make it sound so conspiratorial. I...I thought we should work out all of our options. Pat Ohlmas is moving to Canberra in Australia. But Australia won't take us, we're too brown.'

'Too *brown?*'

'Too brown,' he replied.

'Pat is Ceylonese too!' Nala was very fair, everyone knew that.

'Pat is a Burgher – she can show Dutch heritage and she doesn't look brown. She looks European. Australia will only take Europeans.'

'Well, we were colonised by the British, which should count for something,' she retorted. 'Anyway, I don't want to move. This is our home; we built this house and your practice. We were here first,' she finished petulantly.

'That argument didn't work with the Portuguese, Dutch or the British.'

'I don't mean that. I mean that we have lived in Colombo for much of our lives. This is our home and we shouldn't have to leave.'

'Nor should we have to raise our children in fear,' he raised his voice a little.

'Rajan, you are the only one who's afraid.'

'You *should* be afraid, Nala. Look around you and see what I am seeing.'

She was offended: first she was considered too brown and now she was being called blind.

He looked down at his mango. 'Things will be safer somewhere else. Every generation should have the chance to be better and freer than the one before it.'

'Who said that, your mother?' she scoffed.

'No, I said that,' he replied harshly, pushing the plate away.

She blinked back tears of frustration. She could never explain herself to him properly. 'Rajan, this is our home. We were born here; we buried our dead here, we-'

'And we must protect our living, Nala,' he interrupted her.

'What about Amma and Archi?' she asked. He was quiet. There was also Dhara's mother to think about. They helped her too, and Dhara would never agree to leave without her.

'I need to think more. I need to think – but we still need to leave,' he replied.

She paused before playing her trump card, 'And what about your mother? We couldn't take her with us; no country in the world would want our little retirement community.' She knew as she said it that she had won, for the moment.

✷

Philomena de Silva had aged well. When she laughed her mouth barely moved, which made her laugh sound like a hiccup, sometimes a cough.

'Laugh lines, darling. They are the scourge of any woman in her forties,' she said, inspecting her reflection in the silver tea set. Philomena was in her fifties.

'You have a beautiful home, Nala – so simple and yet sophisticated. Like you.' She lifted the corners of her mouth slightly.

'Thank you Philomena. I'm so pleased you could join me today, we don't see each other nearly enough.' Nala's heart raced. She hadn't slept well for weeks, not since she worked out what she was going to do. She sipped her tea and tried not to wince when it scalded her.

'How are the ladies?' she asked.

'Well, last year Viktoria died finally. She had most certainly overstayed her welcome. And Felicia – that was shocking. She left the Judge for her son's English tutor. Apparently they'd been carrying on for years. Judge only realised when the tutor was still popping over even though the boy had finished his A-Levels and gone to Cambridge. You must have heard about that – such a scandal – and a surprise. It's always the quiet, ugly ones you have to watch out for.'

Nala didn't laugh. She remembered Felicia Gunawardene. The older lady had always been kind to her.

'Where is she living now?'

'Who?' Philomena asked.

'Felicia – where is she living?'

'Oh, Kurunegala – I think she's hiding in her family home. Judge gave her the dowry property back. He's alone in their big house in Kandy. Utterly broken by it all, he is. They say he comes to court, drunk – drunk, at ten o'clock in the morning! They're calling the tutor the Literature Lothario – isn't that clever!'

Philomena caught herself before she laughed widely.

Again, Nala didn't laugh. She had a plan. She tried not to vomit.

'I miss the hill country, Philomena. We were very happy there. We painted, we had teas together and talked about the future. Life was... uncomplicated.'

'Yes, life in Colombo is terribly complicated isn't it? Everyone expects more from you here; even servants make demands in the city. Melvin is an MP as you know – his constituents simply will not leave him alone. Thank you for your contribution to his campaign by the way, I hope you got the note from our office?'

'Yes, yes, thank you for that. Rajan and I were happy to contribute. He deserves it; he deserves to represent the people of Kandy; *all* of the people.'

'Yes, I know that,' Philomena raised an eyebrow. Anyway, it is a very demanding job; I don't think people understand what it involves. Everyone thinks the election was the hard part – not at all – keeping the electorate happy and running for *re*-election - that is the hard part.'

'I'm sure he'll be fine. Melvin is a very clever man.' Nala put her teacup down and adjusted it in its silver saucer. She had been given the set by Philomena when she left Kandy but had never found an occasion to use it. Vasanthi had polished it for today.

'When we were in Kandy, I had the opportunity to meet some of his constituents, in the villages,' she said slowly.

'Yes I remember, you were terribly keen on helping them Nala darling. But there is a natural order to these things, and it's best not to...*upset* that, shall we say? The more you give those Indians the more they want.'

'Those Indians looked Ceylonese to me, Philomena,' she paused. She could feel the clenching in her stomach rise to her chest and to her voice. She continued quickly before she lost her nerve.

'Some of them looked as Ceylonese as Melvin.'

Philomena put her teacup down and looked at Nala carefully.

'Rajan has applied for a teaching position at the University College Hospital in London.'

'I heard,' Philomena replied, relieved. 'He's the strongest candidate – but I'd be happy to put a word in with my brother, if you wish? Aubrey is now the chairman of the selection committee, as you must know. He reviews all the Sri Lankan applications.'

'Yes, thank you – I don't want him to get it.' She adjusted the teacup once more and forced herself to look the other woman in the eye.

'Philomena, he will apply for teaching and consultant positions in London again and again. I know my husband. He's very determined. I don't want him to get those either. Do you understand what I'm saying?'

'Perfectly, Nala darling, perfectly,' Philomena replied and allowed herself to smile broadly.

✧

Rajan placed the letter on his table. Its vanilla parchment glowed against the dark teak. He flattened out its creases and felt the University College emblem, like Braille against his fingers. In the bin next to him, he shoved the map he had torn from his study wall. He filed the letter with the others.

✧

Nala rearranged the frames on her side table; her right hand paused on her belly and her left on a photograph of her and Mohan, taken on Archi's verandah when they were children.

Dhara read the newspaper article to Nala, stopping at times to make sure she was still listening. All of Colombo was talking about the recent execution of Talduwe Somarama, the bhikku who had assassinated Prime Minister SWRD Bandaranaike three years ago. Imprisoned since 1959, he had converted to Christianity shortly before his hanging.

'You smile just like your Appa,' Nala said softly, straightening the frame.

Dhara heard her but she didn't stop reading. She rarely talked about Mohan. Nala knew the child was still tied to terrifying memories of his death. She said a silent prayer for the baby inside her.

When Nala had made her announcement about the pregnancy, Rajan had been very upset with her. There were other pregnancies before Nandan – but those had ended without a baby.

'You are thirty-four-years-old. You can't be pregnant,' he declared.

'Well I am pregnant, Rajan. It's little late to think about my age now, isn't it?' she had replied defiantly.

Rajan blushed. 'It's risky for you and the baby,' he said before disappearing into his surgery next door.

Although it was too early to begin her confinement, Nala had become reclusive recently, weighed down by the fatigue of pregnancy, and even more so, the fear that came with it.

Dhara insisted on checking on her, every day, as soon as she came back from school. Sometimes, she stopped at Nala's favourite sweet store on the way home. It was run by a Bohra family who served as many Indian sweets as Ceylonese ones. Dhara bought the jalebi she was partial to, even though Rajan had warned her the fried pastry would give her gestational diabetes.

'Are you tired, mami?' Dhara asked her, bringing her back to the newspaper. 'If you're tired, I can stop?'

'No mahal, keep going. I like to hear your voice.'

Dhara blushed. 'It says here that Bandaranaike's assassin converted to Christianity shortly before his hanging, so that he could save his executioners the Buddhist sin of killing another Buddhist. And Bandaranaike was born a Christian but he converted to Buddhism so he could join politics. That's ironic isn't it?'

'Ironic?' Nala smiled. 'You sound like Rajan mama.' She shifted her belly uncomfortably in the chair and tried to re-plait her hair; it was a mess.

Dhara went to the kitchen and returned a few moments later with warm sesame oil. She made Nala sit back and carefully rubbed a little oil into her curls, unravelling and massaging gently.

'Mami... when the baby comes, will I still be able to stay here... with you?'

Nala opened her eyes and turned around, wincing from the movement. 'Dhara, you can stay here with me forever. We-'

She stopped in mid-sentence, a rush of warmth and wetness on her feet. She pushed herself up from her chair, knocking it over as she did so.

'Mami, what's wrong? Are you alright?' Dhara asked.

'It's too early, it's too early. Please God, not yet. Not again...'

Dhara helped her to the ground and called out to Ayah.

'Call Rajan mama,' Nala whispered.

Dhara made the phone call to Rajan who was seeing patients at Colombo General. He could get home in ten minutes.

Nala was curled in a ball on the floor. She pressed her hands tightly between her legs. The blood was coming faster and thicker and there was nothing either of them could do.

It was over quickly; there was no time to do anything. No time to drag her to her bed, no time for Rajan or the doctors to arrive, no time for the child's lungs to breathe, for its heart to beat.

Nala lay on the floor, folded up like a baby – like the baby she could not see because she would not open her eyes. Dhara held her as she wept, stroking her hair and rocking back and forth to soothe her, like Nala did when she was little. When Rajan arrived, they were still like that – the mother wrapped in the child's arms, lying in a pool of dark blood. Dhara tapped Nala's back, lost in the rhythm of her own memories.

Bending down, Rajan moved Nala gently and extricated the baby from between her thighs. Her face was streaked with tears and pain as she held her arms out. He hesitated before passing the child to her. He was small and perfectly formed, and yet not formed. His skin was translucent and thin, revealing the web of tiny veins underneath. His eyes were sealed shut, framed by only the whisper of eyelashes. He held his hands together as if in prayer. Nala ran a finger over her son's naked body, tracing his head, down the small ridges of his spine, the curve of his soft bottom, to his tiny toes and back up again. She stopped at the place where she should have felt a heartbeat and then traced the perfect line of his lips. She kissed them gently and whispered something in the shell of his ear.

Rajan touched her shoulder and slowly took the baby from her, Nala's hands clinging hard, first to the child, then to him. He swaddled the child carefully in the blanket Ayah had brought, reluctantly covering his face. After a few moments he spoke, 'Nala, I'm going to carry you to the ambulance, hold on to me.'

She wrapped her arms around his neck as he said to Dhara, 'Stay with her in the ambulance. Kamini mami will meet us there. I'll follow with some clothes for both of you.'

At his words, Dhara looked down at her school uniform and saw that it was dark and sticky with blood. She closed her eyes against the image of the baby that should have lived; and the other images that were freefalling around her. She started to cry too. He shook his head.

'There's no time now, she needs you,' he said brusquely, carrying Nala to the door. Dhara watched as Nala rested her head on Rajan's chest. She heard his voice catch as he swallowed hard, fighting back his own tears.

✿

'Nala, it says here that Sivaji Ganeshan will star in a new movie about Karna. We should see it. Sivaji would make an excellent Karna. He looks like a cursed warrior.' Rajan showed her the picture of Sivaji on set. The rotund hero of hundreds of Tamil films was dressed in ancient armour and large sunglasses.

When Nala didn't respond, he talked on. 'I wonder if the movie will cover the entire *Mahabharata*. It could go on for hours. The actual war was supposed to be eighteen-days long, which by today's standards would be nothing more than a skirmish between cousins.'

He looked at her as she lay silently on their bed.

'Laugh Nala, please laugh,' he said softly.

She lifted herself up. 'Do you believe in karma Rajan?'

'What?'

'Do you believe in karma? We're all taught it, even the Buddhists believe in it. Do you think we'll be punished for the things we've done wrong?'

'No Nala, please don't talk like this. You're a... you're a good person.'

'Karna was a good person too.'

Nala got what she wanted – this was the fourth time Rajan had taken her to see the film *Karnan*.

He didn't like the cinema. It was expensive and unhygienic: all those people breathing in each other's air, sweating into seats that others would then sit and sweat in too. When he took the girls, he made them bring towels to sit on.

Nala tried to hide her tears. She had made it through most of the movie surreptitiously wiping her eyes whenever she thought he was too engrossed to notice. Of course he noticed everything: from the movie, to his wife's tears, to the uncontrollable shaking of the man three rows in front of him – Parkinson's.

It was funny that after being married for almost two decades, she still thought she could hide things from him. When she watched a film and cried, he knew it wasn't just the film she was crying about.

Although he complained about wasting his money to see *Karnan* with her repeatedly, he was secretly pleased when she asked every weekend. He was even more pleased when, at the moment that Karna was struck by the fatal arrow in his chest from his brother Arjuna, she would reach out for his hand and not let go until the end of the film.

Karnan was by far Sivaji Ganeshan's greatest masterpiece. He had outdone himself, capturing the warrior's sadness with every word, song and twitch of his manicured moustache.

Karna's life moved relentlessly towards tragedy. On the eve of the great war, Indra, King of the demi-gods, and Arjuna's father, interceded to protect his son. He asked Karna to give him the breastplate which would protect Karna's life during the battle. The armour was fused to Karna's body and he bled as he cut it from his flesh, knowing that his death in the war was now inevitable.

It was hard not to cry during the film. The final song that Lord Krishna sang as Karna lay dying was beautiful. It expressed grief and glorified Karna as the hero that he was. The film's Lord Krishna sang of the tragedy that grandfathers would tell their grandchildren, and grandchildren would tell their grandchildren. It could only be expressed in Tamil. There was something about their language; its poetry and its pain.

Their language. Sinhala Only. The Tamils no longer had a language with which to communicate with the State – and the State would no longer listen to them. Chelvanayakam, the Tamil politician, kept saying in English that they were voiceless now. In Tamil he would then ask: 'How long do you think it will be before we are nation-less too?'

In the north, Tamil people refused to comply. They did business in Tamil, they stuck Tamil number plates on their cars over the Sinhalese ones, and they issued their own Tamil postal stamps in their own post offices. The State feared the beginnings of a separate state and so it sent in the army to the homeland of the Tamil people in the Jaffna province. The army did as the army pleased and the Tamil people could no longer take refuge there, as they had once done.

Rajan had chosen a path for his family. They had not left Ceylon – it had been years since he'd tried. Nala's brothers had migrated to Canada. Kamini and her family had stayed.

And now they would need to stick to this path, like Karna had. The final scenes of the film began. Arjuna would be remembered forever as the greatest warrior of the *Mahabharata*. It was to him that Lord Krishna gave the *Bhagavad Gita*, the Song of God, the Lord's path to liberation. But it was Karna that Hindus would love. It was the actor Sivaji Ganeshan's Karna that Tamils would remember – chubby yet handsome, righteous yet flawed, heroic yet human.

As Arjuna shot the final arrow into a dying Sivaji, Rajan's heart broke and Nala cried openly, clutching her husband's hand.

7

COLOMBO, 1966

Nala scowled at her husband. He could be so stubborn sometimes. Since his mother's death last year, he was getting worse.

'You spoil him too much, Nala. You should be forcing him to study instead of letting him play cricket in the street all the time. He doesn't have the discipline for medicine.' He was lecturing her about Nandan again.

'He's only ten years old, let him be, there's still time,' she replied defensively. She didn't deny that she indulged him, but Rajan did too, only differently. Nandan did, said, and wanted things that his sisters were not allowed – and her husband just looked away.

'At his age, I was teaching myself human anatomy.'

'At his age, you were a lot less fun,' she rolled her eyes at him.

'Priya should study medicine. She'd make an excellent doctor,' he said.

'She'd make a terrible doctor, Rajan. She doesn't even like science.'

'Still, she'd make an excellent doctor. We should talk to her about it.'

'You can't force her to do medicine because you want one of your children to be like you. Anyway, you know what happened to her in her dissection practical,' she pleaded her daughter's case.

'Medicine is nothing like those practicals, although it's a shame she's so easily nauseated. She doesn't have to do surgery, she's a girl,' he replied.

'Exactly, she's a girl. We should be looking for husbands for our daughters instead of pushing them to study,' she said. 'Priya will make a wonderful wife. She mothers anyone who comes near her. She has an instinct to look after people that could only come from you,' she smiled winningly at him. It worked on other people.

'Think of it this way Nala: marrying a Tamil doctor is highly competitive – *being a* doctor would obviously give her a better chance of *marrying* a doctor herself.'

'Ah, but she is the daughter of a doctor. She doesn't need to study medicine herself!' Nala refused to be outsmarted.

'She could be wonderful at both. So many girls are going to university now. She's clever – she could be more than an office clerk or a teacher,' he replied.

Or a wife, she thought.

'It's getting harder to get into medicine these days,' Nala tried again.

'I know, but I can tutor her.' As usual, he had an answer for everything.

'It's harder than it was in your day.' She didn't want to offend him but it was true. 'There's talk of a new system. Priya might need more marks than her Sinhalese friends to get into medical school – there are too many Tamils in the professions.'

'I know, thank you Nala. I read the papers too. Quotas will be introduced: one Tamil for every six Sinhalese students. I will tutor her and she will get in. I'll talk to people.' He rarely talked to people, he was fair and honest.

She thought about the conversation that was to come. Priya had already shown her the prospectus for home economics at Aquinas College. She loved cooking.

'You always get what you want, Rajan,' she said softly, bitterly.

'So do you Nala. And you're wrong about me,' he said after a long moment. 'I don't want her to be like me. I want her to study medicine because she may need to help her husband, when we find him for her. The world is changing and the financial burdens of life maybe too much in the future for a man to carry alone. It was easier in my day but those days are over. I know that now.'

She nodded slowly. Priya was a smart girl; she would get the marks she needed. She might have to repeat her A-levels but she would get in eventually. After that, she would marry and have children, so would it make any difference what she studied or didn't study, or whether she fainted at the sight of blood or not? As long as she married well. She said a quick prayer to Amman, the Mother Goddess, *Please let her marry well.* She added for Rajan's sake, *and please let her get into medical school.*

☼

Priya looked down at her hands, the fingers of one pushing back the cuticles of the other, exposing the half-moons of every ridged nail.

'I wouldn't be very good at medicine, Amma,' she blinked back hot tears as she argued with her mother.

'Mahal, please don't cry. Appa has made up his mind,' Nala started to cry too.

'Tell him Nandan will study medicine. I'll talk to Nandan, I'll tutor him, there's still time. Appa would prefer it if it was Nandan; someone to carry on the family name and profession,' she implored, silently cursing her little brother and his ridiculous career plans. Most recently the little maharajah had declared he was going to be an international cricketer or a businessman.

'It's not about that. Your Appa wants you to have a career that could help your family, if you need to.'

Priya tried again, knowing it was futile. 'Force Nandan, Amma – make him study. We all have to.'

'I can't mahal.' Amma replied.

'No, of course you can't. You won't make him do anything; he's so precious.'

'That's not fair, Priya,' Nala's tears fell faster but Priya refused to feel sorry for her mother.

'I would be much better at home economics. Maybe even teaching – Kamini mami says I would make a wonderful teacher.' She had written to colleges in Colombo and Kandy. She had a plan but was too afraid to ask Appa for permission.

'Please Amma, you speak to him. He might listen to you.'

Her mother simply replied, 'What to do, mahal? You know what your father is like. He only wants the best for you. Please just hear what he has to say.'

Priya shook her head angrily. No-one listened to her except Dhara and Ayah. She didn't want to hear what her father had to say.

☼

Nala had taken Dhara and Nandan to the temple for the Friday night poosai, leaving the house silent except for Ayah's periodic scoldings to anyone who crossed her path. Rajan cleared his throat the way he did whenever he was about to say something important.

Priya had prepared a response for her father but she struggled to remember the words she and Dhara had rehearsed. Dhara felt certain she would get the marks she needed. 'I'll help you,' she offered. 'We can study every day together for the next six months.'

'We already study every day together,' Priya had replied, laughing tearfully. Going to university with Dhara would be her only consolation, if she wasn't able to convince Appa.

He cleared his throat again. 'Mahal, I'd like to talk to you about something. Your university application form needs to be submitted soon. Dhara is applying for medicine. I'd like you to apply too.'

She said nothing. Snippets of sentences taunted her but she couldn't piece any of them together coherently. Somewhere in her mind were full paragraphs that she wanted to tell him. They had been sitting there for days, some for years, waiting for an opportunity to be heard.

'I've looked over your last few exam results and spoken to your teachers,' he continued. 'They think that if you work extra hard from now until the finals, you will make it. Your teachers have confidence in you Priya; you're a good student. They think they haven't seen your best yet.'

She'd never heard her teachers – or her father – talk about her like that. Dhara was the more studious one. When she remained silent, he spoke again. 'I think I haven't seen your best yet, mahal. I think you could be more; I think you could do more in life than –' he stopped short.

'Than Amma?' she finished for him.

'No. More than me,' he said.

No-one was more than him. 'Do you like medicine, Appa?' she asked suddenly.

'Like it?' he asked, confused.

'Yes, do you like medicine? Are you happy being a doctor?'

'I've never thought about it, mahal – and no-one has ever asked me that. I became a doctor because it was what my mother hoped for; what every parent hopes for. Medicine has given me a livelihood that is better than most, and because I have that livelihood, I can support my family. That's enough for me and I'm grateful for it. Does that answer your question?' he asked, a slight smile tugging at the corner of his serious mouth.

'Yes, thank you Appa,' she replied, sitting up straighter in her chair. 'Is it hard?' she asked quietly. 'Medicine, I mean.'

'It is hard, but everything in life is hard, mahal. The Gita tells me to try harder. My Amma told me to try harder. Is there anything else you'd like to know?'

She looked down and shook her head.

'I've dropped my Saturday afternoon clinic so I can coach you every week,' he said. 'We could start with the renal system. I've made some diagrams...'

He never dropped his afternoon clinic. Suddenly she was more afraid of forgetting the parts of the renal system and confusing it with the hepatic system, than she was of anything else.

'Alright, Appa,' she replied, rubbing a tear in the skin around her nail. It hurt. 'I'll try – I'll study medicine.' He patted her hand awkwardly and she smiled back, a little tearfully.

Rajan reached towards the temple lamp with his hands. Then he touched his face, taking his final blessing from the priest. He placed a donation in the box by the statue of Lord Ganesha and lay face down on the temple's stone floor, arms outstretched in front of him. He offered himself prostrate before the elephant god at the beginning and end of each temple visit. He followed a routine for prayer.

Nala approached the deities a little more spontaneously, depending on which god or goddess she needed particular help from, or which of her friends were praying in the temple that day.

As he stood up, he straightened his clothes and scanned the congregation for his wife. She was in the corner of the hall next to the Amman deity. Not surprisingly, the Mother Goddess sat benevolently ignored, as Nala and a group of ladies chatted and laughed. She waved jauntily as he crossed the temple towards her. He stood on the outside of her circle and whispered, 'I think we should go now, your Amma will be waiting for us at home and Archi needs her medicine.'

He gave Archi her medication, not trusting Ayah or even Nala to do it. Archi faded in and out of reality but somehow for him she was always present and smiling.

He guided Nala to the exit, 'I've finished praying and I don't think you've even started.'

Her nose reddened. 'I've been praying for the last hour actually. Who are you? My spiritual invigilator? The Prayer Police? We have two daughters who'll need to be married soon. Where do you think those marriages will be arranged? In your surgery? Hardly.' He tried not to smile at the word 'marriage'.

On the way home they stopped at Vani's house to pick up the girls. Although Dhara hadn't moved back with her mother, she spent more time there now. Vani had set up a little room for her but Dhara preferred to sleep in her mother's arms when she visited, even though she was twenty-years-old.

On the drive back, he suggested they have an ice cream at Galle Face Green. Nala raised her eyebrows.

'No, I'm not unwell,' he replied. 'It's a tenth of the price if you buy it by the pound or in bulk, or on sale, or not at all. But I thought you might like a treat.'

They took their ice creams down to the beach: strawberry for Priya and vanilla for Dhara, just like when they were children. They would each eat half before swapping cones. Rajan remembered he and Lali did the same thing. Once a year their grandfather would buy them an ice cream from the restaurant next to the Dutch Fort in Jaffna town.

Rajan was too afraid to go inside, begging Lali to stay with him on the glossy terrace as he hopped from tile to tile excitedly. Their grandfather would walk confidently in, wearing his only suit that had been pressed for this annual extravagance. Rajan would choose plain vanilla every time but Lali was more daring, often picking toppings at random, forcing him to try something new.

Nala sat on a bench with him and took out her notebook as they watched the girls, luminous in the sunlight. They didn't go in the water, standing playfully together at its edge. Priya was wearing an enormous striped hat that matched her dress, protecting her fair complexion from the sun. Dhara was only a few months younger, but didn't care about her appearance.

'They're so young but it's almost time,' Nala said as she opened her notebook at the right page. 'I was already married and pregnant at their age.'

'I think I may have found someone,' he said quietly.

'What?'

'I think I may have found someone.'

'For what?' she repeated.

'For Dhara.'

'For what?'

'For marriage.'

'What?' she exclaimed.

He laughed. The conversation was obviously not quite what she was expecting for a Sunday afternoon stroll on the beach.

'Who is he?' she collected herself and ran through her checklist with Rajan.

'Who is he, where is he from, what does he do, who is his family, how is his character and is he fair?' She was a seasoned interrogator, but he was used to it. He answered her questions confidently and thoroughly.

'I don't know if he's fair enough for you Nala, but he's certainly fair enough for me.' Skin colour didn't matter in a man but he knew she was proud she had produced two beautiful children, despite having married a dark man like him.

Rajan was pleased with himself too. 'It will be an excellent marriage for Dhara. The family are good people. They see past Vani's caste and what happened to her.' He wasn't sure he could say the same of everyone in his or Nala's family.

'His name is Siva. He comes from my village in Jaffna and he's training to be a cardiovascular surgeon. He's the eldest son of six children.' He paused, waiting for her response.

'The eldest son always carries the biggest burden for the family.'

'I know that Nala. He carries the family.' Rajan was the eldest son.

'Who recommended him?' she asked, not yet persuaded.

'Kamini's father-in-law, old Uncle Tharmo. He met the boy at a Tamil Federal Party rally, but assures me he wasn't there to participate. He had only brought his parents.'

'Well, are they political?' she asked.

'Everyone is becoming political, Nala. I told Uncle Tharmo I don't want a son-in-law who's involved in the party. I want someone who will work hard, provide for her, make her happy and have children.' Maybe even a son-in-law who would allow her to look after all of them. He would save enough so that he and Nala would not be at the mercy of others, but he had watched his own mother wither. He would need his children.

'He's been offered a position at Colombo General and he's applying for overseas scholarships as well. He's very clever and hardworking. People speak highly of him and his family. Uncle Tharmo said he couldn't recommend his own son more highly. That's a little troubling as his son *is* married to your sister.' Rajan smiled at Nala but she didn't smile back.

He continued. 'Uncle suggested we do a horoscope matching first and if the charts are compatible, the families can meet.'

'Will this boy allow her to finish her studies first? I want her to graduate before she has children, don't you?' Nala asked. 'If he wants to marry into our family, he will wait, surely?'

Rajan answered simply, 'He is a doctor.'

'And you are a doctor and she is a medical student,' she pushed, 'so she's worth waiting for.'

'Don't be foolish Nala – you were the one who wanted them to marry rather than study. I don't want them to wait – I want her to marry and begin her life, hopefully in a new country; a better country than this one.' He had said too much. He didn't want a son-in-law involved in politics. He needed one who would help Dhara escape politics.

'You're marrying her off so she will leave?' Nala asked.

'I am not 'marrying her off' – I am marrying her well, to a man who has integrity, drive and ambition; a man who sees what's happening to Ceylon and can make his way in the rest of the world. You trusted your father's judgement and respected his wishes when he told you it was time for your marriage. Now trust my judgement and please respect my wishes.'

He turned away from her, his eyes stinging from the rebuke of her angry tears. Priya and Dhara had finished their ice creams and were standing at the water's edge, staring into the horizon. The breeze caught Priya's hat and skirt: she grabbed both, pinning them down. He loved his children's laughter; it was rich and unfettered. Once Priya started, she couldn't stop. Dhara followed her, laughing too: both of them linking arms and letting the water lap at their feet.

In that moment the girls were so young and free and happy, watching the water together. The Indian Ocean was bluest around Colombo he thought fancifully, more stunning than the depths of a Ceylon sapphire. It was a beautiful day.

The horoscopes had not matched. Dhara and Siva were astrologically incompatible. Old Uncle Tharmo asked his astrologer to check the charts again and again. He confirmed Dhara's time of birth, the Hindu astrology almanac was consulted and her chart was redrawn from scratch. The new chart was compared with Siva's once more – and once more it revealed an incontrovertible astrological incompatibility.

The astrologer quietly explained to Nala that the planets in Dhara's chart were not favourable for marriage at the moment, or for the next few years. Rajan thought the astrologer was an idiot and told her so.

By this time, Nala had made her own enquiries about the young doctor and had fallen into a state of maternal love with him. She quietly asked Uncle Tharmo to check Siva's chart, which she now knew by memory, against another, different one. Siva and Priya were highly compatible.

✪

Dhara unfolded the soft cloth, revealing an array of scalpels, forceps, clamps and retractors. She had two small bone saws, surgical sheets and piles of gauze, which she pulled out of a bag at her feet. She laughed as Priya's eyes widened in disbelief and admiration.

'How on earth did you get those?' Priya asked, shaking her head.

'I told the theatre nurse they were for Rajan mama,' Dhara was very pleased with herself.

'You lied?'

'Yes, but in the name of medical research,' she laughed as she arranged the implements in order of blade size the way her uncle had shown her. She wouldn't have dared take scalpels from his surgery.

Together the cousins spread surgical sheets on the cement floor of the family kitchen, weighting the corners of each with Ayah's heavy pots. They were meticulous in their work, lining up the edges of the sheets, the same way they made their bed together every morning. They stood back and surveyed the makeshift operating theatre. They were ready.

Ayah hobbled in with Thiru, the mas karaya. He had been selling meat to and flirting with Ayah for decades. He was an old man now, skin wrinkling over his incongruously muscular body. He had upgraded his ice cart for an insulated box with wheels but he still had to pull it from house to house, yoked to a harness across his back. His sons worked in Kollupitiya, selling meat at the market and no longer making house calls.

'The market is a far more profitable approach, but I still enjoy bringing meat to certain special customers.' He gave Ayah a gappy smile and surveyed the kitchen, nodding his approval.

He left the room and returned moments later, carrying a stiff, skinned goat. Staggering a little under its weight, he placed it gently on the floor.

'Hundred rupees, thangachi,' he said cheekily to Ayah, winking at the girls.

'Fifty, and I'm not your thangachi,' she snorted back, hands placed belligerently on her hips.

'Aiiyoh thangachi! I've come all this way by foot. You couldn't even take a taxi to Kollupitiya market for fifty rupees.'

Ayah appeared unmoved by his efforts.

'Eighty, but no less – you are beggaring me,' he wiped his face tragically on his sweaty shirt.

'Fifty,' she repeated flatly.

'Done,' he replied holding his hand out for the crumpled note she pulled from her sari blouse. He kissed it and winked at her again. Her scowl relaxed as she laughed and smacked him on the shoulder. She was aiming for his head but he was at least a foot taller than her.

Ayah handed him three large paper bags filled with mothahams. She had been making the small steamed dumplings all morning, pushing the girls away whenever they tried to steal them. The whole house smelled like the succulence of palm sugar, fresh coconut and boiled green gram. Dhara's mouth watered as Thiru juggled the bags out the door.

She turned to see Priya standing over the goat carcass, breathing in deeply through her nose, and out noisily through her mouth.

'You're not going to hyper-ventilate again are you?' she asked. They had been practising dissections on animal parts and frogs at the university laboratory together, but Priya always stood well behind her, concentrating on staying conscious. Lately, her sister had progressed – instead of fainting she had started hyper-ventilating.

Their first dissection examination was coming up next week and Priya had yet to dissect a goat heart by herself.

'Acca, I'm going to make the first incision from the thoracic cavity to the abdominal cavity. There'll be a lot of blood and it may smell.

Ayah, I want you to be ready with the gauze and the cloths, you're on clean-up duty.'

Dhara stretched white plastic gloves onto her hands. She gave a pair to Priya and one to Ayah who threw them away with a superior sniff.

'I will reach in under the lungs and feel for the heart. It will be easier for me if I can find it without cutting through the sternum, but I've brought a saw just in case. Now, you need to watch me. Watch my hands. The first incision needs to be confident and slow.' Dhara spoke clearly, copying Rajan word for word. He had been showing them how to dissect aubergines since they were children. She now enjoyed spending her spare time watching him operate at the university hospital. He used the same opening words with his medical students.

Priya shuffled back and sat on the ground, her skin paler than usual and her breathing erratic as she swallowed rapidly.

'Imagine this is an enormous aubergine,' Dhara tried again, patting the taut pink dermis layer of skin. It was embroidered with a labyrinth of tiny violet veins, leading inwards, seeking the animal's hidden heart. The goat smelled like palm sugar, fresh coconut and boiled green gram. She brought scalpel to skin and heard a dull thud as Priya slumped to the floor.

Dhara relaxed as Priya finally opened her eyes. They smiled at each other, Priya sheepishly. Dhara pulled back the sheets and slid into her side of the bed.

'How are you?' she asked.

'I'm pathetic,' Priya replied turning her face away.

'Dissections are hard, acca, don't worry. We'll try again tomorrow.' Dhara had located and removed the heart, storing it at the back of Ayah's refrigerator.

'What happened to the goat?' Priya rolled over to face her sister.

'Ayah, mutton curry,' she replied and they both laughed at the thought of Ayah disposing of the evidence. Carlo, Nala mami's Great Dane, would have bones for weeks.

Priya propped herself up on her pillows. 'Dhara, can I ask you something?' She smoothed the sheets around her compulsively. 'Are you angry about the proposal? Because if you are, then I will tell Amma that I can't marry him…'

Dhara didn't look at Priya as she considered her answer. She stared at the mosquito net that hung from the ceiling. Every morning she lifted it off the bed and tied it into a high knot. Every evening she untied it, letting the soft folds of muslin spill over the bed, encasing the two of them in its protective arms. The barrier could not keep out the demons that stirred when the Sun God slept.

'No acca, I'm not upset. I'm happy for you and I'm relieved for me. I'm not ready for marriage yet; maybe not ever, I just don't know. The astrologer has saved me for at least a few years.'

'Appa said that astrologer is an idiot,' Priya replied.

'You should marry the doctor. He sounds nice and smart and astrologically excellent,' she laughed.

Since the proposal, she had been thinking about marriage. She couldn't explain to Priya what she feared about it. She thought about her Amma who had been dependent on her Appa's life and destroyed by his death. Her parents had loved each other. They had disobeyed and fought with their families to be together. They had never truly been forgiven for their decision. For a moment, she allowed herself a memory of her father, with his quick laugh and safe embrace. She didn't want something in her life that could be so hard won but so easily lost.

The proposed marriage to Dr Rajan's daughter was a big opportunity for Siva and he knew his parents couldn't turn it down. When they entered the driveway, his heart leapt a little. It was a magnificent house, elegant without being imposing. He had heard that Dr and Mrs Rajan had designed it themselves and on his previous visit he had tried to identify which parts had been designed by him and which parts by her. The oversized, ornate mirror in the hall-way was definitely her. The grandfather clock was apparently him, his one willing concession to colonial furnishings.

The Rajan family had not been to their house yet. Siva had heard his mother Radha talking to his father about borrowing cane furniture for their visit.

He looked at his gift with excitement. He thought it was perfect but his mother wasn't sure.

'Mahan, take something more conventional for your second meeting. The Rajans are originally from Jaffna but they've lived in Colombo for many years. They're from Colombo 7 now – not Wellawatte where people might appreciate your thoughtfulness.'

His parents had recently moved to Colombo for his father's work. They preferred Wellawatte with its middle-class Tamils. It was comforting, although it wasn't always safe. Whenever trouble occurred in Colombo, the Sinhalese mobs knew where to find them.

He listened to Amma respectfully, but he was adamant about the gift. His bride-to-be would love it. He smiled with relief when he saw Nala.

'Hello mahan,' Nala reached forward and kissed Siva on both cheeks. She ushered him into their drawing room with Radha.

'Hello Aunty, how are you today?' he asked, his eyes trying not to search the room for Priya.

'I am very well, thank you mahan,' she replied as she reached forward and kissed his mother. 'I'm very sorry to hear Kesavan won't be joining us today, I've made some of my butter cake for you all.'

Siva's throat tightened a little at the thought of his father. Kesavan was working in the eastern province this month, trying to earn extra money at Batticaloa Central Post Office. Although Dr Rajan would pay for the wedding and offer a considerable dowry, Kesavan wanted to contribute. He didn't have to, he had his own daughters to pay for, but he didn't want Dr Rajan to think he had agreed to this marriage because of the wealth Dr Rajan could offer.

He smoothened the wrinkled letter he carried from his father to the doctor. He didn't know what it contained but he assumed it was an apology from Kesavan. 'It is a very *thick* letter,' his mother had worried. 'What else might your father want to say? He can be so honest and emotional sometimes. Colombo 7 people aren't like that. Perhaps we should open it first?'

Siva had refused and took the letter from his mother, saying 'Amma, please relax. Remember what Appa says: if this marriage is meant to happen, it will happen.'

Dr Rajan entered with Priya, his niece Dhara and Nala's younger sister, Kamini. Everyone stood up nervously. Pleasantries were exchanged and Rajan gave them all permission to sit. No-one spoke. Siva awkwardly thrust Kesavan's letter forward.

'Dr Rajan, my father is very sorry he couldn't be here today. He is working at the Batticaloa Post Office this month. But he sent you this letter.' Siva handed the letter to him. Rajan thanked him and slowly walked out to read it. He was an awkward man too, Siva thought.

Once more a silence. Siva's eyes wandered as he tried to think of something to say. He rubbed his bare feet against the soft Persian rug on the floor. The strings on the edge of the rug were all uncommonly straight, as though someone had combed them, making sure each one was uniform and parallel to the next.

Nala hurried in with her servant girl close behind her. As tea was served, she offered everyone some of her 'world famous butter cake'. At the mention of the words 'world famous', Siva saw Priya smile and look down.

The cake was warm, soft and buttery. It had just come out of the oven and was melting in his mouth.

Nala smiled knowingly as a satisfied silence descended. She leaned over and whispered to his mother, 'People love my cake, they always do. Rajan never believes me when I tell him and now he won't even see it with his own eyes! Man may be able to walk on the moon, but can he make a butter cake like this?'

'It's corn flour,' she continued. 'I weigh the eggs first and use as much American flour, sugar, and butter as the weight of the eggs. Then I take out two to four tablespoons of the American flour and I replace it with corn flour. It's a secret, don't tell anyone. I'm only telling you because we're going to be related. My friends in Kandy taught me the recipe.'

While Nala and his mother were distracted by the cake, Siva cleared his throat nervously, stood up, and offered Priya his gift. She smiled shyly, accepted the large box and stood holding it, unsure of what to do next.

'Well, open it acca, it looks exciting,' Dhara prompted her.

His mother flinched at the word 'exciting' and Nala shook her head too late at her daughters. It was not polite to open the gift until the guests had left, but Priya's fingers were faster than her mother's cautionary look. Radha flinched again as Priya pulled out a plastic heart. Chaotically, pieces started falling off.

Both Siva and Priya bent down, chasing after the pieces that were rolling everywhere. 'It's not broken,' he muttered, more to his mortified mother than to Priya. His face was red underneath his dark skin, 'It's detachable. The parts are detachable; I thought it would be helpful for anatomy. You can see the four chambers, the atria and the ventricles; that's the superior vena cava right there, it's very detailed,' he kept going.

Please stop talking, he said to himself, *please stop talking now*. He couldn't look up at his mother or Priya, instead concentrating on the pieces of a plastic heart scattered over the beautiful woven rug on the floor.

Suddenly he heard laughter. Priya was taking the pieces from his hands and putting the chambers of the heart back together as he continued to collect them. She was beautiful when she laughed; and was laughing so hard that she had started to cry.

Rajan returned to the room to find his daughter and her prospective husband laughing and reconstructing a plastic human heart together. He sat down but the letter wasn't with him. Nala looked at him, one eyebrow raised artfully. He ignored her question and reached for a piece of butter cake. Siva watched the steam rise from the cake – it was still warm. Rajan smiled at him and then spoke to his mother, 'Shall we talk about the wedding?'

✿

Priya wondered what Siva would look like with his frontal-lobe puff of hair all messed up. The puff looked difficult to achieve – it had elevation, uniformity of direction and considerable shine. The third time they met, they were allowed to go to the Galle Face Hotel for ice cream, accompanied by Dhara, Kamini mami and Nandan. She took the opportunity to study his hair and noticed that it didn't move in the wind when they walked on the Green. The conversation was stilted but pleasant.

'What is your favourite flavour?' Siva asked politely as he ordered and picked up a handful of paper napkins. Kamini mami nodded her approval as he paid for all of them.

'Strawberry. Yours?' she asked, trying not to look at Dhara who was shaking her head. Dhara had instructed her to ask more probing questions before their marriage.

'Same!' Siva exclaimed, 'That's amazing!'

'It is!' she replied, ignoring the rapid eye-rolling that her sister and now Nandan were both engaged in. Dhara fell behind Priya and poked her in the back.

'What else do you like, Siva?' Priya asked.

'What else do I like?' he repeated, confused.

'Yes, what else do you like, aside from strawberry ice cream?'

'Um, I like chicken curry and okra,' he replied tentatively.

'No, I mean what do you like to do, not eat,' she laughed nervously as Nandan sniggered a little. She would take care of her little brother later.

'Oh, *do*! Well, I suppose I like medicine, I like reading and films, Western and Tamil ones. I particularly like James Bond. Sean Connery is an excellent secret agent – better than that Australian fellow, Lazenby. My mother thinks Bond needs to settle down and marry. I like walking on the beach with friends and one day I'd like to travel – with you. How is that?' he asked shyly.

'That is excellent,' she replied. She could feel Dhara, Kamini mami and even Nandan smiling behind her.

'What do you like, Priya?' Siva asked.

'I like cooking. I can make chicken curry and okra. Ayah taught me those and many other curries. I like inventing my own too. I like playing 3-0-4 with my cousins and reading and I love films.'

'Do you like medicine?' he asked, leaning closer to her. Brylcreem. Perhaps he used Brylcreem.

'Yes, I love it,' she lied.

✷

Priya cried as she carried Dhara's belongings with her back to Dhara's room. They didn't know how to separate their things: clothes, books, study notes, make-up and trinkets. It was theirs, not one or the other's.

'You should take your pillow, you sleep better on it,' she said, holding the pillow tightly.

'If you wipe your nose on my pillow you'll have to keep it,' Dhara replied, pulling it away from her.

'How can you be so calm?' Priya asked her, a little resentfully.

'Because I'll be right next door, with my head under my pillow, trying not to listen to you two lovebirds,' Dhara said, throwing her pillow back onto her old bed.

'That is a *terrible* thought!' Priya was horrified. She'd been so upset about the room and excited about her upcoming wedding, that she hadn't thought about the proximity of the rest of the household to what would now be her marital bed.

'That is a terrible thought,' she repeated, sinking onto Dhara's bed, pulling the pillow under her head. Dhara pushed her over and rested her own head next to her.

Without speaking they both started lifting their legs, performing three sets of twenty lifts for each leg. Then, laughing and breathless they turned on their side towards each other. They propped their bodies up on an elbow and performed another set of side leg lifts. Then they turned, and with their backs to each other, they lifted their other leg.

'I'm worried Dhara. He's so smart. I heard Appa say that he's a strong candidate for a fellowship with the Royal College of Surgeons in London – *London*,' she paused her leg lifts to catch her breath.

'Yes, yes, he's very clever, but so are you, acca. You never have enough faith in yourself,' Dhara replied.

'What am I going to do in London?' she asked, sitting up. She watched as Dhara kept exercising. She was frightened but hopeful too. London was the farthest away from Colombo they could go.

'You are going to Oxford Street and Mayfair and all the other places on the Monopoly board – except jail and the brown properties, they look a little disreputable.'

Priya didn't laugh. 'Do you think he'll be disappointed when he finds out?'

'Finds out what?' Dhara stopped her leg lifts and sat up.

'Finds out that I don't want to be a doctor; that I'm not very good at it,' she said quietly.

'I want you to stop that. What are the symptoms of a subarachnoid haemorrhage?'

'What?'

'You heard me. What are the symptoms of a subarachnoid haemorrhage?'

'Severe headaches, nausea and vomiting, seizures, loss of consciousness and sudden death in one out of ten cases.'

'Yes. You might not like medicine yet, but you can do it – just like your father and just like your future husband. Now can we please do our stretches?'

They both sat on their haunches and stretched their arms out in front of them.

'When Siva moves in, do you think he'd like to join our home calisthenics class?' Dhara asked. Priya burst out laughing and rolled over onto her back again. Dhara joined her, reaching for her hand, holding it as they lay there.

'I don't think so, at least not on the days Ayah does it with us.' She couldn't imagine the serious-looking Siva doing sit-ups with them. She had tried to imagine herself with him in a variety of scenarios – at the cinema, at Galle Face Green, at temple together, in the car together, even in bed together. The last thought made her blush with excitement and a little fear. She thought about touching his hair although in her imagination it was softer than it looked in real life.

8

COLOMBO, 1971

Rajan sat down on the divan slowly. He was fifty-years-old. He felt like an old man. He pulled his trousers up as he leant down to undo his shoe laces. He never kicked his shoes off like Nandan. He undid the laces first, loosened the bridge of the shoe and slipped his foot out. First the right foot, then the left; never the other way around.

Nala couldn't stand it any longer. 'What did Dr Navaratnam say?' He had gone to the Department of Health to see his old friend Dr Nava. The Bandaranaike government had just announced its new policy: all junior doctors would be required to work for five years in the national health system before they could qualify fully.

'He says it's worse than we feared. Junior doctors will not be allowed to leave the country until they fulfil their national service. They will only be released from the obligation, and the country, under exceptional circumstances – such as overseas scholarships. When the exam results are out a list will be sent to the airport. The police will be stopping and checking people soon. The girls have to leave Ceylon as soon as they finish their exams – or in five years. I asked Nava for scholarships.' His friend was well-connected at the Royal College of Surgeons in London.' He put his head in his hands.

'He said he can give us one.'

'That's wonderf-' she stopped, realising what he had said. 'Only one? But we need two for London. Siva is already there, waiting for Priya and…' Dhara.

'I know we need two. Nava knows we need two but he can only get one. I've tried everyone. Everyone. They're all in the same position. They're all trying to get people out.'

Rajan looked down. The grout in the tiled floor was flecked with mould. The damp in the air was suffocating. He wanted to bleach the floor; everything. He wanted to bleach himself. He allowed himself to think about the hospital basement at Gal Oya where he first found Mohan. Bodies lined the corridors and filled the store rooms, covered in surgical sheets, blood pooling on the floor. It seeped into the grout, staining it a rust colour. No amount of bleach could remove it. Suddenly every part of him ached, from his one heart to his two feet.

For the first time in their marriage, Rajan refused to make a decision. There was only one path in front of them and Nala took it. She sent Priya to London on the scholarship and offered no explanation to Dhara. She knew no explanation would be adequate and Dhara said no explanation was necessary.

'Tell Rajan mama that you want to stay in Ceylon to be with your mother. Tell him that you refuse to go, please mahal,' she asked her. 'If we can organise another scholarship, we will.'

'Of course mami,' Dhara replied. 'It's the truth.'

Later, when Nala thought about that time, she realised she hadn't even hesitated.

Nala had stopped going out. She sent Ayah alone to do her errands. She used to enjoy going to the market at Kollupitiya. She went every week, often with Kamini, who considered herself an expert at bargaining with the stall holders. Ayah or her driver Kannan would always accompany them so she didn't have to carry anything except her small purse and her list for the week.

Nowadays, she would even pay a little extra and buy from the vegetable karaya who walked the streets of Cinnamon Gardens, selling overpriced okra and aubergines to over-dressed ladies.

She didn't like leaving the house anymore because when she came home, she noticed everything that was there and everything that wasn't there anymore.

Carlo, her Great Dane, still came running towards her, his nails scratching on the hard floor, his tail hitting photos from tables. She laughed as his long legs slid and scrambled, trying to maintain his balance as he hurtled towards her, like a teenage girl in heels for the first time. Carlo had been named after a handsome tango singer Rajan had taken her to see in Colombo. Both the tango singer and the dog had languid dark eyes. Carlo wasn't supposed to be an inside dog. Rajan and Kannan had built him a large kennel, luxuriously furnished with cushions from their old divan. The kennel sat unused and unloved on the front verandah. Perhaps like his namesake, Carlo had fine taste. He had appropriated the new divan inside the house instead.

Nala noticed the slivers of sunlight that pushed through the shutters of their main hall, thin stripes falling on their dining table like a luminous pedestrian crossing. Ayah closed the shutters before they went out in the morning, anticipating and blocking out the midday sun so that the room was cool when they returned. She wanted to turn on the ceiling fan too, but Rajan wouldn't hear of such extravagant electricity consumption. He said the children could use the fans when they were in the rooms – not before.

The children. The children weren't there anymore.

She missed the laughter and arguments that used to come from Priya and Siva's room. She missed the way her daughter hummed as she helped Ayah in the kitchen, the two of them scolding each other over salt and chilli.

She longed to hear the click of Dhara's key in the heavy brass lock on their front door; the sound as the swollen wood scraped a little against the red-brown cement floor. Dhara had moved to Jaffna Hospital. Rajan was so proud of her and their calls every Friday night were the longest conversations he had with anyone all week. Nala was also proud, but fearful too. She thought about Mohan often – odd things would bring him to her; a sari the colour of a frangipani heart, a ridge of mosquito bites, the smell of freshly churned soil. She had opened the dam this time, and its dangerous current had carried Dhara north.

She had Nandan, but he was sixteen-years-old and no longer interested in spending time at home – not the way the girls had been.

And there was Rajan. It was so easy for him to let the girls go. He made them go. He found Priya a husband who wanted to leave, then gave her money, called in favours and did more to make her go than he ever did to make her stay.

Rajan had helped Dhara get the training placement up in Jaffna too. He said it would be safer for her there, amongst their own people. The south had become more violent than the north.

Sometimes she would sit on Priya and Dhara's bed. She would untie the muslin canopy and let it fall, softly enveloping her. Looking around at the room from under the net it looked a little different, a little better. The gauze muted the room's bareness. She would reach out and touch the lines where Rajan had sewn tears in the muslin. She could recognise his stitching anywhere: it was as elegant as his handwriting. Sometimes she would lie down on the bed. She thought she could still smell the girls. That was ridiculous – the sheets had been changed, the bed had been used by guests. But she still did it. She would lie down, close her eyes, and inhale deeply.

The state of emergency should have ended but it continued indefinitely. Nala thought she would get used to army checkpoints and soldiers laughing in the streets, with guns slung as casually over their shoulders as the cigarettes that hung from their mouths. She thought she might stop noticing it, but she didn't.

The train from Hambantota had finally arrived, an hour late. She stood on the platform with Kannan, both of them nervously searching the crowds for Ayah. The old woman emerged with her small suitcase. When she saw Nala, she collapsed into her arms. Nala and the driver dragged her into the car and held her as she wept.

'They've taken all of the children, all of them,' Ayah cried hysterically in Sinhalese. Words, tears and mucus ran into one. Nala wiped Ayah's face with her sari and held her tightly. What could she say?

Ayah had four nephews in Hambantota; two studied at Ruhuna University but the other two were only boys. They were all members of the JVP, the Sinhala Marxist rebellion in the south.

'I told them not to get involved. I told them this would happen.' She started hitting her head with her hands, calling and cursing the Buddha in turns. Nala wrestled her hands down and pinned them to her side.

'I should have brought them here. I should have made them come to Colombo.'

'Nowhere is safe Ayah, not anymore,' Nala kissed the top of her head. Her hair had wilted, like her body.

By June 1971, Prime Minister Sirimavo Bandaranaike had crushed the JVP rebellion, killing over fifteen thousand young Sinhalese men and women in less than four months.

'Nowhere is safe, and no-one,' she whispered, holding Ayah close.

It was the first morning tea Nala had attended in a while. Rita Matthews had made her go.

'You need to get out. Put some powder on. Get dressed in one of your silk saris. And look at your hair – you need to start dyeing your hair again Nala, all your grey is showing. That's not like you. You can't spend your time in that empty house, waiting for Rajan to get back from work,' Rita scolded. She was right, but now, surrounded by people, she wished she was home.

She forced a smile as the ladies chatted. She found that she was still able to laugh at the appropriate moments without listening to what they were actually saying. The sound was empty but her friends hadn't noticed.

'What does Rajan say about it, Nala?' Dolly Fonseka looked at her earnestly. They had been neighbours for thirteen years, and Nala couldn't remember a time when Dolly hadn't been earnest. She heard the question but not the context. What does Rajan say about what?

'As usual, he says nothing at all about it. You know how he is, Dolly,' she shrugged and gave her best exasperated expression. Dolly laughed, as did the others. The conversation continued.

'I like the new name. *Sri Lanka*,' Dolly repeated the words. 'It sounds majestic and powerful.'

'Technically it's the *old* name, Dolly,' Rita corrected her. Prime Minister Bandaranaike, had declared that Ceylon should revert to its pre-colonial Sinhala name.

'Old name, new name,' she shrugged her shoulders. 'Anyway, I think it's wonderful we have a female Prime Minister again. She was the first in the world, the last time she was elected. I'm thinking about becoming a feminist because of her.'

'As long as you don't become a fascist, like her,' Rita scoffed.

'Rita!' Dolly flushed.

'It's true Dolly, unfettered power suits Sirimavo even better than widowhood,' Rita replied.

'Hush Rita, you'll get us into trouble. The servants might hear you,' Dolly looked around nervously.

'That's right, and you know what might happen to us. Our husbands would find our heads impaled on spikes at a road crossing,' Rita replied angrily.

'My Ayah – her nephews were never found. They were so young, barely more than children,' Nala said, more to herself than her friends. 'It would be terrible not to be found – for the families. There are thousands of families who will never know.'

Her hands gripped the elegant tea cup tightly.

'Sirimavo doesn't make me want to become a feminist, Dolly. She makes me want to be sick. She makes me want to leave Ceylon, finally. I mean Sri Lanka,' Nala spoke softly but clearly.

The servant girl walked in with more cake. Dolly's face flushed as she tried not to cry.

'I'm sorry, Dolly,' Nala whispered. 'I didn't mean to upset you.'

Rita stepped in, looking at her friend carefully. 'Are you all going to the fireworks tonight, ladies?' she asked far too brightly. 'The Galle Face Hotel is throwing a party to celebrate the new name and the new constitution.'

'I'm not sure, Rita, I haven't asked Rajan yet. We'll see,' Nala didn't feel like fireworks or a party and she knew what he would say – the new constitution repealed all of the minority protections that had been put in place at Independence. It was nothing to celebrate.

For once, she was relieved by his dourness, it camouflaged her own feelings.

Rita smiled at her encouragingly. 'If you're not going to Galle Face, come to our place Nala. We can have a quiet dinner and let the young people enjoy the fireworks.'

At the mention of the words 'young people' Nala's eyes filled with tears and she looked away.

That afternoon when she returned home, she went to Priya and Dhara's room. Pulling the muslin over her, she lay down on the bed, closed her eyes, inhaled the sheets and cried.

☼

Nala was very worried now. Rita's preamble was getting longer and although she too enjoyed the art of good storytelling it was time for Rita to get to the point.

'Listen Nala, I'm only telling you this because you are one of my dearest friends and I think you would want to know. If it were my family I would want to know,' Rita said. 'Dennis and I have nothing but the highest regard for you. I've known you for such a long time and these people have only recently married into your family. I feel a responsibility to tell you.'

'Rita, what has happened? Just tell me.'

'Yes, yes, yes,' Rita didn't like being hurried. 'Meena told Malar who told me that your sambanthi Radha was seen at Chelvanayakam's latest Tamil Federal Party rally in Jaffna last week.'

'It's called the Tamil United Front now,' Nala interrupted her.

'Yes, yes – Chelvanayakam can break away and call it anything he wants to. He still wants the same thing. But your Priya's mother-in-law – Radha. She was at the rally with her younger son, Anand. Her husband only recently passed away, so Meena was very surprised to see her anywhere at all. Anyway, Anand – he's studying at Katubedda Technical College. You know he was accepted into Peradeniya University but his marks were down-graded by the new standardisation policy. Such a shame – so many of our children will suffer.

'He was sitting *with* Chelvanayakam. Well, not with him, but at his feet. He was sitting there, listening and winding the old man's watch for him.'

'He was what?' Nala asked.

'He was winding the old man's watch. Yes, exactly, that's why I thought you would want to know. Chelvanayakam is a separatist, Nala. If the Sinhalese had bothered to learn Tamil, they could have read his propaganda and worked it out earlier. Between him and that thug in the jungle, Prabhakaran, there's going to be trouble soon.

'But Nala, that isn't the worst of it,' Rita paused dramatically. 'He's not just handing out leaflets at rallies or plastering posters on walls like some of the other boys. I asked people. He's *organising* protests for Chelvanayakam,' she paused again, expectantly.

'Rita darling, thank you for caring enough to call. I've got to go – there's so much to do: Nandan's tutor is coming soon, he probably hasn't done his homework; Dhara is arriving tonight from Jaffna and Ayah needs to be given her instructions for dinner. I'm exhausted just thinking about it all and I haven't even been to temple yet. I told Kamini I would be there half an hour ago. I will call you later, I promise.'

She put the phone down. Carlo came up to her and put his head on her lap. Distracted, she played with his soft ears and rubbed his chest. The dog was so big that people were afraid of him. He had exceeded their expectations about size and ate more than his fair share, but she loved feeding him, watching him wolf down her offerings. He was the only one who didn't complain when she attempted to cook.

Dhara had been at the recent rally too. She had joined the Federal Party when she was at university. She went to protests and Nala suspected she went to secret meetings. She feared where this path might take the girl, but didn't feel she had the right to stop her.

They had never spoken about what happened in Gal Oya. Dhara was only eight at the time but she had seen more of it than a child should. She had eventually stopped screaming at night but she never stopped waking well before dawn. Ayah used to change the sheets for her without saying a word, and Priya never complained about the regular disturbances.

She would ask her about marriage again tonight. Dhara was twenty-five-years-old, dangerously old for a girl, especially one whose mother was from a lower caste. They had saved a good dowry for her and tried over and over again to broker a marriage but she had resisted. She said she wanted to be self-sufficient but Nala didn't understand why that meant she had to be alone.

Thank God Nandan wasn't interested in politics. He preferred the world of parties and cricket and business. They still didn't understand what kind of business, but he kept talking about it as though everyone knew, so they stopped asking. He had recently graduated with an accounting degree, coming first in his class. She was so proud of him – and of Rajan, who had learned the entire syllabus, making study notes and beautiful diagrams, so he could teach Nandan management accounting. Their son had not thought class attendance particularly important.

It was Rajan who had really won the first prize, she teased him.

She said a quick prayer of thanks to Lord Murugan for sending Priya to London. Her daughter was happy and eventually she would be blessed with a baby. Nala thanked the lord more profusely for keeping her son safe from harm. Boys in the north were arming themselves – it wouldn't be long before they recruited Radha's son. But not Nandan: he would get a job, marry a nice Tamil girl, go to parties, and set up a business, of some kind.

LONDON, 1974

Priya's baby was born three weeks early. Nala watched in horror as a stain spread across her daughter's hospital-white bed. It grew rapidly; it was the ferrous colour of love; of death. Nurses in cloudy stockings and sensible shoes pushed her out of the way, reading charts and pressing alarms. One pale, thin arm cuffed to a blood pressure machine, another stabbed again and again as they searched for a vein. A sack of red and a plastic tube hooked into Priya – Nala followed the colour as it crept forward, confidently but slowly. Too slowly. Droplets when she wished for a river, a monsoon, a rush of strength and life. She didn't hold the baby. She held her daughter's hand and prayed.

High blood pressure and massive blood loss. The doctors advised Priya not to risk her life with further pregnancies. She wept, her hands pressed against the place where life is risked so that life is given. Nala knew that feeling.

She had come to London with Rajan for Priya's confinement. Priya and Siva were renting a one-bedroom place in Croydon. The kitchen was half the size of her pantry in Colombo and Nala didn't know where to start. Her first few meals were overcooked, insipid offerings. Siva smiled politely and swallowed. The problem was not so much the absence of space, but the absence of Ayah. Nala knew what kind of food should be made for new mothers; she just didn't know how to make it. In desperation she called her cousins in London who rescued her, each popping in with plastic containers of shark meat curry, sarrakku okra curry, and garlic cooked in vegetables.

She talked incessantly as she reheated and served food for the family, her monologues rebounding off the stained walls of the apartment. Her continuous chatter deteriorated into a nervous babble as she sensed that her ministrations were annoying her daughter.

Priya was too weak to breastfeed fully and the baby cried constantly.

'Perhaps you should try milk formula, mahal,' Nala suggested tentatively.

'Dr Spock says a mother should be able to understand and meet all of her baby's needs. He says all babies are individuals...' Priya couldn't speak any more, she ran to her room crying.

'All babies are *hungry*,' Nala whispered to Rajan, bewildered.

Priya smiled only when speaking to Dhara in Jaffna, taking the phone into her room and disappearing for hours. Rajan balked at the expense but Nala told him not to interfere.

Eventually, she suggested a devious but clinically sound recovery plan.

'Mahan, what if we buy formula and give it to the baby, just quietly... while Priya sleeps?'

Siva nodded. Nala tied a scarf around her hair, buttoned her cardigan tightly over her sari, and set off down the street with Rajan to the local pharmacy.

She browsed the aisles of Boots, captivated.

'English pharmacies have an amazing range of products, Rajan,' she chatted amiably. 'I'm going to stock up before we fly home. Ah, Oil of Ulay – smell this, it's delicious,' she pushed an open bottle towards him but he shook his head.

'You can buy that at any Cargill's store in Colombo, Nala, don't waste your money here.'

'But it's one third of the price at Boots,' she replied with a smile. Kamini and her neighbours would all like a bottle too.

'Put it down,' Rajan whispered.

'What?' she was still inhaling deeply when he hissed again.

'Put it down, they're watching us.'

She closed the bottle of Oil of Ulay and put it back. She wiped a droplet of milky pinkness from her nose surreptitiously. It really was delicious.

'Who, who is watching us?' she hissed back. Why was he always so self-conscious? She was just testing the bottle that said 'Tester'. If they didn't want her to test it then they should have called it something else.

'The man at the desk and the man at the door, they've been watching us since we arrived. Can we please just get the formula and go?'

'This is my first outing in London and we are at a pharmacy, not even Marks & Spencer. You just go. I'm going to look around.' She went back to the face cream.

'Are you going to buy that, lady, or are you just going to smell it?'

They both turned – the man at the door had now moved closer.

'I'm going to buy it, although not right now. I've come from Colombo to help my daughter with her new baby. Would you mind telling me where I can find the milk formula?'

The man looked shocked rather than impressed. What was he expecting? English people were often very polite, but sometimes they were rather odd. She liked English people in Ceylon better than English people in England. The Ceylonese English were so much more refined.

'We don't have it,' he replied.

'You don't have it?'

'We don't have it.'

'You don't have milk formula at Boots?' she asked incredulously.

'That's right, we don't have it. Try the place around the corner.'

With that, he opened the door for her. Rajan took her hand and dragged her with him. She turned to speak to him again and saw the man from the counter checking the bottles of Oil of Ulay. Rajan ushered her out quickly before she could say anything.

'What was that about?' she demanded of no-one in particular.

'Can we please just forget about it? Let's try the other place and get back to Priya. The baby must be hungry.'

At the mention of the hungry child, she focused on her task. Just as the Boots man had said, there was a pharmacy around the corner. It was much smaller and on closer inspection, it was really only a corner store. The man at the counter was an Indian who greeted them warmly. 'Yes, yes of course we have milk powder, many congratulations on the baby, where are you from?'

'Cey- Sri Lanka. We are from Sri Lanka,' she answered.

The man stroked his moustache proudly as he walked them through his store. Rajan tried to politely decline the tour but she shushed him. If the man wanted to talk, let him talk. Not everyone was mute like him.

'I'm from Kenya – Nairobi. We came here four years ago and I set up this store with my brother. I don't get many visitors from the Indian sub-continent but London is full of East-African Indians. We are building our own temple and we even have a language school for our children here. My children are going to be doctors, I can tell,' the man said proudly.

'That's wonderful. How old are your children?' she asked.

'Eight and six,' he replied.

She laughed but camouflaged it into a coughing fit as Rajan gave her a look. 'Do you know the Boots Pharmacy on the high street?' she asked him.

'Yes, yes, yes of course, it is a very big store. One day we will be like that. I will call it Patel and Sons, or perhaps just Patels. That sounds good, doesn't it?'

'Do you shop there, Mr Patel?' she pushed as Rajan tried once again to keep her quiet.

'There? Oh, no, no, no. We don't shop there unless it's an emergency. They don't like us Indians moving here. What can we do, I ask you? The British took us to Africa in the first place. If Africa doesn't want us anymore and India is no longer our home, where else can we go? You should come to my shop if you need anything. Ask your daughter to come here, we will look after her. She's one of us, after all.'

Nala opened her mouth but Rajan was adamant this time. 'The baby is hungry and we need to get back before Priya wakes up. Thank you so much, Mr Patel, it was very nice to meet you, I'm sure we'll be back.' He paid for the milk powder and helped her out the door.

☼

Nala returned to Colombo and two months later Anand, Siva's youngest brother arrived unwillingly at Heathrow Airport with a large trunk, a short letter from his mother, Radha, and all the money she could borrow.

'Exile,' he said, embracing Priya at the Arrivals Gate. 'I've been exiled, acca.'

Of course, even exiles find ways to do things, and once in London, he quickly gravitated towards other like-minded young men. Many, like him, had been sent out of Ceylon by their families for their own safety.

Priya listened to Siva's side of the telephone conversation. Her husband was upset but not surprised.

'Where is the police station, sir?' he asked, his voice strained. 'I'll be there as soon as I can officer, thank you very much. Yes, I understand. I'm really very sorry. I will talk to him. It will never happen again. Yes, I understand, Officer Singh, it *is* a privilege to live in London. I know that and I think he knows that too.'

He put the phone down and ran his hand nervously through his hair.

'Where is he?' she asked.

'He's at the police station at St John's Wood. He ran onto the cricket grounds with a banner.'

'What did it say?'

'Stop the bloodshed in Sri Lanka. Self-determination for the Tamil people,' Siva sighed.

'It's a little wordy, don't you think?'

'Yes, and he spelt 'determination' wrong. The poster said 'self-destination'. He was never very good at spelling.'

'At least it was Lords, and not some provincial cricket ground,' she said, taking his hand. 'What are you going to do?'

'The only thing I can do,' Siva replied. 'I have to go get him. They've agreed not to charge him. The arresting officer is Punjabi, so he understands.'

'Thank God for Punjabis.' It wasn't funny but Priya had to laugh at Anand's luck. The Punjabi Sikhs of India also wanted their own separate state.

Siva tried to laugh but he looked like he wanted to cry.

She reached up and smoothed his hair back into place.

'I think marriage to me is making your hair prematurely grey,' she whispered, putting her arms around him and holding him close.

'It isn't you. It's them.' He meant home, his family and the monthly letters from his mother telling him about problems Priya wanted to forget.

'I don't know what we're going to do with him,' he said heavily, but relaxing a little.

'Well we can't send him back,' she replied. 'Getting arrested in London is one thing; getting arrested in Jaffna is very different,' she looked at him fondly.

'I almost envy Anand,' she said slowly.

'You envy him? Do you want to be incarcerated at St John's Wood Police Station too?' he laughed, brushing his tears away quickly.

'No, it's just that he has a sense of … homeland.' Anand was tied to something earthy and ancestral. Dhara felt it too.

'Living here, I don't know what I'm tied to,' she mused.

'You're tied to me, and my crazy, militant family. How is that?' he replied and hugged her again, this time quickly. 'I'm not going to tell Amma about him. She's worried enough as it is about my sisters. Poor Amma. Is that ok?'

Yes, poor Amma. What did Radha expect, filling their heads with talk of Tamil rights, then Tamil freedom, and inevitably, Tamil independence? What did she think was going to happen? What did Chelvanayakam think was going to happen?

'That's fine, don't tell your mother,' she pulled away from him but tried to keep her voice neutral. 'You'd better get going. Anand will be waiting.'

✿

Four months later, Anand was arrested again, this time for protesting outside the Sri Lankan High Commission in London.

'Are you angry with me, acca?' he asked Priya as she signed his release form. They walked out of Bayswater Police Station and into the fading afternoon light together.

'No, Anand, I'm not angry at you. But you need to be smarter. You have to think about your future. You need a proper qualification and a proper job. How will you provide for a family of your own? We're all worried about you, especially now – you know we're moving to Australia soon.

'I know acca. I'm sorry,' he replied quietly.

'No thambi. You don't need to apologise. I suppose I should be relieved you're the one who keeps getting arrested, not your brother.' She laughed as he looked at her sheepishly and blushed.

'Siva is a terrible liar, Anand. I know he's involved with this London group of yours and I can't stop him. I just want us to move on, to move forward...' she said softly.

'Is that why you're moving to Australia?' Anand asked.

'Maybe. Australia feels further away from politics but closer to home, if that makes sense. I've been thinking a lot about Gal Oya lately. I don't know why,' she said.

'Your cousin-sister was in those riots, wasn't she? In '56.'

'Yes. Dhara's father was killed. I was thinking about the Sinhalese girl – the one who was raped by Tamils. That's what started the riot.'

'I remember, acca.'

'It was a rumour. There was no girl, there was no rape, there was just rioting and killing. Afterwards there was no punishment, only excuses,' Priya said sadly. Tamil history told them something about their future. In time, people would stop making excuses for the killing; they would simply kill.

'I want to leave all of that behind,' she said.

'You can't acca. *History is like your shadow, it follows you everywhere,*' Anand replied in Tamil, quoting from an ancient poem.

'They say that in Australia the sun burns brighter. Maybe there are no shadows there,' she laughed tearfully and pinched her brother-in-law's arm affectionately.

'Let's go home. Siva's waiting for us.'

9

JAFFNA, 1977

Dhara should have listened to Rajan, when he asked her to come back, but she had loved Jaffna ever since she was a child. She had been to her family's village with her parents, to visit her grandparents and her great-grandmother. Appa had told her stories of hide and seek, of building castles for Nala and vegetable patches for Archi. Later – after – she had returned with Rajan and Nala. Rajan would take the children to the Jaffna Public Library where they would read together for hours.

As a child, she pored through books about the Chola kings who conquered India. A thousand years ago they rode victoriously south to create new kingdoms and build temples all over South East Asia. They took their language and religion to an old world made new by fresh ideas. She revelled in manuscripts and maps about a Tamil empire that was safe; where her culture was celebrated.

The Jaffna Peninsula jutted out into the Indian Ocean, flanked by the Bay of Bengal on the east and Palk Strait on the west. The strait took travellers, smugglers and later refugees to India. The peninsula looked lonely on a map, a bent limb connected to the torso of Sri Lanka by a fistula of land, Elephant Pass. The first time she returned to Jaffna, she forced herself to stay awake in the car, expecting to see elephants walking alongside commuters, but there were none.

Jaffna was the capital of their ancestral kingdom, the citadel that young Tamil boys were swearing to protect for their people, not fully realising what payment that promise would demand. A solitary outpost, exposed to the ocean, it had no route of retreat.

She liked working in the north. It felt like home. Jaffna was the place her parents were born. They had breathed its air and walked on its blood-red soil. They had laughed here when they were whole. When she breathed, walked and laughed in Jaffna, she could feel them with her.

'There's a position vacant in the Infectious Diseases department here. Colombo General is a good place to complete your training,' Rajan had urged. She wanted two specialties – emergency medicine and infectious diseases. Both would be useful. He was right about the training opportunity but she knew he wanted her back in Colombo for other reasons.

Every month, more soldiers arrived in the Jaffna province, under the orders of Prime Minister Sirimavo Bandaranaike. The Tamil United Liberation Front was openly campaigning now for a separate Tamil state; Chelvanayakam's devolution platform had inevitably hardened into a secessionist one.

Small groups of armed Tamil youths, no more than boys with stolen guns, had started to attack army and police stations in Jaffna. The government assumed these wild raids were organised by the TULF. Chelvanayakam denied it, stating he wanted a separate state by democratic, peaceful means. The rest of the country watched, holding its breath fearfully, as these different approaches to the same struggle inexorably converged.

Dhara knew fear in many shapes. There was Ravana, the ten-headed demon king of Lanka, who haunted her childhood dreams. All children are taught the *Ramayana*, the story of King Ravana, who stole Sita, from Lord Rama. Rama took his army of monkey warriors from India, crossing the Palk Strait, to wage war on Ravana and claim back his queen. Rama was a god. The formless divine had taken the form of a man for the sole purpose of destroying Ravana and restoring justice. She had learned her *Ramayana* well. But in the version of her childhood, the one that plagued her nights, Ravana defeated Rama, the demon defeated the god.

Fear also came to her when she started operating. She was afraid of hurting her patients. She asked Rajan about it. He patted her on the shoulder and said, 'I hope you never lose that feeling, mahal. Someone's life is in your hands.'

The advice wasn't comforting. She ran to the bathroom immediately afterwards. The empty stomach had worked though, and it was a technique she used for shorter operations, where she could afford to go without a meal for five hours. She remembered her responsibility to her patients, and it gave her courage even if it couldn't give her a steady stomach. All she needed was a steady hand, Priya would say. Dhara smiled. Priya often knew what to say. Sometimes, it was just the way she said it that helped. When she missed Priya, she could recall her voice, her laugh, her tone. It made her feel better.

Surgery required strength and stamina. There were times when she needed more than a drill to cut through bone. Sometimes it was as archaic as a saw, the torque and lever of her own body weight, and a consistent rhythm. Her supervising surgeons said she was strong for a woman. She had always been small; it was only through surgery that she became strong.

Small beads of sweat formed on her upper lip. The soldier watched as she licked her lips a few times. She sat on a metal chair. He leant in front of her on a metal desk as he spoke. They sat under a metal fan that no-one had turned on. The room was small and windowless. The door opened and the soldier shook his head at someone. The door closed again.

She had spent the afternoon studying at the Jaffna Public Library. When she walked out, the soldiers were waiting for her at the gates. She walked quietly but not calmly with them across the road to the police station. The last thing she saw before the door shut, entombing her in silence, was the silhouette of the old Dutch Fort. In a previous incarnation it had housed their colonial masters, serving as a seat of administration and even a prison. Now the army was using the Fort; its ramparts were still solid and capable of fending off the attacks everyone knew were coming.

She sat in a small metallic room under the shadow of that magnificent stone structure, straining to hear the chaos she knew must be outside; a sound that would connect her to life beyond the room. Esplanade

Street was always so noisy, so full of people rushing about. She was usually one of them.

She wondered whether the soldier would notice if she raised her hand to wipe away the moisture under her nose. It was starting to distract her. She was relieved to have something else to think about. But she didn't want him to see that she was afraid.

Fear had its own tone, she thought as she listened to her voice answer the questions that were fired at her.

'What were you doing at the medical clinic in Tellippalai?' the soldier asked. She had been seen at the village clinic. He had dates and times and a list of her colleagues there.

'I was running a vaccination clinic. It's part of Jaffna Hospital's public health programme.'

'Public health?' he asked, sounding a little more sympathetic.

'Yes, public health, we have WHO funding to vaccinate children,' she replied, praying that he would have compassion for her project, for her.

'WHO? We don't need foreign meddling,' he replied flatly. 'What is the real purpose of your work in Tellippalai?'

She had completely lost track of time and without a window, she didn't know how long she'd been there. She had a lot of stamina, she knew she did. But this was different. She was exhausted already and this was only the beginning.

'The real purpose?' she repeated. Her mind scrambled over words; she didn't understand anything anymore. She licked her lips again.

'Yes, the real purpose,' he said, not changing his voice. He walked around the desk casually, to stand in front of her. Then he slapped her hard across the face.

'I-I was there for the vaccination clinic,' she repeated, tasting blood, 'for children, WHO –'

He slapped her again, harder this time, and stood up. As he left the room he said to her, 'I'll be back in a moment.' His voice was still quiet and surprisingly polite.

'Thank you,' she said. Thank you? What an odd thing to say.

She looked around the room. The fluorescent lighting made a quiet whirring sound: like a mosquito. Maybe it was a mosquito, or ten. It was the right season for mosquitoes. In the north it was perpetually the right season for mosquitoes.

She closed her eyes and started to run through her tropical infectious diseases: dengue, malaria, amoebic dysentery, and filariasis. She went on, first repeating their names, then going back to list the symptoms and treatment protocols for each. She knew her diseases because she had wanted to impress Rajan. He knew infection the way Nala knew gossip.

Small pox, chicken pox, measles, whooping cough, diphtheria, helminthiasis, leprosy and scabies. She went back to the beginning and ordered them alphabetically. Then she went back to the beginning again and ordered them by region of prevalence. Priya had admired her knowledge. She had admired Priya too. Priya was an excellent doctor. She never believed in herself enough but she was an excellent doctor. She couldn't remember if she had ever told her that. She was an excellent sister and doctor.

She tried not to cry. A torn cushion had been incongruously placed on the cold metal of her chair. It smelled like fear. She wondered how many others had sat on that chair, sweating and urinating. It was comforting in a way to know that she was not the only one.

Amoebic dysentery, chicken pox, dengue, diphtheria, filariasis, helminths, leprosy, leptospirosis, malaria, measles, scabies, small pox and whooping cough. There, she had it alphabetically.

Now backwards: whooping co–

The door opened and the soldier returned with someone else. The new man stood in the corner, behind her where she couldn't see him. She could only hear and feel him. She was too afraid to look around. Her back was stiff from sitting in the chair for so long; she couldn't have turned if she wanted to. She couldn't turn and she couldn't run.

She took a deep breath. She wouldn't cry.

'Let's try again. Why were you at Tellippalai? We know some of the militants are from that village – you're working for them, aren't you?' he asked.

'I'm in charge of the clinic there; it's my father's village. I promise...' she closed her eyes and braced herself for the slap. Only this time it was a fist in the stomach, not a slap on the face. She doubled over and focused on her diseases. She couldn't breathe but her vagus would relax in a moment and there was enough oxygen in her lungs to keep her alive. There was enough oxygen in her blood stream to feed her brain for another 2.9 minutes.

Protect the brain, Rajan used to tell her. She had seen men reduced to children when their brains collided with forces stronger than their own. She had seen the hearts of children stop and starve their brains to death. And she had seen people who should have died – but didn't. Someone's life in her hands.

Protect the brain or protect the hands?

The soldier pulled her upright by her hair. She cried out. She wanted to push him away. Instead, she wrapped her own hands around her body, not to protect herself, but to protect her hands. She knew where this was going. Protect the brain or protect the hands? She had heard the stories. She prayed that she would live and that her hands would not be broken.

'Take off your clothes,' he said.

'What?'

'You heard me. Take off your clothes.'

'No.' She was so tired. She tasted more blood. She bent her fingers and closed her palms slowly, sheltering them. He noticed.

'Are you going to hit me?' he asked.

The man behind her laughed quietly.

'No.' She wasn't going to fight, she was going to protect.

'Take off your clothes.'

'No.'

'Take them off or I'm going to take them off you. Tamil women are easy to undress.'

Her fists clenched in earnest.

'Do it,' he said quietly. 'Do it.'

☼

She remembered something: 'The first incision needs to be confident and slow.'

○

She lay on the floor, her hands pressed hard between her legs to stop the bleeding. The room was cold and dark. Scattered around her were fragments of thoughts and memories. There was one, shaped like the shard of a broken mirror that reflected a moment from decades ago. Its edges were sharp and each recollection lacerated her anew.

She was eight and cowering in the corner of her parents' room. Amma lay on the bed, trapped underneath the weight of a demon. Her skirt had been torn from her, exposing her legs, which twisted and kicked with no effect. Her eyes were squeezed tight like raisins, drying in the sun. She screamed as the demon drove himself into her. The demon had ten heads and each one wanted a turn. Dhara didn't know people could make sounds like that. She didn't know Amma could make a sound like that.

The demon slapped her mother and threw her on the floor, like one of her dolls.

'I told you to shut up, you Tamils howl like dogs.' He stood up and shook the bloodied snake that was attached to his body. 'Get me the girl, she's quiet,' he said, motioning to the others in the room. Someone reached towards her. She could see the hairs on his arm moving, black ants poised to bite her.

'No, no!' Amma cried. She tried to stand but couldn't, collapsing towards the demon and holding onto his legs. 'I'll be quiet, I'll be quiet, I promise.'

The demon kicked her away and all of his heads laughed at her, but Amma dragged herself back onto the bed. She unbuttoned her blouse with shaking hands and took off her bra. Dhara looked at the erratic rise and fall of her mother's chest. The demon was looking at something else. He walked towards the bed and Amma lay down, silently. Dhara pushed herself deeper into the corner.

She closed her eyes but she could still see the demon as he walked back into the cold, dark room.

Alphabetically: Amoebic dysentery, chicken pox, dengue, diphtheria, filariasis, helminths, leprosy, leptospirosis, malaria, measles, scabies, small pox and whooping cough.

In and out, in and out.

Now backwards: whooping cough, small pox, scabies, measles…

In and out, in and out. Out, please, out, she prayed silently to the relentless demon; god had been defeated. Her eyes squeezed tight like raisins, drying in the sun.

She could smell the salt from the ocean. That was how she knew she was alive, that she was no longer in the room. She lay on the road where she had been dumped, the morning sun settling on her like a soft blanket. Her eyelids were swollen, almost shut. She could see outlines moving towards her.

Faces bent down, strangers calling to other strangers for help. Someone placed a sheet over her naked, battered body. Someone picked her up slowly, easily, as though she were a child.

She unclenched her fingers slowly and stiffly. She held one hand inside the other, feeling the segments and joints of each, making sure they were intact. Someone's life in your hands.

She rested her head on the stranger's chest, and inhaled the starched shirt and old sweat, burying her face so no-one could see her cry.

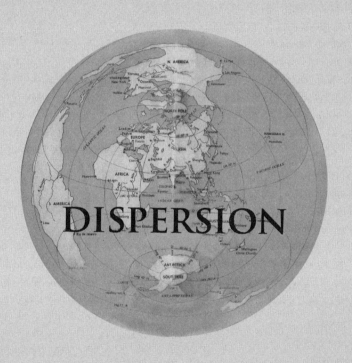

DISPERSION

As Hanuman, the monkey warrior, jumped from house to house, his tail of fire followed him, lighting up the rooftops of the small island. He had escaped the demon king of Lanka, Ravana, whose ten-heads cried out in anger.

Watching from the beach on the mainland, the armies of Lord Rama heard the cry, Hanuman's brothers saw the fire snake through the city, knowing that only Hanuman could cause such destruction. They waited for him to bring Lord Rama's queen, Sita, back from Lanka.

He returned to the lord, bearing not Sita but her jewelled ring and her message. Sita would not be rescued by her husband's soldier. She would wait for Lord Rama to come himself and fight Ravana for her honour. The monkey warrior's tail was burned beyond healing and his mission a failure.

In generations to come, the islanders would remember that night, when they were punished by Hanuman, the son of the Wind God Vayu and the greatest devotee of Lord Rama. The islanders would remember when they were punished for the crimes of their leader; when Lanka burned.

10

When they received the call, Rajan went to Jaffna Hospital leaving Nala behind. He wouldn't allow her to join him. In Jaffna, he cared for the girl until she was able to travel back.

She ate in her room when she ate at all. She spent her days with Nala and Ayah, watching them cook or just sitting in the drawing room, reading. Rajan brought her a wheelchair from Colombo General.

Initially, only Carlo could touch her. Almost blind, he would put his great head in her lap, snorting and salivating kisses all over her. She played with his velvet ears and once, Nala saw her bend down, put her arms around him and weep into the warm scruff of his neck.

Every night Nala slept with her, perched on the far side of the bed. She turned the lights on when the screaming started. One evening Dhara allowed Nala to hold her.

'I'm so sorry this happened to you,' Nala whispered wrapping her arms gently around her. She had wanted to say that for so long.

'Don't be, it's not your fault,' the girl replied. 'Hush now mami, don't cry.'

Rajan, Nala and Nandan ate dinner in silence as they had every night since Dhara's return. Nandan cleared his throat conspicuously. He tried to speak but caught himself and cleared his throat again. Ayah came running from the kitchen and thumped him hard on the back.

'Nandan Baby, Nandan Baby are you choking? What's the matter?' she asked anxiously in Sinhalese. He was twenty-one-years-old but time had frozen for Ayah where her young charge was concerned.

'I'm fine Ayah, thank you. It's just a tickle,' he replied, laughing nervously. When she returned to the kitchen, he tried to speak again.

'Amma and Appa,' he addressed them solemnly, 'I need to tell you something. I met a wonderful girl at university and we want to get married, with your permission. Her name is Shiranthi Perera,' he paused, waiting for the surname to sink in. Rajan understood immediately – he stood up and walked out, without a word. It took Nala a few more moments. She sat for a while until the tears began to fall. Nandan held her hand as she wiped her eyes with the edge of her sari.

'Perhaps this will pass, Nandan. You're young. Don't rush into anything.'

'We've known each other a long time, Amma. We didn't mean to fall in love. Shiranthi's parents will be just as upset as you. She's telling them this weekend too. We've thought this through and we know it's the right thing,' he said.

'What about the children? They will be mixed, what religion will they be? Will her parents allow them to come to temple?'

He was ready for this question. 'Our children will be both Hindu and Buddhist; and they will have both languages and cultures. They will come from two races and be doubly lucky. Amma, I'm sorry to hurt you and Appa. That was never my intention. I want you to think about it. If you don't want me to marry her I will give her up. But I won't marry anyone else.' He kissed his mother gently on the cheek and left her.

Dhara locked the door quietly and closed the shutters, blocking out the morning light. She switched on the lamp by the table, took off her clothes and examined the naked animal in front of her. It looked familiar; she had seen one just like it, years before on the cold cement floor of Ayah's kitchen.

It had bruises that it wore like lace around its neck and body. Some of its skin had been peeled back, revealing the taut pink dermis layer underneath. She put her hand on its flank. It was toned but still soft; rigor had not set in yet. She felt the corrugation of its ribcage and counted the bones: there were twenty-four, the same as a person. That surprised her. She probed underneath the last rib – from there she could reach in and remove the animal's heart. She had done it once before. She scored a line into the arid skin with her fingernail, marking the entry point below the breastplate nature had crafted. It was not impenetrable. The Sun God had not forged it.

She lifted each of the four limbs and then let them drop inertly to the ground. She palpated the purple and blue thigh. Its posterior and anterior dorsal hip muscles were bruised but not torn. She had helped Ayah carve this meat before, she with a scalpel, Ayah with a kitchen knife. This was the tastiest part of the animal; around the hip. It was strong too. Strong enough to support bodyweight; to carry offspring; to kick hard and run fast.

That day in Ayah's kitchen, the animal had seeped scarlet blood onto the sky-blue surgical sheets. But without a living, pumping heart, the blood had wandered, not rushed, out. The body in front of her did not bleed either. It had been drained.

She placed both her hands clinically on the animal. It bore the topography of torture: a patchwork of tearing, scorching, scarring and healing flesh. She pinched her taut pink skin one last time. It was embroidered with a familiar labyrinth of tiny violet veins, leading inwards, seeking her hidden heart. She could reach in and remove it; she had done it once before.

Nala sat with Rajan on their wicker sofa in the early evening coolness. The verandah at the back of the house looked over a rich and chaotic garden. Despite brittling arthritis and dementia, Archi had continued planting, harvesting and replanting until her death last month. She had coaxed life from the earth for almost a hundred years. Her anthuriums sat pinkly and proudly, their central spadix stiff like pointed fingers, scolding the creeping gardenia beneath. Her orchids were shameless in beauty and abundance. The furred petals of her heliconias looked like a pyramid of king parrots, nesting in red and yellow symmetry. Nala mourned her grandmother but she felt her presence in the life around her.

Carlo joined them. He was ageing but he still loped behind Nala like a puppy. He jealously pushed Rajan's hand out of the way, putting his own head in her lap for her to stroke his ears. She pushed back on Carlo and reached for Rajan's hand, taking it in her own once more.

'This is our fault, Nala. We spoiled him,' Rajan said, eyes ahead, voice deflated.

'We have spoiled him. But this is love and he's adamant,' she replied.

'Love? What is love at his age? Nothing but a passing fancy. What does he know of the love required by marriage?'

'The love required by marriage?' she repeated. 'Oh Rajan, you are too romantic,' she laughed tearfully. He pulled his hand away but she pulled it back and refused to let go.

'I *loved* my parents, and I did what was asked of me. He should do the same,' he said quietly.

'Yes, we both did. But children are changing, our world is changing – you keep telling me this yourself,' she replied.

'And now you throw it in my face?'

'I'm not throwing anything anywhere, Rajan. He says he will raise his children as Hindu and Buddhist. They will be both.'

'You can't be both, you are either one or you are the other.'

'And we have always been the *other*, here in our own home. We live in danger because of it. Keeping to ourselves only makes us a clearer target. I see that now. But Nandan and this girl, they will marry, they will love each other and have beautiful children together – imagine the possibility that they might be safer Rajan if, instead of being one or the other, they are the perfect combination of both. Think about that,' she said softly.

✡

Rajan finally accepted his son's choice of wife. Hindu and Buddhist weddings were organised but even Nala, who loved celebrations, wanted to postpone the ceremonies until Colombo settled down.

The Tamil United Liberation Front had won a resounding victory in the Tamil districts of the north and east. The election was inevitably followed by riots against Tamils across the country.

Rajan tried to dissuade his son. 'It's different this time Nandan. President Jayewardene was open and organised about the violence. He's shown his true face – there's no going back now. Let's wait a few months, it will be safer then.'

Jayewardene was a patient of Rajan's. He was an urbane and charming man. Nala was troubled by his recent warning to the Tamils: *If you want a fight, let there be a fight; if it is peace, let there be peace; that is what they will say. It is not what I am saying. The people of Sri Lanka say that.*

But Nandan didn't care about politics or pogroms. He was sad for the hundreds of dead but he wanted to start his life with Shiranthi. There would always be riots in their home.

Dhara tried to sit on the verandah but the gardener walked past her, smelling of beedi. He probably chewed tobacco more than he smoked it, but the faintest smell made her shake uncontrollably. Nala had to put her to bed with a herbal tonic and a shot of brandy.

She traced the constellation of cigarette burns on her left breast. Last week it felt like the shape of a mango. Today, it was the shape of an anthurium leaf. It pointed downwards to the tracks on the rest of her body.

Nala had been applying neem oil to her wounds and scars, massaging her tenderly every day the way Ayah had done with sesame oil when she was little. The hands of women could read the anatomy of a child's pain. *Neem is a great healer*, Nala would say.

Time is a great healer, she had heard one of the doctors say.

Vani visited her every day at Nala's house. Sometimes they sat in silence; sometimes they held each other and cried.

Eventually, Vani said, 'You must leave here, mahal. Leave Ceylon.' She picked the stray threads off the blanket and pulled it across her daughter's legs. One was still in a brace.

'I can't,' Dhara replied.

'I don't want you to stay, please don't do it for me.'

'But I *want* to stay. I've always wanted to stay,' she said.

'When you were born, your Appa said daughters were good luck for a family. He said daughters would always stay with you, but sons, they run away. I want you to run.'

Dhara blinked back tears. Her mother rarely talked about her father.

When she remained silent, Vani spoke again. 'I'm sorry I couldn't be a mother to you, mahal…I wanted to, I really did. It took me such a long time to – recover. I couldn't close my eyes without screaming.'

'I remember, Amma.' She couldn't close her eyes either.

'I wanted you to forget. I gave you to Nala because I wanted a better life for you than the one I could give you. I didn't give you up, mahal,' her mother finally gave her the explanation she'd been waiting for, but it wasn't needed anymore.

'I understand that now, Amma, I really do,' she said tearfully. She took Vani's hand and held it against her bruised and swollen body. 'I never blamed you and I would never judge you. I understand now,' she repeated.

'Leave, mahal. I beg you,' Vani cried.

'No, Amma,' she shook her head. 'If I lie down for a little while, will you watch over me?' she asked, settling back into the bed without letting go of her hand. Vani pulled the blanket around her and nodded.

Nala was excited about the weddings. She spread her new Kanchipuram silk saris out on her bed. She would wear the more conservative peacock blue sari for the Buddhist wedding and the cochineal one for the Hindu wedding. Kamini agreed it was stunning on her. Ayah was soaking her jewellery in bicarbonate of soda; with a soft flannel, the old maid massaged her heavy diamond pathakkam necklace into resplendence.

Even Ayah was getting ready – she had dyed her thin, grey hair black and asked if she could borrow one of Nala's saris. Nandan bought her a new silk sari instead.

That morning she received a call from the President's office.

'The President would like to bless the young couple, Mrs Rajan. Nothing would make him happier at this very sad time for the country,' the aide explained.

When she remained silent on the other end of the telephone, he continued nervously, pitching harder.

'Mrs Rajan, the Daily News would like to cover Nandan and Shiranthi's wedding. They have promised a feature on the front page – not just the social pages.'

She was both thrilled and horrified, muttering disjointed pleasantries as she tried to frame a non-committal yet positive response.

'Mrs Rajan, do it for the country. I know you don't seek publicity or attention, truly important people never do. But this is the kind of story the country needs to hear right now. It will help heal the rift,' he pleaded charmingly.

She was persuaded but Rajan had a different opinion.

'Absolutely not. I will not allow our family wedding to be exploited. Firstly, it will take more than a frivolous story to heal the rift. Secondly, this 'rift' he casually refers to is a great, big *schism*; and thirdly, I don't want my son to start his married life with blessings from that man.'

Rajan was exasperating – after all these years he still had not learned. Where would he be without her? And why did he have to use words like 'schism'?

'Rajan, you have been the doctor to four prime ministers. If he's asked for an invitation, you can't say no. It's an honour, regardless of what you might think of his politics.'

'His politics? His *politics*? This is not about politics any more, Nala; this is people's lives he's playing with. One day it might be our lives. You think we are safe here, because we live in this house, in this neighbourhood? This won't protect us forever.'

She pulled herself up straight and wiped her tears with her sari.

'I'm not stupid, Rajan. That is exactly why we have to invite and honour Jayewardene. You are a prominent Colombo surgeon and the President wants to come to *our* son's wedding. Look at what happened to Dhara. Use Jayewardene, for your son's future and our own.' She softened her argument with a 'Please Rajan, please,' dropping her shoulders and giving him her most imploring look. But it wasn't necessary. She had played her hand well and he nodded reluctantly.

Dhara could hear screaming. It was coming from down the corridor. Somewhere in another room there was another girl screaming for her father.

'*Appa, Appa don't leave me here*,' the girl cried.

Her eyes felt hot; like the first time she had helped Ayah make coconut chilli sambal. She had rubbed her eyes without washing her hands properly and the oil from the chilli had stung for hours afterwards. Ayah had thrust her face into a bucket of milk making her laugh and choke as she cried.

She tried to call out to the girl, to tell her to be quiet. If you made a lot of noise they came back faster. Dhara opened her mouth but she couldn't speak. A strong arm gripped her neck. It was pushing her face into a bucket of cloudy water. It smelled like urine. Her eyes were still burning from the chilli.

Appa, Appa, don't leave me here, she cried.

Priya came from Sydney for the weddings with her three-year-old son Vivek and Siva. She wanted to look after Dhara and Nala wanted to look after them both.

In the midday coolness of the tiled bathroom, Priya poured water over Dhara and bathed her. It trickled around the scar tissue, finding pathways through roughened terrain. She raised the fallen curls at her sister's neck and tucked them back into her loose bun.

'I'm hideous,' Dhara said tearfully. 'It's like I've decayed.' She never left the house.

Priya traced the fretwork of lines that spread all over her body.

'No. This is damage, not decay. Damage can heal.'

'How long can you stay, acca?' Dhara asked.

'As long as you want,' she replied.

'That's not true.'

'I'll stay for a few months, until the baby comes. Siva will go back to Australia without me. I'd like to be here. I'm sorry Dhara,' she said, bending carefully over her.

'For what, acca?'

'I'm sorry I wasn't there for you – with you. I mean – I'm sorry you were alone.'

'I'm not. I'm glad you weren't there.'

'Come back with me. Come to Sydney. It's warm like Colombo and the people are relaxed, not like in London. More Tamils are moving there. Australia wants professionals – doctors like us. Australia *wants* us.' She had imagined that life with her sister in perfect, complete detail.

When Dhara said nothing, she tried again. 'It's safe there – we can be safe and together.'

Dhara shook her head tearfully. There was no explanation she could offer for wanting to stay now.

Nala spat three times. Nandan looked so handsome, like a prince, and Shiranthi, in her fuchsia sari and bridal jewellery, was a beautiful and convincing Hindu bride. She and her family had been open to all of the rituals of the ceremony. They didn't balk when Shiranthi was asked to sit on the wedding dais with the Hindu priest. They stood with her and when instructed by the priest, they symbolically handed her over to Rajan and Nala, who accepted her as their own daughter.

At the Sinhalese wedding, a procession of dancers and drummers started the ceremony, heralding the arrival of the couple. Shiranthi, dressed in a white sari with a veil over her head, walked in with Nandan. They stood on a beautiful wooden platform framed by a canopy of garlands. It was very similar to the manaivarai used by the Hindus. The bride's father handed Shiranthi to Nandan and he tied a gold necklace around her neck, simpler than the heavy wedding chain she received from him at the Hindu ceremony. It suited her understated beauty. They blushed when they had to feed each other from a plate of milk rice. Women in the congregation chanted the joyful blessing for the couple, and it was over.

The Sinhalese wedding took an hour, several hours shorter than the Hindu ceremony. Short and sweet, Rajan called it. Nala left the wedding feeling happy and energised; the Hindu ceremony was so long and complicated that after it was over, she needed a nap.

A few days later, Nala asked the servant boy to buy fifteen copies of the newspaper. She sat amongst the clippings, putting the article into her notebook, Ayah's notebook, her photo album, a frame, and several envelopes to be sent across the world.

Unfortunately the newspaper was black and white so you couldn't see the sari colours in the photographs, but she was relieved that she had kept her eyes open and her smile natural. The headline of the article read *Love Conquers All* and the piece was about the union between two high profile families from different sides of the ethnic divide. Rajan read it and scoffed, 'I told you it would be frivolous.' There was of course a large photograph of President JR Jayewardene, blessing the new and nervous couple.

Nandan came in and sat down on the floor beside her.

'Appa has asked if you and Shiranthi would like to move into the apartment above. It's almost finished,' Nala said, picking up the paper scraps around her.

'I thought he was building that so he could rent it out,' Nandan replied, helping her. The two-bedroom apartment was attached to the main house by a common side door and staircase.

'I think he'd like you to stay close. We could have meals together and see each other all the time – but only if you like…'

Nala found her new daughter-in-law's company surprisingly lovely. Initially, she had been wary. She knew what would happen if she didn't keep Shiranthi happy. Sons sided with their wives; it was just the natural order of things, except in the case of Rajan who always sided with his mother.

Nandan pressed her hand to his cheek.

'You smell like Oil of Ulay. Shiranthi likes the bottle you gave her, thank you Amma. Thank you for everything,' he said, kissing her palm.

'You are very welcome, mahan,' she replied. She pointed to the headline of the article and they both laughed, wiping away their tears.

☼

Dhara heard the screams cutting through the sterile walls. They rushed down the corridor towards her, reminding her that she was next. She twisted and turned on the table but the men had bound her tightly. She felt hands on her ankles, pulling her legs apart. She bent her legs inwards, desperately trying to lock her knees together. The hands yanked harder, opening her body up to them. She kicked against them, against the pain when it started.

Just relax, the voice said.

If you fight it, it will hurt more, another voice said.

A stranger's hands reached inside and pulled back the soft, fleshy folds of her. All that was inside was revealed.

She kicked again and screamed, something low and guttural, a growl from the base of her throat. She tried to jump off the table. People in uniform swirled around and closed in. Hands on her ankles, her wrists pulled back again and strapped to the table with leather cuffs. She was a starfish, trapped and taken out of water. She gasped and heaved, struggling to breathe. She was dying.

Sharp pain radiated up her back, and then it stopped. It started again and then it stopped. She looked around her, shaking the sweat and tears from her eyes. Who was doing this to her? Which man? And why? Why me, she cried and begged at the same time.

She felt the familiar warm stickiness between her legs. It rushed out this time instead of oozing. She was repulsed. She was repulsive. She turned her head and vomited until all she could do was retch. Someone held her head and wiped the vomit from the table, from her hair. She recognised the outline, a reassuring shadow against the white lights that burned over her.

The pain started again.

Someone was inside her again, writhing and pushing against her. He was tearing her open, her body was splitting apart, muscle that had barely healed was ripping once more.

'Dhara,' she heard a voice whisper.

'Dhara, it's me,' she felt a gentle hand on her forehead, wiping away the sweat, smoothening her hair.

'Acca?' she sobbed, not believing what she was hearing.

'Dhara,' the voice said again. 'Open your eyes and look at me. You're safe. Breathe deeply. You're almost there. Breathe again. When the pain starts, do what the pain is telling you to do. Don't be afraid of it this time. The pain will guide you home.'

Pain. Home. Priya.

Her body spasmed again, cold sweat poured from every part of her. Her belly distended and rippled with a life of its own. She looked down, relaxed her hips but hardened her legs against the shackles at the end of her bed. On the second spasm, she pushed with her body, not against it.

Priya. Home. Pain.

Pain.

Home.

Dhara sat on a hospital bed, holding her baby daughter in her arms. She lightly traced the lines of her face, her ribcage, the curve of her bottom and the angles of her joints.

'She's perfect,' she said softly.

'Yes, mahal, she is,' Nala tried not to cry.

Dhara turned her shoulder away from the nurse. 'Please don't do that,' she said quietly.

'I'm just trying to help. She's hungry. You need to feed her,' the nurse reached for the hooks on Dhara's hospital gown again. The baby lay in a plastic crib next to the bed, fighting against the tight swaddle and crying angrily.

'I said, please don't touch me,' Dhara snatched the collar of her gown away from the nurse and pulled the bed sheets up to her neck.

Priya walked in carrying an assortment of bags, some smelling like Ayah's cooking.

'Thank you Sister,' she said politely but firmly to the nurse. 'I'll help her. I remember what to do.'

The nurse left without a backward glance while Priya picked up the baby.

'There, there, *ende chelle cunju*,' she soothed. She wiped the tears from the small puckered face and walked around the room, lightly bouncing a comforting rhythm, murmuring more endearments and soft sounds until the baby stopped crying.

'That nurse is right, you need to feed her,' she said. 'I can only rock her for so long before she becomes enraged again or I get motion sickness.'

Dhara laughed a little but looked down, her hands straightening the blanket over her body instead of reaching for her child.

'Do you like the name, acca – Smrithi?' she asked, nervously.

'I do, it's beautiful, just like her,' Priya sat on the bed next to her. 'I'll help you. It was hard for me, I lost so much blood when I had Vivek, I could never really feed properly. But I've read every book on the topic,' she smiled at her sister.

Dhara swallowed hard. 'Ok,' she said and unhooked her gown, letting it drop a little. She held it over her breasts until Priya shook her head.

'It's only me Dhara,' she said, pulling the gown down and carefully placing the baby in her arms. The child instantly relaxed into her, one fist victoriously emerging from the swaddle, to touch Dhara's scarred breast.

Priya helped position the child and the baby did the rest, turning her head this way and that, rubbing and nuzzling until she found what she was looking for. Her moist pink lips latched tightly onto the dark, swollen nipple and Dhara felt a rush that hardened and heavied her breasts. It was painful and comforting; the child sucked with surprising strength. She felt a lightness and relief wash over her.

Priya untied the muslin net and let it fall softly around Dhara and her baby. Dhara slept on her side, her body curled around the little girl. A shock of black hair rose like a peacock's plume out of the tight, pink swaddle. Priya remembered her smell: talcum powder and eau-de-cologne. She had bathed the child for her sister, gently sponging the creases and extra folds of skin nature had given her, like an outfit that was a few sizes too large. She had massaged away the crust that flaked on the top of her soft head, patiently pulling each individual piece out without pulling the hair itself. She counted each finger and each toe, marvelling at the minuteness that would eventually grow to the size of Vivek and beyond. She kissed the curled ear and whispered the sounds a mother knows how to make to comfort her baby; the sounds she would never make for another baby of her own. She was reminded of the emptiness in her belly.

Smrithi, she whispered to herself. It was a beautiful name.

Dhara stirred and opened her eyes.

'Sleep with us, acca,' she said, reaching over to pull back the sheets.

'You rest, I should go rescue Ayah from Vivek,' Priya replied.

'Just come,' Dhara said, closing her eyes again and nuzzling closer to the sleeping child.

Priya parted the net and gently slid into the bed on the other side of the baby. She curled herself around her too, completing the circle.

11

COLOMBO, 1977

Dhara sat with Smrithi on the floor, wedged into a corner of the shrine room. The lamp still burned from evening prayers. It flickered over the pale photographs of their dead. Her father's face looked at her calmly, his eyes empty of expression, love or judgement.

He couldn't answer her questions or tell her what was right or what was wrong. He couldn't tell her why he had been chosen for such pain. She remembered him picking her up and putting her on his desk. Her small bottom held down the curled edges of a map. He laughed as he drew a pencil line on the thick paper around her thigh.

'Let's call that Dhara's Peak. You will be immortal and sacred like the Himalayas. People will come to pray at your bottom.'

She giggled and watched as he pointed out the contours and colours that marked rivers, jungles, villages and the dam.

'The dam,' he said smiling, 'will bring great life.'

She turned her face into the wall, away from her daughter, and wept confused, bitter tears.

Dhara held Smrithi and walked her around Nala's garden. She pointed out each of the flowers and trees, sometimes holding petals and leaves to the child's tiny nose. She whispered the names of Archi's favourite plants and her father's favourite books. She listed the food she loved to eat and the best dishes Ayah ever made. She rattled off the names of cities she imagined exploring and all the villages in Sri Lanka she had been to. Except Gal Oya whose name she never mentioned. She recited the Tamil alphabet, the one-hundred-and-eight names of Lord Shiva, every prayer her parents had taught her, every temple she could remember and the name of every hit by Loretta Lynn since 1967.

'*I'm a Honky-Tonk Girl* – remember it, Smrithi,' she whispered into the tiny swirl of her daughter's ear. 'It's a classic. It was the beginning of greatness.' She hummed the chorus softly.

She tried to imprint her voice on her child, swallowing back tears and steadying the sound when it quivered and broke, over and over again.

She reached into the warm space between the baby's jaw and neck, nuzzling her and inhaling that perfect smell. She wanted to remember it forever.

When Dhara first asked Priya to take the baby, she refused.

'You can't do that Dhara; she's your child. She needs you, she needs her mother. You'll feel better in a few weeks – all new mothers feel overwhelmed. Amma will help you after I leave and Ayah, she knows what to do. I'll come back as often as I can.'

'It's not that,' Dhara said slowly.

She had thought about this in the months before the baby was born. She wondered if she would feel differently when she held her own child. She did – she felt something tremendous had happened to her. The roots of her were reborn and sunk deep into the earth beneath her feet. They nourished her and gave her a will to live that she had not felt since her father's death. She recognised herself in the mirror with sharp clarity and her purpose with even greater clarity.

She loved her daughter. From the torn and ragged mess that was left by the soldiers, a perfect person had been born. Smrithi had made her whole again, strong again, ready to fight again.

It hurt her to let the baby go – more than the things that had been forced inside her, the cigarettes and barbed wire that had been dragged across her skin, the bones that had been crushed.

It hurt her, but she knew what she was supposed to do, and she could not do it with a baby in her arms. Nor would she allow her daughter to grow and suffer and die in the earth of her country.

'She's your child – you must raise her,' Priya repeated, confused.

'She's *our* child. I can't raise her acca. I can't, at least, not yet. Please take her. Take her for me – take her away from here.'

Dhara cried, clinging onto the baby tightly.

☼

Priya reached forward and lightly touched the statue. It was made of bronze but its colour had dulled with age. Her mother had bought it in India on her honeymoon. It was Lakshmi, the goddess of wealth. She sat buxom and beautiful on a throne, two hands were empty but raised in blessing, her two other divine hands held lotus flowers. Nala said she chose this statue because it was unusual. The goddess was usually depicted with gold coins flowing from one hand, to symbolise wealth.

Rajan had objected to the statue because he said it was the size of two volumes of the Encyclopaedia and weighed as much as four.

'Would those be the volumes you preferred to read on our honeymoon?' Nala had once snapped at him, when she was retelling the story of the deity to visitors.

The goddess sat on a pedestal in the front foyer of their home, facing inwards, bestowing Her blessing on the family within.

Priya placed both hands on the cool bronze. She thought she was going to faint. Her stomach churned. She placed her legs apart and gripped the statue hard; anchoring herself to the goddess.

Dhara had offered her baby. Their baby. Dhara's baby. It was a gift. Her heart swelled whenever she saw the child. There was nothing like it on earth. There would be nothing like it in her life again. She had resigned herself to that – until now – until she saw and held and breathed in this child; this child that Dhara was offering her.

She had begged her sister to change her mind. But with each conversation she had started to fear Dhara *would* change her mind. With each kiss, each cuddle, each innocent stare, each time the child curled her tiny hand around her finger, Priya sank into a primal place where nothing existed except her and her children. Her child. This child.

Priya touched the bronze feet of the goddess, and took her hands to her face to receive Her blessing. Her face was wet. Nala was right about the Goddess Lakshmi – a family's wealth was not in its gold but in its children.

☼

'This is madness Nala,' Rajan spoke softly but angrily. 'Please tell me you haven't encouraged this?'

Nala couldn't meet his eyes. '*Kadaval saithe*, Nala!'

She took a step back, alarmed. Rajan never said for God's sake. His mother had raised him better than that.

'We need to put a stop to this, right now.' He paced the floor of his surgery, stopping intermittently to straighten piles of letters and patient reports.

'Everything is straight,' Nala whispered.

'What?'

'Everything in this office is straight already,' she repeated more loudly and motioned to the perfectly ordered room around them.

'This office – you, Rajan. Everything about you and around you is straight. But there is no straight answer or solution. There is only what Dhara wants right now.' She watched him carefully, her face tight.

'What about what Dhara wants in a month's time or a year or a few years? When she asks for the baby back – think about Priya. How will *she* feel? She will have to give the baby back but it will kill her. And the child, Nala – what about the *child*? This is wrong.' Nala, Dhara, even his level-headed Priya had all gone mad.

'It's just wrong!' He slammed his hands down on the desk.

Nala refused to be swayed. 'What happened to Dhara was wrong. Think about the life Priya could give this child in Australia. That feels right, doesn't it? Think about the love she could give this child that Dhara might not be able to. You know what Vani was like after –'

He cut her off. 'Dhara is nothing like Vani – she's stronger and she'll have us, we can help her.'

'She is stronger. And she's devoted to something neither of us can fully understand Rajan,' Nala replied.

'Are you suggesting that we support Dhara? That we allow her to abandon her child so she can join a group of idealists and ruffians in a doomed struggle?' His voice cracked with incredulity. Nala's resolve unnerved him. She had thought it through and had decided it was right. He couldn't see how.

'The Tamils will lose and then Dhara will lose more than her child, she will lose... more than she has already lost.' He couldn't speak for a moment. An orange robe of fire furled itself around a man he once loved. How many times could he hold a broken and bloodied woman? 'We have to stop all of this now – the baby, the cause, the group she's joined – all of it. I won't allow it, Nala, I won't allow it.'

'You won't *allow* it?' she repeated. 'You won't allow it. You don't understand Rajan – she's not our daughter. We can't stop her. We love her – *I* love her,' her voice broke. She took a deep breath and spoke again, 'But we have never been able – *we* have never been allowed to stop her.'

'It's wrong,' he repeated quietly, desperation creeping into his voice. 'This baby – it will always be Dhara's. Eventually, a mother always wants her child back – and what will they tell her, the baby? Think of the damage it will do to Smrithi, to Priya – to all of them, to all of us, Nala. Please, think of the damage,' he pleaded.

'The damage is already done, Rajan. This part, where a beautiful baby is loved by our daughter and remains part of our family – that is the only thing that feels right.'

Rajan shook his head in confusion and despair.

Dhara and Priya stood in Nala's shrine room again. Dhara placed her finger in the pot of holy ash and touched Priya's forehead and the baby's. She had tried to flatten Smrithi's erratic tufts of hair with sesame oil, giving her whole face a shine. The child looked at her closely, dark eyes fringed by long lashes.

'You could style that into a frontal lobe puff, with enough Brylcreem,' she said to Priya, not taking her eyes from the baby.

Priya didn't laugh, nor did she wipe away the tears that streamed down her face.

'Don't cry, acca,' Dhara said. 'It's the right thing. This is no place for our daughter.'

'Hold her again, please Dhara,' Priya whispered, pushing the child towards her. 'It will never be too late to change your mind. She's yours – the moment you tell me, I will bring her back to you.'

Dhara shook her head.

'Just hold her one more time, she deserves to be held by you,' Priya could barely speak.

Dhara took the child in her arms and traced the lines of her face one last time. It amazed her. She kissed the baby's lips, smelling her breath. She handed her back.

'Go, please. The car is waiting for you. I won't come out. Call me when you arrive safely. Go quickly, acca, it will be easier for me.' She kissed her sister and her child one last time.

The old woman turned the door handle quietly. The house was dark and still. She had heard the soft whimpering for many nights. She knew she would hear it for many more.

For decades she had soothed the pain of other people's children as though they were her own. She didn't resent her lot in life. She fed them, bathed them and comforted them. She watched over them all and never judged them.

She hobbled into the room, guided by the moonlight that flooded through the open shutters. The child didn't like the dark.

She parted the folds of muslin, careful not to startle her, and pulled herself up onto the tall bed. She placed a twisted, walnut-shell of a hand on the child's hair and stroked the curls back from her wet face.

'*Ala vendahm, patty*,' Don't cry little girl, Ayah whispered, in a mix of Sinhalese and Tamil. She bent down and kissed Dhara's head. The girl clung to her and whimpered more, until finally, she slept.

Dhara covered her mouth and pulled away as Shiranthi reached for her face with a tube of lipstick. Every week Shiranthi would take her on an errand, sometimes real but often contrived. Dhara doubted Shiranthi, an accountant, had any need to go to the library at Colombo General Hospital. Once, Dhara had agreed to go to the market at Fort, but half way through their shopping expedition, she couldn't breathe and needed to come home.

Eventually, they had fallen into a pattern of going to the beach at Galle Face Green, early on a Sunday morning with Nandan; and the hospital library on Friday evening when both places were quiet.

'Just try it, acca,' Shiranthi pleaded. 'It's called *English Rose*, which I suppose means it's paler than other kinds of roses. I don't know,' Shiranthi laughed self-consciously, studying the light pink stick. She turned to face Dhara's mirror and pursed her lips. She applied a coat quickly and pressed her lips together.

'Now you –' she turned back to Dhara holding the lipstick out to her.

'English Rose? Are you sure I won't fall prey to post-colonial political mediocrity? Or the heat?' Dhara parried.

'Shall I do it for you?'

Dhara nodded. Shiranthi could be as happily insistent as Nala.

'I'm sorry,' she said.

'For what?' Shiranthi asked.

'For the wedding. I mean I'm sorry I couldn't come. There were too many…people, and I was…' she faltered. She was pregnant. If she said the word out loud then she would have to say other words such as: baby and gone; longing and regret. And more words too, that people, Shiranthi and Nandan or even Priya, would not understand, words like: duty and home and homeland.

'Hold still,' Shiranthi smiled. 'I understood. We both did, acca.' She traced the outline of Dhara's lips, then filled them in with the colour.

'There, what do you think?' Shiranthi asked, turning Dhara towards the mirror. She wore a green cotton shirt cut like a smock. Shiranthi's tailor had made it for her. It billowed out a little when she walked on the beach, trapping the cool ocean air inside it, against her body.

Shiranthi had also bought her the trousers. They were loose fitting, not like the tight bell-bottoms that others were wearing. She needed a belt to hold them in place. Her sister-in-law had chosen a simple one with small shells sewn onto the leather. Dhara stared at her reflection and pressed her English Rose lips together. A deceptively normal woman stared and tried to smile back, tearfully.

SYDNEY, 1978

The baby was still sleeping, and every time she stirred, Priya reached over and rocked the bouncer gently. Smrithi was exquisite. She had never seen anything more perfect than her children. Very slowly, taking care not to wake her, she leant over the baby and placed her nose under her small jaw, breathing in the warm, milky smell.

She thanked the Mother Goddess for her daughter, the blessing she never expected to receive. She spat three times quietly.

Her happiness was overwhelming. It felt boundless, as though she were flying, dipping and spinning and soaring in the sky. And yet, at times, she sensed boundaries; an edge that was tinged with something: doubt, worry – guilt. An end to her present happiness, somewhere in a future she couldn't control.

She felt so happy she wanted to apologise. She did apologise sometimes, many times: to the planets who might realign and conspire to capriciously take away what had been given so randomly; to her father whose counsel she ignored; and most importantly, to Dhara who would eventually change her mind and rightfully want back what had been shared so lovingly.

Siva nervously basted his head with Brylcreem.

'Here, let me do that,' Priya took the comb and created a neat side parting.

He studied his reflection in the mirror. 'You know we stand out in the hospitals. We all have bad haircuts, bad teeth and bad suits.'

'You and the other doctors stand out because you have brown skin and outstanding surgical skills,' she replied.

'No-one would know. I'm a fully qualified cardio-thoracic surgeon with two overseas fellowships, and I'm stuck doing locums and shifts no-one else wants.'

'They will admit you here soon, cunju. Don't lose hope. It will happen, your time will come. There, your frontal-lobe hair puff is perfect. I'm sorry you have to work so hard,' she said, stepping back.

'It's ok. I'm used to it. Back home I worked harder than my Sinhalese friends to get just as far as them. Hard work will take me further here.' He had to believe that.

She kissed him and handed him the toasted sandwiches filled with spicy potato curry. He kissed her back. She was different since the baby had arrived – lighter, more relaxed.

On the weekends he worked as a GP for a radio service. Spending endless hours in a sweaty car, he went to far-off suburbs, misleadingly called Frenchs Forest or confusingly called Castle Hill, which was very different from Castlecrag.

Today his call-outs were in Lakemba. As he threaded through the warren of streets in Sydney's west, he said the same prayer he had said every day for the last thirteen months.

'Please Lord, let my life become useful to others, let me not have left my home in vain.' He took a deep breath and controlled his tears. He remembered the courage of his father, of Rajan, of all the men before him who had worked hard for their families.

He repeated the words of Lord Krishna to the warrior Arjuna: *Who are you to be afraid? Do your duty and leave the rest with God.*

He perched the Gregory's Road Atlas dangerously on his lap and prayed that the patients of Lakemba had seen Sri Lankans before and would not call him names like yesterday's call-out. And, as he saw signs for Chullora, he prayed that he would find Lakemba.

✡

Priya positioned the bouncer next to the paint tray and gave Smrithi the rubber teething ring to play with. Vivek sat cross-legged next to the baby, with a pile of Ladybird books, flicking the pages and pretending to read to himself. She had picked them up from a St Vincent de Paul's shop. *Vinnie's*, she corrected herself, passing him another toasted sandwich.

Siva still couldn't find work as a specialist so she was setting up a GP practice in an old, run-down fish and chips shop. Reluctantly, Siva had asked Rajan for help, borrowing the bond and the first month's rent. Priya quietly asked him for a second, third and fourth month's rent without telling Siva. He agreed without telling Nala.

'You'd like Homebush, Appa,' she said to him. 'There's a growing Indian and Sri Lankan community here; it's a lot like Wellawatte. They need a GP they can relate to, especially a woman. It's the perfect opportunity for us.'

It's the perfect opportunity for us, she repeated to herself.

She surveyed her new surgery with the beginning of hope. Ayah was right about the sugar soap, it cut through the greasy membrane that covered the walls. Siva's shoulders ached, but he kept scrubbing, until the aged colour, an uncertain yellow, emerged.

They were ready to paint but had no idea how to begin. She wished Nala was still with her. Her mother had come to Sydney for four months, helping her with the baby. She had cooked the only curry she could make well – a potato curry – to which she added a secret ingredient that tasted a lot like Heinz ketchup. Nala produced kilos of it and froze it in labelled take-away containers. She had eventually, tearfully, left and Priya steeled herself as she thought about her next visitor from Sri Lanka. Her mother-in-law was coming soon, to help with the children, when she went back to work.

She stirred the paint the way the man at Mitre 10 had instructed her.

'Who would have thought there were so many shades of white?' she said to Siva. She wanted the place to look professional and clean. 'Dhara says it's ironic I've chosen *Natural White*.'

He laughed and placed a hand on the baby's tummy. Smrithi reached down and grabbed his fingers, pulling them into her dribbling mouth. 'Stop that kutty,' he laughed again, shaking the teething ring at her. He picked her up from the bouncer and held her to his chest. Raising her, he blew loudly on her tummy, making her laugh.

'Are you happy Siva? Happy with her – I mean.'

'You need to stop asking me that. She makes me so happy it terrifies me. I'm scared Priya, but mostly I'm happy.' He strapped the baby back into the bouncer.

'Don't be scared, cunju,' she said. 'We'll be fine. For now we are her parents –'

'Exactly,' he dropped his voice, motioning to Vivek who hadn't questioned the arrival of a baby in their lives.

'For now – but what about afterwards, when Dhara recovers? When she realises what she's done – what she's given up. If it happens sooner rather than later, it would be better for the baby…for all of us.'

'Don't say that,' she replied. She knew he was right but she knew her sister too.

'It's true – I just don't want you to get hurt.' He looked at her sadly. It would hurt him as well. He was a good father; a good man with enough love in his heart to accept this baby.

'We won't be hurt, cunju.' She turned to look at her new daughter and addressed the child. 'No-one's going to hurt us, any of us.' The little girl kicked her legs, bouncing herself up and down on the seat.

'Let's paint,' Priya said, smiling at Siva. She stirred the tin one last time.

'Let me do that, it's heavy.' He sat down next to the paint tray. 'The furniture from Dr Wesley is very nice. It was kind of him to offer it.'

She nodded. Dr Wesley was a Tamil obstetrician. He was upgrading his surgery in Strathfield and had given them all of his old furniture. It was much better than the pieces she'd seen at the St Vincent de Paul's shop – *Vinnie's*.

Siva knew Dr Wesley from Colombo General. He was a devout Catholic who had been forced to perform tubal ligations in Sydney, curtailing the propagation of the species and contravening his religious beliefs. He enlisted Siva for an arrangement that was beneficial to both. Once a week at Concord Hospital, Dr Wesley would surgically open the female reproductive system and gingerly hold up the sacred fallopian tube. Saying a quick prayer to Mary, the Holy Mother, seeking Her forgiveness, he would look away. Siva, a devout Hindu, would step in and cut the tube, saying a quick prayer of thanks to Lord Ganesha, the remover of obstacles, for helping his struggling career.

She watched her husband decant the paint into the tray and set it down heavily. He stretched his left rotator cuff, then his right one, wincing a little. She helped him knead out his shoulders. He was only thirty-five-years-old but almost completely grey. He refused to dye his hair like everyone else.

'My mother is an artist, remember? I know what to do with paint. You rest for a moment.' She gently pushed him out of the way, wet her roller and began.

Priya sat in her car, waiting for the pre-school bell to ring. She waited a few more minutes until she saw her friends arrive. She never went in first. She'd rather walk in late even though she always arrived at school early. Her father said timeliness was next to godliness. Or was it cleanliness? It probably was both. Every mother had a group: the Chinese, the Italians and the Whites. She waited for hers – Malathy, Ranji and Shanthi – and walked in with them.

The ladies stood on the side and watched.

'I think you should've bought Vivek a larger uniform,' Ranji teased her.

'I'm going to get at least two years out of those clothes,' Priya replied, hoisting her eighteen-month-old daughter onto her hip.

'You're such a villager!' Ranji laughed. 'You'd never guess you're from Colombo 7.'

Priya laughed too, not taking her eyes from her son. He was friends with all the children, running, playing and laughing easily. When he saw her, he ran over and hugged Smrithi first.

'Amma, McDonalds? It's Friday, please?' he implored predictably.

'OK.' She kissed her friends goodbye with a, 'See you this evening.' They would all meet in a few hours at the local community hall they used as their makeshift temple.

Siva didn't approve of McDonalds. Occasionally they were allowed the Filet-o-Fish but nothing else. Priya secretly took her children every Friday before temple and fed them all the Junior Burgers they could eat.

'Quickly children, we need to get home soon,' she looked around Burwood Plaza nervously.

'Amma, I'm chewing carefully. I might choke,' Vivek said, swallowing his last mouthful.

'You'll choke if you're being cheeky,' she replied, picking up the tray.

'Priya? I thought I saw you.' She turned around and looked into the drooping face of Mrs Segaram, flanked by her three grandchildren.

'Hello Aunty, how are you?' she leant down and kissed the old lady. Mrs Segaram was a friend of Nala's and a regular patient of Priya's.

'I'm well thank you. I'm just giving the children some French Fries, they begged me for a treat, don't you know.' Mrs Segaram looked at Priya's tray and raised her eyebrows.

'Will you be attending temple tonight?' she asked meaningfully.

'Yes...you?'

'Yes, of course. We never miss it,' Mrs Segaram replied.

'Good...well, enjoy your French Fries,' Priya smiled tightly and turned to go. And then she turned back. 'The beef fat they're fried in can be bad for your cholesterol, Aunty, just be careful about that, won't you.'

She ushered her children out, faking the jaunty wave she'd seen her mother do a thousand times.

As soon as she arrived home she called Dhara. They usually spoke after temple but she couldn't wait.

'What is wrong with these people? It's not just one of them, it's all of them,' she complained. 'Why are they all so nosy?'

'By 'these people' I assume you mean 'our people' – and the answer is therefore obvious: thousands of years of inbreeding,' Dhara replied.

Priya laughed. She could hear the smile in her sister's voice. She missed it.

'Don't be too hard on them acca, they're ok. These people keep secrets for us. They have accepted Smrithi as your child, they've cooked you curries and given you more baby clothes, toys and advice than you ever wanted. The community is claustrophobic at times, but also very caring. I don't know if you can have one quality without the other.'

'Thank you Dhara,' Priya replied. 'You are very wise and very right. I'll be nicer to poor, old Mrs Segaram tonight.'

'What time do you leave for temple?' Dhara asked.

'In an hour or so, as soon as Siva gets home. He's so happy to be a consultant, I can't get him to leave the hospital now.'

'Is he still on Deity Duty?' Dhara asked. Every week Siva took a suitcase of deities to the community hall, and like a travelling salesman, he assembled a demountable altar with a selection of Hindu gods and goddesses for worship.

'He is, he takes his duty very seriously,' Priya replied. They both laughed. 'Did you get my letter? I'm sorry it was so long. I feel silly complaining to you; work and playground politics are so trivial.'

'No, acca, I love it. I told you I want to know everything about your life – about her. The more details the better. The photographs were beautiful. Smrithi is changing so quickly. It just happens, doesn't it?

'And Vivek, he's so tall; he must get that from Siva's side. I feel like I'm there with you. It means...so much to me, more than I can say. Thank you for that. I posted my letter yesterday.'

'Good, I can't wait. You don't need to thank me, Dhara. You are here with me,' Priya said quietly. She needed those blue aerogrammes too.

'Is that Dhara mami?' Vivek asked, reaching up for the phone. 'Let me speak to her, let me,' he squeezed himself in front of Smrithi.

'In a moment, darling. Give me some time first, please.' She tried not to push her children away. She just needed more time; there was never enough. The years apart moved too quickly but each day passed slowly. Every Friday when she put the phone down, she counted the days until the next call.

12

COLOMBO, 1979

'My darling Dhara, I miss you. Smrithi is beautiful…'

Dhara read the letter over and over again until she had memorised it. Like all the others, Priya's letters began the same way.

They ended the same way too: 'Please let me tell her. I love you dearly, Acca.'

In between, Priya chronicled the small moments of Smrithi's life: the first steps and words, things that made her laugh and cry, games she liked to play, books she wanted read to her, food she loved and food she spat out.

Priya described the way her hair grew and curled up at the nape of her neck, writing, 'I think she'll have thick, curly hair like you,' and the way she tugged her earlobe in her sleep instead of sucking her thumb. She sent photographs and childish drawings of swirls and random lines, sometimes prints of a small but growing hand.

After Smrithi's first haircut, Priya sent several locks of hair. Dhara touched the hair and closed her eyes, imagining as she sometimes did, that she was holding her child. She put her arms out, then adjusted her embrace; Smrithi would be smaller. But so much bigger than she was before…

Dhara took a deep breath and pushed her way to the front. The Arrivals Gate must be the happiest place in the world, she thought, reaching the railing. From there, she could see Priya walk down the small concourse from the Baggage Section. She craned her neck and stood on the middle rung of the railing to see over the crowd coming out. She checked her watch and glanced at the Arrivals board behind her. She had checked it already but she checked it again, scanning nervously for flight SQ321. It still said 'landed'.

She watched the swing doors open and close. Priya walked out holding two-year-old Smrithi in her arms. She saw Dhara immediately and smiled. She passed the sleeping child to Dhara's outstretched arms without saying anything and they kissed each other. Dhara held Smrithi carefully, anxiously. The fierce, clenched pain in her chest relaxed.

✿

Rajan watched Priya adjust the toddler on her hip with one hand, and unpack her baby bag with the other. She gave Ayah the empty milk bottle and a small jar of baby food.

'Why don't you rest, mahal? You must be tired. Let Ayah take her.' He smiled at the child who was inspecting him closely.

'She's grown so quickly,' he said.

'She looks like photos of Dhara at this age, don't you think?' she asked happily. She handed the child to him and dragged her suitcase onto her old bed.

Rajan was unsure of how to answer. She looked at his confused face and laughed.

'It's ok, Appa. You can say it – say whatever is on your mind. You've never kept your opinion to yourself before.'

'True, but my opinion has never been so divided – or the subject of quite so much criticism from your mother.'

'Is she being mean to you?' Priya asked, unusually cheeky.

'You could say that,' he smiled again. 'Although she'd probably say the same about me.'

'And what would you say about me, Appa – and this?' she stood up and kissed the baby's temple; then surprised him by kissing his.

She was so comfortable in the relationship and more comfortable with herself than he had ever seen her. The unease that had been gnawing at him from the day Dhara announced her decision, swept over him. It tasted like cold metal in his mouth.

He wanted to warn her. He had lost children too and although he had carefully boxed the pain away and allowed time to fog the memory of it, he knew where the pain and the memory were hidden. They were always there.

He didn't want to see her hurt. He didn't want to see any of them hurt.

'Appa?' his daughter, his firstborn, smiled at him. She was so beautiful. She looked just like Nala.

His mother had taught him to speak rarely but honestly.

'I would say that you are an excellent mother,' he replied, not untruthfully.

Nala marvelled at the depth of her daughter's happiness, and through it, she remembered and re-lived her own. She watched Priya walk around the house, explaining old photographs and paintings, telling Smrithi about the places she used to hide and the games she used to play. She talked about Nandan and Ayah and Archi and Dhara – constantly about Dhara mami.

Dhara was always there with them too; her smile at times strained, at times easy. Priya gathered her into the rhythm of their laughter and play.

The little girl followed them both around, unsteady at first, then more confidently, claiming their home as her own. When she called *Amma*, her voice sweet like the sound of Lord Krishna's flute, neither woman hesitated. Dhara stepped back and Priya stepped forward, towards her daughter.

Nala exhaled.

The child sat on the cement threshold to the kitchen, her feet dangling out the doorway. Nala's new dog, Clive lay next to her, his head resting on his padded paws. Occasionally he lifted his head hopefully, eyeing the untouched food on the child's plate, but he knew better than to try. Ayah had a special stick just for him.

Dhara sat with her daughter in the doorway. She had mixed the boiled rice and parappu curry with a tablespoon of ghee, making small balls of food with the palm of her hand. The balls were lined up around the plate, slowly becoming cold.

'No,' said Smrithi. 'No balls.'

'Please darling, Amma said she feeds you like this,' Dhara had read it in the letters: rice, dhal and ghee in balls. It was her favourite. She raised another ball to the little girl's mouth but Smrithi turned her face away, clamping her hands over her mouth.

'Smrithi, please!' Dhara stretched forward and around, trying to reach her mouth again. The child smacked her hand away, sending the rice flying onto the verandah floor. Clive jumped up and took a step forward, looking between the angry child and the tearful woman.

'Go on,' Dhara pushed the dog towards the rice. 'Take it, someone should.' She put the plate on the ground next to his head. 'It's all yours, Clive Lloyd. I won't tell Ayah if you won't.'

Hours later, after Priya returned from the city, Dhara watched her sister feed her child. The same rice, dhal and ghee combined and shaped into balls; then expertly and efficiently thrown into Smrithi's ravenous mouth.

'It's nothing, Dhara. Please don't get upset about it. She's just used to being fed by me. By the end of the week, she'll get used to being fed by you. By the end of the fortnight she will know you properly,' Priya said.

'I know, acca. I'm not upset,' she lied. Priya raised an eyebrow.

'Ok, I am upset. I know she'll get used to me. I *know* that, but I *feel* so rejected.'

'This is the first time you're seeing each other since…well, since she was born. She only knows you as a voice on the phone and the person who is in more photos in our house than anyone else.'

Dhara laughed tearfully. 'Thank you, acca. Thank you for doing that. And for bringing her.'

'You know you don't have to say that. Dhara, I...I love her. I love you. I feel I should thank you more for what she brings to our life. But...you must tell me if you...if you...when you want her back. You have the right to ask for her.' Priya tensed and looked down as she said this, a tremor in her voice.

'Thank you acca, but nothing has changed for me. This is a holiday – I want you to take her back to Siva and Vivek at the end of it, and not because she doesn't like the way I make her rice balls. You have as much right as me to keep her, and Colombo is still no place for her.' She turned away so that Priya wouldn't have to hide her relief.

That night they lay on Priya's old bed, each on either side of the sleeping child. Dhara watched the easy rise and fall of her daughter's small chest. She saw her tug her earlobe. She saw her roll over and reach for Priya, who in her sleep, held her tightly; the little girl's leg thrown over her mother's hip, her hand finding its way under Priya's cotton pyjama top to rest on her mother's warm belly. They were so entwined.

Dhara had imagined her reunion from the day Smrithi had left Colombo. The reunion was never just her and Smrithi. It was always her, Smrithi and Priya. Life had never really been without Priya, and now she could not imagine a life without Smrithi. They were all so entwined. She moved closer to her daughter and her sister, and gently put her arm over both of them.

VAVUNIYA, JAFFNA PROVINCE 1980

She was on a rural placement with Ahilan to the District Hospital there. In a fortnight they would return to Colombo. With other doctors, they were sending supplies to the boys in Jaffna, where small camps were growing and hiding in the jungle. Colombo General was the biggest hospital in the country – she and her friends could skim supplies without being noticed.

Ahilan carefully tied the blindfold over her eyes. She could feel his breath on her hair as his fingers fumbled with the cloth. She heard him step away and reached out.

'No, Ahilan, please...' Dhara tasted beedi and a thick tongue in her mouth. No-one was touching her.

'Please take it off!' she raised her hands towards the blindfold but Ahilan caught her.

'You have to. I asked them not to do it but it's the rules. I'll be here with you, take my hand and try to relax. We'll be there soon,' he whispered.

He smelt like ice cream. They'd stopped at a small roadside café before the meeting. He said he didn't want any but he ate half of her vanilla anyway. She liked sharing ice cream with him.

She held his hand tightly as the car turned corners, sometimes slowing down, sometimes speeding up. There was traffic in Vavuniya, even late at night.

Her stomach jolted as the car braked suddenly. She hadn't been this far north in three years. Ahilan led her out of the car and into a room. She didn't know if it was a house or a building. She could hear people around her but didn't recognise any of the voices. He helped her sit.

'Close your eyes, I'm going to take off the blindfold and your eyes will hurt for a moment. Open them slowly.'

She did as he instructed, trying not to breathe hard. The light was still sharp and a low sound escaped her throat.

'I'm here,' he said, taking her hand again.

She was in a small room full of young people, mostly men but a few women too. At the front of the room stood a man she recognised from leaflets. He was shorter and heavier in person with a thick moustache. He looked like everyone else. He could have been the thosai kadai man near the Kollupitiya market. She expected him to offer her hot, spiced tea with her pancake.

The room quietened respectfully as he began to speak.

'Vannakam,' he nodded his head but did not fold his hands together. His voice was surprisingly high-pitched, almost child-like.

'Five years ago today, I walked into the courtyard of the Krishnan Temple at Ponnalai,' he said softly, clearly. 'I looked the Mayor of Jaffna in the face as he prayed. He was a traitor and I shot him dead.'

Dhara remembered it well. The room murmured its approval. Rajan said Duraiyappah had a family who mourned him, just like everyone else.

'Less than a year later, I founded the Liberation Tigers of Tamil Eelam. We have been persecuted covertly, through laws on language, education and jobs. And now we are being persecuted overtly – there is a permanent military base in Jaffna from which the army attacks our people.'

There is also a Dutch Fort in Jaffna, she remembered. She pushed the smell of beedi away.

'There are those – the TULF and others – who would negotiate with the Sri Lankan government. They plead for devolution of power, for greater autonomy in the north and the east – for the scraps of independence that the government will throw to us like bones from the dinner table. Are we dogs, grateful for little while our master eats well?

'I am no dog and I have no master.'

The room erupted in cheers that were quickly hushed down by others. Dhara wondered where they were.

'The time for peaceful protest has passed. The time for a political solution has passed. Now is the time for war.'

The boys jumped to their feet but he held up his hands, urging them to sit.

'There are other groups – you have heard of them – TELO, PLOTE, EROS – some of them were started by people I know. These people were my friends. I do not believe in friends anymore.

'There is only one group that will fight for Eelam, for a separate Tamil state, and there is only one group that will win that separate state.'

'I do not believe in God – God, like my old friends, has forsaken us. I believe in the Tamil Tigers and I believe in Eelam.'

The young people went crazy and this time, the man allowed them to cheer. Ahilan let go of her hand and cheered with them.

✿

Rajan liked the library of the Colombo General Hospital. On the way home from his ward rounds, he would stop there to read and sometimes to think. Often he just looked at the books, his old friends. They knew each other well. He was happy there, surrounded by words, with no pressure to speak.

Colombo General was a teaching hospital and its library was outstanding. It contained everything he needed: texts and journals on every specialty and even a sub-section on infectious diseases, which he had set up for the hospital when he was a younger, more ambitious doctor.

Nala teased him about the seriousness of his preferred reading material. There was nothing wrong with the Encyclopaedia Britannica, just because she didn't like it. There was only perfection in its leather binding, gold edging, and wafer thin paper. There was the smell and the weight of it in his hands, and the sound it made when he opened it up. The cracking that told him this volume had never been read by anyone before. He was the first.

He loved the precision of medical words. They were descriptive without being trite. They honed in on a meaning and a message, and stopped there. Medical words didn't meander aimlessly. They didn't say one thing and mean another. They spoke truthfully and then ceased, comfortably silent.

Language was everything to him even though he was frequently accused of not using it enough. He had been educated in English like most Tamils. The earth of the north was too hard – it would not yield enough food or wealth, so the Tamils knew they had to study to aspire to more. The American missionary schools in the northern and the eastern provinces had given many generations perfect English, which they used to access universities and jobs in the civil service.

'English is your ticket,' Rev. Harding used to say. The other boys would laugh but Rajan understood. English was their ticket until successive governments made Sinhalese the ticket. His English had allowed him to travel, to win a fellowship in England, and to converse with all Sri Lankans, as they were now known. His English would give him one more ticket, which he would have to use very soon. They were running out of time, even if Nala refused to acknowledge it.

But Tamil was the language he loved most. He missed the way his mother spoke to him – the endearments as well as the orders she gave him. Nothing expressed love the way their language did. Nala would argue that he never expressed his love, at least not to her or even the children. She was wrong. Rajan prayed every night for his wife and children and when he did, it was in Tamil. When he was proud of his family, when he feared for them, when he was happy to see them, his heart soared in Tamil, even if his voice was silent.

He remembered going as a boy to the public library in Jaffna, with his mother. The community loved the library: they could see its value for them and their children. Families and temples started to give books and manuscripts to the library, some written on palm leaves, which had been preserved and passed down for generations. There were original documents recording the history of the Tamil people in Ceylon and India, as well as new works by Tamil writers and thinkers. There were newspapers published in Jaffna and even old photographs of the past century.

He remembered the piles of books, scattered everywhere. He liked to hide amongst them, reading and sometimes organising them. They comforted him. The first time in his life he had broken the rules, was by staying at the library past its closing time. Sometimes he stayed deliberately, sometimes he simply lost track of time and place, as he read.

He sat in the library of Colombo General Hospital, almost half a century later, thinking about Mr Kanagasabai, the curator of the Jaffna library.

For over a year, he and the curator cleaned and filed the manuscripts that would form one of Asia's greatest collections of Tamil literature. Wearing soft white gloves, he tenderly turned the yellowed pages, often stopping to read aloud to the old man. Later, Rajan moved to Colombo for university but he returned to Jaffna whenever he could.

By 1953, the community realised its library was overflowing with knowledge that needed to be preserved and housed better, and the construction of the Jaffna Public Library began.

The library was not just for Tamils, it was for everyone. It was going to be a resource for the world, or at least those who were interested in the Tamil culture that had come from South India and taken on a shape of its own on their small island. The people were so proud: the library contained not only their history but also their communal memory. It represented how far they had come and gave them hope for how far they would go. At the height of its collection, there were almost a hundred thousand books, by Tamils and about Tamils.

It was to be a stately building, the most beautiful in the region, and although the first wing of the Library was only opened in 1959, long after he left Jaffna, he had seen, and would remember forever, the treasures it contained.

An orange robe wrapped itself around him, around his books. He opened his eyes to survey the hospital library once more. His hands trembled a little as he smoothed the pages of his Tamil newspaper and traced the date – 2 June 1981. Nothing had been reported in the national papers. He had already read the article several times and it was finally sinking in.

The Tamil United Liberation Front had held another rally in Jaffna on the weekend, resulting in attacks on the temple and over one hundred Tamil homes and shops. Eyewitness reports from two Sinhalese Cabinet members who watched the main attack from a nearby rest house, called it 'an unfortunate incident'. The politicians did not express regret: they reiterated that if the Tamils were unhappy, they should leave Sri Lanka.

Rajan folded the paper and held it to his chest. He could remember every word although he did not want to believe it. On Sunday night, the police and the army had started the burning, emboldened by government support. It hadn't taken long; one night was all they needed.

The Jaffna Public Library – and every book inside it – was burned to the ground. Rajan had no words and no language. He closed his eyes and wept.

COLOMBO, 1983

Dhara and the driver weaved their way to the front of the crowd. The Arrivals Gate was her favourite place in the whole world. Every year she stood at the same spot in the airport – from there, she could see Priya walk down towards the gate. Each time travellers opened the door she would catch a glimpse of her family as they wheeled their heavy suitcases together. She could watch them for several moments, before they saw her, the doors opening and closing like a mechanical shutter into a private world she had relinquished but also longed to join.

Priya walked out first, holding five-year-old Smrithi in her arms. Vivek was helping his father with the baggage trolley. She saw Dhara immediately and smiled; she knew where to find her. She passed the laughing child to her outstretched arms and they kissed each other.

Dhara held Smrithi tightly, the ache subsiding as she breathed in the familiar smell. She closed her eyes and cursed the tears that fell every time.

'You're home,' she whispered to all of them and to one of them, 'you're home.'

Dhara shook her head when she saw Priya's suitcases. They were full of gifts for cousins and friends in Ceylon – blocks of Kraft cheese, Vegemite, chocolate-covered macadamias and clip-on koalas. She unpacked rapidly – emptying suitcases that would be re-filled with rainbows of silk. She was eager for the sari shops of Colombo and even Madras, if she had time.

'How are things?' she asked.

'Not good acca,' Dhara said, refolding the pile of 'I ♥ Australia' t-shirts. 'The library changed everything; it showed us our place. The army has set up more bases in the north. People are afraid. Skirmishes are happening more often. At least the Tamil Tigers are better organised and armed than they were before.'

'Amma asked me to talk to you. She's worried about you.'

'She's always worried about me.'

'No, Dhara. She's really worried about you. She says you're involved with them although she can't work out how exactly. She says you disappear for meetings late at night.'

'I've started salsa classes.'

'This isn't funny. They will use you.'

'I hope so, acca,' Dhara turned away.

'Look at me. Whatever the army has done; whatever they will do; these boys will match it. The Tigers are even crushing other Tamil groups – they're killing Sinhalese *and* Tamils.'

'You don't know them, acca – and you don't know me,' she said quietly, without anger.

Priya reached for her arm and turned Dhara towards her. 'I know enough. I know your dreams and I know your nightmares. I love you and I don't want you to die for a strip of land.'

'It's our homeland.'

'And you are my home, Dhara. Think about Smrithi.'

'I think about her all the time – every day, acca. I think about her and what I want for her.'

'Then tell me, what do you want for her?' Priya challenged.

'I want her to grow up and to grow old, and to never fear the things I fear; to never dream the terrible things I dream. I want her to be proud of me for the sacrifices I'm willing to make; and to forgive me for the sacrifices I'm not willing to make.' Her shoulders slumped forward. 'I want her to be safe,' she whispered.

'And I want you to be safe, Dhara. Move to Australia – live with us. Let go of this god-forsaken place,' Priya's eyes filled with tears.

'I can't, acca,' she responded. She had tried.

'I don't accept that,' Priya shook her head. 'Be a mother to Smrithi, not just a mami. You could even think about marriage. You could have a husband and children and a family.'

'I already have a family,' Dhara replied.

'You could be a wife…' Priya said.

'No. No-one will marry me after what happened. I'm fine about it, really I am. The Gita says disappointment is just disappointment.

It's one of many temporary emotions. I've grown used to it and the freedom it gives me. I'm comfortable with my life now, acca. I have everything I need.'

'I can't believe you're quoting the Gita,' Priya replied, tears falling down her face. 'You could be a mother, Dhara. There's still time. I wouldn't blame you if you asked for her – she's always been yours. I feel like I've just borrowed her.'

'Don't cry acca. You shouldn't feel that way. Nothing is borrowed between us. We are the Pandavas – everything is shared. You are the mother and I am – I am a soldier.'

Priya didn't say anything.

'Are you sure you brought enough clip-on koalas this time?' Dhara asked, lining up the small toys.

Priya wiped her nose and tried to smile. 'Ayah asked for them.'

'Do you think she might be running a clip-on koala business on the side?'

Priya laughed a little and reached over to her sister. They held each other before pushing each other away.

Vivek's eyes widened as Smrithi emptied the pot of holy ash on the carom board. A grey mist rose from the board game making them both cough. Ayah was in charge of the children. From the verandah, the children could hear the clatter and clang of her daily meal preparation in the kitchen next door. Smrithi put her finger up to her lips, motioning to him to be quiet.

'Are you sure you're supposed to do that?' he whispered.

'Yes, I'm sure. The board needs powder to help the pieces slide,' she replied, rolling her eyes at him.

'The board needs a particular *kind* of powder to help the pieces slide, mahal,' Dhara spoke, laughing as the startled children instinctively moved in front of their crime.

She had been watching them for a little while. She could have stopped them and saved Nala's pot of holy ash. The powder had been respectfully brought all the way from the Thirupathi Temple in South India. Nala would not be happy but Dhara liked to watch the children play.

'Mami, you won't tell on us, will you?' Smrithi asked, giving her a well-practiced smile.

'No mahal, not this time,' she replied, squeezing the little girl's cheeks. They compressed like Ayah's pineapple fluff pudding, then sprang back to their delicious place.

'Can you teach us how to play carom, please?' Vivek asked, eyeing the game eagerly.

Dhara nodded and began to assemble the black and white wooden discs on the board. It was the size of a cards table but made of lacquered plywood, and marked with lines like a square tennis court. In each corner was a hole.

'The red disc is the queen. She's the most valuable piece so she sits in the centre. All of the other pieces go around her in a circle.' She clustered the eighteen black and white discs in the middle of the board, protecting the queen at its heart.

'Where's the king?' Vivek asked.

'There isn't one,' she replied.

'Why not?'

'I don't know, I never thought about it. Perhaps the queen isn't married,' she laughed.

'Like you?' he asked, spreading the holy ash around the surface of the board the way he had seen his grandmother do with her carom powder.

'Yes, like me.'

'What about that man who came to the house yesterday, Dhara mami? Is he your boyfriend?' Smrithi asked. Dhara took the child's left hand and arranged her fingers on the board, her index finger hooked over her middle finger, spring loading it.

'Position your hand like that Smrithi, and flick the striker disc with your middle finger. Aim for your colour. So if you're white, use your striker disc to hit the white discs into the corner.'

Smrithi tried to keep her fingers locked in the posture she had created. Vivek was not as easily distracted.

'Was that your boyfriend? *Ahilan?*' he asked again, stating the name he had heard from the conversation yesterday.

'No, concentrate on the corner. He's just a friend from work. Did you hear us chatting, while you were spying, children?' she asked.

Chastened, the children looked at each other and he spoke for both of them.

'No mami. We tried to, but Ayah caught us.'

'So she should.' Dhara was relieved. Ayah knew who Ahilan was and the old woman had heard the conversation before.

Ahilan often spoke to her in lists: 'We need sterile surgical packs, but the heavy duty ones with extra dressings, sutures and needles. Also: gloves; Savlon packs; pain killers, not just paracetamol, strong ones too – morphine and pethadine if you can get it. This time, I'll get: plaster of paris kits, IV fluid packs, antibiotics – oral and injections, blood substitutes – '

The list went on. Each month it became longer.

Dhara hadn't lied to the children; he was a friend from work.

'He's handsome,' Smrithi ventured, with a naughty smile.

'Yes, actually, he is,' she replied, flicking her striker disc hard into the centre of the board. The circle broke and the pieces scattered, leaving the queen exposed.

Smrithi dropped to her hands and knees and pushed Clive out of the way, using her entire body weight to move the dog.

'He's getting fatter,' she groaned and shoved him carefully, one last time.

'He's just getting older, like all of us, mahal.' Dhara smiled and sat next to her in the doorway to the kitchen. The midday sun had moved to the other side of the house, leaving the kitchen shaded and cool.

'What kind of dog is he?' Smrithi asked.

'No one knows. He's an exotic and unpredictable mix. Your Ammamma had an enormous Great Dane for a long time, but he died just after you were born.'

'Carlo, I know.'

'Yes Carlo. Nandan mama named this one after a famous cricketer, of course. I've made you some lunch – it's your favourite,' she said, showing Smrithi the plate of boiled rice, dhal and ghee.

'Feed me,' the girl commanded.

'I would love to,' she began mixing the food together with her right hand. The ghee melted and pooled in the valleys of rice. She blew quickly on the first steaming ball which she put into her daughter's mouth.

'Ah – ah – ah – hot!' Smrithi whimpered, opening her mouth wide. Dhara reached over and blew hard into her mouth, cooling the rice.

'Better? I'm so sorry, mahal, let's wait a few minutes. Shall I tell you a story in the meantime?'

'Yes please, mami. From the mabara please. Amma tells me those stories at night.' The little girl leant back onto Clive's prone body and made herself comfortable. He beat his tail once and then conceded.

'The mabara? The Ma-*ha*-bhara-*ta*.' Dhara laughed. 'Perfect. Has Amma told you her favourite story from the *Mahabharata* yet?'

Smrithi shook her head against the dog.

'Her favourite story is about the marriage of Draupadi. She was a beautiful princess from a very wealthy and important kingdom. Her father, the king, held a competition to find her a husband.'

'A competition? You mean like a spelling bee? Vivek won his. He can spell anas – anas – the doctor that makes people sleep,' Smrithi sat up and opened her mouth for a rice ball.

'He can spell anaesthetist? That's impressive. This competition was a little different from a spelling bee. Princes from all across India came to the competition.'

'To win Draupadi, the princes had to be able to use Lord Shiva's divine bow, and hit the eye of a fish that was hanging from a string and spinning around. *And* they were not allowed to look at the fish.'

Smrithi's eyes widened. 'How could they shoot the fish if they couldn't look at it? That's unfair!' Dhara licked her finger and wiped a smudge of parappu from the side of Smrithi's mouth.

'Hold still. The king was trying to make it very difficult, so that only the greatest, most worthy of princes would win his daughter. The princes were only allowed to look at the *reflection* of the fish in a bowl – they had to work out how to shoot it from that.'

Smrithi shrieked, waking up Clive who stumbled to his feet and immediately collapsed again, exhausted from the effort.

'That is impossible!' she shouted.

Dhara laughed. 'Not impossible – just very, very difficult. Now which prince in the *Mahabharata* was such a skilled archer that he could do that?'

'Arjuna, of course!' the little girl replied, triumphantly. 'He was the best.'

'He *was* the best,' Dhara agreed. 'He was the only prince who could do it, so he won the princess Draupadi –'

'And they got married and lived happily ever after?' Smrithi asked.

'Not quite – when Arjuna took Draupadi home to his mother, he knocked on her door and said, 'Amma, look what I've brought you.' His mother didn't turn around to see what he was talking about. She simply said: 'Share it equally with your brothers, son."

'What?' The child looked at her with confusion.

'Exactly – Arjuna's mother told him to share it equally with his brothers! He couldn't disobey his mother so he had to share Draupadi. All five Pandava princes married her. And that is the story of Draupadi's marriage.'

'Wowee, mami – imagine if you had five husbands! If Amma told me to marry five boys, I would never. I'm not marrying one boy!'

Dhara laughed. 'Amma would never tell you to marry five boys mahal, don't you worry about that. But Amma does tell you to share everything you have equally with your brother. That is the moral of the story – everything you have is his and everything he has is yours. You can't gain anything by taking it away from him.' She looked at her child closely, leant over and pressed a kiss to her forehead.

'It's a big story for such a little girl,' she whispered, tears in her eyes.

'Someone should tell Vivek that story, he took my Princess Leia figurine and he won't let me play with his Millennium Falcon.'

Dhara laughed and looked away, wiping her tears quickly.

'When do you think you'll be old enough to make your own rice balls?' she asked, smiling, hoping the child said 'never'.

'When I'm forty-two,' Smrithi replied confidently.

'Forty-two? That's an enormous number.'

'It's the biggest number I know, after one hundred. How old will you be when I'm forty-two Dhara mami?' she asked. She swallowed her rice and opened her mouth waiting for another portion and the answer.

'Let's see – I'll be forty-two plus twenty-nine equals seventy-one. I'll be seventy-one-years-old – even older than Clive or your grandparents are now. I'll be so old that you'll have to ball up my food and feed me!'

Smrithi laughed loudly, waking up the sleeping dog again. Her small body rocked back and forth with mirth.

'You laugh just like your mother,' Dhara said. She wanted to scoop her up and hold her.

'Amma says I laugh just like you, mami,' Smrithi replied, opening her mouth for more food.

☼

That night, Dhara lay in bed with her daughter. The child's leg was thrown over her hip and her small hand found its way to her belly. She wondered if Smrithi would always sleep like this, or would she change as she grew older and would Dhara be there with her to see those changes happen. She tried to remember how she slept when she was a child, in bed between her parents.

She thought about her favourite story from the *Mahabharata*. It was the life of Karna, the older brother of the five Pandavas who was not raised as one of them. When the great war finally began, Karna had a choice: he could either be embraced by his real mother and fight alongside his Pandava brothers; or he could remain loyal to the

Kauravas who had befriended and depended upon him. Would he follow love or duty; his blood or his dharma?

Karna made his choice. He was killed on the battlefield by his own brother, his body bathed in the last light of the day. He was watched and he was loved and he was mourned, as he had always been, by his father, the Sun God.

✪

Priya kissed her daughter and her sister and pulled the light bed sheets over them. She had promised Vivek that she would sleep with him and Siva. She closed the door to Dhara's room and stood there for a moment, her head resting on the heavy wood.

Smrithi slept in their shared childhood bed, peaceful and unaware of the dreams that tortured Dhara in her sleep. She loved to watch her daughter sleep; and she never took the serenity of that sleep for granted.

Nothing is borrowed between us, Dhara had said. Nothing and yet everything. She couldn't gain anything by taking it away from her sister. They both knew that.

'Thank you, Dhara,' she said quietly, as she did every night. 'Thank you.'

✪

The house whispered. The adults were taking their afternoon naps and the children were pretending to take theirs. Rajan slept in his study. It was cooler and he didn't like to disturb Nala who accused him of snoring during these daily naps. He denied the charge, outraged. He would detect an adenoidal dysfunction if he had one. He lay on his back, hands on his stomach, fingers locked.

He thought back to yesterday with a smile. It was Krishna Jayanthi, the birthday of Lord Krishna. Ayah had cooked milk rice and churned fresh butter and curd for the little blue god. She had muttered all morning in Sinhalese, scolding them for having so many gods with so many birthdays and so many favourite foods. The Buddhists had one Buddha with one birthday.

Nala had assembled their grandchildren: two from Australia and two from upstairs, in the shrine room where the offerings were laid out. As a boy, the god was renowned for stealing butter from his mother's pantry. All children loved the tales of his pranks.

Smrithi was given the honour of making Lord Krishna's footprints. Nala had been about to lift Smrithi's feet and place them onto a tray of rice flour. She would then be allowed to leave her small, white footprints in a trail from the door of the shrine to the altar where the food sat.

'Wait, Amma,' Priya stopped her. 'Let Dhara do it.'

Nala hesitated but Priya pushed Dhara forward with an encouraging smile. Dhara lifted Smrithi onto the plate and together, they laughingly made a mess of the shrine room floor.

Rajan suddenly remembered something from his childhood – a fragment of a story thrown randomly into his mind. Lord Krishna was stolen away as a baby to save his life. He was given to and raised by another. A familiar coldness rushed through him.

'Lord Krishna, forgive us,' he prayed. 'You taught us that everything around us is an illusion, it is all Maya. Our attachments to each other, our love, our desires, even our fears – this is all Maya.'

The child should be told. The lies – Maya all around him closed in. He shook his head and prayed again.

The children padded quietly across the tiled floor of the study. They gathered around to inspect his withered toes. Their strength and speed were legendary. Rumours had traversed the Indian Ocean and spread quickly amongst them – rumours that despite their aged appearance, his toes had the reflexes of Bruce Lee, even if he did not. He stirred, his eyes closed as they prepared to assess the claim passed on by their parents.

Vivek, the eldest at nine-years-old, was not the bravest. He nominated Smrithi, the naughtiest, to offer her tiny fingers as a sacrifice in this experiment. The rest of them stepped back a little, putting a safe distance between themselves and the famed vice-like grip of those pedestrian digits. Rajan, still pretending to be asleep, tried not to smile as Smrithi scratched the constellation of mosquito bites on her leg one last time, took a deep breath and reached towards her grandfather's toes.

☼

The holiday was almost over. Priya, Siva and Vivek had gone to India for a week of shopping, leaving Smrithi with the family in Cinnamon Gardens. As soon as Priya heard the news about the riots in Colombo, she cut short her expedition. The new plan was for Priya and Siva to fly from Madras back to Colombo. They would stay in the airport for three hours, giving Rajan enough time to bring Smrithi to them. Then they would fly back home to Australia.

Rajan usually loved the smell of Colombo at this time of the year. The frangipani trees were in bloom and they competed with the white starry jasmine, filling the night air with its seductive perfume.

Tonight was different. He tried to turn his head away from the smell of Colombo. The acrid smoke had penetrated the protection of Colombo 7, even if nothing else had, and he could not wash it out of his clothes, his hair, or his memory.

Red clouds illuminated the night sky as he worked. He placed their little granddaughter's bag in the back seat of the car but changed his mind again, moving it to the boot. Ayah had prepared a flask of coffee for him, a bottle of water for all of them, and potato curry sandwiches for the little girl. 'Her favourite,' she commented proudly to no-one in particular as she wiped her eyes.

She had also placed canisters of water, wet towels, and wet blankets in the boot. They were creating a small pool at the back of his lovely Peugeot, ruining the upholstered base that he cleaned every weekend.

He didn't chastise Ayah. He removed the little bag from the boot, silently closing it. He doubted the water would help them if it came to that, but he recognised the love behind the futile gesture.

He argued one last time with Nala. 'I'm taking Smrithi to the airport by myself. It's a ninety-minute drive to Katunayake and back. I won't be gone long. I'll be fine.'

'Nothing is fine about this plan. Try the President's office again,' she implored. 'They will help you, they'll send a driver.'

'I've tried, Nala, the phone lines are jammed, I can't reach anyone.'

'If you're going then I'm going with you.'

'Nala, there's no point in both of us taking a risk.'

'You admit then, this is a risky journey,' she cried jubilantly. He shook his head, defeated. Of course it was a risky journey but they had no choice. Dhara objected to the plan too. She begged him to let her take Smrithi.

'She's my child. It's my duty,' she argued.

'No mahal, you have done your duty,' he replied. 'You are *my* child and she is my granddaughter, this is *my* duty.'

He should have spoken to Priya and Dhara – he should have made them change their mind about the child. It was too late now. All he could do was this one thing.

He checked the route to the airport over and over again, although he had made this journey many times. He memorised a new route that would take them through the Sinhalese neighbourhoods, then along the outskirts of one Tamil neighbourhood, then into the country roads where it was safer. He couldn't find a path that circumvented all the Tamil neighbourhoods, or what was left of them. They were all so intermingled in Colombo, so intermarried until now. He calculated the mileage to get there and back, and factored in that he might need to make deviations if he encountered the mobs. He calculated the petrol he would need for the journey, giving himself a generous buffer, and filled his tank accordingly.

Nala watched him and said, 'Fill the tank right up. You're so economical, even now. You're so... so Tamil, Rajan.'

'Yes, I am Tamil,' he replied, closing the cap, 'I won't give the mobs my petrol. I won't be bathed in it. They can use their own petrol for that.'

He saw her bite hard on her lip. He called in Sinhalese for the servant boy who had just returned from the outside and was relocking the heavy gate. The boy was carrying a packet wrapped in newspaper. Rajan took the packet and walked over to her.

'Is everything ready?' he asked quietly.

'I think so. I just need to get the child. She's sleeping.'

'Let her sleep, it will be a long journey.' He opened the packet and her eyes filled with tears as he took out a jasmine garland, the kind she bought every week outside the temple: their temple that was now blackened beyond recognition. She tried to pin it to her hair but he stopped her.

'Not yet, leave it in the shrine, for when we get back,' he said gently. She understood.

'It's time,' he whispered.

Rajan knew the Negombo area around the airport well from his days as a young house officer at Negombo Hospital. He liked the refuge of the beach town. It was quiet, people only spoke when they had something to say, and they generally meant what they said. Not like the people they socialised with.

He knew that the main route to Katunayake Airport would be targeted for Tamils trying to escape the country, so he had planned to go to Negombo and swing back to the airport from behind. If there were any problems, he could stay at Negombo Hospital, the staff would recognise him.

He packed his car, stocked his medical bag, and set off with his stubbornly protective wife and sleeping grandchild.

'Are you sure you know where we are?' Nala asked. He could sense her trying to control her voice and the rising panic. They had doubled back so many times. She even asked him if they had accidentally re-entered Colombo.

'I'm sure – I know where we are. Stop asking me,' came his terse reply. She was worried, but he couldn't deal with her fear as well as his own. He just needed to focus. At every turn he knew he was getting closer to the airport. But he could also see the fires ahead in the darkness, forcing him to make another turn away from their destination. He could see the fire dancing and knew that it was moving from torch to body. He had underestimated the neighbourhood, he had made a mistake and now he needed to focus. This was an exam question, nothing that could not be solved with a deep breath, an enquiring mind, and an excellent memory.

Left and then left again would bring them out on Ave Maria Road, five blocks from the hospital. If they could just make it to the hospital they could call home, call the airport, call anyone, and wait until the roads were clear. He saw Ave Maria Road, there it was. Four more blocks. What was the Sinhalese word for four? Why did he think of that? What was the Sinhalese word for bucket, he asked Nala repeatedly.

She scoffed at him. 'I know the word,' she said angrily. 'I know why you're asking, but I know as many words in Sinhalese as I know in English, as I know in Tamil. Have you forgotten I am an educated woman?'

He barely heard her but he hoped her irritation would distract her for a few moments. He forced his eyes ahead.

'Don't look,' he whispered. Cars upturned like Darwin's giant tortoises, stranded, limbs flailing and then still, stripped of their tyres. Scorched objects by the side: charred and collapsed; blackened and fused to smoking garlands of rubber. Some were large but some were small, the shape of his grandchild, sleeping in the back.

At the end, all were foetal.

'Don't look, Nala,' he whispered again, wiping the tears away.

Three more blocks. They couldn't breathe. But neither of them wanted to open the windows. Glass and metal were the only barriers between them and the smell that would wrap itself around their memories forever. Suddenly he thought about the day his sister Lali died, like a fast flashing scene on television, its incandescence glimpsed between changing channels. He shook the picture out of his mind and focused.

They were almost there. There were precisely ten houses between this junction and the next. Then one more block, one more right turn, and they could stop. They could survive.

And then he saw it. He saw it before she did. Then she saw it too, and for the first time in thirty-seven years of marriage, she didn't say a word. There was nothing to say. He wanted to say *bhaldiya*, the Sinhalese word for bucket. He held onto that word like a prayer, saying it over and over in his mind, willing her to remember it too.

The crowd swarmed around the car, lighting the interior with their torches. Their shadows moved with the flames and the wind coming in off the ocean, creating an erratic dance of dark and light. The mob formed a tight circle around them, thumping on the car and shouting at him to get out. He opened his door and was quickly dragged out. He turned back to see Nala pulled out behind him. Smoke filled her lungs and she reached for her sari pallu to cover her mouth and nose, but couldn't find it. She was wearing borrowed slacks and a shirt. He had insisted: no sari, no wedding chain, no potu on her forehead, no garland in her hair. Nothing that could identify her – differentiate her – except her beautiful features and her voice, which he knew was trembling.

He took a deep breath, gagged on the smell and started talking in perfect Sinhalese. He had rehearsed his story and was relieved to hear it flow out of his mouth.

'My name is Dr Fonseka. Here are my papers and this is my wife, Dolly and our granddaughter. The head of surgery at Negombo Hospital, Dr Samarasekera – perhaps you know him. He has asked me to assist at the hospital. They're short-staffed as you can imagine. I'm concerned for my family but Dr Samare is an old friend.' He tried not to exhale. If they could make it to the hospital, Samare would support his story.

The head of the mob surveyed him as he stood calmly. Rajan had spoken in Sinhalese; perfect Sinhalese; almost too perfect. He knew he was too composed, too well-spoken, and too dark. But there was nothing he could do now except wait.

The man ordered someone to check the car. Inside they found Rajan's medical bag filled with supplies and more papers identifying him as Dr Fonseka. He had been careful. He had removed the Ganesha statue that normally adorned the dashboard of the car, as well as all traces of holy ash. He had been very careful.

A man yelled back, '*Okkoma hurri.*' Seems fine, he said, slamming the car door shut. The mob prepared to move on.

The little girl finally awoke, hungry and confused. She opened the door and, barely noticing the circle of angry strangers around them, went to her grandmother and pulled at her shirt. 'Ammamma, Ammamma – I'm hungry,' she said in English.

Ammamma. Amma's amma.

The man turned and smiled an ugly, triumphant smile. He held up a bucket and looked at Nala. '*Meka mokaddhe?*' What is this? he asked in Sinhalese.

✿

Pain coursed through Nala's body.

'Stop, stop, stop!' she could hear someone shouting. She wasn't sure if it was Rajan. A child was screaming. Her granddaughter, it sounded like her five-year-old granddaughter. Someone was holding her and she must be screaming. No, it was Rajan. Someone was holding him and he was screaming. Like a small child. Nala was screaming too. And rolling. Rolling as her husband had instructed her to do when they were preparing for this journey.

'If you get caught, don't run,' he said, 'it will only make it worse. You must roll.'

Roll, roll, roll. What was the Sinhalese word for roll? *Bhaldiya.* That was the Sinhalese word for bucket. She had said it. She remembered it. Rajan made her practise it over and over again, each time correcting her accent. It hadn't mattered. The little girl had given her away the moment she called her name. Ammamma. She loved that word.

'What was that smell?' she thought. It was terrible. Familiar, but terrible. Burnt, salted sugar. She couldn't brush it away.

The air was on fire. It hurt to breathe. She couldn't breathe.

Roll, roll, roll. *Urulathal*. That was the Tamil word for roll. Darkness dropped on her.

✿

'Stop, stop, please stop!' begged the old man while his son rushed forward out of the crowd, shouting, 'He's the President's doctor, the President's doctor!'

The inner circle opened up a little and retreated, twisted faces suddenly fearful. The President's doctor. The words were whispered back and people moved faster, moving on to the next Tamil.

Rajan broke away from his captor and ran to the boot of his car. He pulled out the cans of water and the wet blankets and poured them over his wife, crying as he did so.

'Help me,' he sobbed. 'Help me, somebody help me.' Only the old man and his son were left. They both looked familiar to him but he couldn't think. He had to focus. Focus. The younger man helped him wrap Nala carefully. The water and blankets had worked quickly. Ayah had been right. 'Thank you Ayah, thank you,' he muttered.

'Come, Iyah, come. Negombo Hospital is just here. We must go, we must go now.' The younger man was looking around him. The mob had already passed but they couldn't be sure of the next one.

'Come Iyah, we'll drive you.' He helped Rajan carry Nala to the car and put her on the backseat. Rajan sat with her, her head cradled in his lap.

The child; where is the child? Fear surged through him again. Before he could speak, the younger man opened the front door and got in, carrying Smrithi, who was cowering in his arms. He stroked her hair and spoke softly to her, soothing her in Sinhalese. The old man sat in the driver's seat. He reached for the keys where Rajan had left them in the ignition. The man was comfortable in a stranger's car as he took them quickly to the hospital. It was only one block away. So close, they had been so close.

13

COLOMBO, 1983

Nala didn't move. She smelled pine. It was sickly sweet and incongruous with the shimmering coldness of the white walls and sheets and floor. She could recognise hospital disinfectant anywhere. Rajan's hands had a faint trace of it. She lay on her bed quietly as he rattled off words. Third degree, partial second degree, tissue oedema, infection, emergency escharotomy, hypertrophic scarring, grafts, flaps. The words continued. She couldn't feel them so she didn't need to understand them.

He arranged the sheets around her body carefully. She was breathing, surviving, but she was raw. The burning had melted back layers. It revealed something unhealed, unfinished inside. She cleared her throat. The tube had been taken out of her mouth a few days before.

'Do you believe in karma, Rajan?' she asked him softly.

'What?'

'Do you believe in karma? Do you think we are punished for the things we've done wrong?'

'No Nala, please don't talk like this, you're a good person.'

Was she?

'Perhaps,' she replied, unsure – unable to lie to herself for a moment. 'I don't think so.'

She awoke early to find him slumped in the chair next to her hospital bed. The stiff lines of his collared shirt had crumpled around him. She coughed loudly, and he stirred, confused at first, sleep still clouding him. He rubbed his face with his hands, and became clinical again, as he began the first of many daily examinations of her injuries.

'Don't,' she said, reaching for his hand weakly.

'Don't what? Does it hurt?' he asked, worried, pausing for a moment. 'The wounds are too deep; they shouldn't hurt.'

She laughed at that. 'No, it doesn't hurt.'

'Then what?' he asked, returning to his examination. He had a routine that he liked to follow.

'Don't,' she swallowed the dryness in her mouth, 'treat me like a patient. Sit. Talk to me,' she said softly to her husband.

He sank back into the chair and she reached out her hand to him again. It was the only one she could still move. He took it and pressed it to his lips. She smiled and didn't remind him about his views on kissing and infection control. She waited a long time and finally, he spoke.

'I thought you were going to die,' he said simply. 'I saw them hold you down. I saw the fire and I couldn't help you. I thought you were going to die,' he wept, covering his face with his hands.

'There was fire everywhere; around you; the fire Nala, the fire.' Heaving forward, he dropped his head next to her bandaged body. He clenched a fist and pounded the side of the bed. She stroked his hair gently, until eventually, exhausted, he stopped.

'It was the same colour, the day Lali died. It was the same fire, Nala,' he whispered.

Dhara shook her head at Nala. 'You know you should be wearing a hospital gown mami. They're sterile,' she said as she pulled Nala's batik kaftan up over her head.

'Yes, but they're not very stylish are they?' Nala winced as she spoke.

Dhara unravelled the bandages slowly, taking care not to tear the thin layer of skin that had started to form. It looked like tissue paper that had been pulled taut; light pink and mottled white with the slow return of pigment and strength. She washed Nala every day, the way Rajan had shown her. Nala sat quietly, allowing Dhara to undress her, soak her wounds in saline, pat her dry with a sterile muslin and redress her wounds and her body. The nurses at Colombo General were trained to do all of this, but Dhara insisted.

'We are leaving, mahal. We have to go,' Nala said softly.

'I know,' she didn't stop her work. She wrapped the clean bandage along the length of Nala's right arm.

'Please come with us. Come to Australia. Rajan mama said you've refused, but I beg you –'

'Don't mami, please don't beg me. I can't leave…' She couldn't look at her aunt. There was an emptiness in the base of her chest. It would be so easy, so tempting to fill that space. Fullness was within her reach. It had always been there if only she would take it.

She continued wrapping, her hands moving with a practised rhythm. Rajan said consistent motion was essential for bandaging. He said people always thought bandaging was easy but those people had never seen burns and the other devastations of war. Dhara had prepared for this and more.

'Is it because of your mother? I've spoken to her Dhara and she wants you to leave. Look at me, mahal. Amma wants you to leave. Priya wants you there, in Sydney, we all do. Nandan and his children are coming too. You should be with your… family,' Nala sobbed. 'There's no shame in leaving all of this.'

'I know mami. And I'm grateful. You are my family and I will miss you. It's not just about Amma – it's about Appa too. I owe it to him to stay. I want to be here for him. I want to be here *with* him. After everything that happened to him – to us – I can't leave.'

Nala tried again. 'I loved Mohan, and I have no doubt that he would want you to be safe and happy and away from this place.'

'That's probably right mami. Parents want that for their children but children want to be with their parents.'

'Promise me then, promise me you won't go to the north. Stay in Colombo, it will be safer here,' Nala insisted.

'Mami…'

Nala caught her hand as she tried to work, forcing her to look at her. 'You must promise me that you will not fight – I'm not your mother but

I love you Dhara and you owe me some obedience too. Promise me you will not go to Jaffna – that you will live. I couldn't bear it if...'

'I promise,' she said reluctantly. She wanted to wrap a bandage tightly around the longing that seeped out of her like a constant, open wound. It wouldn't heal, it couldn't be cauterised, the pain could only be managed.

She clipped the edges of the bandage in place and admired her handiwork tearfully.

Rajan checked her charts again. She shook her head at him but the tight skin on her neck wouldn't allow the full movement she needed to convey her irritation.

'Your blood work is normal, Nala. You're lucky not to have any secondary infections,' he spoke into the clipboard.

'I know that,' she replied, 'Dr Wijesinghe explained that to me an hour ago.'

'Did his wife bring you those?' he asked, eyeing the dodol, milk toffee and other gifts on her side table.

'This will be the first case where Type 2 diabetes has resulted from a third degree burn,' he said disapprovingly.

'Nandan says you're not sleeping well,' she reached forward to snatch the clipboard away from him. 'He says you go to bed very late and wake up very early.'

When he said nothing, she continued. 'He says he can hear you in the middle of the night, walking around. What are you doing?'

'I'm thinking,' he replied tersely.

'You think a lot,'

'I do.'

'What are you thinking about?' she tried again.

'I'm thinking about why my son has nothing better to do than monitor my nocturnal activities.'

'You admit then, that you have nocturnal activities when you should be resting?' she replied.

'You should have been a prosecutor.'

'Yes, I should and could have been many things. Instead, I'm your wife and I'd like to know what you're doing up at midnight, Rajan.'

He took the clipboard back and held it tightly against his chest.

'I can't sleep without you,' he replied quietly.

'What?' she heard him but she wanted to hear it again.

'I said I can't sleep properly without you.'

'I'll be home soon,' she wanted to take his hand but the clipboard was between them.

'Good,' he replied, looking at her blood work results one last time.

Nala shouted into the phone. It was a long-distance call to Australia, their weekly ritual that gave her peace of mind for the next seven days. She only spoke to her daughter for ten minutes: any longer than that was charged at a higher rate and was too expensive for Rajan who still saved money like the impoverished villager his mother raised him to be.

'Please don't overdo it Amma. Dhara says you're healing well but you need to rest. Shall I come back? I can help with the packing,' Priya said.

'No, mahal, it's fine, the packing is fine,' she replied. 'We can manage. Ayah is helping us. Dhara and your Appa are fussing over me constantly. I'm going mad resting.

'We'll only bring the essentials. We can ship one load this time and I'll bring the most important things in my camphorwood chest. I don't know how I'm going to choose which belongings to take. Your father can't reasonably expect me to leave so much behind. He's only agreed to pay the excess luggage for one chest but I really need at least two. Anyway, everything else will wait until later.'

Later. She didn't know what would happen later, she kept it undefined and sequestered in a distant future.

'What have you decided about the house? Siva and I – we really think you should sell it, Amma. You could use the money in Australia. It's an expensive country and you will be here for... a while.'

'No.'

'I wish you'd listen to me –'

'No mahal, I said no,' Nala tried not to raise her voice. She didn't want to fight again but she was keeping the house. 'For now, Shiranthi's parents will rent the main house. Vani has agreed to move out of Kotahena – what's left of it. She'll move into Nandan's flat upstairs with Dhara. They'll be protected in this house if the Perera's are here with them. Appa says the mobs won't stay out of Colombo 7 forever.'

'And Kamini mami – how is she? When is she leaving?' Priya asked. Nala's younger sister had escaped the riots, hiding in her neighbour's home. But her house – their father's house – in Wellawatte had been burned completely.

'She's ok. Getting on, I suppose. She's leaving a week after us. Her son-in-law has already found work in Sydney. Ayah is the one I'm worried about. She's moving down the road to work for Dr Fonseka. They'll look after her well but she's devastated. She keeps giving Shiranthi cooking lessons.'

Priya laughed. 'How is Appa coping with all of this?' she asked.

'The same as always – silently. He's organised his Australian medical registration so at least he'll be able to see patients there and get out of the house. I'm far too young for him to retire,' Nala replied.

Priya laughed. 'Amma, you're incorrigible. And Clive Lloyd? He's going to miss you too.'

'He's going with Ayah. That dog has lived a happy life, thanks to my cooking.'

'Ayah says that's due to her cooking,' Priya teased her mother.

'Ha! Your Appa says it's the cocktail of vitamin supplements he's been giving him.'

'And the war?' Priya asked finally. 'How are things in the north?'

'The same, worse I think. What is there to say?' she sighed sadly. The riots last July precipitated an inevitable war.

'You need to tell Dhara to come with you, Amma. It's too dangerous for her there. Tell her she must do this for Smrithi.' Priya dropped her voice. 'She is her mother and mothers should be with their children.'

They had had this conversation before.

'You are also her mother, Priya. You need to accept that – Dhara has,' Nala corrected her.

'That doesn't matter now. What matters is we get Dhara out of Sri Lanka. She'll be alone there. Make her come, Amma,' she started to sob into the phone.

'She won't be alone mahal; she'll be with Vani. I've asked her so many times. I can't *make* her do anything.'

'I don't believe you, Amma. You can make anyone do anything you want. You made me…' Priya's voice shook and then faltered.

'That's not true, mahal. I only ever made you do what I felt was best for you, because you're my daughter.' Nala would have cried but today her skin felt hot, as though the fire was still sitting in the cells of her body, turning her blood and tears and the life she loved to vapour.

Priya cleared her throat. 'I should go; Appa won't like it. Let's talk later. Goodbye Amma.'

'Mahal, please –' Nala tried to reply but Priya put the phone down. The heat in her skin remained.

She sat on her bed and surveyed the contents of her room. There were photographs of the children, her parents and even some of Archi. There was one photograph of Mohan and her on her grandmother's verandah in Tellippalai. She could feel the mosquito bites itch on her eight-year-old legs. She traced its worn edges and placed it on the 'to take' pile with the others.

There was a formal photo of Rajan's family posing in a studio in front of heavy curtains. Her father-in-law sat with his British raj moustache and studio walking cane. Rajan's sister Lali was seated next to him. She had died shortly after it was taken. It was the only one Rajan had of her. Nala's mother-in-law was there too, preserved imperiously in sepia. Little Rajan was perched on a raised chair, squeezed in between his parents. She smiled at his oversized head on top of a tiny body, the freshly starched shirt with the collar tightly buttoned, socks pulled right up to his bulbous knees. His mother had borrowed the shoes and shirt from the headmaster's son. While they were all taking their seats, she had lovingly spat on his dry, scratched knees and rubbed them. When he recounted this story to Nala decades later, his eyes filled with tears in a way they would not do for any other woman.

She studied the photograph one more time and her hand hesitated before she placed it on the 'to take' pile.

She picked up a photograph of Archi and her family. It was her favourite – it showed her, Priya, her Amma and Archi – all four generations together. It was taken in 1969 on the verandah of their home.

She remembered that day so well. Archi had been unusually lucid and pain free. She was her old self, talking and joking, passing wind as freely as she laughed. She had wanted to play Three-Nought-Four with Nala and Amma. Nandan was at cricket practice and Ayah had prepared his favourite crab curry, ready for his triumphant return.

At Archi's request, Ayah had agreed to take a short break from the kitchen and join the game. Archi was old enough to ignore the hierarchies of caste, class and race. Her grandmother said that she and Ayah would die as equals, withered, decaying and farting symphonically to the very end.

Archi cackled as she won another hand. Nala hated to lose and was becoming impatient with Archi's unfortunate lapse out of dementia. She was about to lose yet another hand when they heard the gates open and their Peugeot 404 drove in. She was proud they could afford a new car.

'Nandan Baby, Nandan Baby,' Ayah crowed with delight as she scuttled off to the kitchen for his food. The boy came running out of the car, his cricket whites stained green and brown. He started to recount the highs and lows of his afternoon in his best Richie Benaud voice. When he took a breath, Ayah would place a ball of steaming rice and crab curry in his mouth. He was thirteen and too old to be fed, but from her arthritic hand to his mouth, was how it had always been for the old maid.

A few moments later Rajan emerged, holding a large box from the boot of the car. The box was moving and he was smiling. A small toffee brown head poked out.

Rajan stroked the silken ears of the little dog.

'It's a Great Dane. I want a big dog: something that looks frightening but won't *be* frightening.'

'A puppy,' Nandan whispered in disbelief. 'For me, Appa, for me?'

'No Nandan, not for you, for Amma.' He looked at his wife and caught the delight in her eyes. She smiled at him and he smiled shyly back.

Nala lingered on the black and white image. She loved that photograph – she loved that Archi was able to know her children before the light went out in her eyes; she loved that Amma had seen her do well in life; she loved that Priya would go on to marry well and have her own beautiful children. And she loved that underneath her sari, as Rajan was taking the photo, there sat a little toffee coloured puppy, licking her toes and making her laugh. It was a beautiful day.

Nala finally came out of her bedroom and after so many years of marriage Rajan still caught his breath at the sight of her. She looked at him expectantly. He said nothing. She waited.

'You're healing well,' he said.

'I'm healing well?' she repeated.

'Yes, and your hearing is excellent.'

Today was her first real outing since she'd been released from hospital several months ago. She *was* healing well. The body has a remarkable ability to recover and regenerate, if given a chance.

She had been given a chance – they both had. He said a prayer to Lord Ganesha and an obligatory salutation to the planets, in particular Saturn, for their protection and generosity *this* time. The planets could be fickle in their favour and he would not risk a next time. All they could do was pay the local temple priest and wait for the alignments to change accordingly. Lately, the priest had seen a significant move for them, a move from an old home to a new home. He didn't have to be an astrologer to predict that. He didn't even have to be a surgeon or a President. The President of a small but complex island, he thought, as he took Nala's hand and helped her to the car.

She closed her eyes for most of the journey and didn't see the magnificent manicured garden or the hedge-lined driveway. Queen Victoria watched over them, her marbled pallor aged and serious.

When they arrived at the pillared front door of President's House, Rajan tapped and held Nala's hand for a moment. A dark, thin boy in a white uniform guided them to a large reception room. His jacket was missing one of its brass buttons.

'Thank you for coming, thank you so much for coming,' President JR Jayewardene repeated, each time more emphatically, less earnestly. 'It's so good to see you Doctor. Mrs Rajan you look beautiful as always. How are you both?' He didn't wait for a reply, prattling on with pleasantries about their drive, the weather and the selection of teas his servant boy could offer them.

Rajan smiled, wondering if his garrulous wife had finally met her match. The President didn't need to pause to breathe in-between his monologue. He must have a very special respiratory and otolaryngological system in order to achieve that conversational marvel. Nala would be jealous. She usually had to pause in order to take a breath. She was only human. Jayewardene on the other hand was no ordinary human. After his role in the riots, many Tamils believed he wasn't human at all.

Not used to being silent for so long, Nala launched her own strategic attack of social homilies. 'Thank you, Mr President, thank you so much for having us today. You didn't have to, you must be so busy.'

'Didn't have to?' Jayewardene countered, 'Of course I had to. There is no way I could allow the best surgeon in Colombo and his fair wife to leave without a proper goodbye. I would never be too busy for you –'

She interrupted him. 'Yes, but you must be particularly busy at the moment. It's very kind of you to see us.'

Rajan smiled quietly at her nerve. She would not be talked over.

'Yes, yes, yes, there is so much to do at the moment with all the troubles,' the President agreed.

The troubles. The Troubles. Trouble. Rajan thought it such an odd word for the carnage that happened last July and the fighting that was tearing through the jungles of the north now. Decades of latent anger unleashed through canisters of petrol and a match.

'Yes,' the President said. 'Doctor, I don't know how Black July happened – and so quickly. I was just as shocked as you were,' Jayewardene paused.

You couldn't have been quite as shocked as we were, Rajan thought bitterly.

Jayewardene continued, 'One moment we were burying those poor soldiers who'd been killed in Jaffna. Thirteen dead you know – damn those Tigers. We were burying our soldiers at Kanatte Cemetery. We chose to do that so we didn't cause a disturbance, you know. We didn't want to pour fuel on that fire.'

Poor choice of words. Even Jayewardene realised and stumbled on quickly. 'Anyway, Dr Rajan, I just don't know how it happened. It was ugly, so ugly,' he repeated, 'and so unnecessary.'

The English language was clearly limited. There were other words for what happened in July: words in Tamil and words in Sinhalese. But in their common medium of English, the harshness of what one had done to the other was muted: neutered, politely sanitised into socially acceptable conversation pieces.

'Terrible business you know, all that.'

Three thousand people – how long would it take to count to three thousand? Six days: that's how long it took to kill three thousand people, if the mobs used petrol, if the police watched it happen, if the President wanted it to happen.

The killing was efficient because a government minister had given the mobs the electoral rolls, listing the address of every Tamil in the city. Neighbours turned into a raging, faceless mob – except that Rajan could remember their faces, all of them. His eyes strayed to Nala's neck, which she kept carefully covered with her sari.

He wondered how long they would have to stay there, when suddenly Jayewardene's servant boy entered bearing an ornate jewellery box. The President stood up and cleared his throat ceremoniously. He handed the gift to Nala who offered her thanks and stood awkwardly. At Jayewardene's urging she opened it.

The silver clasp on the box opened with a little clicking sound. Inside was a set of twelve silver dessert spoons. Set into the carved handle of each spoon was a gemstone: Ceylon's finest, cut and polished to perfection. Rajan had never seen anything like it before – because no-one eats dessert with jewellery, he thought. Nala was silent. Unusually, he stepped in and spoke on her behalf.

'Thank you Mr President, thank you very much. You didn't have to, it was unnecessary but very thoughtful of you,' he lied.

'Nonsense, I couldn't let you leave Colombo without something to remember your home by. It is sterling silver and each spoon has a different Ceylon gem. I had it made especially for you.'

Rajan stirred himself again to make the appropriate responses. Nala's fingers lightly touched the jewelled handles before she shut the box.

'Thank you sir, that is very kind of you. You didn't have to,' she said, echoing her husband's words.

'Nonsense, nonsense. Now you will have something to remember Colombo and me by, every time you have dessert.'

Her hands twitched. She gripped the box and smiled tightly.

That night Nala sat on her bed. She looked at the camphorwood box and started a list: photographs, diaries, her wedding sari, and the portrait she had done of Rajan.

There was the jar of paddy rice her mother gave her when they had moved into their new home. Amma had boiled milk for her and as the milk rose and bubbled over they all prayed for a life of abundance, a life filled with the riches of health, happiness, children, and grandchildren. Amma's rice was paddy and its husk seemed to have protected it, keeping it fresh during the twenty-five years since they had moved to Cinnamon Gardens. Nala had used the rice in the wedding ceremonies of two of her children, including both of Nandan's weddings.

Rajan said keeping the rice for decades was either unhygienic or scientifically impossible, twenty-five years being too short a time for the grains to have ossified into permanent preservation. His heart was ossifying. Her mother's rice was as fresh as the day she had been given it, and it had nothing to do with hygiene or science. It was a miracle. She could feel her mother as she emptied the jar onto her bed and spread the grains out. She opened the window, allowing the cool evening breeze in. It carried the scent of wet earth from the garden. She wished the smells of her home would seep underneath the skin of the husk. She wanted to store her memories for another twenty-five years, opening Amma's jar from time to time to breathe and remember.

She put the rice back in the jar and closed the lid tightly. Her daughter had told her not to bring any food items to Sydney; the Customs officials were very strict. She only hesitated for a moment before rebelliously packing the jar in the chest. She looked at the set of spoons in their blood red velvet box. She traced the sharp lines of the carved handles and lightly touched the jewels. Then she emptied the spoons into her bedside table drawer and placed the fragile remains of a small yellow kite in the box. It had soared once, hopeful and strong.

Finally, she looked at her saris. There was no way this could be done. She lifted her wedding sari gently – that had to be packed carefully. It was thirty-eight-years-old and made fragile by time, unlike her. One day, she thought, she would use it in the wedding ceremonies of her grandchildren. She smiled – things wouldn't be so bad over there. She would be with her children and, more importantly her grandchildren. She placed her wedding sari in the large camphorwood chest and surveyed her room once more.

14

Nala had been to Australia once before in 1978, when Priya brought Smrithi back to Sydney. Her impressions of the country were limited to a small apartment, a paediatrician's office and an airport.

Her daughter described the local shops as a large mall, which contained clothing boutiques, a supermarket, a few hairdressers, offices and so on. This off-hand but detailed description had made her apprehensive about her first appearance.

She wore one of her good saris – a Mysore, not a Kanchipuram silk – she didn't want to seem ostentatious. She wore a hairpiece, covered with her newly dyed hair, held in place by several clips and a fine hairnet. Around her bun, she pinned a small garland of jasmines she had deftly picked from her neighbour's garden. She applied Oil of Ulay, which she could buy in Sydney for half the price she paid in Colombo. Then she powdered her face with her Max Factor compress: colour Candleglow. There wasn't another Tamil in Sydney who could use Candleglow. They were all a shade of Bronze or darker. Finally, using a small nail, she applied the red pottu in the centre of her forehead. She was ready.

She quickly realised she had overdressed for Strathfield Plaza. She had overdressed for Australia. The mall and its inhabitants were not concerned with appearances at all. Australians were a criminally casual race, all attired in shorts of varying lengths from just under the buttocks to mid-calf. Few men wore collared shirts, most favouring what she considered an undershirt, referred to as a t-shirt.

Noticing that none of the ladies wore much jewellery, she surreptitiously tucked her heavy wedding chain into one side of her sari blouse and pulled out her handkerchief from the other. She had doused it in eau-de-cologne, and she pressed its cooling freshness against her.

Thankfully Rajan had agreed to accompany her on her maiden voyage to the mall. He was also staring at the hundreds of under-dressed Australians that surrounded them.

'Aunty, Aunty! Are you lost? Can I help you?'

She turned at the sound of the familiar accent and looked into an unfamiliar but unmistakably Tamil face.

'*Vannakam*, Aunty,' said the young woman, using the formal greeting without folding her palms together.

Nala didn't respond; she couldn't recognise her. The lady tried again. 'Priya told me you were coming. You look just like her. I mean, she looks just like you. I mean, I would recognise you anywhere,' she laughed nervously, trying hard to fill the void with words. 'You are Priya's mother, aren't you?'

Nala inhaled deeply on the handkerchief. 'I am Nalayini – or Nala – and this is my husband, Dr Rajan. Yes, Priya is my daughter. We've just arrived from Colombo.'

During the rest of the brief conversation, she was distracted – the Tamils of Strathfield had unfortunately adopted the sartorial sins of their host country.

Later that night she stood in the bathroom with her husband. The fluorescent light flickered, then steadied, illuminating the plain bathroom tiles. Every sixth tile bore a posy of what looked like wilted roses.

Rajan tipped his precious blue powder onto his toothbrush.

'Do you think the spice store imports the powder here?' she asked him.

'I hope so,' he replied.

'Toothpaste is nice and it's more convenient. You should try it. You might like it,' she said dubiously. There was only so much change a man could take.

She cleaned her face with a wet cloth, starting with the vermilion pottu in the centre of her forehead. She wiped it sideways. The remnants looked like a shooting star. Priya didn't wear a pottu any more, unless she was wearing a sari. She mostly wore slacks and shirts, even t-shirts. She wasn't as tall as Nala or as fair but she was still very beautiful.

'What did you think about the lady we met today?' she asked.

'Which lady?'

'The one at the plaza – the Tamil one who knew Priya. She was funny.'

'Funny?'

'Yes, funny. A little strange or rude or something, don't you think?' She tried again to get support.

'She seemed fine to me. It was quite nice of her to introduce herself and help us,' he replied.

'I don't know if she was really trying to help us, to be honest. She had a funny way of talking. She referred to me as Priya's mother.'

'You are Priya's mother.' Rajan was irritatingly rational.

'Yes, but in Colombo, no-one would come up to me and say, 'Are you Priya's mother?' What a ridiculous way to introduce yourself. Everyone knows who I am.'

'Well, we're not in Colombo anymore,' he sighed wearily, turning the lid tightly on the last of his teeth-cleaning powder.

At 6:30 in the morning she and Rajan went down to the fish markets at Flemington to choose the largest, meatiest crabs. The market reminded her of Kollupitiya, but teeming with Australians and a surprising number of Chinese people shouting at each other. The language was different. She liked the smoothness of its consonants, which were at variance with the harshness of the hand gestures that accompanied it. Colombo had its share of Chinese restaurants. The food was sweet and sticky, not like their food. But she had never seen so many Chinese people before and she realised she was staring.

She wasn't sure what crabs she was looking for. Ayah usually chose them while flirting inappropriately with the crab karaya. The old woman would circle the Pingo baskets in the dust outside the front gate, her bowed and rickety legs causing her to walk with a lateral rocking movement, much like the animals she was inspecting.

Dark and mottled shells: that was what she needed, she remembered now. She pointed out a few of the larger crustaceans at the back to the vendor. He was intent on selling her the smaller, greener ones writhing at the front of the stall.

'You don't get to choose, love. You just tell me what weight you want and I give them to you,' the man insisted again.

She would not be dictated to by this simpleton in bloodied overalls. She pulled her nylon sari tightly around her shoulders, wincing less this time as it rubbed against her. Its embroidered hem was trailing in the undefined liquid on the ground. She raised it up to her ankles, the way her mother had told her never to do. Her mother had never bought crabs from an irate man at Flemington Market.

'As I said, I will have those four large ones at the back,' she repeated, pointing to the crabs she wanted.

'Listen, love, maybe you don't speak English proper – you don't get to choose. Jesus, you people. If you can't speak English, you should go back to your own country,' the fishmonger said impatiently.

'Today's customers are as fresh off the boat as today's catch,' he whispered to his son. The younger man laughed and replied in a different language.

She straightened her shoulders, lifted her head and replied haughtily with her best convent-educated accent, 'Young man, two hundred years ago we were colonised by the British. Of course we speak English and we speak it properly. Now I *will* have those crabs and I will have them immediately.'

At home, she tried to re-create the crab curry. She roasted the fenugreek and mustard seeds without burning them. She fried the onions, ginger, garlic and curry leaves separately and added it to the seeds. She washed, cut and veined the crabs and coated them in the spices before adding the coconut milk, salt, coriander powder, cumin powder, chilli and turmeric.

It should have been perfect. It was too salty. She licked her tasting finger in despair. She remembered instructing Ayah back home about how to make the dish. No matter how severe she was with her, the old maid cooked the curry just as she liked it. Decades of eating Ayah's crab had made Nala's hand too heavy with the salt.

She frantically called her younger sister Kamini. Priya and Nandan would be arriving in an hour with their families. The crab was not ready and her hair was still wet and wrapped in a towel. Priya had bought her a hairdryer but she preferred to let her hair absorb the sun. Rajan used to love the feeling of her warm, thick hair bathing them both. This had been a surprise to her.

Kamini arrived breathless and dishevelled from her daughter's apartment down the road. She respectfully pushed Nala out of the way and tasted the crab curry – it was too salty she agreed, but all it needed was a full lime just before eating, and the confidence to use it. She opened her handbag and pulled out a lime, a small tin of coconut cream and got to work.

With barely concealed disappointment that no further remedial cooking was required, Kamini complimented her sister's curry as was expected and helped her set the table.

Nala wanted everything to be perfect. She wanted everyone to know that she and Rajan were fine in their new home. She paced the inner perimeter of the place where she was expected to live: three bedrooms, half as many as before, a kitchen the size of her old pantry, and a living room the size of her old verandah. It was fine.

She thought about re-lighting the spitting lamp in her shrine, now reduced to a few shelves in the study. Rajan usually lit the lamp for her every morning. She didn't like the sound of fire, even small ones. She pressed her finger into the small pot of holy ash and applied some to her own forehead. She took more for the black and white photographs of her parents and in-laws, all dead for many years now.

Next to these photographs, Rajan had put one up of her girls when they were no more than ten, sitting on the steps outside their kitchen.

Priya was hugging Dhara so tightly that their cheeks were almost fused together. They still hugged each other like that. She checked her wristwatch. It was eleven o'clock. Dhara would be awake in Colombo soon and Nala would call her, as she did several times a week. Rajan said nothing about the money; he was as desperate as she was to hear Dhara's voice.

She remembered the last time all her grandchildren were in Colombo, sitting on those same steps. It was only a year ago. They were lined up in a row with their little legs pressed against their chests like shiny scratched bosoms. With their mouths open, they waited for her to mix the rice into a mushy, perfect ball – each one contained a little paruppu and chicken curry in just the right proportion, which she threw into their hungry mouths. It was a beautiful day. She would have more days like that in Sydney, she told herself.

She checked the crab curry one last time – it needed a little more lime, but aside from that, it was perfect.

Nala returned from her daily walk with the other Colombo ladies who had moved into her neighbourhood. Rajan called them the Kaftan Kusa Kusa Club. They had all boldly exchanged their casual nylon saris for lighter cotton kaftans. Sydney's heat was oppressive, radiating relentlessly during the day and night. Nylon only seemed to make it worse, trapping the sweat against their bodies, almost steaming them.

She saw her daughter park her car outside her apartment.

'Amma,' Priya called. 'Amma, you should be ready by now – we'll be late for temple.'

'Temple can wait. I am absolutely speechless,' Nala began. 'Did you know that old Dr Mahen's granddaughter is getting married? The wedding is next month at the Strathfield Bowling Club and we haven't received an invitation.'

'You're not invited, Amma. Let's go inside and talk about this please,' Priya whispered, leading her to her building.

'Of course we should be invited,' she scoffed, opening the main door. 'We knew them in Colombo. Dr Mahen was your Appa's anaesthetist at Colombo General for many years. We were so sad when they moved to Canada. I will speak to Meena Mahen about this. What time is it in Canada? Will she be awake yet?'

She heard her daughter sigh as they walked up the four flights of stairs to her apartment.

'Aunty Meena will be coming to Sydney early for the wedding, Amma, and you can speak to her when she arrives, but please don't ask her for an invitation. And please, *please* don't call her in Canada.'

'But I'm sure there's been a mistake, mahal. We've been friends for such a long time. No-one knew Mahen when he was just a junior, but your Appa supported him. It would be a shame for us not to be there at his granddaughter's wedding. I'm sure he'd want us to give the young couple our blessings.'

'Amma, people can't afford to invite the entire community here. They have to be selective.' They had now arrived at the door to her apartment.

'Selective?' she repeated. '*Selective?*' She tried to control her pitch but it was rising. 'Mahen's father and my father were from the same village. They are known people to us. We moved in the same circles in Colombo and your Appa helped him, his career, and his family. Mahen and Meena attended your wedding and Nandan's. In fact, they attended both of Nandan's weddings. If Mahen's daughter is *selecting* anyone for her daughter's wedding, then she should be selecting us.'

Priya shook her head. 'Weddings are different in Australia, Amma. The last wedding we went to was intimate. There were only two hundred people. This isn't Colombo. You won't be invited to everything. You need to accept that,' she said, not unkindly.

'Are you invited?' Nala had to ask.

'Yes, we are,' she replied, reluctantly but honestly.

'Get me Meena's number. What's the time in Toronto?'

A month later, Nala attended Meena Mahen's granddaughter's wedding. The Strathfield Bowling Club was once again transformed into a wedding hall: saris were admired, marriages were brokered and few people paid attention to the bride and groom. Nala and Rajan were seated at Table 25, somewhere in the middle of the wedding hall; disappointingly far from the front but reassuringly far from the back.

○

Rajan still said nothing. She couldn't understand it. What was wrong with him? He had been offered a part-time job with an old friend from Colombo, Dr Pasu – and he had said no. He was sixty-five, the retirement age for some men, but she couldn't believe that was the life he wanted. This was an excellent opportunity to start working in a clinic in Sydney. Pasu's practice was famous in the community; it was expanding and he needed an experienced partner like Rajan.

'Do you want to just keep seeing patients here in this apartment? Do you want *this* place to be your surgery for the rest of your life?' she asked, her voice becoming increasingly shrill. She tried not to think about the beautiful surgery in Colombo that he had designed himself. She tried not to think about what they had left behind.

When patients came to the apartment to see him, she loved the company and conversation, even if it was about illnesses. Perhaps especially if it was about illnesses; her personal lexicon on the subject was impressive. But she also hated showing people where her husband now worked.

The apartment was small and the lighting was insufficient. But with a desk lamp and his reflecting mirror, Rajan could focus a beam of light into a patient's ear, nose, or throat and create the environment he wanted. Sometimes she would hold an additional lamp over his shoulder, apologising to the patient as she assisted him. Rajan didn't notice or mind. She could almost see his brain, eyes, and hands connect as he put on his microscope glasses and focused the loupes. He only noticed the 'paining' parts of local Tamils. He never charged them more than the Medicare rate. He loved working; he didn't have to be in Cinnamon Gardens – Strathfield in Sydney was fine, as long as he had a lamp and loupes.

'I want you to work,' she shouted at him.

'I am working.' He didn't raise his voice.

'I know, but I want you to work somewhere better than this,' she replied, motioning to their apartment.

'If this place is good enough for us to live, then it's good enough for me to work. Plus –' he paused.

'Yes, plus?' She prompted, raising her eyebrows. He could be infuriating.

'I *am* working somewhere else,' he said.

'What?'

'I've been working somewhere else for the last few months. I'm seeing patients at the Holsworthy Barracks Hospital, in the south.'

'What?'

'I've been seeing patients at the Holsworthy Barracks Hospital,' he repeated.

'Yes, I heard you. What does that mean?'

'It means that I've been seeing patients –'

'I understand what it *means*; I want to know what *you* mean.' What on earth was going on? Other women's husbands had secret mistresses, sometimes secret wives. Hers had a secret job.

'Once a week, when I tell you I'm going to the Strathfield Library, I'm actually going to the army hospital where I treat soldiers and their families.'

'Why didn't you tell me?' she asked.

'I didn't tell you because I knew you would think the job wasn't good enough for me – or you. *I* like the job. The soldiers are good people. I think I'm helping them. I like the job and I'm going to keep it. I don't want a new one or a better one. I want this one and you need to accept that.'

That was the end of the argument but it had given her a reason, an excuse, to be angry.

A week later she was still trying to punish him. It had been almost a year since they'd left Colombo and she was still furious with him.

'That's enough Nala.'

'That's not enough rice, you need to eat more,' she said, brusquely forcing more food onto his plate. He was eating less these days, even though her cooking was improving.

'I said it's enough, and I'm not talking about the rice,' he said quietly.

'What?'

'Enough. You know what I'm talking about,' he replied.

She put the spoon down and walked out of the kitchen. He was right: it was enough but she didn't know how to stop. She had never been like that before but life had never been as it was now. Before was so much better. Before, before, before. She closed her eyes and wished for before.

He followed her out of the kitchen.

'Don't you think I wish we were still there? Don't you think I want that life too? Do you think I wanted this?' he said, motioning to the room around them. 'I did my best. Maybe I should have moved us earlier. Maybe I should have taken a chance and kept us there. I don't know. I don't know what I should have done, but every single time, Nala, I did my best.' When she didn't reply, he spoke again.

'If we sell the Colombo house, we could buy a bigger or better place in Sydney, if you wish?' he said.

'What do you wish, Rajan?'

'I wish that you were happy,' he replied slowly. 'This apartment, where I live – I don't care. I grew up in worse. Simplicity suits me. I miss Colombo, I do. But I'm relieved to be with the children. I'm relieved that at least two of them are safe.'

'I can't sell our home. I can't,' she said, shaking her head.

He sat down on the sofa and straightened the lace doilies she had placed on all the arm rests. They were thoroughly impractical, but they were pretty. She tried hard to make their apartment pretty. The furniture was too large, too ornate for the small, simple walls that contained it. The Persian rugs were too elaborate for the worn, polyester-mix carpet they hid. The apartment would never be elegant or stately, but they were both getting old now and would never be elegant or stately either. They would just have to be: in this apartment, together.

Tears rolled down her cheeks. He patted the sofa cushion next to him and she sat. 'I just expected more. I wanted more,' she said.

'I expected more too,' he said quietly. 'I wanted more for you and I'm sorry. But you need to forgive me now and accept the path we've taken – the path I have taken for us.'

'It wasn't just you Rajan,' she replied. 'I chose this path too. I've been watching this black woman on television. Oprah, her name is. She says disappointment is only disappointment. We can choose to let go of it.'

'Really? Did she say how?' Rajan asked, trying not to smile.

'I don't know, but she seems very clever. What's it like out there? Your new job, I mean,' she asked.

'It's different, but I like it. The soldiers, they're driven by duty, even though most of them have never been to war. Sometimes they're scared of the things they're being trained to do. The families are nice and sometimes they're scared too. They're young and many of them don't even remember war. They're in training and waiting, watching the horizon for something terrible to happen. War is always on the horizon, it's in our nature isn't it?' he said, more to himself than her. 'I'm sorry,' he repeated, looking at her.

Her anger receded a little, replaced by shame. 'Don't be. I'm sorry. I'm sorry too,' she said.

'I'll take you home, Nala. I promise, as soon as we get our Australian passports. Colombo is supposed to be safer now; the fighting is only in the north. If we stay in the city, we'll be safe.'

He passed her a doily to wipe her tears and she laughed.

A week later, Nala emerged from the bathroom and declared, 'I'm coming with you today, Rajan.'

She was fully dressed in a simple but pretty sari. She didn't want to overdo it for her first visit. Olive green was not her best colour but the sari had a yellow trim and she thought that was appropriately patriotic.

'What do you mean, you're coming with me?' he asked. He was also dressed properly in a long-sleeved shirt, tie, and shiny shoes. He polished them once a week.

'I mean, I'm coming with you to Holsworthy Barracks. It's a long drive and a long day for you. I think you need the company.' She put a package of toasted potato curry sandwiches in her handbag and smiled benevolently at her irritated husband.

The drive south-west was forty-five minutes long and she used the captive opportunity to talk to him about all the topics he had avoided during that week. Later, when she became a regular at Holsworthy, she used the time to talk about all the topics he had avoided during their life.

The route was beautiful, taking them through a national park. Although the terrain was no longer new to her, she still found the smoky blue haze of eucalyptus forests breathtaking. There were certain bridge crossings and small gorges for which even she stopped talking. Tourists must look at the gentler green hills and palm-fringed beaches of Ceylon with the same awe. She was suddenly sorry she had never noticed the detail and design of her home enough.

The barracks themselves were enormous but well-organised, like a small monochrome world unto itself. In Colombo she was afraid whenever she saw soldiers, but not here. Men and women at Holsworthy walked around with uniforms and guns, and greeted them respectfully. General Andrews shook her hand warmly, as though they were old friends.

'Good morning Mrs Rajan, your husband has told me a great deal about you.'

She was so distracted by the compliment that she didn't know how to respond. She laughed prettily in return. Rajan excused himself to begin his clinic.

'You'll have to stay in the waiting room after the tour. There's nothing for you to do you know. I suppose you could watch television or there are magazines in the waiting room.'

'I'll be fine,' she said to him sweetly. He scowled in return. She turned to General Andrews and gave him her best smile, 'Shall we begin the tour, General?'

After that first visit, Nala joined Rajan on his weekly clinics and quickly made friends with the many wives and fewer husbands who volunteered. She started with small jobs in the administrative office but grew bored quickly. After a few months she decided she would visit the Recovery and Rehabilitation Unit.

She stood at the door and inhaled the sanctity of clinical cleanliness. She pulled her sari tightly over her shoulder and stepped into the ward. Australia's army had not fought a war for years. It played its part keeping peace in a world order that she didn't understand. But the pain of war, the terror of memory, and the process of healing – that she understood.

Her own injuries had taken months to heal well enough for her to leave Ceylon: one month in hospital to protect her from infection and another three months sequestered in her home. She could have ventured out of the house earlier, but she didn't want to. Her body was a patchwork of skin grafts: pieces borrowed from her thighs and buttocks to replace pieces that would not re-grow.

She knew she was very lucky – lucky the burns were not as extensive as they could have been; lucky Ayah had put wet blankets in the boot of their car that night; lucky her husband was a respected doctor who could access the surgery she needed. When Nala looked at the memorial plaques at Holsworthy she knew she was lucky to have survived at all. Every country had its lists.

In that place, surrounded by limbs rendered and ripped, skin flayed and scorched, all that was inside was revealed. From the shadow of her jaw to her right hand to her sixth rib at the back, her skin was warped. It had never fully regained its original pigment or texture. The new layers had thickened, hiding her pulsing jugular but they were coarse and imperfect. She was able to pin her sari shawl around her shoulders and hide most of it. She wore sari blouses that came down past her elbows, as though the three-quarter blouse was perpetually in fashion, regardless of the season, the occasion, or the time of day.

At Holsworthy, she stopped pulling her sari shawl tightly around her neck. She let it drop over her left shoulder as it was supposed to, modestly hiding her chest but naturally showing her neckline. It was liberating: scars didn't matter here – they were almost a badge of honour. They gave her entry into that closed world of complex medication protocols, physical therapy schedules, psych testing, and counselling. At first she stopped caring about her scars as she tended to the scars of others, eventually she stopped noticing her scars at all.

She offered to do what she did best. She joined the kitchen at morning teatime and forced her butter cake recipe on the head chef after swearing him to secrecy. She supervised the baking and helped with the serving on the rehabilitation wards. Once a week, the soldiers of the Australian Army were greeted by an ageing but beautiful lady in a sari who chattered endlessly, while smiling and serving them the best butter cake in the world.

'Which box are we?' Nala whispered to Rajan as he studied the form. The census taker was watching both of them as they argued in Tamil.

'Sshh,' he hissed, concentrating. 'Why don't you ever stop talking?' Forms and officials made her nervous and nerves made her more talkative than usual.

'Don't sssh me! I hate it when you do that. In Australia, men don't shush their wives. Wives are encouraged to speak and participate,' she hissed back.

'Sssh!' he said again. The form was long and complicated. The government was undertaking its five-yearly census. In two more years, Australia would celebrate its bicentenary.

Rajan's heart raced. He surreptitiously took his pulse. Nala noticed and he moved his hands back to the form. They had started to quiver. He dropped the form and scrutinised the census taker: t-shirt, jeans and name-tag on a string. For something as important as a roll-call of every citizen in the country, the man could have at least worn a collared shirt. He would never understand the commitment to casualness. It was too pervasive to be an affectation; it must be an actual cultural trait.

'Just tell me, which box are we?' Nala repeated. She was reading the form over his shoulder and pointed out that they didn't have a box. There was no category for Sri Lankan Tamils. He was surprised she hadn't asked for a box just for Colombo 7 Tamils.

His cousins in the UK told him that they were called British Asians and on official forms, there were boxes for Asians from India, Pakistan, and Bangladesh. The Sri Lankan Tamils didn't have their own box – they fell into the 'everybody else' category of British Asian Other, which they were deeply offended by. The British Asians of East African, South African, Malaysian and Singaporean descent were probably offended too. No-one wanted to share a box and the cultural, linguistic, and historical differences between all of these Asians were obvious, to the Asians anyway. His cousins should be grateful they got any kind of box at all.

'There aren't supposed to be boxes for everyone. There are so many people here from so many backgrounds; there wouldn't be enough space on a form to give us all boxes. Two boxes are fine, Nala – citizen and non-citizen.'

'Perhaps I should come back?' the man enquired politely, unsure of what to do. When the couple didn't say anything or raise their heads from the form, he tried again. 'Do you need a translator, sir?' he asked politely.

At this question, both of them looked up sharply. 'No, thank you,' Rajan replied, placing a hand on his easily offended wife. 'We speak English, but it's kind of you to ask. If you could come back by the end of the week that would be excellent.' And, as if to prove that he could read English, he added, 'The form states that we have until Friday to complete it, correct?'

After the census taker left, Rajan stared at the form again. His hands shook as he turned over its pages. He tried to focus on his wrist first. He visualised the eight carpal bones of the joint followed by the branches of the five metacarpal bones that formed his hand. He then focused on each finger, each segment, each knuckle, willing his usually compliant and capable hands to be still. His hands continued to shake.

He pushed the form at Nala and rasped, 'You fill it out.' He walked over to his writing desk and sat there, pretending to sort through papers. He tried to take a deep breath. He counted to twenty-seven, the day of his mother's birth. Two plus seven was nine, an auspicious number. He counted again. He felt his hands steady and his heartbeat slow down. He looked at Nala as she concentrated on the form.

In Ceylon, census figures had shown the government where the Tamils lived. The government had used those figures to send thousands of Sinhalese families into the regions that had belonged to them. New Sinhalese districts were created in old Tamil ones, making the Tamils a minority in their own homelands.

Later, census forms and electoral rolls had been used to find and set fire to them. He took a deep breath again. They were in Australia now. They were Australian now and this country didn't do that to its citizens. It didn't do that to anyone. This country had opened its doors.

He took the form from her with steady hands. He sat back down at his desk and filled in the boxes.

COLOMBO, 1986

The plane door opened and the languid humidity of Colombo put its heavy arms around her. She had longed for it. She had imagined it, dreamt about it, she could almost taste it.

And when it finally held her, she couldn't breathe.

The thickness passed through her nose and down into her lungs, drowning her in the smell of fuel, of rubber scraping against tarmac until it smoked blackness into a clear, blue sky. The shouts of porters and drivers became angry chants. Sunlight became torchlight and a child entered the circle.

'Ammamma, Ammamma – I'm hungry,' her granddaughter said in English, pulling on the green and blue paisley of her shirt.

'What is this?' the man asked in Sinhalese, holding up the bucket. She could see flecks of ash, stuck to his forearm. They were dissolving into his sweat, black streaks sinking into his skin.

He shook the bucket, rattling the battered tin against its handle. The crowd tightened around her. Rajan struggled, shouting in Sinhalese, men in dirty sarongs held him back, laughing.

'Bhaldiya,' she whispered. She refused to look down at the child, lest she remind them that she was there. If she could hold his gaze, he would see only her, and not the little girl.

She lifted her head and looked him straight in the eyes. They were red and watery; his slow smile, exultant.

'Bhaldiya,' she repeated, loudly and clearly, the way Rajan had made her practise.

The man lifted the edges of his sarong up and tucked them into his waist. He could move better that way. He picked up a canister of petrol at his feet and shook it easily.

'It's almost empty,' he said, shrugging his shoulders as he stepped towards her.

Sampa, sampa, sampa – burn, burn, burn. The words echoed around her.

'Nala!' Rajan pulled her through the mass. People stared; some laughed. Dhara clasped their baggage trolley, her face fearful and wet with tears. Rajan held her to his chest. He was a small man but his strength loomed tall and wide around her. The arc of her terror ended where all comfort began.

'Don't cry Nala, I'm here,' he said. Somewhere nearby she heard a plane land. 'I'm here,' he whispered firmly, as she relaxed into him.

Nala stepped over the threshold with her right foot. She couldn't remember where she'd learned that superstition, it could have been her mother decades ago, or it could have been Chun Hei, the Korean beautician who plucked her eyebrows in a fluorescently luminous salon in Burwood last week. She had made sure her eyebrows were immaculately groomed and her hair dyed Midnight Black before she boarded the plane for Colombo.

Nala prayed to all gods and she observed all superstitions. She spat three times quietly as she looked around, relieved that the house had not changed very much. Nandan's in-laws had of course brought some of their own furniture to replace the pieces she'd taken to Sydney, but the house still looked like it belonged to her and Rajan. It would always belong to them.

Instinctively she walked towards the kitchen, looking for Ayah, ready to give her instructions for the day: string hoppers and a milk sothy for breakfast; rice, snake beans and fried prawn curry for lunch; and a simple puttu, coconut chilli sambal and green chilli omelette for dinner. Her mouth watered at the memory as she peered inside the kitchen. Ayah wasn't there; she hadn't been there for two years. Dr Fonseka and her dear friend Dolly down the road would be enjoying Ayah's fiery sambal instead of her.

But the memories of a lifetime were strong and insistent.

She looked at the empty kitchen and saw the old maid squatting on her wooden seat. Attached to the small platform was the blade she used to scrape the soft white flesh from the hairy brown skull of the coconut. She held it tight in her crooked hands, still powerful despite their age. Ayah's head was bent over her work, her shoulders hunched as she rocked back and forth, peeling away moist layers of the fruit with each movement. Later she would grind fresh red chillies with the coconut, rolling the heavy pin against the stone slab that also sat silent.

Nala turned and walked towards her children's bedrooms. Nandan, her beautiful boy was still bowling a pomegranate down the corridor. 'No Nandan, don't! It will break, it will stain the walls,' she shouted at him. 'Don't worry, Amma,' he laughed back. 'I'm practising; it's called a leg spin. See?' he said, rubbing the red bulb on his leg and twisting his fingers, snapping the fruit into the air. It spiralled up and then down. She caught her breath, waiting for it to hit the ground, and split open into a thousand rubied pieces. But Nandan laughed again and caught it with his chubby hands. 'Just like Richie Benaud,' he winked at her as he ran down the corridor. She laughed as she remembered. Nandan didn't wink anymore.

She stopped outside her daughters' room. This was the most beautiful room in the house. Its large canopied bed was a chariot that tore across the Kurukshetra battlefield, taking Karna to safety, far away from the arrows that killed him in the *Mahabharata*. Priya played Karna, Dhara her loyal charioteer and Nandan, when he was admitted into that intimate circle, a footman.

With the help of extra bed sheets the chariot transformed into a palace. Priya and Dhara were twin princesses, dressed in their temple finery, re-draped to reflect the style of the Mughal Empire they ruled over. If he asked nicely, Nandan was allowed to be a servant boy, running hither thither to satisfy the whims of his mistresses. She closed the door on the majestic palace and entered the final part of the house she had longed to see: Rajan's surgery.

It had been closed up the night before they left. The room was full of labelled boxes and sheets thrown over furniture now. She sat on his swivel chair, feeling the indentation of his weight on its leather seat – years, decades of his life imprinted on its ageing skin. She faced the empty patient's chair in front of her, where thousands of people had sat, listing their pains, their problems and their fears. Rajan had listened and nodded. When they grasped his hands, he held them back tightly, showing strangers more tenderness than, for decades, he could show his own wife. She leaned back into his chair and let it hold her.

✿

Rajan waited for Dhara at the counter. As usual, she carried a large pile of books, which she set down carefully.

'I'll pay, mahal,' Rajan stepped in front of her with his wallet open, flicking through his rupees.

'Rajan mama! I'm not a little girl anymore. I'm thirty-eight – I should pay for you. I've been earning for a while, you know.'

'I know, and I still like to buy my children books,' he pointed to one on his pile – Charmaine Solomon's, *The Complete Asian Cookbook*. 'It's a first edition.'

'It's a classic!' Dhara laughed. 'Priya will love that – Ayah will hate it. She says all those fancy Sri Lankan chefs are stealing her recipes and making lakhs of rupees out of her.'

'Ayah could be right,' he said, smiling, 'She usually is. Ayah says you seem well – a little quiet but well.'

'Did you ask Ayah to spy on me?' Dhara asked, not troubled or surprised.

'No, I asked Dr Fonseka next door to spy on you. Ayah is a free agent, she spies on everyone and helps everyone,' he replied, watching her face carefully.

'I am well, mama. Honestly. I miss her terribly, and Priya too. I feel a pain…' her hand rested on her heart, then moved down to her belly. 'An ache, a constant ache – what can I say?' Her voice trailed away, she looked at him hopelessly.

'You can say that you want her back – you can ask for her back, mahal,' he answered softly. He had said it finally. He had betrayed one child's needs to meet another's.

She shook her head and in spite of himself, he felt relieved.

✿

Nala sat on the steps of the back verandah. Her hips still ached from the plane journey. Perhaps they just ached from age, she was almost sixty-years-old although Dolly Fonseka said she still looked as young as the day they moved in. Rajan suggested Dolly see Dr Puvanachandra, the head of ophthalmology at Colombo General.

Dhara sat on the step below her, and leaned into her arms.

'Mahal, I'm quite sure you don't have lice,' Nala said, running her fingers through Dhara's thick curls.

'You're probably right mami, but check anyway. You know what Rajan mama says about cleanliness.'

She laughed and ran the comb slowly through the younger woman's hair. Dhara never wore it out in public, always plaiting it or tying it into a demure bun at the nape of her neck. Now unfurled, it spilled around her shoulders. Nala poured warm sesame oil slowly onto her head and massaged her. Dhara's hair was thick but there were chunks missing, where it had been ripped out, not from the root but with the scalp.

Dhara sighed deeply. 'I've been thinking a lot about Smrithi and Priya, mami,' she said without turning around.

'They think about you all the time. They always talk about you. Priya misses you very much.'

'I know. I miss her too. I miss all of them. I've been thinking,' she hesitated. 'How are they?'

Nala arranged Dhara's hair to cover the barren, scarred skin. 'They are happy, mahal. They are very happy there. Vivek will start high school next year and Smrithi, she's the cheeky one, always testing Priya and charming Siva. They're all very happy,' she repeated. What more could she say?

'She's the same age as I was, when I came to live with you. I realised that the other day. I wanted to buy anklets for her. I found such a dainty pair, with small bells. I think Smrithi would like them. I was thinking – I only lived with my parents for eight years, but by then, they were my parents and even though I loved you and Rajan mama for three decades afterwards, I still – I still loved them more.'

She turned to look at Nala. 'Do you think those eight years – the first eight years – were what made me theirs and not yours?' she asked.

Nala's heart pounded. She knew the answer to that question – Dhara belonged to her parents because she was born of them, just as Priya and Nandan belonged to her more deeply than Dhara, as much as she had tried to love this child as her own.

Which was why she lied.

'Yes, mahal, I think the relationship a child has with their first parent, bonds them to that parent forever. It can't be broken or replaced. It shouldn't be broken...for the child's sake,' she added. She prayed silently for forgiveness. God would understand, surely He would agree it was best to leave things as they were. How would hurting Smrithi and Priya help them, or Dhara? No-one should have to feel the loss of a child. She remembered it too well.

'I understand,' Dhara said, turning back, her shoulders lower. 'Will you give the anklets to Smrithi for me when you go back? I bought comic books for Vivek; Priya says he's always reading. What do you think?' she asked sadly.

'I think you're a wonderful mami, Dhara.'

'I had a wonderful mami to teach me,' the younger woman rested her head on Nala's knees and Nala spread her hair out in the sunshine.

The man set his father down gently on the divan. Through the wrinkled gourd of his face, he smiled at her, toothless. His body had atrophied on his once-broad frame, and his frame had bent over itself. He looked like a crumpled paper bag. Nala could not remember a time when Thiru had not been strong.

For much of his life, he had pulled a cart with an icebox of meat, through the streets of Colombo. When mass refrigeration and butchers put him out of business, he and his two sons found work, digging roads and drainage between Colombo and the shining hotels that sprouted along the coast.

After the '83 riots, Thiru and his family escaped with the cinders of their lives. He lost his daughter-in-law and three grandchildren. They had been trapped and slaughtered in their home in Dematagoda. It had taken several knife strokes from unpractised hands. Thiru had always shown the animals at the abattoir the mercy of skill, speed and precision. His grandchildren were shown no such mercy.

What was left of the family went back to their village in the east. They worked on banana plantations; long days of hacking through the tough, sticky harvest that fought back against the rhythm of their scythes. Together, father and sons hoisted the heavy stems onto their shoulders, the bananas clustered in tiers, hanging like a chandelier of leathery, yellow fingers. Each stem weighed as much as a goat and had to be carried, unblemished, back along the dirt tracks of the plantation, to the waiting trucks. They were strong and hard workers, Thiru and his sons.

'Was it difficult for you to come here?' Nala asked, placing a cup of sugary, milky tea in the old man's hands.

'Thank you Amma,' he smiled again. 'It was no trouble,' he lied. 'My youngest son, Senthan brought me here. You won't remember him, but sometimes he used to do my deliveries.'

'I remember him. Ayah said you loved her mothahams the most,' she replied.

'Thank you Aunty, I did. Your Ayah was very kind to us. She told us you were back in Colombo,' said the son. He looked at his father uncertainly.

'Doctor is not here at the moment. He's visiting his old colleagues at the hospital. I'm sure he's sneaking in a few consultations as well. He would have liked to have met you too,' Nala said.

'Doctor is very busy, Amma. I've come to ask you for something,' the old man looked down at his hands, spindly fingers wrapped tightly around the teacup. He motioned to his son who took the cup from him. He put his hands together. His fingers wouldn't straighten so he looked like he was cupping his hands. Nala knew what he was doing and she shook her head at him.

'There's no need, Iyah,' she said respectfully. 'How can I help you?'

'Ayah says you need a houseboy, to help your relatives who still live here. Please take my son, take Senthan. He can cook, clean and drive. He will watch over the family and he will never steal from you, on my life.'

Nala looked at the younger man closely for the first time. 'Senthan, you are too old to be a houseboy, don't you think? You must be forty plus?' she asked.

'I am forty-five-years-old Amma, but I can work like a young man,' he replied, raising his head proudly but gently.

Thiru continued talking. 'I will die a labourer. My oldest son will die a labourer. Perhaps we will all die in the war, the fighting has spread to the east now. The plantations are being abandoned. But my grandchildren will study. They will leave this island. Senthan can earn here for them, he can help them more than I could.'

Senthan brought out a parcel from a plastic bag on his lap. 'I brought you something Amma, I hope you don't mind. Ayah taught me how to make it once. Hers are still better.' He opened the sweaty newspaper wrapping, revealing ten perfectly formed dumplings, their tawny cheeks pressed against each other. Nala leant forward and inhaled. The palm sugar, coconut and green gram pulp inside made her mouth water.

Ayah had told her Thiru's story, and his loss. She thought Thiru would ask her for money. Ayah was a sharp judge of character and the house needed the presence of a strong man. Old Mr Perera was no more able to ward off would-be-thieves than Rajan. At best, her husband could have bored intruders with his exhaustive knowledge of acoustic schwannomas of the vestibular cochlear nerve.

She looked at Senthan again. He was burnt dark by the sun, although his face was etched with more than just age and hard work. He was from a different caste but Nala realised she could no longer tell caste or class as easily as she once could. Everyone looked degraded by the conflict, no matter which caste or class they had been born into.

Nala was a Vellala, from the land-owning caste. Her family hadn't held farmland for generations but by the lottery of birth, her caste had more currency than Thiru's. They were the same but different. Mohan said there weren't enough Tamils in Ceylon for the Vellalas to keep differentiating and discriminating.

He was right. War had no such bigotries. It didn't care that some Tamils had been brought by the British to pick tea or that others were Muslim. War didn't ask about the pedigree of your Tamil origin before it took your life. And it certainly didn't ask if you liked to build things or had a cousin-sister who loved you or a daughter who needed you.

Senthan reached forward to offer her the food and she could see scars all along his forearm: fresh burns. Catching her stare, he quickly turned his arm over. They all had their scars, she thought, pulling reflexively at her sari pallu: some were more recent than others, some were more healed than others, but none were more important than others.

She knew she ought to wait for Rajan to return from work. He would need to agree to hire Senthan.

'I'll talk to Doctor, Iyah,' she said, picking up a mothaham and holding out the packet towards the old man. 'I'm sure he'll say yes.'

15

Priya reached the phone on its fifth ring. 'Hello, hello?' she answered, breathless.

There was no sound on the other end of the line.

'Hello?' she asked again, slipping her handbag off her shoulder and dropping the car keys onto the side table. It was carved sandalwood, a gift from her parents. She was about to hang up when a man spoke.

'We'll burn you all out,' he rasped.

'What?' she heard him but didn't know what to say.

Silence. As though words were being arranged to give voice to hatred so deep it could not be fully articulated.

Silence and then the voice.

'We'll burn you all. You think we only hunt tigers in the jungle? We hunt them here too. We know who you are and what you're doing.' The floating voice had found its rhythm and poetry now, he didn't falter.

'We'll find you and we'll skin your tiger stripes from your body. You and your family, we're watching and we're waiting. Tigers are not the only ones hiding in the jungle. Tell your husband we called.'

'Guna?' she asked.

Silence.

'Gunatilake? Is that you?' she asked again, her voice shaking. Guna's family and hers had been friends in Sydney for years before the troubles started.

Until now.

The phone clicked off. All she could hear was the sound of her own short, panicked breathing. Her jaws were fused together. She wanted to open her mouth, to breathe better, to speak, to cry, but the muscles of her mouth wouldn't work. She held the wall and lowered herself to the tiled floor. An apricot colour with undertones of fawn: autumnal, she had read about it in House & Garden.

She closed her eyes and tried to concentrate on the tiles.

A man in a khaki brown uniform appeared, then another and another and another until she was surrounded.

I told you, I told you what happens when you get involved, she said to Siva.

It wasn't her they had come for, it was him with all his stupid letters to politicians, endless petitions, protests outside the high commission and even more letters. For every letter he wrote, tens of thousands and then hundreds of thousands were displaced in the north and east. *Why*, she asked him, *why? There is nothing you can do for them.*

I can't believe that, he said, handing her a bundle. Post them please cunju, he asked nicely. He always asked nicely.

Dhara said sometimes the men asked nicely too. Please take off your clothes. Please don't scream. Please don't move your legs while we insert this pipe, you see we can thread barbed wire into it and when we remove the pipe the wire remains and we can pull the wire out slowly or quickly or any speed we feel like. Or any speed you feel like if you ask nicely.

Priya thought of Dhara and Siva and the places men in khaki brown uniforms took people like them, like us, like her to. Khaki, was that autumnal too?

She held onto the heavy legs of the side table. The wood was still fragrant. Sandalwood was hard and strong, but soft to the touch. It smelled like temples, the burning of incense, the sound of prayer, warm sunlight on cool stone. She pressed her face against the wood and let its smell fill her lungs. The temple was inside her, helping her breathe, helping her stand, helping her move forward.

The calls stopped as suddenly as they had begun. She fought with Siva, arguing once again that his involvement made it impossible for them to return to Colombo, to Dhara. He declared he would never return until their people had their own homeland.

'Well then, I guess we are never going back,' she said with more sadness than malice as she gathered the school bags. 'I'll see you at the surgery after the school run.'

✿

Priya pulled over, turned off the engine and opened the car window. She leaned back in her seat. It was 9:23am. The small park was empty at this time. Her children were at school.

A majestic gum tree towered over the banksias and wattles that lined the boundary. When the wind blew, sunlight dappled and danced between the leaves, as though refracted through a crystal. The marbled white-grey trunk was muscular yet lean. Someone, a caretaker perhaps, had planted a tapestry of colour around it. Some people could make things grow.

Green fingers, the Australians called it.

Archi's fingers, Nala called it.

Slowly the birds descended. She didn't know if they were a flock or a family, the same birds or different ones each time. She'd never noticed birds in Sri Lanka but here she noticed them everywhere, especially in this place where she could watch and think and be. The rainbow lorikeet. Rainbow. Lorikeet. It was a perfect name. Like Vivek or Smrithi. Their name told you exactly who they were. You could close your eyes, say their name, and see them in your mind. You could call them to you and they would come. Like Dhara.

Dhara, she called silently.

Priya saw the iridescent blue and jungle green. She saw the ruffled chest of an orange sun bleeding into a yellow sky. Wings opened and a burst of red took flight. Colour uncontained. Flight with no path foretold. She soared freely, following the rainbow and herself. She rested, breathless in the hollow of a gum. She wasn't a daughter or a wife or a doctor or a mother. She was no-one to anyone. She was nothing and she was everything. Whatever she was, it was for herself.

'Rainbow lorikeets mate for life,' Vivek once told her. 'They are always in pairs. A husband and a wife,' he said.

'A mummy and a daddy,' Smrithi added.

'No, not to me,' Priya said.

'Then what?' they asked, their small faces turned towards the sun, towards her. She looked up and watched the rainbow glide between the trees.

'A sister and a sister of course,' she said smiling.

It was 9:38am. Siva was expecting her. She started the car again.

'Leisure in the age of technology,' Vivek read from the Expo 88 brochure, deepening his voice. 'It's educational. Expo is about cultures around the world. Multiculturalism is a wonderful thing children; we shouldn't be afraid to embrace new cultures and new experiences,' he said, mimicking his father's accent. 'As long as we don't marry them of course.'

'That's enough, mahan,' Priya cautioned him turning away so he couldn't see her smile. Nala laughed.

'Ammamma, Amma, there are so many stalls, you wouldn't believe it!' Smrithi came running back, with Siva shouting at her to wait for him. 'There's food from Italy and Greece and Singapore and Thailand and –' Smrithi paused to check her map of World food, 'there's even a pavilion from Sri Lanka, here,' she said pointing to a red circle on the paper.

Priya was exhausted and hungry. She'd been queuing at the Japanese Pavilion for over an hour because Vivek wanted to see the enormous television and robots. At the words 'Sri Lanka', she looked up hopefully at Siva who looked away.

'Cunju?' she asked her husband.

'There's a pavilion – it's obviously sponsored by the Sri Lankan government. There's nothing in it about the troubles,' Siva replied.

'Did you go in?' Nala asked, surprised. His protest against the war was multi-pronged. He boycotted functions held by the Sri

Lankan High Commission, cricket and anything that could be seen as supporting the Sri Lankan government, however tangentially related.

'No, I had a quick look from the outside. The staff were all speaking Sinhalese. It's just a big tourist advertisement for the country. Come to Sri Lanka,' he mocked, 'elephant rides down south and genocide up north.' Vivek rolled his eyes and Priya shushed him.

'Not here Siva,' she said, looking around to make sure no-one heard him. 'It's supposed to be a big tourist advertisement, all the countries are doing it. What food are they selling?' she asked.

'It doesn't matter. I'm not giving my money to them. Absolutely not, not one cent!' he said.

It was Priya's turn to roll her eyes. 'What food?'

'Hoppers and gothamba roti, from what I could smell.'

She loved hoppers. The thought of the soft, crisp coconut milk pancake made her mouth water. She liked to melt a teaspoon of palm sugar in its moist centre. The queue had barely moved; there was enough time for her to buy the family lunch while Siva stayed with the children. She could eat her hoppers before she'd even left the Sri Lankan pavilion and buy a decoy meal from somewhere else for her pointlessly militant husband.

'I'll get us lunch, you stay here. What would you like cunju – Thai food?' she asked, avoiding eye contact with him.

'I'll help you mahal,' Nala said, also avoiding eye contact.

Siva watched his wife and mother-in-law licking their lips. 'I'll have whatever you're having,' he replied as the children laughed knowingly.

The invitation made her tear the cuticles off her nails A mother-daughter afternoon tea organised by one of Smrithi's friends. Everyone was supposed to bring a plate and the little girls and their mothers would spend the afternoon together.

'Please don't make curried fish patties, Amma. Cream cheese on crackers would be great,' Smrithi suggested.

Cream cheese on crackers? White people missed out on so much, she would never understand it. She looked at the invitation again.

It was a pool party.

'Enough said,' said Malathy.

'More than enough said,' said Shanthi.

'What is wrong with these people?' asked Ranji. 'Why would you want to get darker or wet? There's a reason Sri Lankans don't swim, and we're *islanders*. Do you even have swimmers?'

She didn't have swimmers, she didn't know how to swim and she certainly didn't want to be semi-naked in front of semi-strangers. She scrolled through her list of plausible excuses.

'Smrithi, I just don't think I can make it. I'm running a breast cancer screening clinic…' The clinic was next month.

She expected Smrithi to cry but instead all she said was, 'I'm never allowed to do anything.'

'I'll take her, mahal,' Nala stepped in. 'It'll be fun.'

When Priya arrived to pick them up after the party, she found her sixty-year-old mother in the shallow end with everyone. Nala had stripped off her sari and stood in the pool, wearing only her sari blouse and her full-length cotton underskirt. Her corrugated skin glistened in the water.

'What are you doing?' she hissed while trying to smile at the hostess. She wasn't sure if she should smile apologetically or nonchalantly, her embarrassment just distorted her face into a look of pain.

'Have you lost your mind? Is the heat affecting you?' she asked under her breath as Nala dried herself and quickly draped her sari over her damp underclothes.

'Smrithi asked me to swim with her. The other mothers were doing it and I didn't want her to feel left out. So I got in,' Nala replied casually.

'Like that?' she asked incredulously.

'Like what?' Nala asked.

'Like that – in your underskirt and sari blouse?'

'Yes of course. I don't have a swimming costume. I can't even swim. I nearly drowned once you know. Archi said it was a small wave but it felt very big to me. Mohan rescued me. The swimming pool is beautiful though, much safer than the ocean and all the other mothers were very impressed,' Nala laughed.

'My Appa used to say, 'If you swim, swim together. If you sink, sink together.' He was a very wise man. You should go with Smrithi next time, she'd prefer to have you.'

'Not now, Amma,' Priya said brusquely. She ignored Nala's hurt look and started the car. In the rear-view mirror she watched her daughter help her mother dry and re-plait her hair. They laughed and chatted conspiratorially about the afternoon.

She drove them home in silence.

Priya locked the changing room door, her face flaming with embarrassment. She hung up the swimming costumes and sat on the small bench. It was a stupid idea. She eyed the lycra sheath suspiciously. In Sri Lanka she'd only ever waded in the shallow waters of Mt Lavinia beach with Dhara. If they wandered out too far, Nala would call, pulling them back to the beach like an anxious tide.

As she pulled on a costume and adjusted it around her, she reconsidered. It was hideously ill-fitting, unless it was on backwards? No, it was on the right way, just not designed the right way for her forty-year-old form. If only Dhara could see her now, she laughed. She peeled the lycra off, tried another one, and yet another.

'Are you ok madam, can I help you?' the David Jones attendant asked through the door.

'No, thank you, I'm still trying these. I'll be out in a minute,' she replied. The costumes looked so much better on the mannequins. She couldn't wear any of them. She couldn't even get out of the last one she tried. Trapped in the changing room, surrounded by mirrors, she was unable to escape her growing discomfort. Everywhere she looked she could see herself: out of place.

'Try this one,' a freckled hand emerged from underneath the door.

'What?' she blushed again. She should have brought Shiranthi with her, she knew all the fashions.

'Try this one,' the hand shook the costume at her. 'It's nicer. The other ones were invented to make you look bad. Try this.'

'Thank you.' She knew she must have seemed ridiculous after an hour of sorting through hangers and another half hour of hiding in the changing room. She tried on the new costume. It was higher at the neck and lower at the groin, with a pretty frill around the buttocks. It was suitably modest.

The woman spoke again, 'Just take it before you lose your nerve. No-one looks good in a swimming costume except Olivia Newton-John, and even she looks better in leg warmers.'

Priya emerged from the room. 'Thank you for that. I'm just not sure. That one was definitely better.'

The attendant looked at her. 'You have such beautiful skin,' she said.

'What?'

'You have beautiful skin. Like caramel. My friends and I would kill for skin like yours.'

Priya didn't want to disappoint her daughter again. She remembered her mother emerging from the pool, her underskirt clinging to her curvaceous body. Nala laughed as she stumbled and almost fell back in with Smrithi, who giggled at her side and dragged her out.

It was funny. Dhara would find it funny too. She must remember to tell her.

'I'll take these swimmers. Thank you very much for your help,' she said, before she could change her mind.

Priya stirred the chillied chickpeas, scraping the onions from the base of the pan. Mustard seeds popped and spat angrily at her. She was sick of fighting: with Smrithi, with Nala, sometimes even with Siva. It was draining her. She couldn't believe what she was hearing.

'Don't force Smrithi to do this, mahal, it's not that important,' Nala said. 'Even Tamils in Sri Lanka don't have the ceremony. They're changing, leaving some traditions behind.'

'Leave it behind? You forced me. Of course the ritual is important. This is Smrithi's *Samathia Chadangu*, her age attainment ceremony.'

'I know. Many rituals are important, but rituals, like people need to evolve. You have to change mahal, we did.'

Vivek caught a chickpea as it flew out of the pan, 'The purpose of the ceremony is to tell the community that Smrithi has started menstruating; that she can have children and she's ready for marriage. It's disgusting, Amma.'

'Stay out of this mahan, this is between Ammamma and myself,' Priya snapped at her sixteen-year-old son. She turned to face her mother.

'You didn't change Amma, you've never had to. If we let this tradition go, what's next? We do these traditions to remind ourselves – to remind the children – who they are and where they've come from.'

'Mahal,' Nala took the spatula from Priya and gently nudged her aside. 'Your children will always know who they are and where they've come from.'

Did her mother realise what she had just said – did Smrithi know who she was or where she'd come from? The guilt made her stomach churn; the irony of her mother's statement made her furious.

'You don't know what you're talking about Amma,' she hissed. 'I'm trying to teach her the rules. I mean the rituals. I'm trying to raise her properly. The way…I'm supposed to.' The way Dhara would.

'You are raising her properly. You can let go of some of our traditions and even some of our values, without losing your children.'

Nala tasted the curry and smiled.

'It's perfect, I don't know how you do it.' She shook her head. Priya reclaimed her spatula.

'You don't know what it's like here, Amma. Every day she's asking me about movies and sleepovers and discos and camps.'

Every day I have to decide what's right for Smrithi, she thought to herself. What was right for her daughter? She felt a boundary inch its way inward. She shook her head, trying to banish the thought.

'Soon there'll be boys and maybe drinking and then who knows what these white children do?' she asked Nala. 'I hate being the one that says no but I have to do it.'

'No, you have to stop stopping them. You'll only push them towards the things you're trying to protect them from. You have to let some things go –'

'We let go of our home, Amma. I don't regret that, the way you do. I am happy I'm here, I don't regret that for a moment. But I can't let go of everything. You have no idea what my life is like. I'm working and raising my children without the back-up of an Ayah or an entourage. I'm exhausted from it all. Most of all, I am exhausted from being different. You've never had to live in a place where you're different, where you are the 'other'. You don't know what it's like,' she repeated.

'I don't know what it's like?' Nala echoed. 'I spent the best years of my life being forced to the edge of my own country. I was a fool and didn't see it happening. Your Appa and I – we were the 'other' and it got so awful we had to leave. But I'm here now and I'm learning from so many different others. Being *extremely* Tamil won't protect the children, mahal. I think being extremely comfortable about who you are might help them though. Our culture should enhance your life, not limit it.'

Priya refused to look at Nala. Dhara was the comfortable one.

'It's too late now anyway. I've paid for the Bowling Club already and the caterers. One-hundred-and-seventy people have said they're coming. What am I going to do with thirty litres of frozen aubergine curry?'

She turned the cooker off. 'I'm done,' she said to no-one in particular. She didn't know what else to say – she wanted Smrithi to have her age attainment ceremony, the way she and Dhara had. She just couldn't explain why, to her mother and especially not to her daughter.

✿

That night, Priya called her sister.

'How are you acca?' Dhara asked.

'Tired.'

'The *Samathia Chadangu*?' Dhara asked nervously about the ceremony. 'How is the vote?'

'Split – Nala *against*; Smrithi *against*. Siva and me – *for*. You?' she asked Dhara.

'I'm abstaining on the grounds of conflict of interest. I agree with Nala mami but I understand what you want, acca,' she answered.

'Thank you. I've decided to go with the political strategy of my birthplace and ignore the democratic process in favour of nepotism, bribery and corruption,' Priya replied, laughing wearily. 'I'm going to ask you to convince her and if that doesn't work, I'll pay her off by secretly taking her to see *Pretty Woman*. Apparently it's a romantic comedy about a prostitute – can you imagine?'

'I heard.' Dhara replied, laughing hard. 'Acca, you are a benevolently evil genius.'

☼

The next day, Dhara called, ready with a pre-prepared and hastily rehearsed talk.

'Amma told you to call me, didn't she?' Smrithi accused her.

'No mahal, we speak every Friday.'

'It's Saturday,' Smrithi replied.

'Sometimes we speak on Saturday too,' Dhara laughed.

'It's embarrassing Dhara mami, and humiliating. I can't do it. I have to dress up in a sari – they'll make me look like a bride. I'm only thirteen-years-old. There'll be a hundred people watching me.'

'They're there to bless you mahal. It's an important tradition,' she replied.

'Amma's such a hypocrite, mami. You know we've been quietly eating beef burgers for years, right? That's not very traditional.'

'No it's not very traditional, but a Sri Lankan mother over-feeding her children is a far more deeply entrenched and over-riding tradition. You'll understand that when you have your own children and you can't help your genetic imperative to put high protein food in their mouths. The age attainment ceremony is different.'

'It's to let people know I'm ready for marriage and I won't do it.'

'It's not, mahal. Well it is, I mean, it was,' Dhara faltered, trying to remember what she was supposed to say. 'The ceremony is also to bless you. Your grandmother will use the paddy rice that her mother gave her. We want you to have a full life, Smrithi, like Amma and Ammamma.'

'You mean a full married life,' Smrithi retorted.

'Yes, darling, a full married life, with an abundance of happiness and children. I wish I could be there with you, mahal, to help you understand and to bless you too.'

'But you had the ceremony and you're not married.'

'That's right, I'm not. But I want all of those things for you Smrithi. I pray for them every day. I imagine a future for you that is so much richer than my own life.'

Dhara stopped for a moment. She took a deep breath and controlled the tremor in her voice.

'Mahal, are you listening to me?' she asked.

'I am. I'm listening,' Smrithi replied quietly.

Dhara's voice softened. 'Your mother has asked you to have the ceremony because changing from a girl to a woman means something. It doesn't mean what it used to, but it still means something special. In years to come, your body will create life and you will look back on this change – this gift – and you will want to thank God for it.

'Your Amma wants to honour that gift. Marriage and the rituals of family life don't mean anything to you now, but when you get older they will; and when you have your own children, God willing, they will mean even more to you.'

Smrithi finally agreed.

16

VANNI REGION,
NORTHERN SRI LANKA, 1990

On the day before Smrithi's *Samathia Chadangu*, Dhara took the train
to Vavuniya, the last town controlled by the army. She kept her promise
to Nala and never went back to Jaffna. But every month, she went as far
north as the army checkpoints allowed her.

'I'm training medical students at the District Hospital,' she told the
soldiers in Sinhalese at the first checkpoint. At the last checkpoint she
spoke in Tamil to the soldiers from the Indian Peace Keeping Force.
Her hand strayed to the neckline of her churidah blouse to check the
buttons.

The Indian Army had negotiated a doomed peace accord. The Tigers
would not lay down their arms. The Sri Lankan Army stepped back
and moved to crush a Sinhala rebellion in the south. It relinquished the
north to the Indians and rape, torture and execution simply became
words, buried in the mass graves of their victims.

From Vavuniya station she took an auto to the hospital. A colleague
there had provided her with papers and a regular alibi. She checked-in
and hours later, casually walked out. She was met by the boys. They
travelled by car on the narrow, dirt back roads. She kept the window
down and tapped nervously on the car door.

They switched vehicles twice and continued on foot for hours. The
first few times she did this were exhausting. Later, she grew used to
it. She learnt to wear long-sleeved clothing and thick-soled boots. She
could cope with heat but not mosquitoes or infected cuts.

The jungle dripped darkness. Plants entwined with no beginning and
no end. Hard hues of green and brown were peppered with flourishes
of magenta, pink and yellow; tissue-paper petals fell softly around her.
Palmyra trees rose from the earth like fortress walls. She was unsure

whom they were protecting. She looked up into the camouflage of the tangled canopy above. The only sound was the syncopated harmony of insects and birds; and the disharmony of approaching gunfire. The jungle was ageless and implacable. It waited patiently to receive the dead.

At the camp, Dhara checked the names of the *Maaveerer* first, the martyrs list. Copies were made and sent to each camp as often as possible. It was incomplete, but it was the best they could do. She scrolled quickly for Ahilan and others she knew – and relaxed when she couldn't find their names.

She looked around the operating tent. It was as clean as it could be: bloodied gauze kits, stolen theatre sheets, makeshift swabs, bandages and empty IV and blood packs piled in the corners. The operating table had once been a kitchen table; its orange formica laminate chipped and peeled at the edges, like skin that had been in the sun too long. It sat in the centre of the tent, a citrus fruit that had bloomed out of season.

Around it was a jumble sale of instruments: some stolen and some fashioned out of anything they could get their hands on. Tourniquets from leather shoelaces and plaited strips of silk saris. The better the quality of silk, the stronger the tourniquet. A selection of knives from farmers and wives and fishermen; disinfected and honed to give a degree of surgical precision, alongside stolen scalpels. The instruments were sterilised in alcohol or boiled whenever possible. It was not often possible.

Bullets and shrapnel were recycled; given a second life to take a second life. Blood was recycled; collected and strained through boiled saris before being transfused back into the body. Needles were recycled; most importantly so that anaesthetics could be injected. Sometimes she felt she was recycled.

The first incision needs to be confident and slow.

Blood spurted in arcs, erratic yet graceful; like a monochrome rainbow; its purple-red warm as it hit her face. She clamped the artery and scooped pooling blood out with the cup of her hand. A nurse, no more than a girl, wiped her eyes. She blinked through the haze. The texture of flesh never failed to surprise her. It was so tender. She could pull it away with her fingers. How imperfectly we are made; how fragile we are, she thought. Men, women and children – they were all the same. They all screamed, they all called for their mothers. Meat from a bone; great chunks of it lay at her feet. Sacks used to store rice and vegetables were saved and as the ground became slathered in blood, a nurse dropped them onto the floor. Dhara stepped on re-used sacks and continued her work.

She amputated, clamped, sewed and cauterised. She lanced and helped light into infected darkness when she had finally run out of antibiotics. She tried to plug the holes. Blood beaded, it seeped, and it surged. The body became a sieve.

Bone was the hardest. It required tools she didn't always have. She needed three men to hold down one; even children struggled and bucked and kicked with what limbs remained, begging her to stop, begging her to let them be. She came to hate bone.

At the end of each day she wiped the table down. The slurry. What was she to do with that? Cleanliness is next to Godliness, Rajan mama said. God didn't watch over this hospital.

She looked at her hands – they felt strange after being in surgical gloves for so long – pale, as though they needed to breathe. She stretched her fingers, checking the segments and joints of each, rubbing the calluses that charted almost two decades of surgery. *Someone else's life in your hands*, she remembered. The calluses made her hands look old before their time.

'Join us Dhara,' the young doctor urged. 'Leave Colombo for good. We need you here.' He was in charge of training in the Tigers' medical units.

'No. I'm more useful to you at Colombo General. You know that already – how else will you access what you need?'

She could have moved closer, to Vavuniya or even Kilinochi Hospital further north. She could have disappeared forever into the false night of the dark jungle, into a training camp or a medical unit or an armed unit. She was tied to them, to the struggle.

But something deeper kept calling her back to the sun. She craved its warmth. She turned her face to the sky each morning, eyes closed, head back, palms folded. The demons were only afraid of sunlight. She wouldn't stray too far from it, or the promise of a new day; another day with Smrithi.

'What do you need from me this time?' she asked the doctor.

Together they took an inventory – anaesthetics, antibiotics, blood packs, IV packs and sutures were prioritised. They made arrangements for the passage of supplies – routes, couriers and drop-off points changed constantly. Dhara never carried anything herself; just the medical bag Rajan had given her when she graduated. And in her pocket, a needle and thread.

'I've scheduled a few extra operations for you this weekend, I hope that's ok?' the man asked. He held his clipboard, as though ready for a normal ward round.

'That's fine. I can stay for a week. Ask them to be scrubbed and ready at six o'clock tomorrow morning. It's too dark now to teach properly.'

Tomorrow her family would bless Smrithi's life as a woman.

Dhara remembered the first time.

It was so many years ago. She took Ahilan's hand and showed him the garden. She tended it carefully every day. The branches of the peppercorn tree. Its fruit had slowly aged from green to black. She let him trace its latticed growth across her breast. It had formed the leaf of an anthurium, indigo and shiny. And before that the leaf of a mango. She led him down to the clusters of pink hibiscus; unnaturally sharp but beautiful. They had long since died. The keloid reminded her of where they were buried. The once hot fingers of the fern tree spread across her back. They soothed her now with their touch, like the neem oil Nala had applied. And the orchid. Its purple heart had been carved out with a broken bottle.

She remembered the last time.

It was only months after the first time. Ahilan stopped and looked at her.

'I'm hurting you,' he pulled out of her slowly and rolled over onto his side.

'I'm sorry,' she said again. I am so sorry.

'Please, don't. I'm sorry,' he said gently. She took his hand and pulled his arm around her. She fit herself into the curve of his body.

'I love the smell of your hair. I'll remember it forever,' he said, inhaling deeply.

'I hope so, it smells like chicken curry tonight, and you won't get that where you're going.'

'Stop it,' he laughed and tickled her. 'I would marry you if they let us. I feel married to you already. It's just that –'

'I know. You're married to the cause,' she replied.

'Stop it,' he tickled her again. 'This is very serious. If I have a wife and children, I wouldn't be able to…you know.'

'I know,' you wouldn't be able to die.

She loved him but didn't feel married to him. Like Ahilan, she had given up marriage and the rituals of family life. She slept peacefully in his arms that last night; it was enough.

She looked at her watch again. It would be morning soon in Australia. Priya and the children would be waking up and Smrithi would have to wear her sari. Nala would drape it for her, as she had for them. Priya would take the gold bangles from her own wrist and put them on Smrithi's small arms. Dhara couldn't sleep.

✿

Dhara swung hard at the ball and missed again. The boy laughed as he ran after it. He was conducting his batting drills on a makeshift pitch, where the grass was only a little more barren than the small playing field around it. The land had been cleared for training.

'Acca, don't whack the ball. Watch it closely,' he instructed wisely. Niranjan, or Niri, as he was called at the camp, was sixteen years old. He was small and seemed much younger.

'Tendulkar only whacks when he knows he can control the ball – it is a controlled whack, not a wild whack, acca.' He spat on the ball as he walked back up the pitch, rubbing it vigorously, leaving brown streaks on his clean shorts. His clothes were too big for him.

'You remember I'm not Tendulkar, right?' she asked as he stamped his foot, like a miniature tusker.

'Om, om,' he shouted back, nodding his head sideways, before running as fast as he could. The ball left his hand high and she ducked instinctively as it bounced short and spun towards her head.

'I thought you were bowling to me, not *at* me!' she shouted, dropping her bat and chasing the bowler. Niri ran, laughing as she caught him and wrestled him into a quick embrace. They both collapsed on the dusty field and looked up at the early evening sky.

'You should have gone to watch him play,' he reprimanded her again. 'If I lived in Colombo, I would go to watch cricket every day. I would wait by the gate and shake his hand as he left the field. I would ask him to sign my bat, and my shirt, and my school books. I would ask him to sign everything I owned.'

She turned her head and looked at him as he looked at the sky but only saw Sachin Tendulkar. On this trip, she had brought him and his friends the Kookaburra bats that Nala had sent from Sydney. He had hugged her tightly before remembering himself and giving her a more formal 'Thank you acca.' He was inseparable from his bat, except when he allowed her to use it against his impressive bowling skills.

Tendulkar, the Little Master, had scored his first century in a one-day international game in Colombo last week. He had played at the Premadasa Stadium, which had recently been renamed in honour of the assassinated president. Tendulkar was only twenty-one. By Niri's age, Tendulkar had already been identified as a prodigy and was playing professionally. Niri often sighed when he talked about his hero, rattling off his biography and batting stats as though they were his own.

The boy woke up every morning at five o'clock with his friends. After a gruelling ninety minutes of warm-up exercises, the children had breakfast, morning ablutions and two hours of lessons. This was followed by more skills training until lunchtime. The mid-day meal was served in a mess hall, comprised of a green and brown tarpaulin hoisted over several portable gas cookers. The children sat on the ground and ate from banana leaves. When the afternoon heat was unbearable, they were given more training challenges to complete. The coaches' philosophy was that the children should learn to perform properly under the harshest of circumstances. They were given an hour of rest time before dinner, which Niri used to play more cricket with his friends.

After dinner, the children had history classes followed by bedtime. They followed a strict timetable without complaint and during the day, they embraced the discipline and commitment that was expected of them. Dhara heard crying at night in the dormitory tents but she was not allowed to enter or talk to any of the children. Some of them had nightmares, like her.

The bell sounded for dinner and he jumped up from the ground.

'Niri, Niri – before you go – I wanted to ask you something,' she hesitated, making sure no-one was listening. 'Are you happy here, darling?'

'Happy?' he looked at her and at the mess hall where all of his friends were gathering. He never spoke about his parents or siblings or life before the LTTE camp.

'Yes of course I'm happy! Tendulkar just scored a century!' he said as he ran off with his bat, hitting an imaginary six after six, bowled by an imaginary bowler before him.

☼

Happiness. She wondered how people could feel happiness at the death of others. She didn't feel it. She had tried. She imagined men in the police station, she saw them dismembered by her own hand. It was too much. She re-imagined it, using the hand of another. Something glacial stirred but it wasn't happiness.

She imagined men with their scythes, their iron bars, their toddy-glazed eyes and their yellow teeth. She had never seen the men who came for her father and crushed his skull and let his brain slip through his beautiful curls into the dirt. But she imagined them dead and something ancient stirred, but again, it wasn't happiness.

The human body has so many pieces. That was her first thought when she saw the photographs of Rajiv Gandhi, blown apart by a Tamil Tiger in south India. So many bloody pieces.

And so much jubilation. Men, usually serious, often morose in combat fatigues, ran around the camp smiling and hugging instead. A great day, they said clapping each other on the back, a great day for the struggle. Gandhi; handsome, elegant, patrician, western educated and eastern garbed. You can't win the electorate if you don't look a little *like* the electorate.

Now he doesn't look like the voters or his grandfather; the insides of a Gandhi look just like the insides of all the others he's killed, they said. The men hugged each other once more.

He won't be coming back here again, they said, laughing.

No, Dhara thought, and we won't be going back there again.

Tamil Nadu, the southern state, would no longer hide the Tigers, take their refugees, or provide them with supplies. They couldn't win this war without India. The Tigers had assassinated the grandson of the country's founding prime minister. India would never forgive.

'You don't look happy, acca, are you alright?' Niri asked.

'I'm just thinking, Niri, that's all.'

'About Rajiv Gandhi?'

'No, I was thinking that I won't be able to see my family. It won't be safe for them in Madras; or me – for a while anyway.' The birthplace on her passport said 'Jaffna'. She turned her face away from the boy for a moment. She wanted to scream. Every day she counted the days until her next trip to India. It was the clock that she set and reset her life by.

'Do you miss your family, acca?' he asked. Niri never talked about his. He called his fellow Tigers *brothers* and the nation he fought for *mother*.

'I do mahan, I miss them very much. And you? Do you miss your family?'

He looked around carefully. Everyone was distracted, jubilant, happy.

'Very much,' he answered quietly, for the first time.

When she slept at night, different images plagued her. There was the Demon King, a ten-headed monster who threw her to the ground and tore her open, over and over again. She knew how to kill this monster now. She had only to wake up and wait for the Sun God.

Tamaso maa, jyothir gamaya, she would repeat.

From darkness, lead me into light.

But in her dreams, there was also the man who came to the village, who talked about Tamil Eelam, their homeland. He went to schools, temples and churches. He went to houses and spoke to farmers and fishermen and teachers and clerks and promised them all that the fight – their homeland – was worth the sacrifice. Then he told them the price that each family must give them – give the struggle – one child. Only one child, he said, holding up a finger.

Only one child.

Niri had described how the man came for him. He was only a boy, the oldest of three brothers and a sister. His father had disappeared, taken away at an army checkpoint on his way back from work. No-one knew why and the children had stopped asking their mother when he would return.

The man stepped into their simple home and asked for payment. He looked at the boys and the little girl and knew he would be back to this house in time. Payment was only ever part payment.

Niri stood up. There was no point in fighting. Every family had to sacrifice. He didn't want to leave his Amma. How would she look after his siblings without him? He worked on their small plot of land, took their vegetables to the market, pumped water from the well and carried it for her. But still, it was better him than the others.

He took a step forward; he couldn't look back. The children were crying and holding onto his legs. His mother fell at the feet of the man and begged him for her son's life. She kissed his mud-caked boots and cried and pleaded.

'*Ende mahan, ende mahan*,' my son, my son, she wept.

The man had seen this so many times in so many villages. He had taken his own son from his own wife, given him a gun, trained him to use it and sent him on a mission which no-one survived. His wife had wept and begged and beat her chest as this woman was doing now. He kicked her away.

Niri put his hand out to stop the man. He bent down to his mother. She held him close. She crushed him to her chest with her eyes closed, as if that alone would make all this go away. He could feel the wild beating of her heart. The man reached for him. Niri shook his head, saying – one more moment, please give me one more moment. She clung to him, and finally let go.

Dhara didn't know how to kill that monster. She recited the rest of the prayer.

Mrtyor maa, amritam gamaya

From the fear of death, lead me to the knowledge of immortality.

Dhara didn't fear death.

They sat together, hidden in the forest floor. She held him like a child even though he had done things that even a grown man shouldn't be asked to do. She pushed her fingers through his matted hair, scattering lice. His body was covered in the bas relief of battles past. He carried almost as many scars as her now. He was only nineteen. She let him cry. She kissed the top of his head and rested her cheek there.

'I can't keep doing this acca,' he said. 'They held their children so tightly, these mothers – they wouldn't let go and we cut right through them and the children in their arms. We killed them all,' he said.

He re-lived the story. The Tigers moved at dawn. Their commander told them the villagers had refused to pay their protection taxes for three months. He said that the army was training the villagers. They were arming themselves.

It was a Muslim village. They were the descendants of Arab traders no less, but no more. Like the rest of their kind, they had chosen sides. They fought for the Government.

The Tigers fought for themselves.

The commander reminded them: they are not our people; they have no place in Eelam. Years ago they expelled eighty-thousand Muslims from the Jaffna peninsula, chasing them from their homes. The villagers fled to Puttalam in the west with the clothes they wore and the children they carried.

We are not of the same blood, he said.

The Tigers sat now in the long, dry grass of the east, watching the village of Palliyagodella. They moved as a pack. It was over quickly. The villagers were not soldiers. They could barely hold the guns they'd been given. If they could fire a gun, they didn't know how to reload one. They reached for their tools: their paddy scythes and yam hoes, anything they could grip, anything they could strike with, anything they could throw.

Don't waste your bullets, the commander shouted. They flipped their guns around, one fluid movement they'd made before, a mock military tattoo.

The villagers tried to run. Others reached for shelter; for each other.

When the Tigers killed their wives and children, the Muslims screamed and cried. In Tamil. No more, but no less.

Blood in the grass, on woven palm-leaf walls, on pressed dirt floors. It was as red as his own.

Niri sobbed. He remembered what he'd done. He wrapped his arms around her tightly while she called him mahan, softly. He closed his eyes but all he could see were the villagers.

✿

Faith had faltered for years. A wound that bled slowly, but not fatally. Then they brought him in and faith died. She didn't recognise him at first. It had been two years since he had disappeared into the jungle with his unit. The hair was longer. The skin was older. The body was cleaved, pieces missing.

'Nine lives of a tiger,' he spat out a laugh and clenched his jaw shut.

'Amazing he's lived so long,' they said. He was barely more than twenty-one.

The tiger had been trapped.

'Help him,' his men pleaded as they lowered him to the ground. His men were boys too.

'Hold him,' she whispered. She needed to shout above the cries and the chaos, but her voice hovered in her throat. 'Hold him, please,' she said again, this time loudly. He thrashed against them; against the pain. The bandages on his arm were blood-soaked. She had no new ones to offer him. She cut the shreds of clothing from his body, green and brown stripes fell away. She caught them.

'Hold this,' she whispered, stuffing his clothing into the place where his left arm had been. He screamed, his eyes widened, as if he couldn't believe what he was feeling.

'Hold it hard. Roll him,' she shouted. He was so thin, his body not much bigger than when she'd first met him.

She checked his back. It was gashed and bloody but nothing more fatal than the arm. She rolled him back. She put her hand in her pocket and pulled out the needle and thread. Rajan had told her to always carry it.

'Make sure the needle is already threaded because when you have to use it, you won't have time,' he said.

He was right.

'Hold him down,' she ordered. The boys cried as they each took a part of him and pressed down hard: a knee to his chest, arms to his shoulders, a whole body on his legs. He saw the needle. He jerked, a strangled sound escaped from his split lips.

She reached into the mangled remains of his bowling arm. The flesh hung in torn strips on the smashed bone. The connective tissue was a shamble of knotted ribbons. She pushed it aside with her fingers and the scalpel. She clamped the cluster of arteries that surged blood. She needed to close the brachial artery. She pared back the shredded bicep and surrounding flesh quickly. She'd learnt that from Thiru, the *mas karaya* who brought Ayah her meat. She clipped the limp tube of the basilic vein back so she had more space to work. She adjusted the clamp, lowering it down the cluster, releasing some of the swelling that was building up at the dam.

The dam. Blood burst forth with a will of its own.

She began sewing the artery. Each stitch was small, tight and identical to the one next to it. She was fast and neat, Rajan had said proudly. Like tapestry. But the artery kept snaking out of her fingers, every time he moved. It didn't want to be tamed.

People rushed around her. People called for her. People slipped on the muddy, bloody floor. She didn't look up. There were so many but she wanted to be here for just this one boy. She wanted the river of red to stop. She was almost there. He had stopped moving. The sewing became easier. She wiped the sweat from her face with her forearm, but only covered it with his blood.

'Wake up, Chinna Master,' they cried.

Chinna Master.

Little Master.

Sachin.

Niri.

SYDNEY, 1995

Siva stood in the centre of their living room. He inhaled deeply and exhaled loudly. He raised his hands above his head and stretched himself up, back and then down, slowly. Priya burst out laughing.

'Sai Baba recommends doing the Sun Salute ten times every day. You should join me, it will clear your mind,' he retorted, undeterred by her mockery.

'Does the guru require you to wear thermal underwear while you do it?' she asked him, trying to keep a straight face.

'The guru lives in India; it's never cold in his ashram. This place is freezing,' his voice was muffled as he buried his face into the floor in what looked like a failed push-up.

'Do you need help cunju?' she asked sweetly.

'No,' he strained as he pushed himself into The Cobra and collapsed back down again.

She sat next to him on the floor. 'My mind is already clear. I've been thinking a lot.'

'That's not good,' Siva replied, his smile strained.

'Smrithi is...her own person now. She's almost finished school. I feel like we blinked and things changed and –'

'And what?' he asked nervously, bringing his leg up into the lunge position.

'And, I'm not sure we're still doing the right thing any more. Lying to a child is different from lying to a...a young person.' She felt relieved to have finally said it.

'We're not exactly lying, Priya – we *are* her parents. We just haven't told her the entire story.'

'We just haven't told her the whole story? Siva, this is not like those times when my mother asks me for a recipe and I leave certain ingredients or measurements out. This is the most important thing in the whole world that we have not told our own child!' She looked at him, shocked.

'Do you really do that to your mother?' he asked.

'Of course I do, I thought you knew. I've been doing it for years. Don't change the subject,' Priya shook her head at him.

'Why would you do that to an old woman?' he asked, bending forward and reaching unsuccessfully for his toes.

'Because she drives me crazy – Siva, are you listening to what I'm saying? Are we still doing the right thing for Smrithi? I worry that now – we are doing this for ourselves. Listen to me please,' her face was flushed.

He stopped his attempted yoga and rested next to her on the floor.

'I'm listening. I always listen to you. I listened to you when you brought her home and I don't regret listening to you a single moment after that. You are smart and wise and neither of us know the answer to your question cunju – I certainly don't.'

'But you're the one who always wants to follow the rules...' her voice trailed away.

'I suppose so. I just don't know which rule we are supposed to follow here.' He put his arm around her. 'I don't agree with you on one thing – this is not the most important thing in the whole world. In the north, children are dying in the arms of their mothers in churches. We love Smrithi – you, me and Dhara – and between us we have kept her safe. *That* is the most important thing in the whole world. Call Dhara – ask your sister if she disagrees.'

COLOMBO, 1996

Vani had prepared a simple dinner for Dhara: puttu, omelette and coconut chilli sambal. They had lived together in the small apartment attached to Nala's house for almost ten years, which was longer than they had lived together when Dhara was a child. At first, both of them were uncertain. They weren't strangers at all to each other, but it was strange waking up every day in the same house, sharing a kitchen, a bathroom, observing and accommodating each others' routines and habits. Vani learned to look forward to meal times when she could prepare her daughter's favourite food. Dhara learned to look forward to meal times too, when she could talk to her mother.

She was excited. She took the book out of its plastic bag and showed it to her. Vani laughed.

'Don't you already have that translation, mahal?' she asked.

'I do, but *this* one is a first edition. It was published in 1965 – I bought it for Smrithi.' Dhara walked over to one of her bookshelves and pulled down a copy of the *Mahabharata*. It was by the same author, Kamala Subramaniam, but her edition was published in 1977, the year Smrithi was born.

On family holidays, she enjoyed explaining the war to Vivek and Smrithi who were captivated by its drama. It was full of the richness and depravity of human nature. The five Pandava brothers were good and their cousins, the one hundred Kaurava brothers, were bad. The goodies and the baddies as Smrithi liked to call them. That was the version that was taught to all Hindu children.

It was only much later that she re-read the epic and noticed the many shades between good and bad.

The Tigers took the war to the villages and the cities, their terror widespread, their violence as unrelenting as it was indiscriminate. They cleansed, and in doing so they sullied themselves. They killed all who disagreed with them, even their own. They used their young as weapons; tearing families apart as easily as limbs, as easily as peace accords.

The Janatha Vimukthi Peramuna rebelled in the south. Bodies were found with heads impaled; charred remains wreathed in garlands of burning tyres; young men gutted and left to die, all in public places. The government reacted with equal brutality. No-one knew exactly how many Sinhalese died because so many bodies were never found, but an estimated seventy-thousand of its own people were killed so that the JVP understood the message.

Dhara read the *Mahabharata* and finally understood its message. The heroes were flawed; they were human and therefore they failed. The villains were capable of goodness and greatness.

The Pandavas and the Kauravas: cousins who should have loved each other like brothers. Instead, both sides of the family were destroyed and all that was left were mothers and widows. There was nothing, no glorious kingdom to rule over for the Pandavas. They won the war, but every single one of their sons was killed. A whole generation of their young lost to them. There was only grief and emptiness for the victors.

For the losers, there was no punishment. Of the hundred Kaurava brothers that were brought into the world, not one remained. All of them lay dead on the battlefield, in a pool of the clan blood and their mother's bitter tears. The losers had been punished enough.

In the final chapters of the *Mahabharata*, the Pandavas gave up the kingdom that so many had died for. They wanted to leave the Earth and all of its sadness behind. They journeyed together through the Himalayas to find Heaven, where their dead waited for them – forgiven for their sins and recognised for their virtues.

The *Mahabharata* had helped her understand. Any human endeavour, whether it be a civil war or a fight for freedom, would be flawed. It was the nature of the species. Each would have their moments, their days and years in which they would either redeem or repudiate themselves.

'Smrithi will love it,' she said, touching the first page of the book.

'She will,' Vani agreed, serving more coconut sambal onto her daughter's plate. 'You can give it to her soon. You must be so excited.' She sat down next to her daughter.

'Mahal, are you going to tell her?' she asked quietly.

'No, Amma – I just want to see her. That's all – that's enough.'

She would be meeting Smrithi and the family in South India in two months. It was the first time since Rajiv Gandhi's assassination. Dhara had finally agreed it was safe for all of them to return there.

She felt sick with excitement. She watched the news every day on their small set, expecting – fearing – another bomb blast or assassination that stopped her from travelling. She went to bed each night, anxious but relieved that another day had passed innocuously for her; but then stricken with guilt when she remembered the fighting that continued in the north.

Her days and her nights, her breath and her heartbeat were focused on one thing, and one thing only. Smrithi. In two months she would see her daughter.

And she would see her sister. She craved her child, more and more each day – more than she thought possible – and yet she loved her sister just as much. She could not gain anything by taking anything away from her. They were the Pandavas, blessed and burdened to share equally. It had always been that way between them.

Vani touched her gently on the shoulder, bringing her back to their apartment.

'She loves you so much, mahal. She's very lucky to have you.'

'I'm the lucky one,' Dhara replied.

MADRAS, TAMIL NADU STATE, SOUTH INDIA 1996

The hotel restaurant was crowded as usual. Guests and locals packed in together like sticky, sweaty dodol sweets in a box. Waiters in fake five-star uniforms weaved through patrons, their trays held high, their perspiration sliding low.

Dhara pretended to read as she watched Vivek and Smrithi wolf down puri and potato curry. The puri at the hotel was legendary. When the deep-fried bread arrived, several puris balanced precariously on a silver platter, hot and inflated like balloons, the children clapped in excitement.

She corrected herself: they weren't children any more. They were young adults, Vivek now twenty-two and Smrithi nineteen. Dhara still liked to play with Smrithi's hair, to tug on her earlobe or just gather her into her arms and squeeze her. She'd been watching Smrithi applaud the arrival of puris for years.

'Who's that Dhara mami?' Smrithi asked between mouthfuls, pointing to the photograph in the magazine article.

'You should know who that is – that's Velupillai Prabhakaran, the leader of the LTTE,' she replied. 'What's happening to you children? This man is trying to free us. If Tamil Eelam becomes a reality, it will be because of him.'

'He looks different. He's put on weight and his moustache is bigger. He looks like Ravana,' Vivek said.

She shook her head in dismay, but Smrithi agreed, 'I think you could be right, anna. Prabhakaran *does* look like Ravana. It's the fiendish facial hair.'

'Well, it's not Ravana, it's Prabhakaran,' Dhara hadn't meant to sound curt, but she was upset and didn't like Prabhakaran being likened to the mythical king of Lanka. She knew the demon well and the man, not well enough.

'*Freedom fighter or brutal dictator?*' Smrithi read the article's headline. 'What do you think, mami?'

'I think that no matter how depraved the Tigers become, the government has done and will do worse to the Tamil people, if the Tigers did not exist at all.'

Smrithi didn't look satisfied with that answer. Dhara wasn't sure she was satisfied either. Disappointment was only a whisper away from disillusionment.

'You know that families are being forced to give the Tigers everything: their money, their property and their children. I can't understand that mami – can you? I can't imagine what that must feel like, for those parents or those children.'

'I know, mahal,' Dhara looked down. Priya reached for her hand. Her sister always knew what she was thinking, even when she didn't want to be thinking it: children torn away from their parents; the emptiness that yearned to be filled.

Priya gave Smrithi a warning look but her daughter continued. 'The suicide bomb at Colombo's Central Bank killed almost a hundred people. Over a thousand more were injured. I know the Sri Lankan Army targets Tamil civilians. But to hit back like that – do you think that's right?'

'No mahal, I don't. But they are sending a message – if nothing is safe and sacred for the Tamils, then nothing is safe and sacred for the Sinhalese.'

'But mami, it didn't achieve anything. Now the international community has condemned the Tigers as terrorists.'

'The international community always judges the actions of the Tigers but never the actions of the Sri Lankan Army. A school girl was abducted by the army recently Smrithi. Her name was Krishanthy – and when they found her body it led them to another mass grave. Where is the UN investigation into that and all the other graves in the north? ' she asked. The army controlled Jaffna once again, and people were disappearing, once again. She was angry but hadn't meant to let her daughter see that.

'The BBC said that a lot of children died in the bank bombing,' Smrithi said, chastened but not defeated.

'The dead children were only reported because they were lying next to the dead foreign tourists. Children die in our part of the world and go unnoticed all the time.' Dhara regretted her words as soon she said them. 'I'm sorry, mahal. I'm just tired: tired of it all,' she said, looking at the girl's troubled face.

'You don't know what it's like, mahal, to lose your home – to have it taken away from you; to be treated as though you are nothing; to be hunted and killed as though you are nothing. After a while you either believe it or you fight it.'

'Yes, but surely how you fight says something about who you are. If you fight like this, are you better than nothing?' Smrithi replied. She was only giving voice to a conversation each of them was having inside themselves – Dhara far more than others.

'Neither of us has fought for our lives or the lives of the people we love. I don't have the courage and, God willing, you will never have the need. It's hard to judge; I wouldn't presume to judge.'

'But we do judge, mami. We judge all the time,' Smrithi countered. 'We judge the army, we judge the Palestinians, the Hutus, and the Serbians. We judge them all and it's only right that we do. Judgement is part of what makes us a civilised species.'

'Perhaps that's the problem, mahal. We're not really a civilised species, are we?' Dhara replied, heavily.

'You know mami,' Smrithi said, looking at the magazine cover again, 'Ravana was a good man as well as an evil king. He was a great devotee of Lord Shiva wasn't he?'

Dhara laughed a little. She tore her last puri in half and gave a piece to each of the children. 'Yes, Ravana was good and evil. We all wrestle with the Ravana inside us, I suppose.'

Priya shook her head at her daughter, motioning to her to stop talking. It was time to change the subject. She took the magazine away from Smrithi and gave it back to her sister, saying, 'I don't care if he's the leader of the Tamil Tigers or a demon king. His wife needs to take better care of him. If he doesn't lose weight and start eating better or exercising, he's going to look like a heart attack before he turns forty-five.'

COLOMBO, 1998

Dhara wiped the tears from her eyes. Priya made her laugh until she cried. In this week's call, she was doing an impersonation of Nala. It wasn't unkind but it was uncannily accurate and Nala wouldn't have liked it.

'Stop it acca, you are terrible,' she laughed into the phone.

'I know, I know, but she makes me so mad, Dhara,' Priya laughed back. 'Listen, Siva wants to talk to you about the latest news. Do you have time?'

'Of course, although he's more supportive than me,' she replied. Her own politics were changing; a stealthy subversion creeping into the cracks of her Tamil nationalism, creating larger fissures that longed to be filled with peace.

'You know what they say: absence makes the heart grow more rabid,' Priya said, calling Siva to the phone.

'How are you Dhara?' he asked politely.

'I'm well thank you, anna,' she replied. 'How are you?'

'They're going to be outlawed,' he said abruptly.

'I'm surprised they weren't outlawed earlier,' she replied. What was there to say? The Tigers were becoming braver and more brazen in their civilian bombings.

'Anna, the international community has no option but to respond to the attack.'

'They could ignore the civilian bombings, the way they ignored the civilian bombings in the north,' he said, referring to the recent bombing of St Peter's at Navali. 'It was a church, Dhara, almost a hundred Tamils died, seeking refuge there,' he said, as if he had to remind her.

'I know it was,' she replied. 'And now the Tigers have bombed the Temple of the Tooth, one of the holiest Buddhist shrines in the world. The army has captured Jaffna and the Tigers have bombed Kandy. It just keeps going.'

For what? she thought.

'If the Tigers are outlawed by other countries it will be harder for the diaspora to help them and the refugees,' Siva was worried.

She was just tired.

There were hundreds of thousands of Tamil refugees living in camps, in poverty, and in fear. They were called Internally Displaced People – IDPs: horror sanitised with an acronym.

'The Norwegians are willing to help us, they want to mediate and broker a peace deal,' he said.

Help us, not *them*.

'Will the Tigers listen? Do you think they will put down their arms this time?' she asked. The government maintained that the Tigers didn't want negotiations to succeed, although the same could be said for the government. The war had its benefits for both sides and while no side continued to win, the Tamil people continued to lose.

'Yes, the Tigers will listen,' he said.

They all had their connections but she didn't want to talk to hers any more.

She wanted to feel faith; she missed its reassuring, justifying whisper. But all she could think about was something Martin Luther King said. She had used the quote last month in the religion class she taught at the Wellawatte Sai Baba Centre.

'I want to read you something. It's from Dr King. I'll send it to the children, they're closet pacifists so they'll like it. He says: *The ultimate weakness of violence is that it is a descending spiral, begetting the very thing it seeks to destroy. ...Returning violence for violence multiplies violence, adding deeper darkness to a night already devoid of stars. Darkness cannot drive out darkness; only light can do that. Hate cannot drive out hate; only love can do that.*'

'The time for love has passed, Dhara. You know that,' Siva replied.

'Yes. But surely there is something more than all this violence, all this death?' she tried again.

'They will not stop until we're all dead. You know that too.'

We – except that it's only me that is here, she thought.

'Thank God for the Norwegians then, I suppose,' she said, closing the book.

He agreed, 'Yes, thank God for the Norwegians.'

'May I please speak to the children?' she asked, exhausted.

'Yes of course, Smrithi's waiting,' he replied.

17

Nala stood next to her daughter, watching her closely as she cooked. She was convinced that whenever Priya gave her recipes, she omitted ingredients. She faithfully reproduced her daughter's dishes but they never achieved Priya's tantalising flavours.

'I've called Mr Venkatraman over tonight, Amma. He's coming after dinner.'

'Why do you need the astrologer? Is everything alright?' Nala asked, worried.

'I don't know. It's Vivek. He's been acting strangely all year. I need some advice. I'm sure Saturn is affecting him badly at the moment.'

Nala cleared her throat nervously.

'I need to tell you something.'

Priya didn't stop cutting onions. She cut quickly and beautifully; gracefully and uniformly. She had Rajan's hands. She was making her own seeni sambol. No-one made their own seeni sambol anymore; the onion chutney was too difficult. Most people bought it in a bottle from the local spice store.

'Vivek has found someone,' Nala paused. 'She's Italian and Catholic.'

Priya stopped. She spoke, without looking at her. 'How long have you known Amma?'

'Just a day,' she lied quickly and comfortably.

Priya picked up the knife and continued cutting, tears falling into the food.

Nala hurried through her prepared speech.

'They studied together at university, she's also a doctor. Vivek says it's serious for both of them.'

The tears fell faster and Priya had to stop to wipe her face. Nala's nose reddened in sympathy. She had had this conversation before, many years ago. Boys – it was always the boys.

'He said he's been trying to tell you for the last few months. He didn't want to lie but he's afraid of your reaction. That's why I'm telling you. Her parents were informed last week.'

'Does anyone else know about this?' Priya asked.

She didn't hesitate before she lied again.

'No, just me and a few of his friends from university I think.'

Nala, Smrithi and all of Vivek's cousins were party to his clandestine relationship. They had been instructed to feign surprise when a formal announcement was made.

Priya spoke quietly, 'Will he leave her if I ask him?'

'Don't ask him to do that,' she said gently. 'He loves her; please don't make him choose.'

'But what if they marry, what about the children? What will the children be? She'll make him convert.'

'Vivek is a good boy, he won't do that – you have to trust him. Trust the way you raised him.'

'Trust? It's too much, Amma – a Catholic – a white – it's too much. He will lose everything. We – we will lose everything.'

'No mahal, please listen to me. Don't cry,' Nala reached out but let her arm drop. She wanted to hold her daughter but it had been a long time since Priya had allowed that.

'I know what you're going through, mahal. We allowed Nandan to marry Shiranthi –'

Priya interrupted her. 'You *allowed* Nandan to marry Shiranthi because you *allowed* Nandan to do anything and everything he wanted. You spoilt him.'

Nala faltered. Priya was right but it was more complicated than that. She wiped her face with her sari pallu and spoke again.

'We did spoil him but we also changed Priya. Sometimes Sydney reminds me of Colombo. We each had our own suburb, the Tamils in Wellawatte, the Muslims and the Sinhalese had their places too. Just like here – you all live in your own neighbourhoods and you think you're safe, that your children are protected because you keep to yourselves.

'Your Appa and I, we learned that if we wanted to live, we had to mix and we had to marry. I loved that Colombo, but it had no future. Maybe it still has no future. But you, in Sydney, with Vivek and these Catholic Italians – you have a chance.'

Priya's shoulders dropped. She was already dialling Dhara's number, tears falling unchecked. She took her cordless phone and left the room. It was early morning in Colombo.

Nala thought about Rajan, who vowed to disavow his only son but could not; instead giving Nandan the Hindu and Buddhist weddings he had asked for. He chose to embrace the marriage, not just tolerate it.

Siva and Priya would learn to do the same; they would learn because there was no other way forward. These things just take time, she thought to herself, taking the abandoned knife from the cutting board. She adjusted her glasses and slowly, less uniformly, finished cutting the onions for dinner.

✿

'Oh Dhara,' Priya cried. 'What are we going to do? He thinks he's in love!'

She gave Dhara a summary of the problem unfolding in Sydney, between sobs of disappointment. She wiped the phone; it was covered in tears and onion.

'*We* are going to calm down, and by that I mean *you*. You are going to calm down. The best-case scenario is that this is just a passing fancy. If you try to forbid the relationship, he'll go all Romeo and Juliet on you and that ended badly for everyone.'

'Dhara, this is no time for jokes!' she tried to stifle her laugh.

'I'm not joking!' her sister replied. 'You need to think strategically, not hysterically. The worst-case scenario is that they get married and live happily ever after, which is actually a lot better than the Romeo and Juliet scenario. You're on a good wicket, as Nandan would say.'

'You're not helping,' she dried her tears and blew her nose into a tissue. More tears fell. 'Plus, I'm not taking advice from my inter-racially married younger brother.'

'Your happily married younger brother. Acca – just give Vivek time to work out what he wants. He's a sensible boy; he'll do the right thing. It might not be the thing that you wanted or expected or planned for him. But he'll do it well and if you ever want to see your future grandchildren, you'll support him,' Dhara replied, trying not to laugh.

'My future grandchildren are going to be called Carmela, Sofia and Luca!' Priya managed to laugh at herself, if not her predicament. 'How did you become so wise and Western?' She could finally speak clearly; her voice was congested but steady.

'It's one of the many benefits of not having to do the hard work myself, acca,' Dhara replied softly.

'You do different work, Dhara. How is everything there?' she asked her sister carefully.

'Same as usual. How is Smrithi?'

'Same as usual,' Priya replied, distracted from one worry by another. 'She's an adult now – a woman. She deserves to know, Dhara. I think she senses something isn't right between her and me. She must know, on some level, surely…'

'Everything is as it should be between the two of you, acca. Mothers and daughters fight. It's a rule. I think I read that somewhere in the *Vedas*,' Dhara replied.

'No Dhara, in the *Vedas* you read: *Mathru devo bhava* – our first God is our mother.' She felt the tears cloud her eyes and fall down her face again.

Mathru devo bhava

'She should have a chance to know you – as her mother.'

'She already knows me and she loves me – it's enough for me,' her sister replied.

'It's not enough for me.' It wouldn't be enough for me, Priya wanted to say.

Mathru devo bhava

How many times had she recited that at temple as a child? How many times had she looked at her daughter and whispered it to herself, begging God to forgive her for not telling Smrithi, begging Smrithi to forgive her.

Dhara spoke after a long while. 'It's enough, acca,' she said softly. '*Mathru devo bhava*. You are her mother. God forgives all things and so must you. Now put down the phone, stop crying and work out how to make friends with these Italians you might have to marry.'

✧

After Vivek's announcement, extended family members suggested more astrologers, threats and expedited arranged marriages. Shock eventually gave way to resignation and then concern that he might *not* actually marry the girl, shaming their family in front of The Italians.

'My only concern is that the girl still doesn't know how to cook a curry. That boy might starve,' Nala declared, stacking slabs of butter cake in Priya's freezer.

'Amma, when you got married, you didn't know how to cook a curry either,' Priya replied.

Nala ignored her.

'I've labelled all the cakes, mahal. There's one for the Italians too. I don't know what Vivek is waiting for, he needs to propose.'

'Leave him be, Amma. He has time, it will happen. It's Smrithi I'm worried about. I can't even talk to her anymore. She won't listen to me. She wants to study overseas now and she won't meet a single boy we've suggested.'

Priya stretched another shirt over the ironing board and changed the setting.

Nala closed the freezer and inspected the fridge. 'She's only twenty-two-years-old, mahal. She has some time too. You can't give Vivek space but refuse it to Smrithi, it isn't fair.'

She hadn't meant to say anything; the words just slipped out. Rajan said she lacked discretion and tact, which according to him was a bad combination of skills not to have. She said it was easy to have discretion and tact if you never opened your mouth.

'It isn't fair?' Priya repeated. 'It isn't *fair*? You let Nandan do as he pleased but you made me follow the rules. Was that fair? Did Nandan ever once have to do what you wanted? Did he become a doctor like Appa wanted? Did he marry a Tamil girl like Appa wanted? Did he?'

Nala wasn't sure if she was supposed to answer those questions. It was hard to look at her daughter. She tried to imagine what Oprah would do in this situation. She wanted to defend herself, but Priya wouldn't let her speak. There was more.

'Don't you talk to me about treating children differently. Can you honestly say you treated Dhara and me the same? Dhara would never criticise you, but I would.'

Priya took a deep, ragged breath. She looked shocked, as though the words had spewed forth on their own, ambushing her as much as Nala.

'Amma...' she stepped back. 'I just...please, just don't tell me how to raise my children now. You're the one always advising me to let them go – this is what happens when you let them go. My son will marry an Italian and my daughter won't marry at all.'

Priya's voice had dropped but her words still made Nala flinch.

What could she say? Nala had treated all of her children differently and she would treat them differently again if she had to. She struggled to speak. 'I tell you to let go mahal, because you hold on to her too tightly,' she began.

'I hold on because she's not mine, Amma – you know that – you of all people know that.' Priya was sobbing now, her face contorted in pain. 'She's not mine and I'm terrified of losing her.'

'You could never lose her mahal – talk to her, instead of fighting with her.'

'Smrithi won't listen. She doesn't love – I mean she doesn't... respect me.' Her face flushed a deep red. She wouldn't look up.

Nala's heart ached for her daughter. She never doubted her daughter's love, even when she spoke to her like this. Priya was hers in entirety, in absolute, even when she didn't want to be.

'She respects you and she loves you. You are her mother.'

'I don't want to hear it Amma,' Priya regained her composure. 'It doesn't matter. Smrithi will do what I did. I know she comes to you for advice. Please don't make this worse.'

Nala felt the familiar pain in her throat: it was throbbing at the place where her words collected and congealed; words that always remained unspoken.

Tell her why you love her, instead of telling her what you expect from her. That was what she wanted to say.

She dug her nails hard into the palm of her hand and mumbled an apology. She set off back to her apartment. It was a fifteen-minute walk that took her twenty-five minutes these days. Rajan had gone to the Plaza for his daily walk – she would have some time alone to recover.

As she opened the door to her apartment she was greeted by the smell of cooking, incense, and camphorwood. The familiar smells that told her she was home.

Home. Home wasn't the apartment. Home was family: her children and now her grandchildren. It wasn't the home of her birth or the home of her choice. If she could choose, they would all be in Colombo. Not *all*, actually. She and Rajan would be back in Colombo with Dhara, and Priya would be living in Australia, coming for visits that made everyone happy, just like they used to. In Sydney they lived only hundreds of metres from each other but had never been more distant.

She rubbed her palm, her nails had left small indentations. She sat down heavily on her sofa, breathed deeply and let her tears fall. She had been holding them back from the top of her daughter's driveway. There were too many Sri Lankans in their neighbourhood. She couldn't be seen walking the streets of Strathfield crying like some well-dressed mad woman. No, she had far too much pride for that.

The sadness spread from her heart to her chest to her throat and emerged as uncontrolled sobs. She lay down and brought her knees up a little towards her stomach, holding Rajan's TV cushion. It smelt reassuringly of him, even though he wouldn't be able to reassure her. She knew what he would have said: 'What do you expect if you insist on interfering in their lives?'

She wasn't interfering, she was trying to help. Mothers are always judged, rightly or wrongly. She looked at the picture of her mother-in-law on Rajan's writing desk. She was everywhere, his beloved Amma. She was present in photographs and she was present in him. She could see her mother-in-law in her husband's single-mindedness and his stubbornness; in the way he insisted on washing his own shirts and refused to buy non-sale items. She could see her mother-in-law and she blamed her for all of Rajan's faults, even the ones that weren't her fault. It was easier to blame a dead woman.

Rajan said that operating on his patients involved muscle memory: it was a conscious act but also an unconscious one; a learnt and remembered impulse. The heart was a strong muscle. Perhaps the expectations, disappointments, and criticisms that mothers and daughters held for each other were ingrained into it like muscle memory.

When Rajan came home from the Plaza he found her asleep on the sofa, her nose red and her breathing a little ragged. He gently placed a blanket over her.

'How was the Plaza?' she asked, waking slowly, trying to sound normal.

'Fine, I bought you Alphonso mangoes, a whole box from Pakistan. They were selling them at the spice store,' he said, bending slowly to sit beside her. He took his hanky and tidied up the smudged potu on her forehead. He left his hand on her face.

'A whole box?' she loved the small mangoes. They tasted just like the ones back home, not like the insipid ones from Queensland.

'They were on sale,' he replied proudly.

She laughed, closed her eyes again, and kissed her husband's hand. He laughed too and didn't take it away.

Vivek's Hindu wedding was over and the Catholic wedding was about to begin. Priya surveyed the crowd on the other side of the church. Caterina's parents had submitted a guest list as long as their own. Apparently the Italian community in Sydney was even bigger than the Tamil community and everyone was related to everyone. Caterina's mother had said, 'If I don't invite all of these people I'll have to walk around with a paper bag over my head.'

Priya said exactly the same thing to Vivek when justifying the five hundred close personal friends and relatives she'd wanted to invite to the Hindu wedding. Patrizia and Priya compromised – three hundred Sri Lankan Tamils to the Hindu wedding and three hundred Italians to the Catholic wedding. Each side invited their own extended family, adding two hundred people to both weddings. It was only fair.

Her eyes wandered. The Italian widows were dressed in black and the Hindu widows in muted saris. Neither wore make-up or jewellery. The older married women on both sides of the aisle wore too much make-up and jewellery.

The Italians were all crying. The Tamils were watching the ceremony, dry-eyed but interested. They had barely paid attention during the Hindu wedding yesterday, but then, no-one paid attention at Hindu weddings.

When the Catholic priest asked Vivek, 'Will you give yourself to Christ?' Siva's hands had tightened on the wedding leaflet. Priya pressed his arm gently. The Hindu ceremony had been allowed to go forward, un-amended. So the Catholic ceremony should be allowed to go forward, un-amended.

'Their children will have both, faiths,' she had told Siva. *They will have both faiths*, she repeated to herself.

The church was a beautiful building with sweeping stained glass windows and pews all organised in respectful worship facing the main altar. It didn't have the chaos of Hindu temples and Priya understood now why her Archi often preferred churches. The small, quiet enclaves were perfect for solitude and prayer. Temples had no furniture. People walked and prayed, they talked and prayed, they ate and prayed. There was so much 'else' – sometimes too much 'else' – to do at a temple.

Looking up, she was concerned by the enormous figure of Jesus, nailed to a cross and suspended from the church roof. Christ's pain was palpable: droplets of sweat and blood at his brow, the tension in the muscles and ligaments of his arms. Her eyes followed the line of his torso down to his narrow, almost feminine waist. She counted the ribs: they were all there. Quick physiological and diagnostic checks were a habit she had inherited from her father. She shuddered as her eyes stopped at one of the iron nails. We are a universally cruel species, she thought; we are sadly and happily more similar than we are different.

Vivek's new father-in-law had given him an iron nail to put in his suit pocket, to ward off the evil eye. She had spat quietly on her son three times to do the same, as she pointlessly straightened his cravat. She rubbed his forehead where his skin was still creased from the turban he had worn the day before.

'Eight hours in a turban is enough to scar a man for life,' he laughed. She laughed too, because it was wonderful to see him so happy; to see how he looked at Caterina as she wafted down the aisle in a voluptuous taffeta gown, like a complex dandelion with purpose and grace.

She stole a look at her father. He was crying quietly while Nala patted him, her face wearing a familiar smile: half sympathetic, half embarrassed by his rare show of emotion.

She had been thinking about her brother's wedding a lot lately. She remembered it well, even better than her own wedding. Most of all, she remembered her parents. Proud and hurt, they had accepted Shiranthi's obeisance as Hindu custom dictated at the end of the ceremony. When they raised her from the floor where she sat at their feet, they embraced her and loved her as their own child.

Priya took a deep breath in and let it out, wiping away the tears. The priest nodded at her. She stepped forward and put her arms around her new daughter.

18

SYDNEY, 1999

'Stand up straight and smile,' Priya barked shuffling Smrithi over to the azalea bush. It was green and hadn't flowered yet, creating a more neutral backdrop for the photos Priya wanted.

Smrithi was still unmarried. Priya angrily straightened the pleats of her daughter's heavy, silk sari.

'Siva,' she instructed her husband, 'take headshots, then a few from the chest up and a few full length so they can see the sari. Chin up Smrithi, look straight into the camera.' She stood back, giving Siva a clear shot of his reluctant child.

'Smile Smrithi, please,' he said.

'I am Appa.'

'No, that's a grimace. You have to look happy.'

'But I'm not,' she replied.

'Not that again, Smrithi,' Priya scolded and Smrithi braced herself for the rest of the familiar conversation. 'I wish you'd just listen. If you don't marry soon, you're going to miss the boat and you'll regret it for the rest of your life. Everyone has to get married. It isn't a choice or an option. It's a necessity. It's our duty to find the right man for you and your duty to accept him.'

'For god's sake, Smrithi, smile. I can't send these photos to your aunties if you look like you're at a funeral.'

Nala created space on her cluttered kitchen table. Smrithi placed the bowl of coffee trifle pudding down. It was Rajan's favourite.

'Amma sent this for you. Where is Apps?' she asked, looking around.

'He's gone to the doctor's for an eye check-up,' Nala replied.

'But it's Sunday.'

'He's gone to check the route. His appointment is tomorrow but it's at a new clinic…he doesn't want to be late. You've lost more weight, darling. How is everything going?' Nala asked.

'I'm fine, Ammamma, I'm fine,' Smrithi replied, her eyes filling with tears. 'Amma is really mad at me.'

'I know. What did she say today?' Her daughter had a harsh tongue at times.

'She said if I don't marry soon, I'm going to miss the bus or the boat or something.'

'She's just trying to help you Smrithi. Your Appappa and I did the same thing for her when she was your age. These days children are given a chance to get to know each other. Amma will find a nice boy and you'll be allowed to meet many times. If you don't like each other, you could even say no.'

'Did you meet Apps before you married him?' Smrithi asked.

'Me? No! We met once but didn't even speak to each other. I remember walking into the room with a plate of sweets. My Amma told me to keep my head down so I barely saw him. He spoke once that entire meeting – that should have told me he was a mute. Our parents checked our charts, the planets were a good match. Four months later we were married.'

She laughed at the look of horror on her granddaughter's face.

'It wasn't so bad. It was expected of us and it was what we expected. But as you know, I'm a very modern grandmother. Have you thought about finding your own husband?' she asked.

'Maybe, Ammamma. I haven't had much time to date,' Smrithi replied.

'Hmm, always studying. Vivek dated – it can't be that hard,' Nala laughed again. 'Do you *want* to get married, Smrithi?' she asked more seriously. 'You've finished your journalism degree now, what is stopping you?'

'Nothing is stopping me, I want to get married but not just yet,' Smrithi replied, 'I want to study more. I've been accepted into a Masters programme in London. I could travel and work before marriage. That's not too much to ask, is it?'

'Perhaps not. Your Amma would be happy for you to do those things, from within the safety of marriage,' she replied, trying to sound casual.

'Women don't need the safety of marriage any more Ammamma, it's not like when you were young, or even when Amma was young. Is she disappointed in me?'

Her granddaughter was hurt. 'Not disappointed Smrithi, she's afraid for you, but she doesn't do a good job of explaining that.'

'Ammamma, when you chose Appa for Amma, were you ever afraid that he wasn't the right one for her?' Smrithi asked.

'The right one? There are many 'right ones', darling. Look at your Appappa and me: we are always boxing each other but we love each other. That love took time to come. First there was respect, then affection, then sex and then love.'

'Ammamma!' Smrithi blushed.

'Ah Smrithi, there was a time when your grandfather was very amorous, you know.'

'Ammamma, please!'

'On our wedding night, even I was shy. I was a young girl, you know, but I had read novels so I knew what to expect. I was waiting for your grandfather to begin – that is the man's job,' Nala continued, 'But when Appappa came to our room, he got into bed, turned over and went to sleep.'

'He went to sleep?' Smrithi was relieved.

'Yes, he went to sleep. Most disappointing, but he learnt what to do later. As you can imagine with your grandfather, he worked hard to ensure he excelled.'

'Ammamma!'

Rajan walked in to find Smrithi covering her ears and Nala grinning wickedly, her wrinkles jostling for space with the lines of laughter across her face. 'What's going on?' he asked nervously.

'I'm just talking to her about love, marriage, and wedding nights,' she explained.

Rajan looked like he wanted to cover his ears too.

She shook her head at her husband, who was blushing under his dark skin.

'My point is that all the important things will happen over time. Listen to your grandmother, Smrithi, I know these things. Your deepest feelings will come after you marry.'

Rajan blushed even deeper, but nodded his agreement before he fled the room.

Early morning light filtered into the room, soft strands settling on Dhara's bed. She wedged the phone between her ear and shoulder and stretched her body. Lately her back had started to ache at night. The alarm in Priya's voice was becoming a regular wake-up call.

'She'll be twenty-four by the time she returns from London. She should have been married by then. What on earth is she going to do with a Masters in international relations?'

'Did you want me to answer that, acca?' Dhara asked, stifling a yawn.

'This is serious, Dhara. There are only a finite number of Tamil boys in the world in the right age group with the right qualifications and the right family background. If she doesn't marry soon she's going to –'

'– miss some form of transportation, yes I know.'

Priya laughed in spite of herself. 'Stop it. I need help.'

'Yes, you do. You sound like Nala mami from thirty years ago. Acca, she's won a scholarship to the London School of Economics. The world will offer her an infinite number of paths and people. She will choose one and it might not be the right one but it will be her one.'

'How can you even say that?' Priya asked. 'You've had a stroke, haven't you? What kind of Tamil girl is given choices?'

'Smart ones, like Smrithi – with smarter mothers, like you.'

'How can you be so brave? What if something happens to her, Dhara?'

Dhara understood her sister's fear. There were so many things that could happen to a young girl.

'I think about Karna's birth sometimes. I wonder what his mother thought, when she put her baby in the basket and placed it in the river. She must have been afraid too.'

'Oh Dhara...' Priya's voice choked.

'Don't cry, acca. I think she knew that the Sun God sees all things, and that is all any mother can ask for. Do your duty and let her go. It's terrifying but it's time.'

Priya lit the lamp in her shrine room. She held a stick of incense to the lamp watching it light. She shook it gently, putting out the flame, leaving the smoking ember at the tip. The small room was filled with the sweet perfume of sandalwood. She waved the incense in front of each deity and then placed it in its holder.

She pressed her finger into the pot of holy ash and tapped it on the side of the pot. Rajan taught her how to do that when she was a child, so she didn't spill any.

She reached up and pressed her finger to her daughter's forehead, leaving a smudge of ash.

Smrithi bent down to touch Priya's feet, but she stepped back, raising her daughter. She didn't deserve that honour. She gathered her in her arms.

'Come home soon,' she whispered, kissing her tearfully.

Smrithi knew how to make a bed. Her grandfather had taught her in Colombo when she was only five. She remembered the yearly holidays to her grandparents' home. As soon as Rajan woke up, he would make his bed and explain to her, 'If you're going to do something child, you should do it properly.'

She smiled as her grandfather talked her through it again.

'You need to line up the top sheet with the frame of the bed,' he said, smoothing the sheets with his elegant hands and proudly demonstrating the parallel lines to his granddaughter. His movements were slow, giving the lesson greater gravity.

'Lord Krishna taught Arjuna that, in the *Mahabharata*,' he said, straightening his pillows. It was, he told her, important to dust off any ectodermal tissue that had shed during the night.

'Lord Krishna taught Arjuna how to make a bed?' she asked.

He laughed. 'No. Krishna taught Arjuna that you must do what you have to do.' His face clouded over and he looked at her, suddenly sad. 'You must do the right thing Smrithi, whether you want to or not – and you must do it to the best of your ability. That's all that is asked of us, even though sometimes it seems an impossible task.'

She hugged him. He felt smaller now in her arms, his shoulders narrower, and his body shorter. His hair was still jet-black. Every month he dyed it. It was his one concession to vanity and no-one was allowed to tease him about it. His routines were slowing down but they were intact.

'So, you're going on a big trip,' he said wiping his eyes. 'I've asked Ammamma to give you the names and addresses of our people around the world. If you have any problems, call them. They know you're coming.'

'I'll send you and Ammamma a postcard from every city I go to, ok?' she said, hugging him again.

After she finished her Masters, she wanted to visit some of the ageing Tamils on Ammamma's list. Smrithi had her family tree, her journal, and her camera ready. Her grandparents might not be able to travel anymore, but she could travel and record for them.

'I have something for you,' he said. He didn't give gifts and she assumed he would take her to the shrine for one last blessing before she left for the airport.

Instead, he handed her a videocassette. It was the film *Karnan*, starring Sivaji Ganeshan, in the lead role of the tragic hero.

'Watch it with your relatives when you visit them. They will explain the language to you. I'm sorry you won't be able to understand it yourself, but you know the story better than anyone,' he said.

She was sorry too that she couldn't understand Tamil, but it was true, she did know the story. She cried every time she read it.

Nala came in to find her husband and granddaughter scrutinising a videocassette. 'What is it?' she asked.

'It's *Karnan*.'

Nala touched the cover gently. 'Sivaji was so handsome, shining in the Sun God's armour. I haven't seen this film for decades,' she said, more to herself than to them.

'Thirty-five years ago,' Rajan said, 'I took your grandmother to the cinema seven times to see it. We were much younger then.'

Nala tried to hide her tears from her husband. Smrithi had to look away.

'I bought one for you too,' he said softly.

LONDON, 2000

Smrithi's leg shook under the table as she waited for her coffee. Prashanth reached forward and put his hand on her knee, steadying it. He moved his hand up a little but she pulled away.

'Careful, someone might see you,' she looked around nervously.

'It's an overpriced café at an even more overpriced yoga centre in an extortionately priced suburb of north London. No self-respecting Sri Lankan Tamil would come here,' he replied.

'Except us,' she laughed taking his hand under the table and placing it tentatively back on her knee.

'Yes, but we're not very good Sri Lankan Tamils are we?' he reached over the table and took her other hand in his. It was liberating to do that in public. Primrose Hill was far enough away from Strathfield or even Walthamstow where her extended family lived.

'Speak for yourself,' she laughed again. An impossibly limber looking waitress brought two mugs to the table. She placed the chai latté and fair-trade decaf cappuccino between them and smiled, her potu moving with her blonde eyebrows as she said, 'Namaste, enjoy,' and left.

'My father would die if he saw me here,' she said, looking around the café and waiting room. 'He's been trying to teach me to meditate for years.'

Men and women milled about in designer yoga gear, stretching, reading or meditating. Aromatherapy candles scented the room with lemongrass.

'He'd probably tell me that we invented the Sun Salute and now these vellakaran hippies are making a fortune out of it.'

'He's right; didn't you just pay £20 for a forty-five minute jyothi meditation class your father could have given you for free?'

'Yes, but for some reason I'm more likely to do it when my father isn't making me.'

'Is that why you won't marry me? Because you know your father would want you to?' he took both her hands in his.

'No, we've been over this already, Prashanth,' she didn't want to talk about it again.

'No, you've been over it with me but I still don't understand how a nice Sri Lankan Tamil girl like you doesn't want to have five-hundred to eight-hundred of her parents' closest friends over to the local community hall for a massive curry-fest and a five hour ceremony that nobody listens to anyway.'

'Maybe that's it. Nobody *listens* to the ceremony; they just do it because they have to, because it's what we've always done.'

'OK, Smrithi, what did you do with your first pay cheque?' he asked.

'What's that got to do with anything?'

'Just answer the question – what did you do with your first pay cheque?' he repeated.

'I gave most of it to my parents and I made a donation to the temple and the Tamil Refugee Organisation. I also bought myself an expensive cardigan from Country Road but it had bell-shaped sleeves so it was totally worth it.'

'Exactly, and why did you do that?'

'Because it's what they did with their first pay cheque, and what my grandfather did with his. Except for the cardigan of course.'

'Exactly,' he replied.

'You're cute, even when you're smug,' she shook her head at him. 'It's a beautiful wedding ceremony. The male and female forms of the divine are joined to make the whole. It's the equal union between two people and two families.'

'You know the ceremony well,' he said, playing with her hand.

'I've been to about a thousand of them. *I* paid attention. It's a sweet ceremony too – at the end the priest throws the wedding ring into a pot of water and the bride and groom both put their hands in. Whoever gets the ring first will dominate the marriage – best of three tries. It's really just to give them a chance to touch each other for the first time.'

'That is sweet. Antiquated but sweet. I like the music – the moment the wedding chain is tied. You can feel the finality of it,' he said.

'Music is everything. Imagine how boring *Star Wars* would be without music,' she said, trying to change the subject.

'I know, let's have a Wookie wedding ceremony.'

'What are you trying to say about my body hair?' she laughed.

'If you love the Hindu ceremony so much, then let's do it,' he said, leaning forward.

'I just want something simpler; something that has meaning because we've given it meaning, not because it's expected of us but because we wanted it for ourselves. I don't feel connected to the community or those traditions any more.'

'Then let's have a wedding at the temple in Walthamstow, family only – simple and fast,' he said. 'We can go to The Banana Leaf afterwards for take-away hoppers.'

'No, Prashanth, I'm sorry. I'm just not ready for that. A temple wedding with only our family is still a few hundred big. Why can't we just go to Camden Town Hall and have a registry wedding?'

'A registry wedding? What kind of Sri Lankan are you?' he laughed and shook his head, bewildered.

'A confused one. There are people in refugee camps who tie string around each other's necks because that's all they have. They make do with wedding chains made of string and food rations that are inadequate because the government lies about the number of refugees in every camp. I just couldn't bear a big wedding, Prashanth, I'm really sorry.'

She was crying now as she sometimes did when she thought about her mami in Colombo, her work and the stories she told.

'Our parents left, Smrithi, and I won't feel guilty about the privileges that come with their choices.'

'I know and I agree. We have left; we are almost born again while other people are dying. To me, that means that the parts of our culture we take with us should be by choice and not blind habit.

'So if you could *choose* to marry me, or call it whatever you want to call it, with or without the ritual – if you could choose to stay with me forever, and have lots of culturally challenged children with me, would you?'

She wiped her tears and laughed. 'Of course I would,' she answered.

COLOMBO, 2001

News arrived in Colombo, via relatives in London and Toronto that Smrithi had found someone. After months of negotiation and meetings between the two families, Smrithi and Prashanth agreed to a registry wedding in London, witnessed nervously by Anand, Siva's younger brother and stand-in.

Priya called Dhara in tears.

'Tell her to come home and have a Hindu wedding here. She can't carry on like this. What will people say? Find out what's going on Dhara, please,' Priya implored hysterically.

Dhara tried to reassure her. 'He's Sri Lankan Tamil, from a good family, acca. She's had a wedding, albeit a short one at an office rather than a temple or a bowling club. All people should say is 'congratulations.'

'You know it's not enough. She thinks she can travel with him, and *live* with him now, just because she's signed a document. She's being stubborn. She's always been stubborn. A Hindu wedding was good enough for me – it should be good enough for her.'

'She's not being stubborn, acca. She's just being herself. She's not listening to you because children often don't listen to their parents. She thinks differently from us, that's all.'

'This isn't Western liberalism Dhara, it's shameful.'

'No acca,' Dhara stopped her sister. This had gone on long enough. 'I know about shame, and this isn't it. Shame crawls under your skin and makes you want to tear at yourself until you are reduced to a raw, basic element of who you were, so you can start over, as someone else.'

She could feel Priya's head sink into her hands on the other side of the phone. Her voice softened.

'This is love, acca. Don't make it into more than that. She's just a young girl, in love, and given that you had to throw your son two ceremonies, your wedding average is unaffected by Smrithi's off-beat approach to life and familial compliance.'

'Will you talk to her…for me?'

'Yes, I will talk to her, for you,' Dhara replied.

That night, she stayed up until midnight. From her balcony she could see the street cats jump up onto the brick wall between Rajan's house and the Fonseka's. They walked like ballerinas in the moonlight, placing their feet carefully between the shards of broken glass that had been cemented to the rim for protection. The cats and London were awake.

'Amma wants you to go home and have a proper Hindu wedding.'

'I know. How is she?' Smrithi asked.

'She's fulfilling her cultural stereotype. How are you?' Dhara asked.

'I'm not fulfilling mine, I guess.'

'Yes, I can see that.'

'I thought perhaps we could come to Sri Lanka, mami. We could stay with you in Colombo. There's a human rights organisation, the Centre for Social & Political Research. They've been helping me with my thesis. They've offered me an internship,' Smrithi said.

She had read Smrithi's draft thesis: *Religious revivalism and the construction of the 'Other'*. It wasn't finished yet but it was excellent. It used Sri Lankan politics as a case study for global lessons in nation building.

'No,' Dhara replied. She knew the centre well. Not so long ago, the Tigers assassinated its director. He was a moderate Tamil.

'What?'

'No Smrithi. Absolutely not,' she spoke more harshly than she had intended. Fear had its own tone.

'Why, mami? It would be wonderful. I could help you with your work. I've been fundraising for you at Uni, everyone thinks your medical projects are great.'

Dhara didn't say anything.

'Mami, I miss you,' Smrithi tried again. She sounded like she was going to cry.

Dhara wanted to cry too. 'It's dangerous, mahal,' she replied finally. 'The fighting is getting worse. The Tigers have re-claimed the Vanni region and they're heading towards Jaffna. There are hundreds of thousands of Tamils displaced and living in refugee camps. You don't want to see that Smrithi. I won't let you.'

'I will stay in Colombo, with you.'

'Even Colombo is dangerous mahal. The police are on high alert for suicide attacks and there are army checkpoints around the city. They have unlimited power to arrest and detain people. This is not a place for a young girl.'

'But –'

'No. No 'buts'. I can't protect you here, do you understand? Amma will never allow it, and neither will I.'

She felt her chest tighten with panic. She had tried so hard for so long to keep Smrithi away from Sri Lanka – away from the Tigers who stole and seduced the young; and the soldiers who – she stopped herself. She must breathe. She closed her eyes and allowed the sunlight into the shadows of the Dutch Fort. It warmed the cold metal and cement of that room. It held her in its embrace. It was the same sun that watched over her daughter.

She must breathe.

'I'm so proud of you mahal,' she said quietly, calmly. 'But researching from the safety of London is very different from working in Colombo.'

'Please mami, if you agree, Amma will let me.'

'No – I don't want you here,' she willed her voice to relax. 'Please understand, Smrithi. Colombo is not the place for you. Not right now.'

They argued until they both cried and Smrithi finally agreed to give up her plan. Dhara put the phone down and as usual with these calls, she immediately remembered all the things she had forgotten to say.

'I miss you too, mahal,' she said quietly to herself. 'I miss you too.'

SYDNEY, 2001

Nala rarely left Strathfield, unless it was to attend a wedding or a funeral in another suburb. Even then she had to rely on her children or Rajan to take her. She thought about her driver Kannan in Colombo. He once took her and Kamini all the way to Kandy to visit her old friends there.

Priya and Siva would be attending a cardiology conference in Chicago soon.

'You should try to visit Oprah,' Nala said, heaping more soya curry onto Priya's plate.

'Oprah? How do you know about Oprah?' Priya asked.

'I know Oprah child, I'm not a villager. I've been supporting her for years, before she was famous. Do you think you'll see her?'

Priya laughed and shook her head.

Oprah said if you didn't like something, you should change it.

Nala took a deep breath and spoke clearly. 'Oprah says the more you meet other people's expectations of yourself, the more they expect of you. She says disappointment is just disappointment, it's a temporary emotion and people shouldn't be so afraid of it.'

'What?' Priya asked, confused.

'Oprah says we shouldn't be so afraid to disappoint others. She says we should just do the best we can and not be afraid of other people's expectations. Like Smrithi,' Nala added. 'Don't close the door on her, mahal. You will only regret it later. She loves you.'

Rajan and Siva both looked up sharply from their curries. She stopped talking, her heart pounding hard. She looked at Priya, expecting a response or an explosion or both, but her daughter just stared back at her, speechless. Emboldened by Priya's silence, Siva stepped in.

'I thought Lord Krishna said that to Arjuna in the *Bhagavad Gita*. Wasn't that in the chapter on duty?' he asked.

Nala shook her head; Siva thought everything clever came from the *Bhagavad Gita*.

'No,' Rajan replied. 'Oprah plagiarised that and the rest of her commercially successful philosophy from Karna's life.'

'No she didn't,' Nala corrected him. 'She says we should be true to ourselves and she thought that up all on her own.'

'No, Nala – we're not having this argument again. Oprah took that straight from Karna's life. He was surrounded by the expectations and disappointment of others. His mother expected him to leave Duryodhana and fight with his Pandava brothers instead of against them. Duryodhana expected him to be loyal and defend him in battle. He was torn. In the end, Karna chose to embrace and follow his duty.'

'But that's exactly what Lord Krishna said to Arjuna on the battlefield. Oprah took it from the *Bhagavad Gita*,' exclaimed Siva. 'Lord Krishna said: 'Do your duty to the best of your ability, Arjuna. Focus only on that and detach yourself from everything else, from the consequences of your actions, from the rewards of your labour."

Nala wasn't interested in the *Bhagavad Gita*. 'It was Oprah, not Lord Krishna or Karna. Oprah says you should know who you are and just own it. She's a funny one, that woman. She's not married either but she's very clever, like Smrithi. If you see her in America, tell her your mother said hello.'

LONDON, 2003

When Smrithi announced her pregnancy, Priya packed her bags, stocked the freezer for Siva, and left for London, proposing to stay for three months.

'I'm going to be helpful,' she declared to her husband.

'Why are you going four weeks early?' he asked nervously.

'To nurse her through her confinement obviously. You can join me in London when you've finished writing letters to the UNHRC,' she replied defiantly.

'Whatever you do, don't talk about the Hindu wedding,' Nala warned her.

'What Hindu wedding?'

In her hand luggage she carried a 5kg block of deep-frozen chocolate cake, Smrithi's favourite, made for her by Shiranthi and Tupperware containers of frozen aubergine curry from Nala.

As soon as she arrived, she rearranged Smrithi's spice cupboard the way she liked it. She reorganised the fridge so the restorative cooking and bulk freezing could begin, explaining, 'Smrithi, the coriander and cumin in sarrakku powder will heal and act as a natural antiseptic, the okra will lubricate your stools, in case of tearing and constipation, the garlic will release your uterine wind, and the shark meat helps breast milk production. Everyone knows that.'

Everyone except her daughter.

Smrithi gave birth to a girl, Ahalya. The baby looked like a little bird, fresh from its shell. She was covered in a soft down of black hair with folds of skin hanging loosely over her tiny frame. She was mesmerizingly beautiful and terrifyingly fragile. The new parents and grandparents were in awe and in love.

Smrithi read books on birth, babies, and breast feeding, and she had her own ideas on how to recover post-pregnancy, how to feed, and how and when to put the baby to sleep. Priya was amazed – why were there so *many* books on this topic? And who in God's name made Gina Ford the boss of everything?

Prashanth seemed just as committed to doing everything 'by the book', and together, the young couple would pore over them as though they were textbooks or instruction manuals, highlighting sections, bookmarking pages, and colour-coding chapters.

'Why don't you ask me, mahal? I've been through all of this before. I'm your mother, I… I could help you.'

'I know you can Amma. You are helping me,' Smrithi smiled, examined her baby and calmly referred to her book.

She couldn't help herself: while Smrithi slept, Priya added finely chopped shark meat to the chicken sarraku curry. At the back of the pantry cupboard she hid a tin of formula milk and gave the baby a quick top-up feed while rocking her to sleep instead of that outrageous swaddle-and-leave method that Smrithi was trying to adopt.

'I'm so proud of her, Amma. She's independent and capable. It's hard to believe she's mine,' Priya said tearfully to Nala on the phone.

'It's not hard to imagine that at all, mahal. You raised her and she's just like you.'

'She's a lot like Dhara too, Amma. I'm so proud of that as well. I've asked her to take the baby to Colombo while the ceasefire lasts. Dhara needs to see her grandchild; it's important for all of them.'

It was important to her too. It helped stem the unease that had existed on the edges of her happiness for years, slowly inching towards the centre; towards her heart.

'I just wish Smrithi was happier I'm here. I wish she…needed me.' The way I need her, she thought.

She re-stacked her daughter's freezer as she spoke to Nala. She had cooked four weeks worth of curries for her. Things with the baby would become easier after that.

Finally, when it was time for her to return to Australia, both she and Smrithi hugged and cried at the airport. She boarded the plane feeling that the trip had not been what she thought it would be. The disappointment was confusing but as she relaxed into her uncomfortable seat she realised she was relieved to be leaving.

19

PINNAWELA ELEPHANT ORPHANAGE,
NORTH-EAST OF COLOMBO, 2004

Smrithi took a sip of her tea and winced at its sweetness. Tourists would leave Sri Lanka with a distorted view of the country's most famous export.

'Prashanth, I want you to know I'm writing this news piece, if you can call it that, under protest.' She kissed him and her baby daughter and stood up. The fluorescent light on the café wall flickered erratically as it attracted and killed another mosquito.

'It's alright cunj. This story has provided us with a much needed tax deductible holiday,' Prashanth took out the bottle of repellent and liberally doused Ahalya.

Smrithi flicked through the script she'd written for the journalist, once more. She shook her head. 'They're going to film in the afternoon. Apparently the light is better but I think Finuala just needs the extra time to memorise my words.'

Prashanth laughed. 'Don't be mean Smrithi, it doesn't suit you. If you want to tell stories about Sri Lanka then you shouldn't front them. You'll be recognised here and you'll never be allowed close to the truth. There are many stories in this country – stay quiet and you'll learn more.'

'You sound like my Appappa. He's the quiet and knowledgeable type. It's the Tamil variation of strong and silent.'

'That's me. If you don't have to work this morning then let's pretend we're tourists like Sunhat Lady over there.' He motioned to a pale lady in an oversized woven hat.

'The feeding has almost finished and I've paid for a few bottles,' Prashanth stood up and strapped Ahalya to his back in a harness, saying, 'best to avoid sudden death by stampede.' He took Smrithi's hand and they joined the group of tourists at the elephant stalls.

One of the mahouts was collecting payment chits and handing out bottles of milk in exchange. He tucked the chits into a fold in his sarong. The baby elephants jostled each other, craning forward with their supple trunks raised. Smrithi laughed with delight as she thrust a bottle into an eager mouth. The elephant was no taller than her chest.

'Hold onto it hard, they've got a strong suck!' she shouted at Prashanth over the sound of babies crying for more milk and attention. She gripped both hands around the bottle as the baby quickly emptied it. Prashanth exchanged his last chit for two more bottles and gave her one.

'They're like children!' Prashanth shouted back. 'That was amazing. I feel a whole new sense of sympathy for you cunj,' he held his own chest in mock pain.

Smrithi handed her empty bottle back to the mahout.

'Stand back everyone, stand back,' the mahout said, cracking his stick on the side of the stall several times. The five babies huddled together and moved to the back, waiting. A man in a white safari suit stepped forward. He straightened his badge and cleared his throat ceremoniously.

'Good morning everyone, my name is Asela Jayasinghe and I will be your guide for today. I hope you enjoyed the feeding session. You are welcome to show your gratitude to our mahouts at anytime. They accept all major currencies but prefer US dollars.'

The crowd laughed, some uncomfortably.

'In half an hour we will take the elephants down Rambukkana Road to the Mal Oya River. We have seventy-seven elephants here at Pinnawela at the moment, including twelve more babies at the nursery.

'Sadly, our numbers are growing due to the war which I'm sure you all know about. Now that there is a ceasefire and a chance for peace, my rangers are making trips into the jungles of the north and east, to rescue these gentle giants from those terrible Tigers.' He lingered on the word 'tigers', elongating the last letter. It sounded like he had mosquitoes in his mouth.

'When we find the orphans we can integrate them quickly into the herd. Female elephants are very community-minded and when a mother dies, another mother in the herd will adopt the calf. She will feed and protect the calf as if it was her own.

'We offer them a home here – more than simply food and shelter. We offer them a chance to recover from trauma, and to rebuild their herd, their family, through our internationally renowned breeding programme. Are there any questions yet?' He looked around.

'Where are the bulls?' Sunhat Lady raised her hand politely, revealing an intricate brown henna design on her white palm and wrist. She wore an embroidered gauzy blouse, shaped like a short kaftan, over cotton pants. The blouse clung to her fulsome body when the breeze strengthened. She hadn't noticed but the mahouts had.

'We keep them in a separate section at the far end of the compound. The tuskers, or the bulls with tusks, are each kept alone, with their own mahout. We do this for your safety of course madam.'

Sunhat Lady took her hat off. Her perfect ash-blonde hair was arranged in careful layers and hid the years well. Smrithi guessed she was in her fifties. She instinctively tried to tidy herself.

'She had a colour, wash and blow-dry at The Colombo Plaza before she left Colombo this morning,' Prashanth whispered. Smrithi smacked him.

'Do the elephants get to choose who they mate with in your breeding programme?' Sunhat Lady asked, this time revealing more of her accent.

'English and moneyed,' Prashanth whispered again.

'I'm sorry madam, I don't understand the question...'

'Do the elephants get to choose their partners?' Sunhat Lady asked again. Smrithi looked down. 'I mean, it seems awfully cruel. You said some of these elephants have been through a war. I just thought it would be kinder not to force a partner on them and let them choose or breed more naturally.'

'Ah yes, I see. Well, here at Pinnawela, we try to mimic the habitat and the, how shall I say it...the rituals of life that occur in nature. We create a safe environment and we allow *nature* to take its course. In this way, we successfully bred fourteen calves last year.

'Now, if there are no further questions, enjoy your playtime with the elephants and please make sure you are wearing closed shoes. The orphanage is a charity, not a commercial enterprise, and we cannot accept any responsibility for injuries incurred while you are here. Welcome to Lanka.' He clicked his heels together sharply and smiled graciously at the crowd.

The gates of the stall opened and the babies rushed towards them. Smrithi reached her arms out to one but a mahout stepped forward and tapped it away with his stick.

'You like touch elephant?' his smile was stained yellow. He held one hand out to Smrithi, and with the other, raised his stick at the baby. He never took his practised gaze or smile from her.

'Yes, I like touch elephant,' she replied, pushing dirty notes into his hand. He lowered his stick and the baby rushed towards her, its trunk rapidly searching her body for food.

She laughed as the gentle prodding became more insistent and daring. 'Stop that!' She pulled the trunk away as the baby tried to lift her shirt. She reached into her bag and retrieved the tamarind pods she'd been saving.

'Here, try these but don't tell anyone,' she said, leaning down to play with the leathery flap of its ear.

'You are beautiful,' she whispered, catching the sticky, brown jam that slipped out of its mouth. 'That's the best bit, don't waste it.' She offered the tamarind paste back to the baby's trunk and rubbed the forehead between its almond eyes.

'Are you trying to mother that elephant? I heard you telling it to eat more,' Prashanth stood between Smrithi and the mahouts who were circling for more 'gratitude'.

'I can't help it, they're so beautiful. Even when they're young, their eyes look so old, so knowing.' The baby wrapped its trunk around her and pulled her closer. She bent down and put her arms around its enormous head. She could smell crushed coconut and jackfruit.

'It's the Ganesha in them,' Prashanth said, bending down so Ahalya could reach forward and touch the animal.

'Good morning, could I please pat your elephant?' Sunhat Lady joined them.

'Of course, although it's not my elephant,' Smrithi replied.

'Thank you, those mahouts won't leave me alone.'

'Are you enjoying your holiday here?' Smrithi asked.

'Is it that obvious I'm not a local?' She wrinkled her peeling nose.

Smrithi burst out laughing. 'We're not locals either. We're from London. My family is originally from the north of Sri Lanka – Jaffna – you wouldn't have been there.'

'No, we've been to the tea estates in Nuwara Eliya though. And Sigiriya of course. We climbed to the top of the mountain. It was exhausting but the palace was worth it. The view was spectacular.'

'Have you been to Yala yet?' Smrithi asked. 'I'm researching puff pieces about the rise of eco-tourism in Sri Lanka. I work for a lifestyle channel,' she said apologetically.

'Eco-tourism?'

'Yes, well, we've taken quite a loose definition of Eco, it's more like animal tourism and the successful integration of nature reserves with tourism here, instead of just a beach-based industry. Apparently it's all the rage with western tourists.' She needed to find a better way of explaining what she did for a living.

'Yes, I suppose so. I never thought of it like that. I didn't even know there was a war here until my husband suggested we visit! It's such a surprising country. We are going to Yala. I'm very excited – imagine a 5 star chalet in a jungle, with wild animals wandering all around you.'

Smrithi nodded and gave the elephant another tamarind pod.

'I'm sorry to gush!' Sunhat Lady said.

'Don't apologise,' Smrithi replied. 'They're all beautiful places, the highlights of Sri Lanka, really.' The ash blonde highlights.

'I know!' Sunhat Lady nodded emphatically, loosening the layers of her hair. 'I love Sri Lanka. I could live here.'

'Yes, it is a very pretty country. Nice beaches and nice hotels,' Smrithi tried to sound sincere.

'It's more than that – the people are so friendly. There's something spiritual and serene about the place.'

'Spiritual?' Smrithi repeated. Ahalya had started to wriggle free from the harness and she helped Prashanth pull tightly on the straps, locking the little girl against his sweaty back.

'Yes, spiritual. It says so much about your society that you'd look after these poor creatures. Where else would you find an orphanage for elephants?'

Only in Sri Lanka.

'It must be part of your Buddhist mentality,' Sunhat Lady smiled.

Prashanth cleared his throat loudly and stepped forward. 'Yes, that must be it. It's been lovely to meet you but I think our daughter is itching to throw herself into a herd of elephants.'

'Yes, sudden death by stampede – best to avoid it,' Smrithi echoed weakly. She allowed Prashanth to usher her away quickly. Tomorrow they would head back to Colombo, and to Dhara.

Dhara held onto Smrithi's hand tightly; she couldn't see a train. She'd been crossing the tracks on her own for more than twenty-five years but suddenly she felt nervous, as though the young woman's presence opened up small crevices in her confidence, through which strange, previously unthought-of anxieties crept through. She looked both ways once again and pulled Smrithi quickly across the aged iron lines, careful not to trip in the sand and weedy tufts that grew around them.

This was Smrithi's first visit to Sri Lanka since 1983. Neither of them had ever spoken about that terrifying night when the ashes of people and homes billowed into the sky like black storm clouds. Dhara wouldn't talk of it now; there was so much else – so much more – she wanted to say, if she dared.

Together they faced the narrow stretch of beach. The ocean was advancing, gradually eating at the boundaries of the island. The broken granite boulders on the sand's edge couldn't hold it back forever.

'Colombo has some excellent restaurants, you know,' Dhara said.

'I know, mami. I just thought we could sit on the beach and eat kadalai,' Smrithi replied, smiling at the chickpea vendor. He shuffled over, hobbling under the weight of his steel basin, brimming with freshly boiled chickpeas. He set it down in the sand.

'How many?' he asked in Tamil, wiping his hands on his sarong before retying it quickly.

'Two, thank you,' Dhara replied. The man took a square of newspaper from the basin and deftly twisted it into a cone. He scooped the chickpeas into it, squeezed juice from a tired looking lime, and finished it with a generous sprinkling of chilli powder. He swirled the cone three times without spilling a chickpea, and brandished the delicacy, properly seasoned, towards Smrithi.

'This looks great,' she inhaled.

Dhara laughed. 'We could make a real Sri Lankan out of you yet.'

'Thank you, I'd like to be a local with you,' Smrithi replied, throwing more chickpeas into her mouth.

Dhara flinched. 'Tonight I'm taking you to Shri Balakrishna's,' she said quickly. 'They make the best vegetarian lamprais in the city. They use soya curry instead of any meat. It's delicious, almost as good as your mother's.'

'My mother's?' Smrithi asked, coughing on her food. 'My mother makes lamprais?'

'Yes,' Dhara replied, patting her daughter's back hard. 'She used to make amazing lamprais. Her flavours were complimentary and complex, but then she'd make one of the lamprais curries a little edgy, a little contradictory, just to shake things up.'

'She never told me! She's never made it for us. No-one makes their own lamprais in Sydney, we buy it from the Sri Lankan caterers.'

'Your mother has many talents she doesn't boast about,' Dhara replied. 'There's a reason no-one makes lamprais; they require skill, patience and meticulous attention to detail.

'You need to make four or five curries – the meat, the fish cutlet, seeni sambol, prawn blachan, fried plantains, spiced rice – it's endless. And if that hasn't exhausted you, you need to wrap individual portions of rice and curries in a banana leaf and steam it.'

'I can't believe Amma used to do that. Why did she stop?' Smrithi shook her head.

'She had you. She put all her lamprais time and a lot more into raising you.' Dhara crumpled the oily newspaper cone into a ball. The crows recognised the gesture and bobbed closer.

'She's a good mother, isn't she,' Smrithi said, more to herself than to Dhara. 'I see that, now that I have my own child. I realise how hard she tried; still tries. So much of parenthood comes down to time – how much time do you have, how much can you give to your children?'

'Your Amma gives a lot, she gives everything,' Dhara replied. She stared out into the blue. The waves gathered at the break like rebellious pleats of a sari, yearning to free themselves and stream away, back over the horizon.

Priya had given her daughter all the time she had. She had held nothing back for herself. She had devoted and divided that time between her children and her husband. It was a simple equation with the beautiful distilled clarity of a couplet from the *Thirukkural*.

Time would wear away the granite boulders and the Indian Ocean would claim more of the beach for itself. How much time would God give Dhara with the people she loved?

'I feel like time is the only important thing I need, mahal,' she said, picking up the remains of kadalai from her lap and throwing it to the crows. 'Time to give to my work, time to be with my family, time to be with you. I pray that I... I have more time.'

'You make it sound like you're dying, mami!' Smrithi touched her arm.

'No, mahal,' Dhara tried to laugh but the sound that came out was disjointed and forced. 'I'm completely fine, a picture of outstanding health. I just wish I could see you all more, especially that beautiful little daughter of yours. She is at the beginning of time.' She exhaled deeply and then inhaled the sharp, salty air.

'And you are only half way through yours, mami, remember that,' Smrithi leaned over and kissed her hard on the cheek.

Dhara stood up and reached for Smrithi's hand again. She would lead her back over the tracks, more confidently this time.

✿

She held the sleeping child, watching the familiar rise and fall of her chest, the indentation between the pink bottom lip and the chin, the balled fist that sometimes jerked, then relaxed and opened against her smooth cheek, the small nails with half moons at their roots, the faint lines on the padded palm telling the story of a life barely begun. She looked just like Smrithi.

Dhara closed her eyes and prayed. She asked Lord Ganesha to remove the child's obstacles from her life; she asked Saraswathi, the goddess of learning, to teach her wisdom, and Lord Vishnu, the Protector, to watch over her. She begged Lord Shiva, the Destroyer, to keep His distance.

She knew these gods were just different forms of the one, formless Divine, but found herself reverting to stories from her childhood: stories her father told her about a time when gods walked the earth and heard the prayers of the devout.

She was devout. She prayed and prayed every day – for courage and for forgiveness. Please God, she asked, help Smrithi understand, make her forgive me, keep her safe. Please God, she begged, help me finish the path I started. Help me do my duty. I have chosen my dharma, she said.

She gently placed the child down on her bed. She kissed her on the lips and froze when the little girl stirred, but didn't open her eyes. She lay next to her, careful not to wake her. I have chosen my dharma, and it is mine, not Smrithi's, she repeated and closed her eyes again.

The next day Dhara drove Smrithi and her family to the airport. Prashanth tried to make small talk about the traffic, cricket, the weather; anything to fill the silence and sadness between them.

Finally, Smrithi spoke. 'I don't want to leave you here, mami.'

'I live here, mahal. This is my home. Now it's time for you to return to yours.'

'I just wish… I just wish we had more time,' Smrithi replied, echoing Dhara's earlier words. 'I can ask for more projects in Asia, or even look for work in Sri Lanka.'

'No, Smrithi. We've talked about this before – and you have a child now. You have a responsibility to keep her safe; to do what's best for her. This ceasefire won't last, it never does. When the fighting starts – well, this just isn't the place for you.' She didn't know how else to explain it.

'If it's too dangerous for me, then it's too dangerous for you, mami,' Smrithi said softly.

'This is my home,' Dhara repeated. 'I have a duty to be here. You have a duty to your daughter; to love her and give her the kind of life she couldn't have here. We'll see each other again.' She wiped the tears from her face with the back of her hand. She couldn't look Smrithi in the eyes.

'Perhaps I'll find a way to come to London. I'd like to see this Primrose Hill you always talk about. I'm glad we had this time together, though.' She pulled the car into the drop-off lane and turned off the engine.

While Prashanth assembled the bags onto a trolley, Dhara held the baby one last time. Pressing her face to the baby's she noisily kissed her cheeks, her hair, and her hands. It made the little girl laugh so she kissed them all over again, laughing with her and finally, crying. She gave the child to Prashanth and held Smrithi for a long moment.

'You are a wonderful mother,' she whispered.

'You are a wonderful mami,' Smrithi whispered back. Dhara felt a pain in her chest.

'I need to go now, I'm not allowed to park here.' She kissed Smrithi one more time and started the car without looking back. She didn't want to watch them leave.

COLOMBO, 2004

The agar-agar jelly at the Galle Face Hotel was palm green. Management hadn't changed the colour in the fifty years that Dhara had been drinking faloodah there. Management probably hadn't changed the colour in the one-hundred-and-thirty-eight years since the hotel was built from the skeleton of a Dutch villa.

She sipped her drink slowly as she read Priya's latest letter. Despite email and weekly calls, they both still enjoyed writing. She sat in the hotel lobby instead of at her favourite table on the verandah. It was unusually windy for May. She liked to suck the jelly pieces up her straw first, rolling the gelatinous emeralds around in her mouth before swallowing them. Then the basil seeds – they were swollen and sat on the surface of the rose syrup like fish roe on a pink pond. She lifted her straw and sucked those next, grinding them between her teeth. She glanced around to see if anyone heard her.

No one was listening. The magnificent colonial lobby was quieter than usual. Even the Galle Face Hotel had been affected by the recent state of emergency. She had barely noticed it. Another year drifted by and another ceasefire drifted with it. Under the watchful eyes of the Norwegian mediators, both sides had finally conceded to a federal solution – the Tigers had relinquished their objective of a separate Tamil state; and the government had agreed to devolve some power to the Tamils in their own provinces. An agreement written in sand, washed away by the rising tide of war. You can't hold back the tide. Its surge and swell was primal.

Last month's election had consolidated power for President Kumaratunga, Bandaranaike's daughter, and her new Prime Minister, Rajapaksa. Neither wanted a federal solution. She doubted the Tigers had ever really wanted one either. Some aspirations were too deeply embedded in our DNA.

The Tigers of the eastern province had splintered from the Tigers of the north. Now these factions fought each other. Colonel Karuna in the east and the Tamils' Supreme Leader Prabhakaran in the north: the army still hadn't entered into the conflict, they didn't need to. They could afford to watch. Like an auto-immune disease, the Tigers had begun attacking their own body.

Dhara continued to work with all sides of the conflict. Her only priority was the movement of medicine and equipment into the Tamil provinces. Those areas had become more accessible since the ceasefire.

She kept her promise to Nala, and had not been back to Jaffna since 1984. But she also kept a different promise she made to herself, years before that, when she vomited a viscous saltiness from her body and invoked the sun, begging it to scorch her clean.

She paid her bill – Five hundred Rupees. Rajan would be horrified. She had to agree, it was extortionate. As she left the hotel and tried to hail an auto, she looked across the Galle Road. A white van was there, as she knew it would be.

TRINCOMALEE,
EASTERN PROVINCE OF SRI LANKA, 2005

Dhara was in Colombo when the tsunami happened. Even there she could feel the shudder. Later, she imagined white, foamy froth, riding on the crest of a stone-coloured wall. Similar to an image her father had given her, a memory from his childhood that plagued hers. It came back to her now, when she thought about entire villages swallowed by an angry ocean. Families, homes, graves, memories swept away. Nothing but the heads of palm trees, lifting their chins out of the water, gasping for air. The earth bowed and stumbled under the weight of so much water.

She applied for a government permit to join the NGOs in the eastern province. Her friends at *Médecins Sans Frontières* were quick to offer her a job, they knew she had excellent experience although no-one had quite the right experience for this crisis. She packed a small bag, a crate of her own medical supplies and a needle and thread.

'Have a drink with me tonight,' the man said in Sinhalese, sitting down next to her. He took his MSF tag off and put it on the table, rubbing the back of his neck. He was darker-skinned than her, his black hair shorn down to his scalp.

'I'm far too old to have a drink with you,' she replied in English. He was handsome in that unwashed way that only camp doctors could be.

'How old are you?' he replied, undeterred.

'Is the entire Belgian Unit this forward?'

'Only the French members. The Flemish are not as interesting,' he shrugged his shoulders. He refused to speak in English.

She laughed. 'You are neither, what's your excuse?' she asked in Sinhalese. She didn't like the taste of it in her mouth.

'I don't need an excuse to flirt with you. What's a nice doctor like you doing in a place like this?' he asked, motioning to the dark canvas walls and simple folding beds and chairs that served as their communal mess area.

'I could ask you the same,' she reverted to English. 'What is a Sinhalese doctor like you doing in a camp for displaced Tamils?' she asked, not maliciously.

'The same thing as you. I'm trying to help. I heard the need was greater here. I've been stationed in West Africa for the last few years with MSF but after... what happened, it didn't make sense to me anymore. My family still lives in Colombo. I just wanted to be useful here. My name is Suren, by the way, in case you were at all interested.' He held out a hand to her.

'I hope you washed your hands?' she hesitated, half-mocking, half-serious.

'Twice, like I was scrubbing for surgery. And you?'

She too knew the need was greater here. When she arrived at the MSF camp, she wondered if God hated them. After everything she'd seen with the Tigers, all the bodies of young men and women, boys and girls really, that she'd sewn back together or whose pieces she'd thrown away, she wondered whether God felt that carnage was not fast enough and a simpler solution was required. He brought a dam wall down and allowed a cleansing such as they had never seen before. She wondered what they had done to be so forsaken, so wiped from the face of their small island. She wondered how they could be worth less; how they could be loved less than others.

She shook her head, at no-one in particular, at herself, at God perhaps. Suren was looking at her, studying her face brazenly, waiting for an answer.

'I always wash my hands,' she replied, laughing again.

'You are beautiful when you laugh, you should do it more often.'

'There is little reason to laugh,' she replied, standing up. Her shift had started.

✧

Dhara held the child over the latrine. Her legs were braced on either side of the narrow pit. She gripped her under the arms, suspending her above the wooden seat. The girl was still too weak to squat on her own and Dhara didn't want her to touch anything inside the makeshift hut.

'There, good girl,' she said, holding the child against her when she'd finished. The stench in the hut was oppressive. She would never get used to it; or the blood and mucus that laced the diarrhoea, like oil in a river.

'Lean on me. Now what do we do?'

'We wash our hands,' the little girl replied softly.

Yes, Dhara thought, we wash our hands with contaminated water.

'Remember chutie, when you wash your hands ask for the sari-water.' Dhara pointed to the sign above the pump. It showed water dripping from a filtration bag made from an old sari. Nala used to have hundreds of saris.

The doctors were trying to make people use the latrines, but many were too weak to move. They lay in their own faeces, under canvas tents that were meant to shelter them from the sun. Those closer to death were moved to makeshift warehouses, where they slept on top of plastic sheeting. It could be rolled up and replaced.

People lay in endless orderly rows, making disorderly sounds: low moans of pain and raw cries of grief. IVs were rationed; children and mothers first. Peanut-butter-like protein paste was squeezed from their wrappers; the wrappers were torn and licked shiny clean.

The seasoned disaster-relief staff waited for the sour smell of rotting fish. They feared it more than the mighty waves that had carried them to this camp where people lay like pustules on a corpse. The elderly didn't speak, they had seen cholera before, and they didn't dare say its name.

The tsunami had drowned parts of the south where the Sinhalese lived, and more of the east where the Tamils lived. Tens of thousands killed and hundreds of thousands displaced, more efficiently than any civil war could do.

Sewage pipes broke and burst, vomiting death into freshwater supplies and seeping insidiously into the groundwater. Men and women layered banana leaves on the floor of their shelters. The parquetry formed a flimsy barrier against the earth made soft by quiet toxins underneath.

In the south, foreign-aid rebuilt houses, hospitals and villages quickly. Little girls had schools in which to study. They had ceramic toilets and entire sanitation systems in which to defecate.

President Kumaratunga had stopped tsunami-aid to the parts of the eastern province held by the Tigers. She said she was preventing them from stealing a cut.

Dhara helped the little girl stand. Her arms and legs were shrivelled like the spindles of a murunga plant. When she breathed, a deep hollow sank in and out frantically beneath her ribcage. Her name, Jayanthi, her age, eight and village, Mutur, had been registered. She waited now for her family to find her. Her mother and father and anna and ammamma and thambi. And Parameswari, her little goat. And the hundreds in her small fishing village: men who would have unfurled the canvas from their boats and pushed them out that morning, women who tended to their fires, made thosai for breakfast and said their prayers. Children, like her, who wanted to swim in the sapphire blue and find treasure on the shallow ocean floor instead of going to school. She waited and she remembered.

She was dragged between rooftops of submerged buildings until she was pummelled and trapped against a palm tree, its mighty spine bent from the weight of too many people sheltering at its peak. A man shimmied down and protected her from the lashing waves. Another followed him pulling her up to safety, her small weight dropping the head of the tree an inch closer to the rushing water below. Someone put a trembling arm around her. No-one spoke.

The girl bent forward and vomited clear fluid, tinted with a streak of bile. It splashed on her bare feet. She didn't notice. Dhara held her as her wasted body cramped and faeces rushed again from her corroded insides. More blood and this time pus. Suren was at her side, helping her. They settled the child onto her plastic sheeting.

LONDON, 2005

Dhara was in England for a conference on infectious diseases at the London School of Tropical Medicine and Hygiene. She was presenting a paper with Suren, on 'Disease control after a disaster' based on their tsunami-relief experience.

She tried not to think about work. She was with Smrithi, surrounded by children for whom the future stretched limitlessly ahead of them. She watched with pride as Smrithi deftly balanced a phone between her shoulder and ear, while putting a nappy on her new son. The baby, Rishi, looked back at his mother through the longest eyelashes she had ever seen.

'OK Amma, I will. Of course I will. Speak to you soon,' Smrithi said, grimacing a goodbye to her mother and dropping the phone with relief.

'Amma wants me to make sure you eat properly, Dhara mami. She's asked me to take you to Hopper Hut in Walthamstow for some authentic hoppers.' She laughed, as did Dhara. Dhara could get the coconut milk pancakes from her local hopper restaurant in Colombo. Priya wanted Dhara to make sure Smrithi was eating properly. She was under instructions to go to Walthamstow in east London, bulk-buy Sri Lankan food and restock Smrithi's freezer. Priya had been in London for the birth of Smrithi's second child a few months ago and she was concerned her daughter's freezer might have already run out of food.

As Smrithi juggled the new baby, her toddler Ahalya and various other tasks, Dhara felt confident her daughter could pull together a meal or two.

Smrithi handed the baby to her. She took him gingerly. Like Ahalya, he was exquisite; created perfectly in the image of his mother. She lowered her face to his, inhaling the space between his jaw and neck. It was warm and milky.

Smrithi laughed again, 'Amma does that too. It must be a Sri Lankan thing.'

Dhara smiled self-consciously. 'I am still amazed by how beautiful they are,' she said.

'Me too,' Smrithi replied. 'Appa always laughs when I say that. He tells me that even the blackest mother crow thinks its chicks are golden.'

'He's quoting an old proverb. It sounds better in Tamil,' Dhara laughed.

'Appa says everything sounds better in Tamil.'

'He's right. I'm deeply sorry you never learned Tamil, mahal. It is your...mother tongue. It's important to...us.' She stopped for a moment and began again, more lightly.

'But as he knows, you are no crow Smrithi and your chicks are as golden as the sun itself.' She swaddled the baby and put him in his basinet on the floor. Sitting down next to it, she held her arms out to Ahalya who joined her.

'Amma tells me you're moving back to Sydney soon,' she said.

'Yes. Prashanth has agreed but he's worried. We both are. He's only ever been there for holidays. It's been years since I lived there and I guess I've changed too.' Smrithi straightened the play mat in front of her, combing its tasselled trimming with her fingers.

'Not as much as you think you have, mahal.'

'Dhara mami, do you think you'll stay in Sri Lanka forever?' Smrithi asked.

'I do. Is your Amma plotting another extradition attempt?' she asked back.

'She's always plotting one for you,' Smrithi replied. 'Amma says... Amma says that if you'd moved to Australia with them, your life would have been different.'

'I know Amma says that. She's right I suppose.' She looked down, unsure of how to explain her choices, but desperately wanting to try.

'The *Vedas* say that man has four stages of life. First you are a student, then a *grihasta*, or householder with a family, then you are a... actually, I forget the other stages.' She laughed nervously, swallowing the dryness in her throat. 'But the stage of *grihasta* – which you are in now, with a husband and children and a home – I think that was never meant to be, for me.'

She had known that for a long time. The *grihasta* had been broken, left in a cold, dark room somewhere in the shadow of an old Dutch fort. She had been catapulted into a different stage of life whose name she could not remember; perhaps the *Vedas* had not envisaged such a stage and therefore not given it the validity of a name. Whatever it was, it was hers and on most days, she had made her peace with it. On some days, like today, she wished it had been different.

'Can I be a *grihasta* if I'm not actually married?' Smrithi asked.

'You're a naughty girl. You should just have the Hindu ceremony,' Dhara laughed at her, adding, 'It would make your mother happy.'

'Do you regret it? Not leaving, I mean...' Smrithi asked.

Dhara looked at the baby in the basinet next to her. She suddenly remembered the name of the last stage of life before death – the *sanyasi*, or one who has given up all attachment to the world and is ready for liberation.

She wanted to pick the baby up and hold him again, to cuddle him with the little girl on her lap. She had learned not to regret. It required a soldier's discipline and a sanyasi's detachment. She had learned to live through her sister's joy rather than begrudge it.

But these children, her grandchildren – life began again with them. She found her discipline faltering and her detachment a mirage. An old, suppressed, almost physical ache began to pulse, once more, deep within her belly.

'No. I have no regrets, mahal,' she lied. 'People say that nothing good comes of violence – it's not completely true. I think violence teaches us to long for peace. I long for peace and I hope the work I do brings some peace to others.'

'Appa says Rajapaksa means to finish this. You know he doesn't long for peace. Why don't you leave now?' Smrithi asked. Rajan, Nala, Priya – they all asked her the same thing.

The new president hadn't taken long to make himself Minister of Defence and Finance as well. He was hiring his brothers, cousins and friends for other positions, like a cancer metastasising through the country.

'The abductions are increasing – Sathya Ponnusamy's uncle was taken in a white car and never came back. That was months ago.'

'It would have been a white van,' Dhara said quietly.

'What?' Smrithi asked.

'A white van – they use white vans, not cars, to take you.'

'Mami, leave while you still can, before they take *you*; before the fighting starts again. You could come to Sydney with us.' Smrithi was struggling to speak, tears falling against her wishes, as she felt the familiar frustration rise. Ahalya went to her mother and she held her close.

Dhara said nothing. There were no words to explain. She was tied to her home, an umbilical cord that nourished her just as easily as it could strangle her. For the first time in years, she found herself wanting to pull against it, hard.

SYDNEY, 2007

The early disappointments of their new life in Australia shook Smrithi like airplane turbulence. She assumed it was temporary but was silently fearful it might be fatal.

'Migrating is terrifying,' Nala had warned her. 'Migrating back home may even be harder. You expect so much more of it – so much more of yourselves. What would you like me to cook for you when you get here?'

Prashanth turned off the television in disgust. 'Do you think other Australians will think of our children as Australian?' The local news didn't fill them with confidence, in particular, stories about boat people. The debate about border security and a global refugee crisis had been sidelined in favour of political mileage.

Smrithi answered carefully. 'I don't know cunj, we just haven't been here long enough to know how people classify us.' She tried to keep her response neutral. He was worried that in Australia, you were either Australian or you were a migrant.

The word 'migrant' held a sense of 'other' that made both of them uncomfortable. It delineated and excluded ownership or the right to an equal place in Australia. Names, categories, and words: they could be corrupted and weaponised.

'In Britain, I was proud of being British and proud of being British Asian,' he replied. 'I just don't see different ethnic groups accepted in the public space. Politicians, television shows and journalists are pretty white with the occasional indigenous person, Pacific Islander or Chinese. Diversity isn't part of the national image – the prevailing concept is still white, even though a lot of faces we see are not. It makes me wonder what image of normal our children will absorb – how will that make them feel about themselves?'

There was nothing she could say. Ahalya would join the local public school soon and she was disappointed to find that the only scripture classes offered were Anglicanism and Catholicism. Her children could either learn about Judeo-Christian culture; or they could learn how to colour in with all the other infidels.

She missed the British Asians of England. She missed George Alagiah and Mishal Husain from BBC World, even if their latest news was about the escalation of fighting in Sri Lanka, where the Tigers were cornered in the north.

She missed being lectured on human rights and the draconian state they lived in by Shami Chakrabarti, the strident British Asian leader of Liberty. She missed waiting jealously for the latest British Asian writer to emerge from East London via Oxbridge.

She even missed watching out for Prashanth's brother, Praveen, who was an actor. He had represented the full versatility of the British Asian identity on television. He was a regular on *East Enders*, *The Bill* and *Spooks*. He had played a doctor, gangster, terrorist, corner-store owner and someone forced into an arranged marriage. Later in his career he had played the Every British Man, rather than the Every British Asian.

She thought there was scope for Praveen to be written into *Home and Away*. They really did need an Indian family to move to Summer Bay. She could see it now: the family would be called the Kumars. The Kumar parents would own the local convenience store although the Kumar father used to be a doctor back in India. The Kumar daughter was studying to be a doctor and had an illicit white surfie boyfriend. Whenever people were injured on the beach, the eccentric but charming Grandma Kumar would rush out and sprinkle turmeric on the injury.

The Kumar son, convincingly played by Praveen, was quietly hiding his secret identity as an Al Qaeda sleeper agent. Of course the writers, who would never be employed by the more culturally sensitive SBS channel, had overlooked the fact that the family was clearly Hindu and not Muslim.

In Season 432 of *Home and Away*, the Kumar family would invite all of Summer Bay over for a BBQ tandoori kangaroo to celebrate their new-found citizenship (and perhaps the release of the extended Kumar family from Christmas Island). Little did the residents of Summer Bay know that due to poor writing, the Kumar son would fulfil his racial stereotype. He had been 'activated' and had of course spiked the tandoori marinade with anthrax.

'Smrithi, you have to stop daydreaming about the Kumar family. They are never moving to Summer Bay,' Prashanth snapped her back to reality.

'How did you know?'

'It's obvious when you start talking to yourself in your head. Focus please. I want the children to be proud of being Australian, but within that national identity I want them to feel proud of being Tamil as well.'

'Sri Lankan Tamil,' she corrected him.

'No cunj, just Tamil; Australian Tamil in fact. Sri Lanka is far less our country than Australia,' he replied.

'But it is our country of origin; it's where our people came from. My father would say we are Tamils from Tamil Eelam,' she said.

'Yes, your father *would* say that. Tamil Eelam doesn't exist. So putting that on a form is only going to get us arrested under a Prevention of Terrorism Act.'

'OK, OK. we are still Tamils from Sri Lanka, aren't we?' she replied. 'We are Tamils with no relationship to the birthplace of our parents. We're a floating diaspora that has to ground itself somewhere,' he put a hand up to stop her from interrupting as she impatiently tried to correct him. 'Smrithi, our identity isn't tied to Sri Lanka beyond our history, which –' he put his hand up again, '– is very important. Where we came from *is* important. But where we are now is also important. We are ethnically Tamil, which makes us Tamil Australians or Australian Tamils – whichever you prefer.'

'Australian Tamils. I feel sad. It's like we have no *oor*, no village.' She felt like crying but she wasn't sure why. She'd never even been to her parents' *oor*. It was such a small word but it held a lot of meaning. Your village was not just about where you lived; it was about who your family was, about who *you* were. It told others about your character not just your ancestral location. Your village mattered.

'Cunji, you're so dramatic. You get that from your grandmother,' he replied, cuddling her. 'We have an *oor*, here in Sydney. It's not so much a village or a place the way it used to be, but a collection of people. We have an *oor* in our community of cousins and friends.'

She felt a little happier.

'I'm not trying to be contrary, I just want being Tamil to be considered a valuable part of being Australian.'

'I don't know if it is or it will be,' she said, pensive. 'But maybe we should start watching SBS in the meantime.'

Priya rolled her eyes. 'What's the point of moving to Sydney if you're going to live on the North Shore. Everyone else is in Strathfield.'

Smrithi sighed. 'If by everyone else, you mean the rest of our extended family, I know they're all in the inner-west. We've tried to like it, honestly Amma, we have. But we prefer the North Shore.'

Her parents' suburb of Strathfield was also known as Strathpuram for its high concentration of Sri Lankan Tamils. Rajan called it the

Wellawatte of Sydney. But its ethnic face was changing, becoming increasingly East Asian.

'Amma, we have no problem with Sri Lankans, or South Asians, or East Asians or any Asians. We used to be British Asians. We just don't want to live in a suburb that's dominated by one or a few ethnic groups, even our own. Prashanth is worried about Sydney's 'ethnic ghettos,'' she said.

'Seriously mahal, you forget that I too lived in London. Golders Green, Hounslow, Tower Hamlets and Tooting could also be described as 'ethnic ghettos'. You lived in Primrose Hill for ten years – from memory, it had an exciting ethnic mix of international expats. It was hardly demographically representative of London, or Britain either.'

Smrithi hated it when her mother was right. In London they only saw a diverse mix of British people when they left Primrose Hill and the business district to go to Heathrow Airport, and then they were reminded of why they lived in Primrose Hill.

'OK Amma. I don't expect you to support our decision, but I would really like it if you could visit us 'up north' if it isn't too far away from Strathpuram. The North Shore has a good mix of cultures, excellent schools, efficient public transport and enormous houses. I think you'll like it.'

'Perhaps,' Amma replied. 'Your grandfather calls it the Cinnamon Gardens of Sydney. He thinks it's ironic you want to move there.'

'Appappa thinks everything is ironic,' Smrithi laughed.

20

NO FIRE ZONE,
IN THE NORTH-EAST OF SRI LANKA, 2009

No. Fire. Zone. Three inaccurate words. She must remember to tell Rajan; he would appreciate the irony. Dhara loved Rajan, Smrithi, Priya and Nala. She loved Nandan and Siva. And her Amma and Appa. She loved reading Rohinton Mistry novels, eating puttu, omelette, coconut chilli sambal, and listening to American country music although she never told anyone about that. As she worked, she tried to remember the words to 'Don't Come Home A-Drinkin' by Loretta Lynn. That woman could sing.

They used the church as a hospital. It was large. Its four walls and most of its roof were intact. It had been stripped of its pews, the precious wood used for cooking fires. The pulpit remained and they turned it on its side, fashioning its sturdy teak front into an operating table. They stored their equipment and meagre supplies in suitcases and bags in different parts of the building. It was safer than keeping everything together.

Each wing of the church was a ward: children in the chancel and sanctuary; operating theatre in the right wing of the transept; priority post-op and ICU in the left wing; triage, burns and everyone else in the knave. The dying and the moderately malnutritioned were left to camp outside, under plastic sheets, old sacks, cardboard, palmyra mats, anything they could scrounge or make to provide shelter from the blistering sun and the last of the monsoonal rain.

On the battered and scabbed roof of the church, they painted a blood red cross. It drew the sick and the dying, and they prayed it would deter the army. The drones could see it and it was all they could do to protect themselves. The steady beat of shelling was getting louder.

'Suren, call them again!' Dhara shouted at her friend. She was gloved and cutting open the collapsed vein of a two-year-old to insert an IV. The child jerked when she made the initial incision but then he just looked at her, eyes empty and drained, too tired to cry from the pain. His mother sat with him on the floor, holding his arm steady with one hand, and stroking his hair with her other.

Suren ran to the portable radio phone and made the call, his hands shaking as he shouted their GPS co-ordinates into the mouthpiece. They had advised the Red Cross of their new location two days ago and again yesterday when they realised the shelling was coming closer. The Red Cross assured them each time that they had informed the army.

She heard the running before she heard the explosion. People picking up their children, picking up their injured, and running. She could hear running, then an explosion followed by another and another. It started with a low whistle and then a roar. And then screams.

The high beams of the roof started to fall. She pulled the child and his mother into a corner of the chancel. She was coughing and crying. Wood cracked against the cement floor next to her. She shuddered over the cowering mother and child.

Light burst into the shape of an enormous, layered marigold. Like the fireworks on New Year's Eve in Colombo. She looked up and saw raindrops of fire fall from the sky. Droplets burrowed through the clothes and skin of people it touched. They ran, screaming, trying to tear the fire out of their bodies but it burrowed deeper still.

From the fire came streamers of white smoke. The streamers found each other and entwined to create a cloud of the purest white she'd ever seen. The cloud rose and rose. Around her, people screamed. The mother pushed her away, clutched her child and ran into the cloud.

'No!' Dhara cried but it was too late. More fire dripped from the sky. It was seeking the church. The sanctuary wall broke. Suddenly there were others around her. They pushed against the broken stone of the walls, and the splintered beams of the roof. They dug to find whoever remained and carried them out into the madness. She held a child. She didn't know whose. He closed his eyes against her chest. She was making a noise she didn't recognise. She wanted to soothe him but she couldn't form words, just the wheezing that spurted from her throat.

She crushed the child against her with one arm, and with her free hand she grabbed a young girl who was standing, dazed and unmoving. Dhara pulled her hard. She wheezed again, the sound becoming more guttural. She held and she pulled and she wheezed and she ran and ran and ran into the jungle.

✧

'We're leaving now,' Suren said to her, pulling the tarpaulin off the jeep. He laid it on the ground and pulled out the scissors from his pack. He cut it into four pieces and gave one to each of the children hovering around him.

'Wait,' he shouted, as they darted away. *Maram kucci*, he yelled in stilted Tamil. *Moondu maram kucci*, he held up three fingers. 'You need three sticks.' He pointed to the mighty Palmyra trees, lying broken around them, but the children had already run off with their treasure. Children learned not to stand still in open places. Three sticks and a bit of tarpaulin: it had proven to be the more effective shelter against the scorching sun. It could be grabbed when the army shelling started again or when the Tigers ordered them to march, herding them with their guns. He found that people were dying trying to grab the complicated UN tents they were given.

After the last attack some of the government doctors had agreed to leave. Suren was the only Sinhalese amongst them. The Ministry of Health had ordered everyone back to Colombo months ago but they had refused.

'Come with us, Dhara. This is the last chance. There is only one way this ends.'

The end.

She had been there at the end for so many people. They looked at her with wild panic and desperation; very occasionally resignation, or worse, relief. She never knew what to say. *Paravaile mahal, padango.*

It doesn't matter, daughter, sleep, she would murmur, holding their broken bodies.

Smrithi was excellent at words. Dhara was better at numbers. There were over one-hundred-and-fifty-thousand refugees in the No Fire Zone. The entire population depended on the UN to eat. Farming and fishing had long since ended. The monthly UN food ration for April was enough for sixty-thousand people for two days. April had thirty days. Dhara was hungry. Around her people starved and shrivelled.

Everything ends. She had felt the end so many times. In the black ants of Gal Oya, the metallic darkness of a police station, the blood-soaked floor of the jungle camp, and now, here.

Here, where children knew when and how to jump into bunkers at the first trilling of missiles the army said it wasn't using. They saw the earth shudder and list like the small fishing boats of their fathers, tossed by a careless ocean; the burst of sound that deafened for a moment, a beautiful, silent moment followed by screaming. Some children, the younger ones tried to clamber out, reaching for their parents if they had any or those who'd carried them this far who were not their parents but someone to hold onto when they'd lost everyone else who'd ever held them before. The older children knew better, they stayed in the bunker and waited, stacked on top of each other like crumbled, dry tea biscuits shoved back in a box.

Here where they lined the children in lifeless rows and could not cover them because they needed the tarpaulins for shelter and the sheets for stretchers and the clothes for bandages. So the flies covered them and sometimes the mothers sat with them and wailed over them and beat their bodies in pain and anger and loss and more pain. They pushed the flies away but the flies came back. They were hungry too.

She begged people to keep digging, deeper into the stone-hard earth. The strong carried spades, picks and hoes and at each stop along the road that was no road, they dug. The strong were not really strong, they were simply stronger than the weakest, but they knew their lives depended on it and they knew their lives were not pitiful or at least their lives had once not been pitiful but proud and happy. They had once dug the earth for yams and planted seeds and prayed for rain. Now they dug for life and planted the dead if there was time and prayed for the end.

And when the shelling started again, mothers left their children because they had others to carry. The old carried the young, the young carried the youngest and the oldest. Sometimes the oldest just sat; they had run enough; they had seen enough. Or they carried themselves because despite all the life they'd had, they still wanted more. Sometimes mothers stayed with their children in lifeless rows if they had no-one left to carry.

They heard the familiar drum of mortar fire, like the heartbeat of the earth itself except the beat was erratic and its inconsistency that kept them guessing, jumping, ducking, running became a consistency that they understood and learnt to anticipate or so they told themselves as they guessed, jumped, ducked and ran, because it made their deaths seem less random, less fickle and their lives something they could control even though they secretly knew they could control none of it.

And the mothers wondered: is this how it ends? They clutched their wasted children around them and placed their wasted bodies over them. They took shelter under the carcasses of fallen trees and fallen people and fallen words of Conventions signed in faraway cities by people who were certain they would see sunset and sunrise and another sunset and sunrise and thousands more. And they were angry not because they'd lost their husbands and their homes and their homeland, but because now they would lose their children. They knew a maddening terror, a chaos in their minds, a surge of adrenalin and vomit and urine because they knew their children would die.

The mother and the farmer and the teacher and the man who drove an auto and had never missed a day of work, ran with the doctor and the mechanic and the woman who sewed dresses and secretly loved her sister's husband. They all looked the same now: clothing torn, feet shredded, bodies covered in the red-brown dust of their village and all the pounded villages they'd marched through, the muck of the jungles, the red of fresh blood and the smelly black of old wounds. They'd often done their best and sometimes their worst, they'd lived as their parents and priests and teachers and the Gita had told them they should. And now they would die as no-one had told them they would.

Scattered, terrified and wondering why them, why like this, why now when so much of life before was suffering and so much of life ahead was unfinished.

And when the sky rained fire they wondered if the sun itself had been shelled and broken into a thousand incandescent stars that now sought the soothing waters of the lagoon they were trying to cross. They gagged on muddy water and pushed through the tangle of bodies that floated and cluttered their path. They looked up at the sun, and felt it thunder down in disbelief.

'Come with us, Dhara. This is the last chance,' he said again.

She remembered driving to Katunayake airport to pick up Smrithi and Priya, the window rolled down, singing a Loretta Lynn tune as she went, something, something, *don't come home a-drinkin' with lovin' on your mind...*

She remembered the Arrivals Gate. She told Smrithi it was her favourite place in the whole world. And even though she had never seen the world she didn't need to. She just needed that one place. Her heart ached to stand there again, waiting for her daughter to return.

'OK,' she said. 'OK.'

COLOMBO, 2009

Dhara licked the ice cream from her wrist. She could never eat it fast enough. Rivulets of vanilla dribbled down her arm. She threw the cone to a stray dog that had been watching her hopefully. She didn't want it; she just bought it out of habit. It was an old habit. The ice cream made her look like she was meant to be there.

She sat at Galle Face Green as the last light of the sun bled into the Indian Ocean. She came here whenever she finished work on time. She liked to watch families go for walks on the promenade: children running into the ocean and shrieking away from it; young men who linked pinky fingers and walked, swinging their hands in time with the waves; even a few tourists, taking photos of the sunset she was watching now.

The man approached her slowly; working hard to appear casual. She tried not to smile. This was a random encounter; one stranger with another. He stopped a few feet away and sat against the stone wall, near her but not next to her. He looked different. He had shaved; the skin on his cheeks was much lighter and smoother than the skin on his nose and forehead. He wore a simple checked shirt, slacks and leather slippers. She was used to seeing him in his stained medical coat and torn trousers. He put his mobile phone to his ear, as though making a call.

'It's good to see you, Dhara,' he said.

'You too, Suren. You look well. You've been eating and bathing for a change,' she said.

'You too,' he laughed, his eyes straight ahead.

'What are you going to do?' she asked. A crow landed on the wall between them, its feathers shone like oil on black water.

'I'm leaving. The CID wants to see me next week. They've questioned some of the others already.' He looked around nervously.

'I know. I met Vigna and Kuhan yesterday. The CID released them as long as they agreed to recant their testimony,' she said. Vigna and Kuhan had been with them in the No Fire Zones. Together they had sent a stream of reports detailing the thousands dead, urgently begging the government to allow medical supplies in and the injured out. The government had refused.

'How were they?' Suren asked.

'Afraid. They looked afraid. They'd been beaten but wouldn't admit it. They were held for almost a week.' She spoke without judgement. She was afraid of the Criminal Investigation Department too. 'They've been told to give a press conference with the others. They'll say they exaggerated their reports; that the Tigers forced them to lie.'

'What are you going to do, Dhara?' he asked, looking at her directly now. 'I can help you leave. My family has contacts at the German embassy. That's where I'm going. Come with me.'

'Come with me,' she echoed.

'I'm serious, Dhara. If you don't recant you know what will happen to you. I know it's important to you, to tell the truth – it's important to all of us that people know what happened. But is it worth dying for?

When the CID takes you, agree to their demands. Say whatever they want you to say. Call me. Or call my brother if I've already gone. He'll help you. I've emailed you his details, please keep them.'

He had tears in his eyes. 'Please Dhara,' he said softly. 'There was so much death... back there – wouldn't it mean more if we lived?'

She didn't answer his question. 'I haven't always told the truth,' she replied instead, more to herself than to him. 'I've lied for a long time. I know sometimes it has its place.'

Sometimes it served a purpose. She felt tired from lying. She wanted to set down its heaviness. She wanted to tell the truth. She suddenly remembered where she was.

'Thank you, Suren. I'm very grateful for the offer and for everything you did for me. I'll miss you. I don't know what I'm going to do. I haven't decided yet.'

'There's nothing to decide. You have no choice. Don't be a fool,' he said loudly, startling the crow. It stretched its wings and sidled away.

Suren jumped down off the wall and took a step towards her. She shook her head and motioned to the people around them. He stopped and looked around, backing away slowly.

'You should go Suren; you'd make a terrible spy. You're an excellent doctor though, I hope you keep working in Germany or wherever you end up. You should go back to MSF, they need people like you.' She wanted to take his hand and hold it in hers, but this was not the place.

'I want you to think about it. Promise me that much,' he said.

'You should go,' she repeated. He nodded reluctantly and shook his head at her.

'Please Suren. I promise, I will think about it. *Poite vahngo*,' she said in Tamil. Go and come back. There was no word for goodbye in Tamil.

He looked down and walked past her.

She turned her face towards the fading light. Nala warned her about her skin getting darker but she had never cared. She loved the feeling of the sun on her. It was the same sun that kissed her father's head every morning when he went to work. It was the same sun that was beating down on hundreds of thousands of people trapped on a narrow strip of beach in the far north-east of the island. For four months, as fighting intensified, a mass of battered people moved as one, eastward, seeking safety. They picked up their remaining children and ran towards the coast, towards the rising sun.

This was President Rajapaksa's 'Zero Civilian Casualty Policy'. The army inched forward relentlessly. The Tigers fell back, using the Tamil people as cover. The militants' final play was as cruel as it was mis-judged: they thought the army wouldn't shoot through a layer of innocents. The army killed and stepped over the morass of bodies without a second thought. The Tigers used the Tamil people, wielding them to their death as they prepared themselves for their last stand. The more fighters they lost, the more fighters they stole from the cadaverous families they'd sworn to protect.

People huddled together on a beach on the other side of the country from her. Hope had convulsed away. The army wouldn't stop and the Tigers wouldn't let them leave the war-zone. The sun had already set on them.

She closed her eyes and tried to say the words of the *Gayatri Manthram*. It was a prayer for protection. Her father taught it to her when she was a child and they had recited it together at dawn and at sunset. She tried, but history's fist tightened around her throat.

She looked north and saw the majestic palm trees at the top end of the beach, leaning ever closer to the earth. After thousands of years of being grazed by the wind, they were bending, in supplication to Surya, the Sun God; in defeat.

SYDNEY, 2009

Priya tried to control the tremor in her voice. She took a deep breath and spoke into the phone again, 'Dhara, I'm not asking you to migrate here, just come for a holiday until Colombo is safe.'

'Colombo and Sri Lanka will never be safe. People don't need to fear the Tigers any more, but they should and will fear their government,' Dhara replied.

Priya knew she was right. In the end, the end was fast. The Sri Lankan Army had a new arsenal at its disposal. The People's Republic stood in the shadows behind the Democratic Socialist Republic: whispering, urging, arming. Artillery, mortar fire, multi-barrel shells and cluster bombs. Words on a shopping list, numbers on a balance sheet, corpses on a crowded beach.

The Tigers died cornered, with a fragile barrier of ragged refugees in front of them and the ocean behind them. There was nowhere to go. And there was no one to see: the UN had been evacuated more than six months before. The Red Cross had limited access and the media had none.

Priya knew what cruelty man was capable of, in the darkness of a small room. Dhara had told her, many years ago, and she had spent a lifetime trying to forget.

'Come back to me, Dhara. Leave, do it for me, for Smrithi, for our grandchildren.'

'But what about our people, acca? What about them?' Dhara asked, as she always did.

'They are dead and you will die with them, is that what you want?' Priya felt angry tears fall down her face. 'I'm sorry. I didn't mean it. I just look at that footage – the soldiers and the...the women.'

Grainy, jerky home videos haunted them all – naked prisoners, hands tied behind their backs, blindfolded and kneeling on the ground. Then shot in the head. The same clip: different locations, different soldiers, different victims. The female prisoners were the most painful; desecrated in life and mutilated after death. Their glassy eyes stared at her in her sleep. She could not fathom the last thing they'd seen; the last thing they'd felt. The trophies of war.

She imagined Dhara like that; her dark curls weeping down her naked body like the long roots of the banyan tree. Her eyes open, unmoving.

'I'm so scared for you. I am scared all the time,' Priya whispered.

'I know acca, me too,' her sister replied.

✿

Siva couldn't stop watching the news. Reports were pouring out of the north after the end of the war. The media was finally questioning the true extent of the loss of life, although it would be too little, too late, again.

The Sri Lankan government promised an independent and robust inquiry into its conduct. Norway and Canada might push the UN to call for a real investigation, perhaps even Obama, he seemed brave. But China would block them – its foothold in the region would become a stranglehold. And magnificent hotels would be built on mass graves.

President Rajapaksa continued to look the world in the eye and say that the army had not used heavy weapons; the army had not targeted civilians. The UN satellite imagery showed that it did; that the army had set up mortar batteries that were calibrated and recalibrated and recalibrated again for the No Fire Zone it had shepherded civilians into.

When asked why he would not listen to international community requests for a ceasefire, the President flashed his blade-like smile. He said that he would deal with the conflict in his own way; that 'ours is a home-grown process.'

When asked repeatedly by the US Ambassador to allow the Red Cross into the No Fire Zone, to provide food and medication to hundreds of thousands of trapped refugees, Gotabaya Rajapaksa, the president's brother replied, 'We are beyond that now.'

When asked if the Tigers could surrender, Basil Rajapaksa, the president's other brother replied, 'We are taking the necessary steps and the President has accepted the conditions.' The Tigers marched out; weapon-less, under the mantle of white flags that Rajapaksa told them to carry. They were executed anyway.

The President said there were only five to ten thousand civilians in the final No Fire Zone, a small spit of land. His own drones and UN satellites showed there were more than a hundred-and-twenty-five-thousand people. If most of those people did not emerge from the No Fire Zones after they had been 'liberated' from the Tigers, then where were they?

For Priya and Nala, the suffering was a narrative that was heard on the news and summarised at annual fundraisers. The small network of migrants who came in the seventies and eighties had grown. There were eventually enough of 'Nala's people' in Sydney to have the ladies' luncheons, the Colombo General dinners and the Hindu College reunions she longed for.

But Siva wasn't from Colombo 7. He was from Jaffna, where the earth wasn't soft and black like it was in the south. In the north, it was unrelentingly hard and people had to work harder to grow less. He knew about hunger, the kind that stops you from sleeping at night.

He knew about fear, the kind that drives you to want something else for your family. He had come to Australia hungry for security and success. He had left his home because he had to, and despite the passing decades in Australia, he could not and would not forget. He felt for his people in Sri Lanka, even more so during the last five months than at any time over the last twenty-six years of war.

The argument between him and Priya was ongoing, the ebb and tide of which depended on the latest news report that he had watched or the latest mood that Priya was in.

'What does it matter?' she asked, not for the first time 'What does it matter if it was two-thousand or forty-thousand or seventy-thousand dead in the final months?'

'How can you even ask that question, what's wrong with you?' He was incredulous, also not for the first time.

'It doesn't matter because it's over now. The war is over,' she replied. Her eyes were weary but her tone was hard.

'Of course it matters,' he shook his head. 'It matters because they are people, they are our people.'

'No, our people are here, in Sydney, in London and Dhara in Colombo. Our people are our children and our grandchildren. It doesn't matter which report is accurate, who's right, who knows – who cares now? You're not helping them so I don't know why you do it,' she continued. 'What do you achieve by watching that Internet footage? Those mobile phone clips are gruesome. Yes, the army is disgusting but your fascination with it is perverse.'

Siva looked down, hurt.

'You and your brother, you're all the same,' she shouted, angrily.

'It matters,' he said quietly, sadly. 'It matters if it was two-thousand or forty-thousand or seventy-thousand because they're people, *our people* and they were slaughtered on a beach like animals.'

COLOMBO, 2009

The streets of Colombo were filled with a jubilation not seen since independence. There were fireworks and parades, parties in houses and hotels. President Mahinda Rajapaksa and Gotabhaya Rajapaksa were hailed as heroes by their people and by leaders all over the world. Sri Lanka had won its war on terror. Gotabhaya, the Defence Secretary, was preparing to teach governments and armies of other nations, how to defeat terrorism. It would be a lucrative lecture circuit.

Dhara smiled as she read Priya's latest letter. The missives were getting longer but more repetitive; a detailed marketing campaign in which she tried to sell the virtues of relocating to Sydney. She must tell her to stop; there was no need anymore.

She remembered her visit to London. Smrithi had asked her to begin her daughter Ahalya's education. It was an honour given to family elders. Dhara had taken the little girl's right hand and shown her how to write the letter 'aahna' – the first letter of the Tamil alphabet – using a plate of uncooked rice as a canvas. Smrithi had wanted her daughter's education to be started in the right way, by the right person. Dhara had been so happy that day; she could have more of those days. She wanted more of those days.

Many of her friends were leaving Colombo. They were afraid of the white vans that now brazenly roamed the streets. If families were lucky, the people who went missing were found days later, dead in a public park. After Lasantha Wickrematunge's assassination, more journalists were leaving too. He was only one of many. The newspapers worked for the State, as did the judiciary, as did anyone who wanted to live. Wickrematunge and the President were childhood friends. It had meant nothing.

Sri Lanka belonged to the Rajapaksa family now, as it had belonged to other great Sinhalese families in the past. The streets were lined with giant billboards from which the god-like Mahinda and Gotabhaya watched victoriously over their kingdom. No-one watched them. There was a buffet of ministerial positions, state assets, reconstruction contracts and foreign naval bases to be feasted on, at this family gathering. The spoils of war. A carcass picked clean.

She looked at the letter and flattened its folds against the glass table. *The air is cleaner in Sydney*, Priya wrote randomly. *The winters are cold but sunny; I'll buy you a fleece and Ugg boots. They're lined with real lambswool.*

She took a small piece of paper from her handbag. It was the name and contact details of Suren's brother. She would call him tonight. He would call his friends at the German embassy. She tried to calculate the hours from Colombo to Singapore to Frankfurt to London to Sydney. It was too long. A small thread had been pulled on the discipline and restraint and denial of a lifetime. She felt herself unravelling and she couldn't wait any longer. The urgency rushed through her like adrenalin.

She felt her heart beat faster as she dared to hope for a time and a place outside this island. The winters were sunny in Australia and it was the same sun that warmed them all. She wondered what real lambswool smelled like. She tried to remember what Smrithi smelled like. She felt her child's hand in hers when she helped her across the railway tracks to the Wellawatte beach, that last time.

She started a conversation she had rehearsed in her mind a thousand times. It terrified and exhilarated her. She gripped the edge of the table and closed her eyes. She could see the smile, hear the voice, almost touch the face. She would tell Smrithi. They both would. Smrithi would understand, eventually.

But first, she would call Suren's brother. She took a deep breath. The air in Colombo was heavy this time of the year, humidity settled on them all like a shroud. The monsoon was coming.

GRAVITATION

Vyasa, realising that he was coming to the end of his earthly life, decided to preserve the Mahabharata *in writing, so that future generations would remember the Great War that shaped their destiny. He asked Ganesha, the elephant god, to be his scribe, but gave him two conditions. Ganesha must not stop writing once Vyasa began the story and Ganesha must understand everything that he was writing. Ganesha agreed to the old sage's conditions, but gave Vyasa one of his own. He declared that once Vyasa began his story, he must not stop; he must narrate continuously until the very end. Narrator and scribe thus agreed the terms and Ganesha broke off one of his tusks, which he used as a divine pen. Vyasa sat down and began…*

21

Rajan rarely left the house, but Siva had been elected President of the Rotary Club.

'I'm the first Sri Lankan Tamil president of our chapter,' he said proudly.

Rajan had avoided Rotary meetings for twenty-five years but he reluctantly agreed to attend this dinner for his son-in-law's sake.

The event was at the Concord Community Centre. He quickly realised he was overdressed in his pressed trousers, long-sleeved Marks & Spencer shirt and Brylcreem-ed hair. Most of the other men were in polo shirts and shorts or slacks. Everyone wore statement watches and drove statement cars. He wondered what statement his sartorial incongruity was making.

He had expected the audience to be homogeneous, similar to the sophisticated gentlemen's clubs of Colombo 7. He had managed to avoid those clubs as well. The Concord Community Centre was filled with the biriyani mix of the local community: white people, Italians, Chinese, Koreans and Sri Lankan Tamils. There must have been others; the Rotary had evolved from an elite philanthropic club to a genuine community society.

He politely declined the fried sausage on a bed of Tip Top white bread and burnt onions. Elderly Rotarians competently manned the sausage sizzle. They smiled at him and passed him a cold beer from the ice-filled garbage bin. The Rotary Club's new Sri Lankan president was flanked by Chun Hei, the vice-president, and former Korean beautician from Burwood. She used to manicure Nala, Priya and Smrithi's eyebrows. Business had obviously been good for her. She wore her casual clothing with a heavy gold necklace and a jewelled pendant the size of a fish cutlet. Her eyebrows were immaculately drawn.

Siva seated Rajan and Nala at the President's table next to Nandan, Shiranthi and members of the Rotary's Executive Committee. He then left to mingle with his constituents. An old man leant over with his hand outstretched.

'Michael Bennett – I'm very pleased to meet you. Siva has told me so much about you both. I'm the Treasurer here.'

'Thank you Michael, it's very nice to meet you too.' Rajan paused and tried to remember some social formalities. He hadn't met new people for a while.

'Have you been the Treasurer for a long time?' he asked. Nala smiled her approval.

'Oh, a very long time. I was Treasurer from 1994 to 1998 and then again from 2002 to 2006 and now. This will be my last term; I'm far too old but Siva nominated me. We've been attending Rotary together for years, decades – ever since he arrived here. He's an excellent Rotarian,' Michael said.

'Thank you Michael, we're very proud of him. The Rotary Club does excellent work,' Nala said, seizing an opportunity to speak. 'Your charity work is very important.'

'Thank you Nala,' he replied. 'It's interesting you raise that. Siva has asked us to consider supporting the detainees at Christmas Island.' He paused while a young man offered them a plate of green rolls. Rajan peered at the food.

'It's *dolma*, rice and mince meat wrapped in vine leaves – it's a Greek specialty. My mother made it,' the young man explained.

Rajan remembered – the evening had a theme, 'Foods of the World, Foods of Australia.' It was Priya's idea; as the reluctant First Lady of the inner-west chapter of the Rotary, she was anxiously in charge of catering.

'Thank you, it looks delicious,' he said, taking one.

Michael continued, 'Siva would like the Rotary to donate schoolbooks to children detained at Christmas Island and the other detention centres. He thinks we should even try to fund a teacher at one of these centres. What do you think?'

Rajan was surprised. Siva hadn't mentioned the idea to him at any of their weekly dinners.

'I think it's an excellent idea. These children – many of them have never been to school. They will need an education – and not just the children, the adults may need help too. If they've come from war...' Rajan's voice trailed off. He hadn't spoken so much in a long time. .

'Yes, I think that's right. It's a hard one though, contentious in Australia. We have to be conscious of all of our members, although I suppose this is the right chapter of the Club to support the issue,' Michael said, looking around at the attendees enjoying the range of Australian cuisines.

'You know, if you ignored the politicians, and asked people, most of us would want to help refugees – the genuine refugees; the ones who are fleeing war, the way you did,' Michael continued. 'Siva told me about your family. We've been friends for a long time.'

'We were lucky. We left before things became really bad. It was much worse for others,' Rajan replied.

'Yes, but the war is over now, isn't it. Why are people still leaving?' Michael asked. 'It's just that there are people in danger that we can't even help. And some people who come on boats are fleeing poverty rather than danger. Their need isn't as great as other boat people or asylum seekers – there are so many, we have to prioritise them somehow. That probably sounds awful to you, doesn't it?' Michael stopped, suddenly appearing like a self-conscious old man instead of a self-assured Rotarian.

It was an important question. The war had ended and the Sri Lankan government was ostensibly rebuilding the north rapidly. The government was rebuilding roads, airports and harbours of the north and east. It was rebuilding the tools it needed to regain control of the region. The militarisation of the north accelerated, but development of the rest of the infrastructure was slow; some thought deliberately so.

Congratulatory aid from international allies was invested into constructing new Sinhalese communities on top of old Tamil ones. The army appropriated land and businesses. Tamil families that were not living in refugee camps were living by the wayside of their former homes, watching as the government waited for neglect to kill them.

For the refugees in camps, it was worse. Anyone suspected of being a Tiger or Tiger supporter was taken away and rarely returned. The soldiers had set up a section for themselves and the female refugees of their choice. Families traded what they could for information about loved ones, and if they were lucky, a secret passage out of the camps. The war was over but the dying hadn't stopped.

When some camps were finally closed, tens of thousands of people had nowhere to go – no homes, no towns, no jobs and no food. They were not in imminent danger but they were desperate; desperate enough to get on a leaky boat. The war was over, but people were still fighting to live.

Michael watched Rajan expectantly. He didn't know where to start so he started with the truth.

'I'm an old man Michael - too old to judge any more. It's the young who have learned judgement but not yet compassion. I am relieved our children live in a country where people can voice their disagreement, their anger, but there is no fear that that anger will lead to bloodshed.

'In Ceylon I saw a national debate about ethnic equality deteriorate into raging mob violence and a war for nationhood. It is so much easier to inflame a debate than to truly engage in it. One of the things I like about Australia is that we have the potential to debate without demonising each other; we might even fight without war. This is a better country Michael and you should be proud of that. I am.' Rajan suddenly felt breathless. Nala's vine leaves were poised in mid-air.

Michael nodded in agreement and challenged him further. 'But don't you think boarding a boat, knowing it is illegal, knowing it forces the hand of Australia, is wrong?'

When Rajan was a young doctor he used to be good at solving problems. He was tired now. He needed to rest. He didn't separate the world into right and wrong anymore; for him there was just the memory of the past and the moment of the present.

'Michael, thirty years ago, when a mob tore through Colombo, it was our Sinhalese neighbours who helped us. People threw their children over burning walls to seek protection. Neighbours opened their doors and offered shelter. Australia is a neighbour and they helped us too. It isn't illegal to seek protection. It is illegal and inhumane to deny it.'

He paused and pushed at the vine-leaf roll on his plate. 'Some of these people who come now – they're not trying to subvert the legal process here. They are desperately trying to live a better life, in a better country. I'm not saying we should let them all in, I understand that we have to prioritise. I am saying that we don't know the traumas of their past or the hopelessness of their future.'

Rajan's mind felt clearer than it had for a long time; lighter but peacefully drained of words.

Michael looked at him kindly and said, 'I'm an old man too, Rajan. There is no good solution, only degrees of difficult solutions.'

'I agree,' Rajan said sadly. 'The difference between each degree is the respect we show these refugees; and the dignity we allow them.'

Michael nodded his agreement and Rajan smiled. The Rotary Club wasn't as bad as he had thought it was.

Rajan sat at his writing table. 'How much do you need?' he asked quietly. He hated being in this position. He didn't want to say no but he also knew that this could be money wasted.

The man swallowed. Bala hated being in this position too. In all the years that Rajan had known him, Bala had never asked for money.

The man cleared his throat, 'Three thousand more, I have the rest,' he spoke softly but clearly, looking Rajan in the eyes.

'How much is it in total?' Rajan had expected it to be more.

'Ten thousand.'

That was a lot of money. He wasn't surprised Bala had saved the rest of it. He was a good worker. He lived a frugal life and whatever money he didn't use for rent or food was sent back home or saved.

'Why do they want to leave? Things are getting better aren't they?' Rajan asked. As soon as he spoke he regretted it.

'Are they ok?' he tried again.

'Yes, of course,' Bala answered politely.

They had known each other at Colombo General, decades ago. Rajan liked him. Bala was a radiographer: clever and decent, he had often helped Rajan to master the changing diagnostic technology at the hospital. Later, in 1984, when Rajan was preparing to leave Colombo, he had urged Bala to do the same. But Bala had a mother, brother and sister. When Rajan moved to Sydney, Bala moved to Batticaloa.

The war went east and Bala's mother and sister did not survive. He was at work when the shelling started and he had stayed at the hospital. He knew enough emergency medicine to be useful. He had called his mother that morning and she said her brother was on his way with a car. He would take them all to a Sinhalese friend's house in a nearby village. He had thanked God for their friends and put the hospital phone down.

In the end, he couldn't leave the hospital for days. He kept calling his mother's house and his uncle's. No-one answered. Finally he returned to his neighbourhood. As he walked through the smouldering remains of his home, he found his mother, sister, and uncle. They had been blown apart, the pieces of his family carelessly strewn around, burned and barely recognisable. His profession was the study of bones and he knew what had happened to them.

It would be years before he could close his eyes without having flashbacks of that day, and more years before he could sleep without dreaming of them. It would take even longer before he stopped wishing he had died with them.

He didn't want to leave Sri Lanka but he knew he had to. His younger brother Kumar had his own children and grandchildren. He had begged his brother to leave with him. His granddaughters were the right age for the army to take and his grandsons were the right age for the Tigers to take. Humanity had long been replaced by something hideous and incomprehensible.

Countries had opened their arms and borders to the Tamils and Bala left in 1990. He brought Kumar's two youngest sons and their children with him to Sydney. He carried a small bag and his education. He had no other possessions or papers but he had been allowed refuge.

News of the atrocities reached Sydney. Rajan grieved for the tens of thousands dead; the countless disappeared, buried in unmarked graves with no certainty for the families left behind – just the endless torture of hope. There were no bodies, no records, and no remorse. He did what others like him were doing. He helped his friends. When Bala arrived in Sydney, Rajan found him a job at Siva's hospital. He looked at Bala's face and asked no questions.

Two decades later, Bala was there with a request for a loan. Rajan would give him the money. But he wanted to make sure Bala knew the consequences of what he was doing. Money went into Ceylon all the time, often to the wrong places. During the war, Tamils thought they were funding orphanages and later found they were arming children instead.

'Are you sure this is safe?' Rajan asked. It was another stupid question he regretted.

Nothing was safe for the Tamils. In the final stages of the war, people died in hospitals and schools where they had taken refuge. Rajan had read the recent Amnesty International Report. The Tigers had used their own people as a shield. But the army, knowing the molecular composition of that shield, had still attacked it, breaking down men, women, and children to finish the Tigers. War crimes, the report called it. War was always criminal.

'Safe? No. I'm not sure at all. The boats are dangerous but staying is hopeless. It's not like it was just after the war ended, it's not better, it's different. There is reconstruction of the country but no reconciliation. It took less than forty years from independence for war to begin and another thirty years for it to end. Without reconciliation, conflict is inevitable.

'My brother Kumar and the children who stayed are all gone. It's only his grandchildren who are left there. I want to do this for my family before I – I'm not getting any younger, Rajan. When we die, the only thing we leave behind is our family.'

Rajan understood. He had sent his child north instead of sending her out, and she had been irreparably damaged. He had allowed the only thing we live and die for to be taken away from her. He had left her behind and allowed her to live in the echoing emptiness of their once vital home.

He must try one last time to get her out too.

'They're sending the oldest grandson. He's smart and he's strong. His father taught him to swim. He will survive the journey. The boat is better than staying.'

Kallathoni, Rajan thought to himself. It was the Tamil word for boat people, used by the Sinhalese to denigrate them. The Tamils *had* come to Ceylon by boat thousands of years ago, and so had the Sinhalese. Did it matter which race had arrived first?

'I will give you the money, not lend it,' Rajan said.

'I will pay you back.'

'No. Consider it a Christmas present.'

'We don't celebrate Christmas, you and I,' Bala said, as he smiled at his old friend. 'I will pay you back.'

'I know you will, but I don't want you to,' replied Rajan.

'Thank you – and Merry Christmas,' said Bala. They both laughed sadly.

Priya was surprised when her father called.

'Appa, wouldn't you prefer to have this conversation with Nandan?' she asked.

'No, I want it to be you,' he insisted.

Rajan and Priya sat at the dining table together, reviewing papers. Nala hovered in the kitchen trying to listen in and cook dinner.

'This is the deed to the house in Colombo; it's for you, Nandan and Dhara. I'd like Nandan's in-laws to live there for as long as they want.' He passed her another worn piece of paper. 'This is the deed to a small piece of land in Tellippalai. There was a house there, once. The village was razed so I don't think it's worth much. It was part of your Amma's dowry. Your grandfather gave it to me, to us. He worked hard for it and I don't want the army to take it. I'm sorry I have to burden you Priya.'

'It's ok Appa, it's no problem,' she lied.

It would be hard to reclaim the small property on the Jaffna peninsula, and probably not worth the effort or even the cost of the airfare and bribes she would have to make. But she understood what her father was saying. People were returning to claim their homes, presenting faded title deeds that were older and more tattered than their owners. The land in the north and east had been destroyed, littered with the debris of war, but people still wanted what was theirs.

'Here are copies of all my accounts: three in Colombo and two in Sydney. Amma will still be entitled to my Ceylon State pension.

'I make certain annual donations, mahal. There is the Hindu College and the orphanage at the Ramakrishna Mission in Jaffna. There are a couple of other places.' He gave her a large box with receipts carefully organised and filed in separate envelopes.

'Also,' Rajan continued, 'Vani and Mohan's family is still back home. I help them, but I don't want to trouble you...'

'I would be happy to continue the help, Appa, we all would. Really, it's no trouble,' she replied. She couldn't look at him. She thought she was going to cry.

'I should have enough savings for your Amma and the commitments back home,' he said.

'I'm sure you do, Appa, but we can also manage it. The three of us have enough. We would be happy to maintain those commitments.'

She flicked through her father's account book. He still noted every deposit and every withdrawal in a small book, using the same ledger system he had taught Nandan years ago.

'What's this, Appa?' she asked, suddenly noticing a withdrawal for three thousand dollars with no description. It was not like him – what could he have spent three thousand dollars on? He only ever went to the fruit market at Strathfield and her house for dinner.

'That is nothing,' he replied.

'Appa–'

'It's nothing. It's done.' His mouth tightened. He folded his hands together. 'One last thing – I have a friend here in Sydney, Balachandran

– Bala, you will remember him. I will give you his phone number. He knows people in Colombo who help…who help people leave. I want you to call him and start making arrangements for Dhara. I have the money.'

'Appa – it's never been about the money – it's…'

'I know mahal. You must tell Dhara and then we must tell Smrithi. It's time.' His hands relaxed and Priya reached over and held them. They were so frail.

'Yes, Appa,' she whispered.

She looked up and saw her mother at the door. Nala smiled at her and motioned to her to come and eat. She had cooked fish curry. Priya went to the bathroom to wash her hands before dinner.

Nala sat at the table next to Rajan. She looked at the account book. Rajan's handwriting was like calligraphy. He had been taught to write by Christian missionaries who valued aesthetics. He had no time for aesthetics but he understood perfection. She ran her fingers over the numbers, 3 0 0 0. It was a lot of money but she didn't ask.

He looked down. 'It was a gift.'

'I know,' she replied. She had seen Bala leave the apartment that day. He had tears in his eyes as he greeted her with the traditional 'Vannakam', his palms folded together in respect.

'Do you mind?' he asked his wife.

She was surprised. He had never asked her if she minded, not once in their entire life together.

'Are Bala's people ok?' she asked, echoing Rajan's first questions to Bala. 'Are they safe?'

'The ones that are still alive are safer than they were before,' he replied. 'But they want a better life. They want to work and they want their children to study. They want to be heard by their government and protected by their police. They don't just want to live; they want to live with dignity – with dreams for their children – always for their children. There's nothing wrong with that, is there?' he asked, looking out the window. He wasn't talking to her. He was looking inwards, remembering another time. He too had wanted a better life but she had stopped him.

'I don't know what the right thing to do is any more,' he said softly, still not looking at her. 'There were so many things I should have done differently, Nala. It was my fault.'

'No, it was my fault, Rajan.' She took a deep breath. It hurt to breathe. She wanted to tell him.

'I have one more thing to do,' he whispered.

She didn't want to talk about Smrithi just yet. 'There are other things I need to tell you…' she began.

His eyes finally focused on her. He saw her clearly. 'No. Let's not do that. It doesn't matter.'

'It does matter, Rajan. You always did your duty. You always did your best,' she replied. 'I –'

'No. It's done,' he replied, gently closing the account book. 'It's done.'

☼

'Mohan, Mohan come out now, I'm tired of looking!' Nala shouted at her cousin-brother. She had checked every part of their small house. Mohan was an excellent hider and she was a terrible loser. She sat on the steps of the front verandah and examined her legs. They were covered with inflamed mosquito bites.

'Don't scratch!' Archi said. Her grandmother sat in her usual place on her rocking chair, her legs covered with a light blanket. From there, she could watch over her domain.

'Don't scratch!' Archi repeated, more imperiously, 'You'll scar yourself. It's malaria season, you should be more careful.'

Nala was inspecting her fair skin, searching for scars when Archi let out a long kusu. The old lady gave a wicked giggle as her chair and blanket began to move with a life of its own.

'Aaaarchiii! What did you do that for?' Mohan shouted as he stumbled out from under her rocking chair, coughing and laughing. Archi's kusus were legendary.

'Found you!' Nala cried.

'That's not fair,' he replied, breathing the humid, clean air deeply, 'It doesn't count.'

He sat himself next to her and they began to compare battle scars.

'Mine are definitely better than yours,' she said pointing to her left calf. 'See how these ones merge into each other, making one big bumpy line. It looks like the Himalayas.'

Mohan didn't laugh. He wasn't listening to her. He had noticed something else. The verandah was trembling. It was an erratic shake, as if the ground was shivering from the cold. Except it wasn't cold, it was August and it was warm, the air dense with the last of the rain. Nala noticed it too. He reached out for her, anchoring her small body to his, as all around them the house and the jackfruit trees vibrated.

And then people were screaming and running, as if to flee the shaking, but the ground was having a seizure; it knocked them down casually like chess pieces. She remembered when her father's dog had a seizure. Appa had to kill it, even though he loved that dog. She remembered the shaking and the frothing; there was so much froth.

White, foamy froth, riding on the crest of a wall of water. Nala saw the froth first and then the wave. It was the colour of stone, not the blue she loved. She couldn't hear the people screaming any more; just the roar of the ocean as it opened its mouth to her and then there was nothing.

Wet, grey stone engulfed her, smacking against her bones, tearing at her skin, clawing its salty way inside her mouth and lungs.

'Nala, Nala, Nala!' It was Mohan. And again, there was nothing.

'Hold on to me Nala!' he shouted. She could feel his strong arms around her chest, lifting her up, lifting her out. Mohan, she thought. Mohan.

'Hold on to me Mohan,' she whispered back, waking finally, 'hold on to me.'

Rajan reached over and put his arms around her shaking body.

Nala called Dhara almost every Friday afternoon. Sometimes she missed a Friday if Dhara was in surgery or distracted with work, but Dhara would call apologetically a few days later; or Nala would call her back, concerned. As Nala got older and her hearing harder, the calls became shorter – but they never stopped.

Dhara hadn't picked up her phone for seven weeks.

Nala lifted the cloth she had used to cover the thosai batter. Usually she rested the batter overnight to let it ferment properly but she had forgotten to make it last night. Despite only having a few hours to sit in the warmth of her kitchen, today's batter had already risen by several centimetres, its surface smooth and shiny like a white balloon. She gave it one gentle stir and oiled her pan with ghee. Priya told her not to use ghee but every now and then she liked to rebel against her children's well-meaning strictures.

She ladled the mixture onto the pan in a circular motion. Her hands were too slow now, her grip on the large spoon slipping as her fingers struggled with its slender stem, her shoulder pushing back against her forward movement. But she was still able to create concentric layers of pancake, just the way Rajan liked it. He said it reminded him of the moon, orbited by thin, crispy rings on the outside. She added a tablespoon of coconut chilli sambal to the side of the plate but no sambar. He didn't like the thick vegetable gravy anymore.

She placed the plate at the table where he was waiting silently, and sat with him.

'You're not eating?' he asked.

'I'm not hungry yet,' she replied. Everything tasted the same to her. Like burnt, salted sugar. She watched him eat a few mouthfuls. She was empty. She wanted to suffer. She wanted to feel pain or sickness, something other than the unbearable weight of uncertainty. Every night her imagination coloured a blank canvas with horrors she had only ever heard about.

'You haven't eaten properly for weeks. Not eating isn't going to help her,' he said softly.

'Nothing is going to help her, Rajan,' she replied, thinking about the dream last night. She had been dreaming about Mohan a lot lately.

She had called everyone in Colombo who knew Dhara. Shiranthi's parents, the Pereras, had a spare key to her apartment. Dhara had lived there with her mother until Vani's death, a few years ago. Then she had continued to live there alone. The Pereras had checked the apartment – it was fine: clean, orderly but empty. Nothing seemed to be missing but they wouldn't know if it was.

Dhara was missing. No-one had seen her. Nala spoke to Dhara's colleagues at Colombo General Hospital. They directed her to the Tamil Medical Institute. Dhara had been collaborating with the organisation, testifying with other doctors and nurses who worked at hospitals in the No Fire Zones. They were documenting what happened. The report, not yet finished, cited eye-witness reports of army and Tiger attacks on civilians in what were supposed to be safe-zones for them.

Nala didn't care. Savagery no longer surprised her.

Dhara hadn't been seen for seven weeks. Her colleagues had done everything they could think of – filed police reports, contacted politicians and the local branch of the ICRC, as well as Amnesty International and other human rights organisations. They had even hired a team of private investigators.

'They won't find her, will they?' she asked. It was a question, but there was no doubt in her voice.

'No, they won't find her. I should have made her come with us. I should have known...' his voice faltered. 'It's time to tell Smrithi,' he said slowly, 'We waited too long. Tell Priya it's time.' His face, the jaw, the mouth were resolute once again.

She felt relief rush through the cracks carved by fear. She saw the froth again. White, frothy foam riding the crest of a wall of water. But the water was cerulean blue this time, not stone. It was the colour of the sky over Colombo, reflected in the mirror of the Indian Ocean. Her chest relaxed slightly for the first time in almost two months; only a notch, but it was enough to let her breathe a little more deeply.

Rajan spoke again, 'I remember... I remember holding her on the bus when we returned from Gal Oya. She was only eight-years-old. She sat on my lap the whole way back to Colombo. She didn't cry Nala, despite what she'd seen, she didn't cry. She just shook in my arms. I told her to put her head against my chest and concentrate on my breathing. I tapped a rhythm with my fingers, on her back. Eventually she stopped shaking and slept. I wish I'd never let her go.'

'We have to let them go Rajan, it's what we're supposed to do. We have to...' she couldn't stop the tears now. 'Dhara used to do that at home too, the tapping, when she was scared. She had those terrible nightmares afterwards. I would lie with her sometimes, and I could hear her tapping her chest to sleep. I always thought it was strange. I wanted to ask you about it but in the morning I would forget.'

She leant back in her chair and closed her eyes. She put her hand on her chest and found her heart, but its rhythm was too painful for her to follow.

Nala rose quietly before dawn and assembled the food quickly. She had cooked everything the night before: puttu, omelette and coconut chilli sambal. It was a simple meal. She took the ice cream from the freezer – home made vanilla. And a glass of cold milk. Dhara didn't like plain milk but she really ought to drink more. Nala stirred a spoon of Sustagen into it, for extra strength. She placed the food at the altar, careful not to wake Rajan. Eight days had passed since they had agreed. Eight days after death, her favourite food must be prepared and presented to her. She must eat and then she must go. Nala placed holy ash on the forehead of her child. The photograph had been taken on their last trip to Colombo. Dhara was beautiful. Nala heard a noise in the kitchen and Rajan entered the study. He shuffled his feet slowly under his sarong. He was also carrying a glass. The suspended green jelly looked like seaweed in a milky pink ocean. 'For Dhara,' he said.

Priya opened her eyes and checked the clock. It was 11:23 on Tuesday morning. Siva would finish his operation in an hour and call her, before seeing his next patient. She got out of bed and turned to face it.

First she pulled the sheets and quilt up to the pillows, folding the edge of the sheet back over the top of the quilt. She ran her hand over the body of the bed, smoothening out the wrinkles. It was cool against her palm. The quilt was neatly parallel to the top sheet that was neatly parallel to the bottom sheet. Every part of the bed found its solace in perfect alignment. She bent down and tucked the sides of the sheets under the mattress, creating a tight seal around it.

The bed was properly made. Rajan would be proud. Dhara would have laughed at this daily activity and forced her to stop. Dhara would have forced her to live. She pulled the top of the sheets back a little, careful not to disturb them, and slowly slipped back into bed.

Nala sat quietly, perched on the edge. She winced as she adjusted her back and tried to balance on the bed without pushing her daughter. Priya didn't move or acknowledge her presence. The curtains were drawn. The air was old and hung watchfully in the room. Nala wanted to open a window and let the afternoon light in.

'I brought you something,' she said tentatively. 'I thought you might need it.' She opened the plastic bag on her lap and pulled out the soft net. She held it up, unfurling it a little. Priya finally opened her eyes.

'It's silly, I know, but when we left home, I couldn't bear to leave it behind. It reminded me of you both.' She placed the muslin gently over her daughter. Priya sat up slowly and fingered the net.

'Your father used to sew the tears.'

They looked like the thin scars made by barbed wire when it is dragged over a body. Skin pinched elegantly into permanent ridges.

'I know,' she replied. Her face had changed over the last few months, the patina recognisable to all who had suffered. She held the muslin up.

'It smells old,' Priya whispered.

'It is old,' Nala shrugged with a smile.

'I always knew you brought everything from Colombo,' she said. It was an old accusation, said without blame.

'No,' Nala replied. 'I left some important things behind. Appa says it's time to tell Smrithi.'

Her daughter nodded and slumped back holding the muslin to her chest. Nala walked around the bed to the other side and lay down. Priya moved towards her and into her waiting arms.

22

Food sat in Nala's kitchen, untouched. No-one wanted to eat after she and Rajan talked to Smrithi. Priya and Siva were there too but they didn't speak very much, neither knew what to say.

Nala told Smrithi what happened the day she was born. She thought of it often and when she spoke, she was simply replaying a memory a little louder, so that everyone could hear what she heard in her mind every day.

Dhara sat on a hospital bed, holding her baby daughter in her arms. She lightly traced the lines of her face, her ribcage, the curve of her bottom and the angles of her joints.

'She's perfect,' she said softly.

'Yes, mahal, she is,' Nala tried not to cry.

'Ammamma, what are you talking about?' Smrithi looked at her grandmother, confused. Nala was lost inside herself.

'Appa…' she asked, turning to her father. He was always rational. He looked at her with tears in his eyes.

Priya cleared her throat. 'You were – you are Dhara's, mahal. Not mine.'

She heard a whimper escape her father's throat but she did not take her eyes from her mother.

'After Dhara was…attacked, you were born. She loved you so much, Smrithi, and she wanted to do what she thought was right for you.'

'Right for me?' Smrithi whispered. They were all staring at her. They had gone mad.

'Yes, mahal. Right for you –'

'How is this right for me? I don't understand what you're saying,' Smrithi replied. She was confused and yet she understood what they were saying.

'You are Dhara's,' her mother repeated.

'*Why*? Why didn't you tell me?' Smrithi asked. 'Why didn't she tell me?' she shouted.

There were other questions later, many angry ones: How could you not tell me? How could you lie to me? How could all of you lie to me for so long? But all of these questions were incidental to the main one.

'Why?' she screamed at her mother again. Her mother, who wasn't her mother.

'Why?' she screamed at her father, who wasn't her father.

Priya tried to explain. 'I begged Dhara – I pleaded for permission, and I was terrified I would receive it.'

'Why didn't you disobey her?' she cried. 'You owed me more honesty than you owed her loyalty.'

'No,' her mother replied simply. 'I owed her everything. I owed her you. She was my sister.'

'And I am your daughter,' she screamed again – except she wasn't her daughter. She was Dhara's daughter and Dhara hadn't wanted her.

Sometimes the tears were silent, sitting quietly, coldly on her face. At other times, wracking sobs tore out of her chest.

Why – why hadn't Dhara wanted her?

She placed her hand on her abdomen. There was a black mass inside she wanted to expunge. She had been told a terrible story about a young woman and unknown men. The memory ticked like a metronome, it was all she could hear. She couldn't escape it. Revulsion shuddered through her. She ran to the bathroom and gripped the sides of the toilet, retching into it. She watched a frothy liquid settle on the surface.

She wept more.

Repugnance receded, momentarily replaced by something else. It hijacked her, travelled freely, propietorially, claiming her as its own. It was grief and it was endless. It threw her carelessly to the ground. It swallowed everything she knew, everything she was. It took her mother, her mami and herself.

She wept again and again.

Smrithi sorted through memories: of her childhood, of trips to Sri Lanka and India, of family holidays. She tried to create order amongst them and extract signs she had missed. But her memories wouldn't listen to her, defying the new jigsaw puzzle she was re-shaping with the pieces of the old. Her memories preferred the old puzzle, and so did she. If only she could put the box away, surely it would hurt less.

Her brother was her second-cousin and her grandmother was her great-aunt. Her mother was her aunt and her mami was her mother and her mother was dead. Her father and grandfather weren't related to her at all. Everyone she knew was someone else, most of all, herself.

Suspicions scuttled across her mind, like rats in an attic. Gnawing relentlessly on the timbers of her memory, they weakened the once steadfast architecture around which her life was built. Inchoate fears seeped out and rot set in.

The stranger and the strangeness. She looked at herself in the mirror – the curly hair, the deep-set eyes, the pointed chin. They were features that used to belong to Nala and Priya and Siva. Now she feared they were those of an unknown savage. Someone who was not of them. Someone who should have died for the crime of life he gave her.

She sat on the toilet and wiped herself. She stared at the toilet paper, smoothening down the edges of the square, holding it in her palm like a miniature painting. Red: the colour of the flame tree, the hibiscus flower, the kunkumam powder worn by Tamil women. Dhara never placed the small red orb on her dark forehead, she had never married.

Half her blood belonged to someone – to something – else. Half her blood ran darker, harsher, crueller than the rest. It was tainted.

She didn't want Prashanth to touch her. She was not the woman he fell in love with. She held her children close and then pushed them away. She didn't want them near the stranger, touched by his violence. She was shame. She was grotesque and they were still sunlight.

☼

Priya made a mixture of rice, sesame seeds, and sesame oil, which she fed to the birds in her garden. It was the month of *Sanni* and she was trying to appease Saturn with her offering.

Helen peeped over the fence. 'Would you like some help?' she asked, her blonde hair catching on the dense murraya hedge. She'd been helping Priya with Saturn for years.

'No, thank you Helen. I'm almost done,' Priya replied.

'I missed you at the Hellenic Club. We've just started the foxtrot. You can't hide at home or the temple forever. You should let your friends help you,' she said as she climbed over the fence. They had cut a hole in the hedge and placed stools on either side so they could do this easily. Helen hugged her tightly.

'She'll come round Priya. It's just going to take some time. Next week I'm going to pick you up for dance class. It took forever to convince you to join, there's no way I'm letting you drop it.'

Priya hugged her back. Together they finished feeding the birds and prayed to Saturn one last time before Helen returned over the fence. Priya went inside and checked her answering machine. There were no messages.

When Vivek and Smrithi left home, Siva and Priya accepted the solitude, resentfully at first, and later comfortably. Priya took over Smrithi's old room with her saris and Siva took over Vivek's old room with his books. Suddenly both of them had more space in their lives.

They built new routines around themselves. Every Tuesday night and Saturday morning they went to the temple at Westmead. It was a beautiful building, a stone carved temple, not a community hall. Siva taught scripture and Priya joined the ladies wing, attending yoga classes and making garlands with her friends.

Every Thursday morning she went to swimming classes with her friend Malathy. On Wednesday nights she went to dance classes with Helen; and every Friday night she spoke to Dhara. For years, Siva and Priya went wherever they felt like, from the local Chinese restaurant to Antarctica.

When Smrithi returned from London, Priya changed her life again. She converted Smrithi's old room into a playroom. She built new routines around her grandchildren and helped Smrithi look after them. Until now.

Smrithi refused to see her. All the years, the decades of sacrifice, of love were erased by a lie – a lie that had been told out of sacrifice and love. They had hurt Smrithi, all of them – Nala, Dhara, Siva and Priya – but Priya had hurt Smrithi the most. She loved her the most too, that she was sure of.

Home alone, the void left by Dhara gaped ever wider in Smrithi's absence. The playroom was empty. She couldn't even enter it. The toys she'd retrieved from their attic didn't remind her of her grandchildren. They reminded her of her children.

She didn't want to change her life again. She wanted to take Ahalya and Rishi to the park and show them the rainbow lorikeets play. She wanted to take them to McDonalds and temple and swimming parties and all the places that made this their home. Her home.

A twin-headed snake coiled tightly around her chest. Grief and guilt, their flat eyes stared at her impassively as they squeezed and choked her. Siva found her sitting on the tiles of her front foyer, her back against the wall and her arm around the warm leg of the sandalwood side table her parents had given her.

'What are we going to do?' he asked quietly, sitting down beside her. He had lost too. He grieved too.

She looked the snake in the eyes and squeezed back.

'I've been afraid for so long – afraid that if we told her, we would lose her. And now I've lost any way. My sister…' her voice choked and she stopped, tears streaming down her face.

'That is enough loss. It's more than I can bear. I will carry my guilt – my failures – with me into my next life, as will Dhara. Perhaps this grief is my punishment for our mistakes.'

'I don't think it works like that, Priya,' Siva replied hesitantly.

'You're not Lord Krishna so I don't think you know *exactly* how the law of karma works,' she rested her head against the wall.

He looked at her, startled. Her eyes were closed, fringed by dark shadows underneath, but the edges of her mouth were almost upturned.

'11,717 days,' she said.

'What?'

'11,717 – I calculated all the days that I loved Smrithi – all the days that Smrithi didn't know Dhara and the days, the thousands of moments that Dhara didn't have with her child.'

'That wasn't your fault – that was Dhara's choice. You can't regret those moments. They were a gift, a blessing, they were lived for both of you... I don't know how to explain it. The two of you...' he faltered again.

'Those moments were... shared. I know,' She pressed her face to her husband's tears. 'They were shared, and yet they weren't. They were mostly mine.

'I promised my sister I would raise Smrithi. I'm going to give her time; and space – as much as she needs. Unless she takes too long. I'm going to keep raising her. For Dhara and for me.

'I need some help. There are boxes in the attic,' she stood up slowly and held out her hand.

The attic housed thirty-two years of hoarding: every postcard their children had sent them, every school report and merit award, cardiology journals Siva wouldn't throw, saris Priya had no time to wear.

Boxes containing letters – hundreds of blue aerogrammes post-marked Sri Lanka. A lifetime of correspondence from Dhara that always began and ended the same way. Priya had kept them all. She had memorised them all. She pressed the skin of the last one to her face, inhaling it. Then she put it back in a box with the others and taped the box shut.

'They're for Smrithi.'

✦

Nala called Smrithi over to her apartment on the pretext of looking at old photos. Smrithi used to love looking at them before – before, she had been happy to spend hours with her grandmother, reading her notebooks and letters, while Nala talked about old times. She had prepared a box for Smrithi today, containing photos of Priya and Dhara as children.

First, Smrithi wanted to make a glass of faloodah. She liked cutting the coloured agar-agar, making sure she had equal portions of the green and red jelly.

'You cut the agar-agar like your mother,' Nala said, 'the pieces are all uniform.'

'*Which* mother?' Smrithi asked. She took her glass and went to the living room before Nala could reply.

Smrithi sat on the floor, cross-legged and leaning against the sofa. Nala sat beside her on the sofa, propping cushions around her aching back and hips.

'How are you darling? Are you managing?' she asked. Smrithi began sorting through the photos and answered without looking up.

'It's been fine, hard at times I suppose, but fine.'

Fine. Smrithi was not one for 'fine'. Neither was Nala.

She tried again. 'Amma says you haven't spoken to each other for a while.'

Again, Smrithi didn't respond. She continued to sort photos, occasionally stopping to sip her drink. She had Rajan's sorting gene.

Nala had asked herself a question for almost thirty-three years: Why didn't they tell Smrithi? The easiest answer was because Dhara made them promise not to until she was ready. It wasn't easy to lie, but it was easier than telling the truth – the truth that Smrithi had been born of violence, but birthed by love. That in recording how she had been conceived, they must remember the inconceivable.

She told Smrithi: 'Darling, your parents begged Dhara to move to Australia. They wanted you to know the truth but as time went on, it became harder for all of them.'

The young woman stopped playing with the photographs and put them down. Sitting on the floor, she drew her knees to her chest and hid her face in them, crying harsh tears. Nala sat with her stroking her hair.

'Ammamma,' she asked finally. 'Ammamma – when Dhara ma... mami gave me away...was she disgusted by me? I can't imagine giving away my child, my own child.' She shook her head, her voice trembling. 'I look at my daughter and I could never let her go. I think I must have reminded Dhara mami of what happened to her. I must have been a constant, repulsive reminder. Did she hate me? Maybe I would hate me too. Maybe I would be disgusted...'

'No, *ende chelle cunju*,' Nala said in a stream of endearments and tears. She reached down painfully to hold her granddaughter.

'She wasn't disgusted. She loved you. You reminded her that she lived when she could have died. She loved you and she wanted to protect you.'

'That was my choice to make, not hers,' Smrithi replied. 'She gave me no chance to get to know her, to love her...as my mother.'

Nala didn't know which *she* Smrithi meant. Her anger for each of them was interchangeable, as was her love and her loss. As were they.

'She took that away from me!' Smrithi cried. 'They both did. They lied and they were only protecting themselves from their lies.'

'No Smrithi, Dhara was afraid that if you knew, you would return to Sri Lanka – you would want to be with her. We were all afraid of that.'

'That was still my choice to make,' the young woman repeated.

'No darling, that is a mother's choice to make – and both of your mothers love you,' Nala replied. 'I'm sorry we hurt you, I am. But of all the lies I've told, this is the one I don't regret. We wanted to protect you.'

Smrithi clung hard to her, speaking into the folds of her sari, unwilling to move or let go of her grandmother's spindly legs. 'It hurts...'

'I know, darling,' she said. 'Your parents did the best they could for you. We each have to choose our own *dharma*, our own path. We choose it and we follow it the best we can.'

Smrithi cried again and half laughed. 'Ammamma, you sound like the *Bhagavad Gita*. Have you been talking to Appa lately?'

'No, it's from Oprah,' Nala replied.

Smrithi dried her tears with her hands and looked closely at her grandmother.

'Ammamma, I'm angry at Amma, even though I...love her...' Smrithi didn't finish her sentence.

'Daughters are always angry at their mothers.'

'Not just daughters – husbands and wives, siblings – we're often angry at the people we love,' Rajan said from the front door.

He had returned from his daily walk to the Strathfield Plaza. 'Mothers can let go of their anger more easily, I think. We constantly fail the people we love. But *losing* a child is far worse than *failing* one.' He leaned against their apartment doorway, tired from the flight of stairs. 'The thought of a future without your children is terrifying. Life can not be comprehended without your children in it.'

Nala hadn't heard Rajan say so much in a long time. She wanted to respond but he raised a hand. 'Smrithi, ask your mother – ask Priya – about her favourite story in the *Mahabharata*. It's the marriage of Draupadi – do you know it?' he asked.

'I do Appappa – her favourite story is about polyandry and blind obedience to one's mother?' Smrithi asked.

'No,' Rajan laughed a little, shaking his head. He looked at Nala but spoke to Smrithi. 'Your great-grandfather used to say, if you swim, swim together. If you sink, sink together.'

'I feel like I'm sinking Appappa,' Smrithi replied, tearfully.

'Then ask your mother for help,' he said. 'I need to rest now Smrithi; it was good to see you. Come over more often, won't you?' He kissed her gently.

Nala looked at him, old and grey, in his precise and crisp shirt and his polished shoes. The edges were fraying. It was hard to imagine they were ever so young once that there was more of their life ahead of them than behind them. He unbuttoned his shirt slowly. He did everything slowly now. He would put on his sarong and have an afternoon nap, as he did every day. His naps were getting longer.

'Don't be angry at your mother, Smrithi. You are entitled to your pain, to all of it,' she said quietly, offering her a curried mutton roll and another tissue. 'But don't be angry. Be grateful darling, while you still have time.'

☼

Nala cast her mind back to a conversation. She couldn't remember if it was the one when Smrithi was a child, or later when she had almost finished school, or university. They were all so similar, the memories. Their frames had faded away, leaving a panorama of repeating images and words in different decades.

Dhara called her. She was ready to talk, to explain, and to reclaim.

'She deserves to know, Nala mami. I want her to know how much I love her. I ache for her every day. I see her all around me. Everything makes me think of her.'

'I know mahal. It must be so hard, I can't imagine how you feel,' Nala replied.

She didn't need to imagine. She still carried the feeling inside her: when Rajan took the last baby from her hands. She loved him no less than the others. She could see the lines of his small body, she could recall the smell of his paper-thin skin, and she could remember the name she whispered into his tiny ear.

'Mohan. Your name is Mohan.' She kissed him and rested her forehead on his. Rajan touched her shoulder. She held on. He insisted. He had to pry her fingers from her son. She watched him gently wrap the child in a blanket, tucking the folds tightly, swaddling him for an eternal sleep. He covered the small face, the tiny peak of the nose, the barely open nostrils, the sealed eyes, the prayerful hands. The perfect lips.

The feeling – the loss – was there, constantly at first, then daily and then less often but still present. Bubbles of pain that rose to the surface, as though from a long-forgotten submarine that slept on the ocean floor, entombing all life within.

'Mami, please help me – help me tell her. I've spoken to Priya and she agrees, it's time. She's scared about Smrithi's reaction, but she agrees. She wants to tell the truth too.'

The words jolted Nala. Priya. She didn't want her to suffer that pain. Of course Priya agreed with Dhara. She always agreed with Dhara, with Rajan, with what was right. She would agree, but she would never admit she wished it were otherwise.

Her daughter loved that child in the confused, irrefutable, unbreakable mess of love that exists between a mother and a child and sometimes between siblings; between these siblings.

Priya would never keep what was Dhara's, no matter what it cost her.

But Nala would. She cautioned Dhara; she convinced her.

'If Smrithi knows, she will come back to Ceylon. Think about your work, mahal. Can you give it up? Can you stop it?' she asked. 'Smrithi will want to be with you and help you. She worships you already. She will want to be like you. I worry...'

She didn't need to say more. She hadn't lied. And she never told Priya or Rajan about the conversations.

Perhaps she was right. If Smrithi knew, she would have followed Dhara and she would have died with her.

Or perhaps Dhara would have given up her work, her faith in a homeland, and moved to Australia.

A dam deep inside her collapsed.

Guilt rose like bile from her gut, bitter and burning from the inside.

A pyramid of boxes arrived at Smrithi's house by courier. Each contained countless letters from Dhara to Priya, that all began: 'My dearest Acca, I hope this letter finds you well. How is our darling girl?'

She recounted the events of her life in Sri Lanka and the people around her. In a letter from 1996 she wrote:

'They found Krishanthy Kumaraswamy finally. And her mother, brother and a family friend too. They worked out what happened. It's unusual for them to bother but there's something about the photographs of her in her pressed white school uniform and her hair. She always wore it in two long plaits, looped under each ear and tied with big shiny ribbons. There was nothing unusual about her. She looks like every school girl in Sri Lanka. Maybe that's why people noticed this time. It's harder to ignore when it could be your child.

'She was going home from school and stopped at Kaithady Army checkpoint in Jaffna. She was taken by six soldiers and never seen alive again.

'Her mother, sixteen-year-old brother and the other man went to report her missing. Her mother would have guessed what had happened to her when she didn't return. But she went to the army base anyway.

'It's been almost two months now, and they were all found there at the base. Her mother and the friend were bound and strangled. Krishanthy and her brother were cut into pieces before they were buried. Amnesty International is working hard to have the soldiers arrested. It's an incredible campaign, the first one of its kind here for a victim, but I'm not hopeful.

'I think about her a lot. I don't know her at all, and yet I feel I know her well. She must have been so happy walking home from school that day. Her exams were over and she might have applied to university. She would have been so frightened. I wish I could have told her the pain won't last forever. There is an end to it, one way or another. She was nineteen-years-old acca, the same age as Smrithi.

'Thank you for looking after our daughter. Keep her safe and far away from all this.'

Smrithi closed her eyes for a moment and saw the school girl. She shook the image from her mind and tried to replace it with another: her mami sitting with her on Primrose Hill, laughing as they did handstands with Ahalya under a pink London sky. Tears fell onto the paper.

The letters all finished the same way: 'Not yet. All my love, Dhara.' Smrithi didn't understand the ending, but she understood the beginning and the middle and that was something.

Smrithi remembered a moment. She was sleeping. Someone opened her small hand and placed something inside it. It was smooth. She woke up.

'Amma,' she whispered, sleep still upon her. Her words caught in her sticky mouth.

'Shh. I'm sorry, I didn't mean to wake you. I had to see you.'

'You're back,' Smrithi said, opening her eyes more fully. 'What did you bring me?'

Priya laughed. 'Open your hand and have a look.'

It was a carved elephant.

'Smell it,' she said, pushing the hair back from Smrithi's face. It smelled delicious and familiar, like the smokiness of their shrine.

'It's made of sandalwood,' Amma bent down and nuzzled her. 'You smell good too,' she tickled Smrithi's neck with her nose. Smrithi moved over, making space for her in the bed.

'Is it a baby elephant, like me?' Smrithi asked.

'No, it's a mummy elephant, like me,' she replied, holding her close. Amma smelled like sandalwood too.

Smrithi sat patiently as her children piled sand around her. *A human sandcastle, Mummy*, they said, laughing as they accidentally put a handful down her swimmers. She ran her fingers through Pearl Beach's soft, white sand. Its warmth was comforting. Children on a beach were comforting.

Watching them play, she couldn't get other images out of her mind. Twenty, maybe forty, maybe seventy, some reports were now suggesting one hundred thousand dead; killed in the final months of the war. Mothers on a beach, digging bunkers in the sand. Sand is so hard to dig: rebelliously returning to its place when dry; hard and heavy to move when wet. Mothers hiding their children, using their bodies as sandbags, as shells rained down. Mothers will do anything.

Smrithi caught Ahalya by the waist and wrestled her onto her lap.

'Mummy, mummy!' Ahalya shrieked, wriggling as Smrithi tickled her.

Smrithi stopped and held her seven-year-old daughter in her arms like a baby, brushing the sand from her face.

'Why are you crying, Mummy?' Ahalya asked, sitting up. She wiped her mother's face with her small hands.

'It's just the sand, darling. I've got sand in my eye, that's all,' she replied, kissing her. She could smell the beach on her daughter's skin.

Smrithi remembered fragments of a moment. She was five. It felt like a dream. A nightmare. A circle of men in sarongs and slippers. They carried fire. Amma told her never to touch fire. The light darted from the fire to their faces to the knives that hung at their sides. Amma told her never to touch knives. They poured the fire on her grandmother. She blazed like a bonfire. The men laughed. Ammamma screamed. Appappa ran into the fire as the skin on her grandmother's arm slid away, like a runny egg. She took a step forward but someone held her back. 'No, bubba, wait,' a man said, picking her up. She was bundled into her grandfather's car, terrified.

She remembered hearing Appappa cry and Ammamma fight to breathe. She opened her eyes. Men and women rushed around her, a snowstorm of white coats and uniforms.

'Stay with her Rajan, I'll take the child,' someone said, a doctor, a friend.

'No,' Appappa wept. 'No. You stay with Nala, take care of her please. I'll take the child. They're waiting for her. I promised her mother I would take her.'

I promised her mother.

Smrithi remembered the ambulance that took her from the hospital to the airport. The sirens keened like a thousand children crying. Appappa sat between the driver and a soldier. He held her on his lap, his blackened hands over her eyes, his heart hammering against her ear.

She remembered the airport. Amma cried, the cadence of it uncontrolled and raw. Appappa held her once more.

'Go home, get away while you can – don't bring her back here,' he whispered to Amma before he left.

Amma clutched her tightly, sobs and words, still shuddering forth.

Words like *Kadaval*, God.

And mahal.

Smrithi put her small arms around her. She knew she was safe. 'Amma,' she cried, 'Amma.'

No-one in the family had been to a wedding or a function since Dhara's death had been agreed upon. There was no body so there was no funeral for her, but each of them had performed the rites of mourning in their own way.

At Priya's request, the entire family was meeting at the local temple in Homebush for Tamil New Year. Nala was a little excited; it was a dormant emotion that had slowly resurrected itself. She liked the Western habit of making resolutions on the 31st of December but by the 3rd of January she had usually broken hers. Having a New Year in April gave her a second chance to 'be nicer to Rajan, don't let the children upset me so much, remember to pray for Rajan's family…'

Smrithi ironed a sari for her; plain lavender with a silver grey border. It was a gift from one of Priya's numerous trips to Madras years ago. According to Priya, the colours were 'too young' for Nala now, but she didn't care.

Nala couldn't even bend forward properly to pleat and set her own sari any more. Smrithi did it all for her, pinning the layers the way Nala had taught her two decades ago. Her granddaughter placed a fake bun in her hair, wrapped her thinning, dyed curls around it, and pinned a fine hair net over it all. Finally, she arranged Nala's wedding chain, moving the pendant to the front and added a few bangles to her grandmother's pale arms. She stepped back.

'You're still a beautiful woman, Ammamma,' she said.

'Do you think so, darling,' Nala laughed, pleased.

Smrithi parked the car and helped her get out.

Nala noticed the fast clatter of the Parramatta train line heading west. Every single face on the street was Tamil. She tried not to think about the face that was missing.

Sandwiched between stocky, red brick apartment blocks, the temple in Homebush was adequate. She preferred the much grander temple in Westmead or even the one in Wollongong. Rajan said that God was everywhere and he would rather pray at home but reluctantly joined them on the hour long drive to Wollongong. Her great-grandchild, Rishi, Smrithi's son, was surprisingly up-to-date on Vedic philosophy for a five-year-old and he assured her that his great-grandfather was indeed correct.

'God is everywhere,' Rishi explained, 'You don't have to worship Him in a temple.'

Nala was a devout Hindu who had prayed happily in temples and churches her entire life. She didn't need to be lectured by a child. She knew that all Gods were one and that He could be worshipped anywhere, including in the comfort of one's own home in one's own sarong, as Rajan preferred. However, she looked forward to going to the temple.

It was a dynamic place, despite its unassuming appearance: marriages were negotiated and arranged; families surreptitiously observed potential husbands and wives for their children; the Year 12 results of young Tamils were compared; rumours were started and scandals exaggerated; births were celebrated and divorces whispered about; Sri Lankan politics was debated and more marriages negotiated. In her prime, Nala could arrange a marriage, a dinner and a game of cards all before she had circumnavigated the temple once. Rajan did not consider this a valuable skill. What did he know? People prayed, they connected with God and with each other.

She proudly showed off her grandchildren and great-grandchildren to the ladies who greeted her warmly. Everyone wanted to kiss her. Rajan told her off, lecturing her that 'this kissing business is unhygienic and unseemly. Especially at your age, you have to be very careful about germ transfer.'

'It's true,' added Ahalya, who shared Rajan's aversion to germs. 'Germ transfer can be deadly.'

Nala laughed out loud, tears in her eyes. Dhara had been so proud of her grandchildren.

'Sshh,' said Priya, 'the priest is coming.' Her face had aged. She held out her arms nervously and then insistently to Ahalya and Rishi. Smrithi couldn't look at her but she pushed her children forward and they ran happily into their grandmother's tight embrace. Priya exhaled.

Nala leaned over and whispered to Smrithi, 'You know, you are very lucky I've lived to see you move back to Sydney. I never thought I would make it.'

'I know, I really thought you'd be dead by now,' Smrithi replied.

Nala burst out laughing again, earning her more annoyed looks from her husband. Smrithi's son ran up to Rajan, offering him a handful of sticky, sweaty sugar candy. Rajan laughed and surprisingly, accepted his unhygienic gift.

Nala caught Smrithi watching the exchange between one of the youngest and the oldest. Her granddaughter smiled, finally looking a little more comfortable.

After they prayed, Nandan took her home to her apartment. The rest of the family was on its way over. She had been cooking for days despite her children's instructions not to 'go overboard'. She would throw Priya overboard if she scolded or advised her one more time.

She straightened her sari shawl and looked at herself in the mirror. She licked the iron nail, then dipped it into the pot of vermilion kunkumam, slowly and steadily re-applying the coloured powder to the middle of her forehead. Priya had tried to make her use the reusable sticker pottus that came in so many colours and styles. Why would she need sticker pottus when she had her kunkumam? She had used the same colour powder and the same nail since she arrived in Sydney all those years ago. Her red pottu was straight and perfectly round. The nail had not aged and despite her increasing frailty, her hand never faltered in this one daily task. Her great-grandchildren were coming today and the little ones liked to press their foreheads to hers, taking an imprint of her pottu onto their own faces. You couldn't do that with a sticker.

Today's New Year menu was vegetarian, and simple. She had cooked as much as she could manage these days: her special vegetable noodles and potato ketchup curry for the children; puttu, aubergine curry, okra curry, and coconut chilli sambal for the adults. She wanted to offer her world famous butter cake for dessert, but Priya had insisted on bringing a pudding. Rajan loved his daughter's puddings, so she didn't say no but she secretly took a brick of butter cake out of the freezer.

She opened the front door to Smrithi and her family. Before she could kiss anyone hello, she was confronted with the bespectacled eyes of Rishi.

'Pooti, when you die will you be reborn?' he asked.

Nala was thrilled that she was a Pooti now – a great-grandmother as well as an Ammamma and Amma. She missed her siblings but she was grateful she had lived so long.

'Hello, Rishi. Yes, I think I probably will be reborn,' she laughed 'But I hope not, I'd prefer to go straight to God. We'll see. How are you?' she asked him.

'I'm a Hindu, thank you very much,' he said, walking past her after receiving his kiss.

She hoped that Rishi would not accost Rajan with the same theological questions; he was resting after the morning's outing and watching *Yes, Prime Minister*. She kissed the stream of children and adults coming through the door and went to get her husband.

She found him sitting with Rishi, engaged in a deep conversation. She didn't know who the Jedis were but clearly they had a lot in common with the Hindus. Rajan was laughing and wiping his eyes and she was about to leave them when she heard Rishi ask,

'Poota, do you think Dhara Parti will be reborn?'

Smrithi had explained Dhara's death to the children as honestly as she could, leaving out certain details. She held her breath. She wasn't sure if she should intervene and save Rajan the pain or Rishi the confusion.

The boy continued, 'I thought if Dhara Parti was reborn she could come live with us. I think Mummy misses her, so does Ammamma.'

'We all miss her, Rishi. I don't know if Dhara Parti will be reborn. That is decided by our karma, do you know what that is?' he replied.

'Of course, Parta told me. Do you think the people who hurt Dhara Parti will be reborn?'

She watched Rajan now as he carefully organised his thoughts. He put his arm around his little great-grandson and spoke. 'Rishi, I think there is greatness and there is God in all of us: in you, and in me; in Dhara Parti and even the people who hurt her. I struggle...to believe in that but I know I must. I am glad you are beginning your relationship with God so early in your life – keep going, it will sustain you in the years to come.'

Rishi thought about this for a moment and then kissed his great-grandfather. 'Thank you, Poota, you sound like Yoda.' With that, he got up and ran out. They had no idea who Yoda was but they both laughed.

As she did every year, Nala had prepared a small shrine in the living room. A coconut was placed in an old steel pot filled with water and adorned with mango leaves. The pot sat on a bed of uncooked rice; her mother's paddy.

'If you sow it,' her mother had said to her, 'it will grow fields of new rice.'

She remembered packing the paddy, decades ago. It had crossed oceans with her, survived a pogrom and even Australian Customs Officials.

The family stood around the shrine. For each child, grandchild and great-grandchild, she had assembled a betel leaf. She placed a token amount of money on each leaf, just a note and a coin, with a small smudge of holy ash on top. She had also made one for Dhara, as she did every year.

Rajan gave each leaf to his family slowly, concentrating hard to control the shake in his hands. It was their blessing for the Tamil New Year – and a symbol of abundance, not wealth – from the hands of someone who had been greatly blessed himself.

23

Rajan picked up the photograph. The sepia had faded but the clarity of the image remained in his mind. The girls were dressed in their best hand-smocked outfits with Nandan in a sailor suit. In the evenings, when Rajan returned home from work, they went to the beach at Galle Face Green together. Walking along the promenade they ran into friends. The children cajoled him into buying ice creams while they played.

All the adults, except Rajan, chatted and laughed together. He just kept a watchful eye on the children as they wet the hems of their dresses in the water. When they went too far, he called to Nala to shout at them. He rarely shouted himself.

They were so beautiful. He prayed for their protection, their health and happiness every morning and every night, and several moments in between. He prayed for forgiveness. He put the photograph back in the box.

Rajan had a strict routine. He woke up at six o'clock to perform his morning ablutions. Standing in front of the dulled mirror of his bathroom, he inspected his greying hair – everywhere from his ears, nose and eyebrows to his chest. Then, slowly, he worked a thick lather from a shrinking bar of Palmolive Gold soap and covered his face. With his razor, he carved smooth, straight roads of brown skin.

He couldn't control the razor anymore. Nandan or Vivek had to shave him every few days. And he couldn't get up at six o'clock. Sometimes he would lie there awake, willing his tired body to move, angry at its slow and stealthy rebellion.

His morning toilet was becoming more painful. Nala tried everything – okra curry, spinach curry, strong coffee, oranges, grapefruit and the worst, high fibre drinks. He had briefly toyed with the idea of giving himself a suppository. A small sliver of the Palmolive Gold should work. He sat down on the toilet seat, poised to self-administer, when he dropped it into the toilet. It was one thing to put soap up his bottom, it was quite another to fish it out of the toilet bowl first. The growing discomfort was preferable.

'What's wrong with you?' Nala asked as he emerged slowly from the toilet.

'There's nothing wrong with me. What's wrong with you?' he countered.

'Nothing. Why did you take so long?'

'Were you timing me?'

'No.'

'Then how do you know I took so long?'

'Don't be smart.'

'I am smart.'

She scowled, huffed and scowled again as she walked away muttering, 'Something is wrong with you. I can smell it. Actually, I can't smell it!' Turning around she cried triumphantly, 'That's what's wrong. You still can't go. I knew I was right, there is something wrong!'

He was already walking away to their study, massaging his bowel as he went.

'I'm going to pray, please don't disturb me with your medical discoveries,' he said without turning back.

The guests were arriving at eleven o'clock. He had already told Nala that he would not be seeing anyone if they came during *Yes, Prime Minister*. Sir Humphrey Appleby could make him laugh so much that he cried. One time, he laughed so much he choked and stopped breathing. Several of his descendants were doctors; all ready and keen to perform an emergency tracheotomy on the kitchen floor with a bread knife and a straw. Luckily for him that time, he was able to cough-start his own respiratory system.

He didn't like talking to people any more. He spoke when it was necessary. It was an economy of words that people mistook for an economy of emotion. He didn't need to speak much, given that Nala usually spoke for both of them. When he was younger, he could review the histories of the following day's patients in his head, while she carried on a one-sided exchange. If she was in a particularly argumentative mood, he could review the whole week's patients while she fought with herself on his behalf.

He used to listen to the BBC World Service every morning on the radio. He didn't even like the news anymore. He'd heard it all before: the decades were different but the problems were the same.

Smrithi tried to tell him about a new group of radical Buddhist monks that had emerged in Sri Lanka. They sounded just like the old group. They were inciting riots against the Muslims now. Sri Lanka was a Buddhist nation, they said, with no place for Muslims. The monks accused the 'Moors' of stealing Sinhala women to take as their wives, and indoctrinating Sinhala children in their ways. Rumours quickly fomented into violence in their infected island. The government did nothing. Rajan asked Smrithi not to tell him any more.

He shuffled slowly to their shrine. It was small but sufficient. He said a quiet prayer to Lord Ganesha and thanked him for removing the obstacles of their life. Nala had placed a bowl of sweets for his deity. Lord Ganesha should cut down on sugar. The incidence of heart disease amongst Hindus was very high and given the elephant god's BMI he was also in a high-risk category for Type 2 diabetes. Rajan laughed and asked the Lord to forgive his irreverence.

He dipped his fingers in the remains of the thirunuru bowl. Vivek had dropped by yesterday with his two youngest children. They had raided the shrine and were found quietly eating the Lord's fruit, covered in holy ash and decked out in several layers of Nala's prayer beads, as well as her enormous brassieres.

He dusted off his fingers so he wouldn't spill ash on the floor and walked to the photographs of his family that adorned the corridor wall. He placed holy ash on each of the dead. Closing his palms and his eyes again, he thanked them for the life they had bestowed upon him. First, Nala's parents who had given him his wife. Then the photograph of his parents, taken when he was only eight. His mother looked so strong. His fingers lingered as he placed the ash on her.

Then the photos of their siblings. To Mohan he prayed for forgiveness. The words *enne manichidu* asked for something deeper than the English language could convey; could perhaps feel.

There were words for most things in Tamil and English and Sinhalese. Widow, widower, orphan – these were words for pain. But he couldn't find the word for someone who had lost a sibling or a child. There was no name for it. Language, in all its complexity and dexterity, could not name the depth of that pain. He must remember to tell Smrithi that language could not describe what Dhara and Priya had each suffered. Language had limits, like the borders of a nation. Pain did not.

Words were leaving him now. They were luminous, tropical birds sensing the approach of a long, barren winter. He liked the stillness. It didn't frighten him. He cried at weddings, refused to go to the almost monthly funerals of their friends, laughed at his grandchildren's jokes, played with his great-grandchildren, and simply stopped talking to everyone else.

✪

Nala walked around the grounds of Rookwood Cemetery. It was a peaceful place. There was a Jewish section, an enormous Chinese section, and even a section for Buddhists – there were graves for everyone, lying harmoniously together in death. She had stopped for a while at the cemetery for Australian soldiers. It was on Remembrance Drive. Remembrance: Australia remembered and revered its dead. It buried its warriors with dignity.

A week ago Rajan had gone to his study for his afternoon nap. He changed into his sarong and placed his neatly folded clothes on the rack next to the mattress he slept on during the day. He napped the same way he had always napped – on his back, hands on his stomach, fingers locked. He looked the same, only lately much smaller. He was shrinking into himself, she had thought: his mind and words turning inwards. He closed his eyes and never opened them.

'It's not right,' she said to herself. 'It's not right that I should live to see this.'

'Would you have preferred it, if it was you first?' he asked her impatiently. 'You need to pull yourself together Nala.'

She turned to look at him but he wasn't there, just a lifetime of scoldings, echoing in her ears.

She had been to viewings before; they were an important community get-together. But she didn't want to look at her husband's body; preserved yet lifeless. She and the mortician dressed him. She chose a yellow, pin-striped Marks & Spencer shirt that she had given him years ago. He didn't like yellow but she knew his dark skin looked better in that colour than the formal blue or muted brown that he insisted on wearing.

They had to have the viewing; people needed to pay their respects, but for once she found herself agreeing with him. He said, 'Respect is better reserved for the living than for the dead. For my own funeral, I want a private cremation, short and simple.'

She replied, 'You'll drive me into an early grave so you should give those instructions to our son, not me.'

The funeral was worse.

Rajan had insisted that his funeral should be in Tamil. Lately in Sydney, Tamils were using Indian priests – Hindi speaking and Sanskrit chanting – for their funerals. He called this new approach a 'fad'.

'People died in our homeland for the protection of our mother tongue. It seems nothing less than ungrateful that since escaping the war, Tamils here think it's fashionable to be sanctified and cremated in Sanskrit, a language that is also dead. At my funeral the priest must speak in a living, breathing language. *And* he must wear a shirt – none of this 'sarong only' business.'

So an elderly gentleman, Mr Vaithalingam, had presided fully-clothed over the funeral, explaining the ritual in Tamil and in English to the enormous gathering of family and friends. Nala found herself wishing she didn't understand what was happening as the old man poured rice into a mortar.

Paddy rice was used at weddings. Husked rice was used at funerals. Paddy rice was living. Husked rice was dead.

Nandan tearfully performed the last rites for Rajan. She remembered at her father's funeral, her twin brothers had been inconsolable. Mohan had stepped forward to perform the duties of a son. Her mind often strayed back to Mohan and Gal Oya these days.

Mr Vaithalingam asked Nandan to pound the husked rice with the heavy stone pestle. The body was dead and the soul needed to be released. Nala wondered if Dhara had been pounded by stone.

She wiped the tears that were falling fast and inhaled deeply. She hadn't brought any tissues. She couldn't believe she had come to a funeral without tissues. She couldn't believe she was at Rajan's funeral.

The old man began to read from the *Bhagavad Gita*, the Song of God. She knew the verse in Tamil. Birth, death and every emotion, expectation, and disappointment in between are only temporary. They are illusory; they are not real, yet we live the length and breadth of human experience as though they are.

Death is natural to all who are born. Death can liberate the soul from the cycle of life, from pain and from suffering. Death is inevitable and should be embraced – it should be accepted.

The body is a vessel, a clay pot to be broken with a scythe, freeing the soul. Mr Vaithalingam handed Nandan the clay pot and she wondered if Dhara's body had been touched by a scythe.

Some souls are freed too early, too young, she thought. Rajan was lucky. His soul was ready even though she was not. The funeral director pulled the curtain across, shielding the coffin from the mourners. He pressed a button and she wept as Rajan was taken away towards the fire.

☼

Nala's coffee table had been converted into an altar, with a large photo of Rajan as the main deity. She placed a chain of gardenias around him and anointed his forehead with holy ash and kunkumam. Specks of the red powder spilled onto his nose.

'Sorry,' she muttered. She wiped his face and continued her work. She had made a plate of thosais for him. The fermented pancakes had come out perfectly. Their edges were crispy and golden. She'd used extra ghee. His heart would be fine. She placed fourteen peanuts on his small silver coaster. He liked to eat them while he watched *Keeping Up Appearances*, with his brandy aperitif. A cut glass tumbler. A gift from Holsworthy when he retired.

The kitchen was a mess and she left it like that.

Priya brought a wheelie Eski containing a dry prawn fried curry, a grated prawn varai curry and a prawn gravy curry.

'Appa's favourites,' she said without tears. Siva carried the heavy Corningware dish of coffee trifle pudding and a box of Mini-Magnums.

'His favourites,' he said, crying as he kissed her cheeks. Smrithi found the pack of Home Brand honeycomb pieces in his study where he'd hidden them. They were no longer crunchy but he didn't like to waste.

They all sat on the floor and looked at her. Nala looked at Rajan. Your tidiness was compulsive and annoying. Those British comedies were tiresome after the second re-run. I hate the news. No-one shops at sale times only. Normal people talk to each other, they chat, even when they have nothing to say. Normal people compromise not just what they want, but who they are. You were hard and harsh. Sometimes you made me cry. Sometimes you held me as I cried. You said nothing comforting, not one word, but you comforted me. Sometimes, often, you made me laugh, even when you didn't mean to. I loved you. For sixty-four years I loved you. You made me love you. But today, on your eighth day ceremony Rajan, I hate you.

She looked at her family and said nothing. Confused, Priya opened the *Ashtothram*, the one-hundred-and-eight names of Lord Shiva, and began chanting.

✿

Priya surveyed her parents' apartment with despair. It looked tired like its owners – owner. The small tables and shelves were filled with photographs of the family, each with a thin film of dust over them. The apartment didn't have any empty horizontal spaces, or even vertical ones for that matter; all the walls were covered in her mother's paintings. What hadn't been mounted in their apartment had been given to the children and grandchildren, who dutifully hung the gifts on their walls.

Nala was watching Oprah. Rajan should have been having his afternoon nap in the study. She opened the door slowly, afraid of the empty room. Four small certificates hung on the wall by his desk. They were the size of postcards, faded but preserved: two to 'V. Rajan for hard work, 1928'; and two to 'V. Rajan for very hard work, 1928'. Certificates given to a seven-year-old boy who, even then, displayed one of the qualities that would help him succeed.

She missed his withered toes. Her fingers reached out towards the lonely mattress, waving in front of it, daring him to grab her. It was silly. She laughed.

She closed the door gently and looked around the apartment. She didn't know where to start but she had to work quickly before her mother realised what she was doing.

Since Rajan's death, the apartment had declined quickly. Priya and Smrithi visited Nala – separately, at Smrithi's request. When they thought Nala wasn't looking, usually during the *Days of Our Lives / Young and the Restless / Oprah* marathon or her afternoon nap, they cleaned.

Both of them had been schooled well by Rajan at a very early age. Each would clean quickly and quietly: disposing of food that was past its use-by-date, wiping crevices from the kitchen to the bathroom, and dusting photo frames to reveal the memories underneath. Each woman would sit on the floor and straighten the frayed edges of the old Persian rugs. Both were worried Nala would trip on the wayward threads and both needed to see the order of straight, parallel lines.

On that day, Priya decided to spend extra time in the kitchen. A slow trail of ants wrapped itself around a sticky bottle of rose syrup, creating a graveyard of intense sweetness. At least the ants drowned happy. Faloodah always made her happy. She remembered sitting with Dhara and Nandan on the back verandah, sipping its chilled milky pinkness with their father. The four of them wouldn't say a word, each silently concentrating on consuming the drink in their own way. Dhara ate the coloured gelatine at the bottom first. Priya and Nandan preferred to suck the floating, swollen basil seeds. Sometimes, when Rajan wasn't there, Nandan inhaled, loaded his straw with seeds and fired them out at his annoyed elder sisters.

She remembered watching her father as he drank his faloodah. He tried to refuse the drink, saying that it contained too much sugar for him. But he was vulnerable to the pleas of his children. He held the rim of the cold glass with two tapered fingers, taking care not to let anything fall on his neatly pressed trousers. He stirred the drink into a small, captive whirlpool, mixing the layers of gelatine, milk, syrup and basil seeds. When the whirlpool reached the correct velocity he angled the glass and took a deep sip, ingesting each of the component parts in just the right proportions. Her father was a genius.

She laughed again. Ayah used to make their drink for them. But that task, like so many others, had fallen to Nala when they left Colombo. She looked at her mother's kitchen and sighed. Nala had eventually become an inventive if not adept cook, but cleanliness and organisation were not part of her repertoire. Priya licked the rose syrup from her fingers and steeled herself for the cooker.

She scrubbed hard around the electric hot plates and felt her right shoulder ache. She wasn't young any more either but she didn't complain about her ailments the way her mother did. She just diagnosed and treated herself and got on with it. She would never understand Nala's need to discuss her pain in loud and copious detail. They were all in pain, including her father who never said a word. Occasionally he approached her quietly for a prescription after he'd done his own research, and she'd realise how much pain he lived with.

She felt her blood pressure rise and her heartbeat quicken with irritation as she returned to the study room where the shrine was kept. It had been reduced to three shelves loaded with deities, vying for space and special recognition from their worshippers.

On the top shelf there was a photo of Dhara. Priya wouldn't let her eyes linger on it. She looked at the prayer talismans, blessed by priests from various temples in Sri Lanka and South India. She picked up one of the small metal cylinders and shook it. The tiny scroll rattled inside and she wondered what that particular prayer was for. Nala had spent her life praying for her children and their offspring. It was one of her pastimes – praying, parties, and pain.

She went back to the photo of Dhara and picked it up. She held it to her chest, trying to remember what it felt like to hold her sister. She still looked at the clock on Friday night, sometimes in between. Sometimes she even reached for the phone.

'I'm sorry,' she whispered. 'I miss you.' She put the photo back.

On the bottom shelf, her mother had kept Rajan's receipts from the Pillayar Temple in a large Roses chocolate box. Priya counted them – there were sixty-four donations to the temple in Colombo, one for every year that had passed since he first saw Nala.

She stopped for a moment. She would not cry today. She quickly placed the receipts back in their box and continued her work.

As she dusted around the deities, a small card fell from the middle shelf. The size of a playing card, it was a picture of St Christopher, smiling with his hand raised. She used to tease her mother for praying to Catholic saints. She turned the card over to see Nala's messy, faded script: *British Hospital for Mothers and Babies, Woolwich, London. 3rd August 1974, waiting for Priya.* That was the day Vivek had been born. She had no recollection of the birth or the days afterwards; it had all been lost in a haze of high blood pressure. Her only clear memory was the doctor telling her that she would not have more children.

For years afterwards her mother told her how she stayed by her bedside praying to St Christopher. Nala's request had been simple: to please, please bring her daughter home from that dangerous journey mothers and their babies make together. She wiped the card, wiped her eyes, and continued cleaning.

✿

The sun skated off the water. The Parramatta River lapped the shore, brown dirty hands on the coarse pebbled beach. It wasn't ideal but it would have to do. Priya made the mixture. Milk, holy ash, jasmines and more ash swirled together in a red Bunnings bucket. It was a cheap one. They would throw it away afterwards. Her mother leant over the bucket and poured a sachet of kunkumum in. She no longer wore it. The red powder swirled and disappeared.

Nandan carried the bucket to the water's edge and set it down. That was when they all noticed the swimmer. He had noticed them already. Large, pointed sunhat, sunglasses and an amply sagging belly in Speedos turned towards them.

Her brother started to panic. 'Acca,' he mumbled, his back to her as he faced the water. 'What shall we do?'

'Nandan, turn around, I can't hear you properly,' she replied. It was late morning and the breeze from the water carried nothing more than the smell of ferry smoke and petrol. It was too hot for all of them to be standing around at Cabarita Park, especially Nala. Siva helped Nala to the grassy bank around the small beach. She stood away from the water, leaning heavily on his arm.

'Just act normal, acca,' Nandan replied, turning around with exaggerated casualness. 'I'm pretending to watch the ferry. That man is looking at us.'

'Of course he's looking at us Nandan mama,' Smrithi joined them at the water. She spoke without looking at Priya.

'Twelve Sri Lankan Tamil's hanging out by the beach, wearing traditional clothing and carrying a bucket. That's not suspicious at all. Plus we've just prayed to the Sun God but it looks like we're worshipping the River Cat.'

Priya laughed. It was good to hear her daughter's voice. Afterwards, she thought, she would ask Smrithi if she could take the children for an ice cream. She felt like pistachio today. Smrithi would say no, but one day she might say yes.

Nandan laughed too, more nervously. 'I'm not sure how I'm going to do this. He might report us.' Priya looked over at the man and inspected him as closely as he was inspecting her. She wondered if he had a phone in his Speedos.

'Don't stare acca,' Nandan hissed.

'I'll do it,' she replied. She let the water lap her feet. It was cool.

'What?' her brother asked.

'I'll do it,' she repeated, holding her hand out for the bucket. Her toes gripped the sand. She felt anchored.

'You can't. I'm supposed to,' he replied.

'Then do it.'

'I can't, not just yet. Let's look for shells or something. Pretend we're here for a reason.'

'We are here for a reason and I want to do it,' Priya replied softly. Nandan stood firmly, ankle deep in water, the bucket handle now clenched in his fist.

'I'm supposed to – it's the tradition,' he replied. They rarely fought.

'Interestingly the *Gita* and the *Vedas* do not address the issue of who is allowed to pollute public rivers with the remains of relatives.' Smrithi held out her hand resolutely to Nandan. When he remained silent, she said, 'I think Amma should do it for Appappa.'

'Amma –' Nandan turned to his mother for help.

'I agree,' Nala replied simply. 'Priya should do it.'

'Fine,' Nandan left the bucket on the sand and stepped away. Priya exhaled. She dipped the bucket into the river and captured a little of it. With a wooden spoon she stirred; solid subsumed in fire and now water. She stirred harder and harder until Smrithi put a hand on her back.

Priya stopped and smiled. It was the first time Smrithi had touched her since they told her. She stood up and waved brazenly at the swimmer. He didn't wave back. The sun kissed her face. It was a beautiful day. She walked deeper into the water so it lapped her knees. She gently poured her father's ashes in.

24

Nala closed her eyes.

Dhara sat on a hospital bed, holding her baby daughter in her arms.
'Smrithi. I want to name her Smrithi.'

Smrti – that which is remembered.

The child had been named after the Hindu scriptures that were passed down by human memory. Her granddaughter had an excellent memory. Sometimes Nala imagined that all of their family stories were filed away in that carefully ordered mind of Smrithi's. She was their family's memory. That thought comforted her – after she died Smrithi would remember her for the family. Nala, Rajan, Mohan, Dhara and all of the others would not be forgotten. Smrithi would remember and she would tell her children. Perhaps they would tell theirs.

She called her granddaughter again.

'Smrithi, I have an idea. I want you to go back to Ceylon. I want you to go back to our home and remember Dhara. Remember her and your mother. Do this for me darling. Your grandfather would have wanted it too.' Her voice shook when she mentioned Rajan.

'I'll start calling people to tell them you're coming.'

She put the phone down after a long conversation with Smrithi and several follow-up calls to Priya, Siva and Prashanth.

'Memory Smrithi, memory,' she whispered to her empty kitchen.

COLOMBO, 2010

Smrithi stood at her grandparents' old dining table with Prashanth and the Perera's. Shiranthi's parents were too frail to move the heavy black wood of the ornate chairs. Senthan, their elderly servant stepped forward but Smrithi asked him to wait. Prashanth moved the chairs for each of them. Sulethi, Shiranthi's mother, held on to Prashanth tightly as he helped her into her seat.

The dining table was one of the few pieces of her grandparents' furniture that remained in the house. Most of it, including Rajan's personal medical library, had been donated to the Jaffna Hindu College and replaced with cheaper, simpler furniture. Nala had tearfully given Smrithi strict instructions before she left for Colombo. She was to organise Dhara's belongings. Letters, photos and jewellery should be brought back to Sydney; everything else should be given to the Ramakrishna Mission orphanage.

'I have a man, Smrithi, who takes my things,' Nala offered by way of explanation.

'What do you mean you have a man who takes your things? Is someone stealing from you?' Smrithi asked, concerned.

'No,' she laughed through her sobs, 'I have a friend, actually he was Rita Matthews' friend. Those Matthews always were very well connected. Whenever I call him, he goes to the house in Colombo and takes whatever I ask him to take – he delivers it to the Hindu College or to Swami Satchithanandan who runs the Ramakrishna Mission in Colombo. The Swami then has it transported to their missions in Batticaloa. It's harder to get items to the north but sometimes he does that too. He's a good man.'

When Smrithi arrived in Colombo, she surveyed her grandparents' old almairahs, expecting to see the colourful reams of Nala's saris and the starched army of Rajan's shirts. Priya and Nandan often criticised their parents for bringing too many of their belongings with them to Sydney. The truth was that most of their belongings had been left behind, in cupboards and camphorwood chests, in Cinnamon Gardens, awaiting their eventual return. Smrithi opened the cupboards but found them empty.

Nala knew they weren't coming back. Over the years, with Dhara's help and Rita Matthews's man in Colombo, she found ways to give their belongings to people who needed them more.

The house looked different from the memories of Smrithi's childhood. It was withering. The once glowing floors had dulled, the tightening of skin causing cracks where previously there had been a flawless complexion. The corners were too far to reach for old hands, and colonies of spiders were appropriating the widening shadows of every room. The air around her was stagnant, where once the powerful lungs of her grandparents' home had refreshed and replenished them all with the easy flex of its muscle.

'What do you want to do with this place, mahal?' Sulethi asked her. Smrithi smiled at her use of the Tamil word. 'We are too old to live here anymore I think.'

'Perhaps. Are you comfortable here, Aunty?' Smrithi asked.

'We are very comfortable, thank you,' Sulethi replied. 'Dr Fonseka's grandson lives next door now. He has moved back to his family home. He checks on us regularly. The servant boy is good-hearted, a little lazy, but good-hearted. We need someone young and strong here. Senthan is getting older too, but he runs the house for us as he has done for years. He and I have taken a wager with your grandmother to see who will go first.'

Smrithi said, 'That's a little morbid isn't it?'

Sulethi laughed, 'I suppose so. Nala has put her money on herself.'

Smrithi laughed too, 'Of course she has. If you're happy, you should stay here, Aunty. I think the house still has a little time left in it.'

Smrithi walked around Dhara's apartment. She had played there as a child when her uncle Nandan lived in it. The apartment was above Nala's house, separate but still connected. She looked at photographs of herself on Dhara's shelves: school portraits, formals, graduations, family holidays, her children. Her life, captured at so many contiguous points that Dhara could feel like she was there with her, observing – if not participating in – her life as it happened.

So much of the story was communal – the memories of two were merged into one and placed in an ageing house. The weight of it was crushing. Smrithi didn't think she could bear it.

In a cupboard in Dhara's study, she found folders of letters, post-marked Australia, and filed chronologically. A lifetime of correspondence from Priya to Dhara that always began the same way:

'My darling Dhara, I miss you. Smrithi is beautiful.' The letters all ended the same way too: 'Please let me tell her. I love you dearly. Acca'

She sat on the floor, her tears blurring the words, as she read more letters. She could see that each one narrated the details of her life; everything from cardinal moments to the banal. The rituals of her existence had been preserved and made meaningful over and over again. The letters held the minutiae that only a mother would notice and record; the minutiae that only a mother would care about and read.

Smrithi wept for her mothers – both of them – and for all of them.

She returned to her bedroom. Prashanth had opened the curtains, flooding the room with the young morning light. She remembered the way she slept as a child: sometimes with Dhara and sometimes with Priya. If she was very lucky, she slept with her grandparents. Nala's stomach was the softest.

She looked at her bed. Prashanth had made it. She remade it quickly before he returned from the bathroom.

'If you're going to do something child, you should do it properly.'

It soothed her: the bed, the memory, the principle.

She missed Rajan. She missed Dhara. She missed her mother and father.

Other things soothed her too: the memory of Appa taking her with him on his ward rounds. She almost came up to his belt, her head level with the Motorola pager that he clipped onto it.

'This is my daughter – Smrithi,' he announced proudly to the nurses, his big hand squeezing her small one.

'She's beautiful, Dr Siva,' they cooed. 'She looks just like you.'

'Thank you,' he replied, never missing a beat. 'She's much better looking than me. When she grows up, I think she'll look just like Priya. She's smart like Priya too – Smrithi, tell them the chambers of the heart.'

The chambers of my heart, she whispered to herself.

She called her father.

'How could *you* not tell me, Appa? How could you love me?'

'There was nothing to tell, mahal. You are my daughter,' he replied. He was so clinically comforting.

'You've always believed in crazy things,' she smiled, wiping away her tears. 'Like Tamil Eelam, and what was that other place – Lemuria.'

'As you well know Smrithi, Lemuria is – or was – a real place. Much of the south Asian civilisation began from this sunken land mass. There was a great Tamil civilisation there from as early as 50,000BC,' he said proudly. 'It predates any other ethnic group in the area. If it wasn't for that great flood, the entire sub-continent could have been ruled by Tamils.'

'That's the one,' she laughed. 'It's a pity it was submerged by the ocean. As I said Appa, you're a great believer in impossible dreams.'

'Have some faith Smrithi,' Siva replied. 'You are my daughter.'

'Goodbye Appa. I'll see you soon.'

SYDNEY, 2010

'What happened next Parta, what happened next?' the children chimed at their grandfather. As a reward for them not using the word 'poo' during their home religion class, Siva had agreed to tell them a story from the *Ramayana*. He was slowly lowering the bar of conduct expected in these weekly classes. As a religion teacher at the local temple, he expected discipline and respect from his students. As a grandfather, he wondered how long it would be before his grandchildren asked about the monkey's bottom.

'You tell me what has happened so far, children,' he replied.

Rishi responded quickly. 'The bad king Ravana stole Rama's queen from her home and took her to his kingdom. Sita was a prisoner in Lanka, which is where you came from.'

'Very good, Rishi. Lord Rama sent his monkey warrior Hanuman to Lanka to rescue Sita. He gave Hanuman his ring so that Sita would trust him and know that he had been sent by Rama.'

'Why didn't Rama just text her Parta?'

Rishi rolled his eyes at his elder sister. 'Because, Ahalya, they didn't have mobile phones in the olden days.'

Siva laughed. 'Hanuman found Sita in the beautiful Ashoka Gardens of Lanka. She was crying. Hanuman approached her carefully so he didn't scare her. The monkey warrior was very powerful and frightening to some. Hanuman presented Lord Rama's ring and asked the beautiful queen to step onto his back so he could carry her to safety.'

'I would love to ride on a monkey,' said Rishi.

'I would love to have a pet monkey. I love monkeys,' said Ahalya. She loved all animals and was waging a determined campaign to get a puppy. Priya walked in with a plate of cut fruit for the children; red apples for Ahalya and green apples for Rishi. She had heard the story from the kitchen and continued it for Siva.

'Sita refused to go with Hanuman. She gave Hanuman her jewelled hair comb as proof that Hanuman had seen her. Sita told Hanuman to tell her husband and lord that she would wait in Lanka. She didn't want to be rescued by Hanuman. Instead, she wanted to remain a prisoner of Ravana, the Demon Lord of Lanka, until Lord Rama himself came for her.'

'That's a bit silly isn't it, Ammamma?' Ahalya asked. 'She should have just gone with Hanuman. Imagine riding on a monkey. That would be wonderful. What happened next, Parta?'

'Well then children, Hanuman was about to leave Lanka and return to Lord Rama, who was waiting for him in India. Suddenly King Ravana's soldiers arrived and captured him. They took him to Ravana who looked at the monkey all tied up. He laughed at how easily Lord Rama's warrior had been conquered.' Siva did his best impersonation of Ravana's evil laugh.

'Poor Hanuman, is he going to die, Ammamma?' Ahalya asked, worried.

'No, not at all – Hanuman escaped but his tail caught on fire. He jumped from rooftop to rooftop, setting fire to the kingdom of Lanka, until he got to the coast. From there he could see Lord Rama and his army of monkey warriors waiting for him at the tip of India. So he jumped over the ocean and arrived at Rama's feet. He gave him the message from Sita and it was then that Lord Rama knew he would have to fight Ravana to reclaim Sita. He knew that war was coming.'

'Is that the war that made you leave Sri Lanka, Ammamma?' Ahalya asked.

'No, that was a different war; a much sadder war,' Priya replied.

'All wars are sad, Ammamma,' said Rishi.

'Yes, darling, they are, they are,' she was silent for a while as she thought about the last time Lanka had been set on fire.

'Ammamma,' Ahalya said, crawling into her lap with a cheeky smile. 'Ammamma, what did the monkey's bottom look like?'

Priya and Smrithi created a new rhythm with each other, footsteps moving forward, tentatively, erratically at first, more confidently later as each step found the comfort of solid ground. They still stumbled into anger and disappointment, but they steadied themselves.

Anger and disappointment were passing emotions, two of many, Nala said Oprah said; Rajan said Karna said; Siva said Lord Krishna said; Smrithi said Nala said. Like hurt. And guilt and regret and longing. And even love.

The door opened and the rituals of childhood emerged.

Rishi brought his copy of the *Mahabharata* to his grandfather and, together, similar but not identical heads bent over the text and transported themselves to the ancient kingdom of Hastinapura, to a time when gods walked the earth with warriors. Siva told his little grandson about Karna, who followed his own dharma. He talked about duty and the importance of doing things properly. Rishi nodded, his head cocked to the side, as he traced the swell of his grandfather's rheumatic hands.

Ahalya came to her grandmother with her comb and elaborate hair ties. Ahalya's hair was just like Smrithi's. Priya slowly and gently pulled the comb through, taking care not to hurt her, as grandmother and granddaughter chatted away. At the end, Ahalya would lean back and Priya held her close. Dhara once said Ahalya smelled like sunlight. She was right.

Every week Priya gave Smrithi a quick kiss and handed her a cooler bag full of curries. Smrithi would sometimes reach out and hug her mother. That day, Priya carried two extra bags. From the first one, she pulled out a pink pavadai sattai, the traditional outfit worn by young girls. Ahalya kissed her grandmother with delight and immediately tried to put the pink skirt on. Priya showed her the pearls she had embroidered onto the blouse.

'It's for your Mummy and Daddy's wedding darling,' she said looking at Smrithi and helping Ahalya into the dress. 'Mummy tells me you're going to be her flower girl.'

'I am! What's in the other bag, Ammamma?' Ahalya asked.

Priya took out a bottle of rose syrup from the second cooler bag and said, 'I'm going to make you a drink Ahalya. It's pink. You'll love it.'

The heat and smoke from the priest's fire was oppressive. The wedding was almost over; Nala exhaled with relief. Smrithi had asked for a small wedding at the Westmead Temple. Only the family *was* invited, which Nala had conceded to happily, grateful that Smrithi was having a Hindu ceremony at all. She looked at the family gathered there with some amusement – it included Smrithi's young daughter and son. It was a very modern wedding but then Nala had always been a very modern grandmother.

Nala asked Smrithi why she had agreed to a Hindu wedding after so many years. Smrithi replied 'it would make my mother happy.'

She shifted uncomfortably. Her hips were aching from standing for so long. From time to time, the smoke made her chest tighten. Priya hovered anxiously, asking her to sit, but she had a duty to perform and it was important to her.

It had been a long time since Nala had stood this close to a fire, a long time since the last wedding, a longer time since a fire had curled its fingers around her. The mix of milk, honey, ghee and flowers were all burning, spitting and fusing together as an offering to the divine. The smoke settled like a heavy blanket around her shoulders. They were more tired now than they were the last time.

Nala didn't like fires, even small ones.

She straightened the folds of her wedding sari out of habit. It was a deep crimson silk, an unusual colour for its time, when all the girls were wearing bright reds. The gold work on the sari was in perfect condition; its elaborate thread work had not been unravelled by the decades that followed. It had survived a civil war, a move to a new country, sixty-four years of marriage and six months of widowhood. It was still very beautiful, although more fragile.

Today, once again, her wedding sari was called upon to provide an important service. It was spread over her granddaughter's wedding seat, the raised platform on which the bride and groom sat during the ceremony. The priest sat on the ground, by the fire, performing the ritual of marriage. It was the only time in a young Hindu's life when they would sit higher than the priest. During the ceremony the couple would be elevated to the status of Lord Shiva and the Goddess Parvathi.

Nala smiled to think of Smrithi representing the supreme Mother Goddess. She reached out a scarred hand to touch the girl but thought better of distracting her. Instead, she waited impatiently, standing behind her and Prashanth under the canopy of garlands.

She straightened her wedding sari again, and counted in her head the number of times it had been used on the wedding seats of her children and grandchildren – five times: once for two of her children and once for three of her grandchildren. After today there would be one more grandchild to marry. She said a silent prayer to Lord Murugan asking him to let her live long enough to see them all married, to give her the privilege of completing the task she had performed for the others, the task she was about to repeat now.

The music reached its peak, signalling that the auspicious moment had arrived. It was time for the guests to stop talking and pay attention. The music was loud enough to drown out the sounds of gheckos and any other bad omens that might appear at the exact moment of marriage, the moment when Prashanth tied the thick gold wedding chain around Smrithi's slender neck, bonding them together forever.

The wedding chain had been blessed by the married elders in the family, investing it with the power of all their dreams and hopes for the young couple.

Nala remembered how nervous Rajan had been when he reached around her with the chain. It was the first time he had touched the perfect line of her neck. His surgeon's fingers, usually so precise, so sure of themselves, struggled clumsily with the complicated clasp. His dark hands shook against her much fairer, pristine skin. Amma had to help him. Standing behind them she had reached forward and it was her, not Rajan, who sealed their marriage.

Nala's hand wandered to her neck and she ran her fingers over its imperfect line. She looked for him in the front row and then she remembered. Sixty-four years – it was a lifetime.

Tomorrow she would make her famous crab curry for the family. He would like that.

'Ammamma, Ammamma, help me,' Smrithi whispered as Prashanth fumbled with the chain.

Nala said one more quick prayer, wishing her granddaughter all of the riches that had been bestowed upon her own married life – children and grandchildren, health and happiness. Her fingers were older than they were at the last wedding, but still steady. She reached down and quickly closed the clasp.

ACKNOWLEDGEMENTS

Thank you: Appappa, for teaching us how to make our beds properly, and Ammamma for telling us stories; Rajan Uncle and Aunty Nalaini, for teaching me how to write those stories.

And to Amma, Appa and Mum, thank you, with all my heart, for teaching and giving me everything else.

This book owes its life to:

My Brother: Narendran, sibling love was the easiest part to write.

My Family: Rachel, Rohan, Noah, Tejas, the Rasanayagams, the K.Pillais, the Pintos and the Cousins. Thank you for your love, faith and deep-fried aubergine curry.

My Book Club: Rohinton Mistry never had such generous and wise people in his corner – Sandra, Narelle, Tina, Carmela, Alex, Angela and Su Lin, you made the book much more than I ever thought it could be.

My First Readers: Kate Kelly, Bekster, Nat, Havas, Terry and Eagle-Eye Franksy – there's a reason you get imposed on first. No more needs to be said.

My Frienditors: Shals, Keda Sivabra, Tim and Latha, Pri, Tascha, Alex W, Renee, Mum Cheney, Mikey, Michael and Phoebe, Gareth,

Sue and Bec Drury, Paula Ellery and Reema. Your lifelong literary sensibilities have been invaluable.

My London Crew: Helen, Em, Sue, Louise, Davina, Colin, Bob and Terri. You will recognise your hunger for justice in this.

My First Supporters: Kerri Sackville, Mia Freedman, Lana Hirschowitz, Bec Sparrow and Jamila Rizvi, thank you for encouraging me to use my words.

My Writing Ladies: Every writer needs a Susan Tenby (and Co). Susan, you are a verb.

My Photographer: Clare Lewis Photography.

My Agent: Tara Wynne at Curtis Brown Australia – thank you for your constant support, careful criticism and faith in my writing career.

My Publisher: Sam Perera and Ameena Hussein at Perera-Hussein, thank you for taking a chance on me.

My Children: Ellora, Kailash, Hari and Sid. Remember Mummy loves you and keep trying to create a better world – you owe that to your ancestors and your children. Also, make your bed properly.

My Cunj, Haran: Don't laugh, but words fail me. Actually do laugh, the sound of it makes everything better.

GLOSSARY OF TERMS

Acca – elder sister

Amma – mother

Amman – the Mother Goddess

Ammamma – grandmother

Anna – elder brother

Appa – father

Appappa (sometimes shortened to Apps), Parta and Thatha – grandfather

Ayah – nanny or nursemaid

Beedi – native tobacco that is commonly chewed

Bhagavad Gita – the Song of God, or a divine message delivered by Lord Krishna to Arjuna, the Pandava warrior, just before the Mahabharatha war begins. (see Mahabharatha below)

Bhikkus – Buddhist monks

Burgher – an ethnic group in Sri Lanka descended from European colonists (mostly Portuguese, Dutch and British) and local people

Cavanam – be careful

Chappals – slippers or shoes

Chutie – a pet name for little girls, meaning little one

Cousin-brother/sister – in Tamil, cousins are referred to as siblings as there is no word for cousin other than 'machal' which is specifically used for marriageable cousins only

Cunju, cunj, cunji – darling

Doddol – or kaladoddol – a sticky, gelatinous sweet made of coconut milk

Dhara – from Dharini, a popular Tamil girl's name, meaning 'earth'

Dharma – one's duty in life; the right course of action

Eelam – Tamil name for the separate Tamil state that the LTTE (or Tamil Tigers) fought for. It covers the northern and eastern provinces where the Tamil people have historically lived

Faloodah – a chilled drink made of milk, rose syrup, gelatine pieces (agar-agar) and swollen basil seeds

Ganesha – the elephant god, considered the remover of obstacles. Many prayers begin with an invocation to him. Lord Ganesha is the son of Lord Shiva, the destroyer and the brother of Lord Murugan

Iyah – respectful term for an older man

Karma – the consequences of one's actions in this and previous lives. Hindus believe that we are born and born again, continuously accruing and expending good and bad karma. When sufficient good karma has been accrued during our lives, man is able to liberate himself from the cycle of birth and death

Kadalai – chickpeas

Kallathoni – Tamil word for boat people, used by the Sinhalese as a derogatory term for the Tamils

Karaya – Sinhalese word for vendor. These men usually brought fish and vegetables to people's houses on carts

Kunkumam – a red powder that is used to make a potu or the dot worn in the middle of the forehead by Tamil women. A red dot made from red kunkumam powder denotes that the woman is married

Kusu – slang word for fart

Lamprais – a traditional Burgher dish comprised of several curries and rice, wrapped and steamed in a banana leaf

Maaveerer – name given by the LTTE for their soldiers who have died as martyrs

Mahabharatha – an epic poem in Hinduism about a great war between two sides of a royal family, the Pandavas and the Kauravas (see Bhagavad Gita, the Song of God above)

Mahal – daughter

Mahan – son

Mahavamsa – a revered 5th century text, that chronicles the history of the Sinhalese kings of Ceylon. This and other religious texts are used to claim Sinhalese ownership of the country and the place of Buddhism in it

Mama – uncle

Mami – aunty

Maya – the concept of illusion. In Hinduism, everything except the divine soul, is considered to be an illusion

Murugan – the deity (or god) most revered by Tamils in Sri Lanka. In Hindu mythology he is the younger brother of Lord Ganesha, the elephant god, and the second son of Lord Shiva, the destroyer

Nathaswaram – traditional music that is played at Tamil weddings, involving trumpets and drums

Navarathri – nine-day festival in honour of the three goddesses – Saraswathi (goddess of learning), Lakshmi (goddess of wealth) and Parvathi (or Amman, the Mother Goddess). On the tenth day, Vijaya Thasami, children are encouraged to begin a new activity and pray for their education

Navura – the evil eye that may be warded off by specific poosais. Tamils often spit three times to frighten off or distract the evil eye

Nona – Sinhalese word for madam

Pallu – the shawl of a sari draped or pulled around a woman's shoulders

Parta – grandfather

Paruppu – a lentil curry (also known as dhal) made from split red lentils

Pathakkam – a traditional gold necklace with a heavy diamond pendant, usually worn at weddings

Pavadai sattai – a traditional outfit worn by young girls, consisting of a long, full skirt and blouse

Pillayar – another name for Lord Ganesha, the elephant god

Poosai (or **pooja**) – prayer ritual usually performed by a priest

Poota – great-grandfather

Pooti – great-grandmother

Potu – the spot placed on a woman's forehead. A potu mark made in red kunkumam (coloured powder) denotes that the woman is married; in black it denotes that she is unmarried

Priya – a popular Tamil girl's name meaning 'beloved'

Ramayana – an epic poem in Hinduism about a great war between Lord Rama, the incarnation of god, and Ravana, the ten-headed demon king of a mythical Lanka

Rasathi – pet name in Tamil for a young girl, meaning 'queen'

Sai Baba – a famous holy man, spiritual teacher or guru who lived and taught in South India

Samathia Chadangu – a ceremony conducted for young girls when they begin menstruating. It is called an age-attainment ceremony

Sambal – chutney

Sambanthi – in-law

Sanni – the planet Saturn which is considered to have a powerful and detrimental influence on the lives of people

Sarrakku powder – a spice mixture of ground coriander and ground cumin. It is a mild blend that is used regularly in food preparation. Coriander (seeds, ground powder) in particular is considered good for the health

Smrithi – the class of Hindu sacred literature that was based on human memory, as distinct from the Vedas, which were considered to be divinely revealed. Also a popular girl's name. From the Sanskrit, smrti, meaning what is remembered

Swabasha – 'self-language' or one's own language

Tamil Eelam – Tamil name for the separate Tamil state that the LTTE (or Tamil Tigers) fought for. It covers the northern and eastern provinces where the Tamil people have historically lived

Thali – gold wedding pendant that is hung on a heavy gold wedding chain (called the kodi); typically worn by Hindu women

Thambi – younger brother

Thangachi – younger sister

Thatha – grandfather

Thirukkural – a poem considered one of the most important pieces of the Tamil canon of literature, comprised of 1330 couplets

Thirunuru – holy ash used during praying

Tholan – a young man or boy who accompanies the groom during the wedding ceremony. The tholan must be related to the bride

Thosai – a fermented savoury pancake made from urid lentil flour

Thosai kadai – shop selling thosais, usually in roadside stalls or in local markets

Tiffin carrier – three steel containers locked together with a handle, each containing a curry

Oor – village. The word has a profounder significance in the Tamil language, meaning the place where you and your family came from

Vannakam – a traditional Tamil greeting or welcome that is spoken with palms pressed together as if in prayer

Vedas – Hindu scriptures that were 'received' by man, directly from God

Vellakaran – white person

Vellala – land-owning upper caste of Tamils

Vershti – the white, sarong worn by Tamil men around their waists. It is generally worn by priests; or by lay people at weddings, funerals and important events

TIMELINE

1948 Ceylon granted independence from Britain under the leadership of DS Senanayake and the United National Party (UNP)

1951 SWRD Bandaranaike forms the Sri Lanka Freedom Party (SLFP)

1952 DS Senanayake dies and his son Dudley Senanayake (UNP) becomes Prime Minister

1953 Dudley Senanayake resigns and his cousin John Kotelawala becomes Prime Minister

1954 Prime Minister John Kotelawala talks about maintaining the parity of status between Sinhalese and Tamil as official languages of Ceylon

1956 SWRD Bandaranaike (SLFP) wins general election to Prime Minister, and passes the Sinhala Only official Language Act

1959 Prime Minister SWRD Bandaranaike assassinated by a Buddhist monk

1960 Mrs Sirimavo Bandaranaike (widow of SWRD Bandaranaike) wins general election to become Prime Minister

1965 Dudley Senanayake and UNP form government

1970 Mrs Sirimavo Bandaranaike (SLFP) wins general election to become Prime Minister

1971 Appeals to the Privy Council abolished. The Janatha Vimukthi Peramuna Party (JVP) launches a Marxist rebellion in the south which is quickly crushed

1972 New Republican Constitution adopted, repealing original constitutional protections for minorities. Mrs Bandaranaike changes the name of Ceylon to Sri Lanka

1973 Standardisation and quota policies for Tamils students entering university introduced

1976 Vaddukoddai resolution signed by the Tamil United Liberation Front, saying that a separate Tamil State is the will of the Tamil people

1976 The Liberation Tigers of Tamil Eelam formed

1977 JR Jayewardene (UNP) wins general election to become Prime Minister

1978 New Constitution of Democratic Socialist Republic of Sri Lanka adopted. JR Jayewardene becomes President

1979 Military occupation of Jaffna

1981 Jaffna Public Library burned

1982 JR Jayewardene (UNP) re-elected President

1983 Anti-Tamil riots in July; official start of the civil war and exodus of the Tamil people

1987 – 1990 Indian Peace Keeping Force (IPKF) enters the north and east to enforce peace and disarm all Tamil militant groups. During this time more than 5,000 Tamils were killed by the IPKF. After prolonged fighting with LTTE, the IPKF leaves Sri Lanka

1987 – 1989 Janatha Vimukthi Peramuna Party (JVP) launches its second uprising during the Indian occupation of the north. The Sri Lankan Army and government are thought to have killed 70,000 Sinhalese rebels

1991 Rajiv Gandhi, former Prime Minister of India and election candidate, assassinated by LTTE whilst campaigning in South India

2002 Ceasefire and peace talks negotiated by the Norwegians. The talks breakdown in 2003

2004 Tsunami hits killing 35,000 and displacing 500,000 people in the east and south of Sri Lanka

2006 – 2007 After sporadic skirmishes in the north and the east, and a further ceasefire and peace talks in 2006, full scale fighting resumes in 2007. The LTTE loses the eastern province

2008 – 2009 The final Army campaign against the LTTE in the north begins, led by Defence Secretary, Gotabhaya Rajapaksa (President Mahinda Rajapaksa's brother) and Gen. Sarath Fonseka

2009 Official end of the civil war and defeat of the LTTE

GLOSSARY OF POLITICIANS

DS Senanayake – leader of the United National Party (UNP) and Prime Minister from 1947 to 1952

Dudley Senanayake – leader of the United National Party (UNP), son of DS Senanayake and Prime Minister from 1952 to 1953 and again in 1960 and again from 1965 to 1970

John Kotelawala – leader of the United National Party (UNP) and Prime Minister from 1953 to 1956

SWRD Bandaranaike – leader of the Sri Lanka Freedom Party (SLFP) and Prime Minister from 1956 to 1959

Sirimavo Bandaranaike – leader of the Sri Lanka Freedom Party (SLFP), wife of SWRD Bandaranaike and Prime Minister from 1960 to 1965 and again from 1970 to 1972, 1972 to 1977 and 1994 to 2000

JR Jayewardene – leader of the United National Party (UNP) and Prime Minister from 1977 to 1978 and President from 1978 to 1989

Chandrika Kumaratunga – leader of the Sri Lanka Freedom Party, People's Alliance and the United People's Freedom Alliance, daughter of the SWRD and Sirimavo Bandaranaike and Prime Minister in 1994 and President from 1994 - 2005

Mahinda Rajapaksa – leader of the United People's Freedom Alliance and Prime Minister from 2001 to 2005 and President (as leader of the Sri Lanka Freedom Party) from 2005 to Jan 2015

GG Ponnambalam – leader of the All Ceylon Tamil Congress from 1944 to 1972

SJV Chelvanayakam – leader of the Tamil Federal Party (FP). The FP splintered off from the All Ceylon Tamil Congress in 1949. The FP later became the Tamil United Liberation Front which Chelvanayakam led from 1972 to 1977

Velupillai Prabhakaran – leader of the Liberation Tigers of Tamil Eelam (LTTE, also known as the Tamil Tigers) from 1976 until his death in 2009

ACRONYMS

UNP – United National Party (Sinhalese-led)

SLFP– Sri Lanka Freedom Party (Sinhalese-led)

ACTC – All Ceylon Tamil Congress (Tamil-led)

TULF – Tamil United Liberation Front (Tamil-led)

FP – Tamil Federal Party which became the Tamil United Liberation Front (TULF) (Tamil-led)

LTTE – Liberation Tigers of Tamil Eelam (also known as the Tamil Tigers)

JVP – Janatha Vimukthi Peramuna Party (Sinhalese-led)

IPKF – Indian Peace Keeping Force

ICRC – International Committee of the Red Cross

MSF – Médecins Sans Frontières

WHO – World Health Organisation